Praise for Sonali Dev

INCENSE AND SENSIBILITY

"*Incense and Sensibility* is a tender, well-crafted novel, as much about finding purpose as it is about falling in love. Dev writes with such rare empathy and humor that I often found myself holding my breath on one page only to be giggling by the next. This is the kind of book you finish with a whole-body, happy sigh and a warm ache in your chest where the characters will live on. Yash and India's story will stick with me for a long time."

—Emily Henry, *New York Times* bestselling author of *Beach Read*

"I ADORED this book. What a polished, sharp, sensual read. I felt each of the characters so deeply. Dev pulled me along by my veins. The writing is so lush and visceral; there were times she described a feeling or action with such vibrance I had to stop and reread it and think about how she came up with that phrase. WHEW! This book holds a galaxy of depth in its pages; it is powerful and loving, sensual and layered. The writing, as always, is glorious. I'm genuinely so in love with it."

—Christina Lauren, *New York Times* bestselling author

"This incredibly romantic, modern reimagining not only bravely addresses the importance of personal integrity in life (and politics), but also gives readers a hero and heroine they'll fall madly in love with. Sonali Dev never gives her characters an easy out. In this book, the emotional payoff for their hard-won journey is perfect."

—Jamie Beck, *USA Today* and *Wall Street Journal* bestselling author

"A deeply emotional story of responsibility and impossible love that will appeal to fans of Austen's classic. It also provides an incisive look at a current political landscape of division and violence, while adding an ultimately hopeful spin. The book's subjects are often serious, but its ultimate focus on being true to oneself and one's principles makes this a satisfying and uplifting romance."
—*Library Journal*

"The story of trauma and recovery in the face of racist gun violence is timely . . . emotionally charged . . . deeply romantic. Dev excels at portraying the fond interconnectedness of the large Raje family. . . . Series fans will be happy to revisit the Rajes and be pleased by the sweet love story."
—*Publishers Weekly*

"Dev masterfully explores the darker moments of being human while leading the reader to a realistic, hard-won romantic ending. *Incense and Sensibility* shares its source text's focus on family, but it also launches Austen's novel into the twenty-first century with its emotional, complex survey of racial identity in America."
—*BookPage*

RECIPE FOR PERSUASION

"A sumptuously multilayered story about the ways love gets tangled in family life and romantic relationships. Highly recommended."
—*Library Journal* (STARRED review)

"Nuanced and powerful. . . . Balances the toe-curling romance with high-octane family drama. . . . Dev's candor and sensitivity in both story lines set this family-centric romance apart."

"This foodie release is a must-read."

"Dev's extended Austen universe continues to astonish, using the beloved second-chance romance *Persuasion* as a scaffolding for a complex, modern romance that celebrates courage, love, and growth."

"A delight from start to finish, both for Jane Austen fans looking for a fresh take and readers seeking deeply felt relationships and complicated family dynamics. In Dev's world, the past is alive in the present; I was wholly engrossed and had plenty to think about. At the same time, the reality TV storyline added a thread of pure fun escapism—something all of us need right now."

"No one writes like Sonali Dev. *Recipe for Persuasion* is a complex, thoughtful exploration of family dynamics, mothers and daughters, and the sorrows we often endure before we find our true place in life. A rich, delicious tale."

"Master storyteller Sonali Dev pens another fantastic Jane Austen retelling with this intricately layered tale of the complexities of familial and romantic love. Full of yearning and wit—and featuring a delicious hero—this book is not to be missed!"

—Jamie Beck, *USA Today* and *Wall Street Journal* bestselling author

"Sonali Dev does it again! In a nod to Austen's classic, *Recipe for Persuasion* dices up family drama and slow-boils the romance between Chef Ashna and footballer Rico Silva as they come to terms with their past and their current feelings *Master Chef*-style. You will gobble up this Dev concoction like it's your favorite dessert . . . and then you'll want seconds."

—Falguni Kothari, *USA Today* bestselling author

PRIDE, PREJUDICE, AND OTHER FLAVORS

"With humor, insight, and culinary descriptions so rich the tantalizing aromas practically waft from the pages, Dev's latest draws readers into a tangled world of class, cultural, and political issues in a delicious riff on *Pride and Prejudice*."

—*Library Journal* (STARRED review)

"Every black sheep needs to bring this read on their next vacation."

—*Good Housekeeping*

"Vivid and deliciously enticing, Dev's storytelling is layered with emotional depth. . . . A flavorful harmony of cross-cultural unions, familial love, and an entertaining ensemble of characters that will leave readers with a serious craving for more."

—*NPR*

"Dev has a gorgeous, lyric quality to her writing voice that she somehow manages to blend seamlessly with sharp humor and comedy, and I absolutely loved it. I really enjoyed meeting the Raje family—a truly delightful read."

—Suzanne Brockmann, *New York Times* bestselling author

"Faces such issues as cultural assimilation, familial forgiveness, and medical ethics head-on. . . . Mouthwatering . . . Ideal for romantics and foodies alike."

—*Booklist*

"A vibrant multicultural feast written with a taste for the true nature of the American stew—not a mush of indecipherable flavors but a celebration of its many ingredients. Sonali Dev is a fresh, unique, and wise voice in women's fiction."

—Barbara O'Neal, *Wall Street Journal* and #1 Amazon Charts bestselling author of *When We Believed in Mermaids*

"This sumptuous novel is rich with complicated personal and family conflicts, mouthwatering food, and the contrast of wealthy vs. modest in a sophisticated urban setting. Dev has a well-deserved reputation for excellence in multicultural women's fiction and fans are certain to love this latest."

— Shelf Awareness

"This book is delicious! A window into a beautifully rich family and cultural life, and romance that made our hearts glow, Dev reminded us again why she has a place of honor on our bookshelves!"

—Christina Lauren, *New York Times* bestselling author

THE EMMA PROJECT

Also by Sonali Dev

Incense and Sensibility
Recipe for Persuasion
Pride, Prejudice, and Other Flavors
A Distant Heart
A Change of Heart
The Bollywood Bride
A Bollywood Affair

THE
EMMA
PROJECT

a Novel

SONALI DEV

AVON

An Imprint of HarperCollinsPublishers

P.S.™ is a trademark of HarperCollins Publishers.

THE EMMA PROJECT. Copyright © 2022 by Sonali Dev. All rights reserved. Printed in the United States of America. No part of this book may be used or reproduced in any manner whatsoever without written permission except in the case of brief quotations embodied in critical articles and reviews. For information, address HarperCollins Publishers, 195 Broadway, New York, NY 10007.

HarperCollins books may be purchased for educational, business, or sales promotional use. For information, please email the Special Markets Department at SPsales@harpercollins.com.

FIRST EDITION

Designed by Diahann Sturge

Library of Congress Cataloging-in-Publication Data has been applied for.

ISBN 978-0-06-305184-3

22 23 24 25 26 LSC 10 9 8 7 6 5 4 3 2 1

For Devieka and Isha, for all the love, the laughs,
and the pride. (And for Yokos, of course.) Your atya
cannot wait to see you take the world by storm.

THE
EMMA
PROJECT

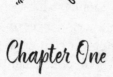

Chapter One

*V*ansh Raje wasn't hypocritical enough to see his life as anything but charmed. Handsome: *Vogue* had declared him the most gorgeous of his siblings, and even he wouldn't argue populist opinions about beauty with *Vogue*. Smart: Not book-brilliant like his siblings, but cleverer than all of them put together, as his grandmother always assured everyone, and who would argue with a grandmother about the intelligence of her grandchildren? Rich: that, of course, was the most tangible of labels, so no reinforcements of proof were necessary.

Add to that a loving—fine, make that doting—family, and a contagiously sunny disposition that was his greatest asset, and Vansh had made it halfway into his twenties without ever facing anything to throw him off his admittedly spectacular game.

"Well, don't you look all pleased with yourself, Baby Prince," Naina Kohli said. She had known Vansh his whole life and had the only voice on earth that had this particular impact on him. A potent combination of reprimand and amusement that made Vansh want to wipe his face like a toddler caught eating dirt, while also making him feel like no one else ate dirt quite as impressively as he did.

"And don't you look resplendent, Knightlina," he said, raising his glass of celebratory bubbly at her.

A flash of anger slipped past her guarded brown eyes. She hated her given name—enough to have legally changed it at eighteen. Vansh was the only person on earth who got away with using it anymore. And he only used it when that tone of hers made the otherwise nonexistent orneriness bubble up inside him. Then she smiled and did a quick half turn showcasing her charcoal-gray silk pantsuit.

"Not bad for the spurned ex, ha?" she offered.

"Not at all bad for the spurned *fake* ex," he countered.

She shrugged as though she cared not a bit for anything, least of all that distinction. They drank to that, and took in the night sky reflected in the pool on Vansh's parents' estate. Naina had chanced upon him here after Vansh had made his way to the private alcove behind the pool house to get away from the thousand-odd guests celebrating his brother's historic election win.

Yash, Vansh's oldest sibling, had just won California's gubernatorial race in one of the closest elections in recent history, also known as a bloodbath. Or that's how it had felt in that last week of campaigning when Yash's opponent had dropped the gloves and every modicum of decency and gone after Yash as a liar, a cheat, and when nothing else worked, as a foreign-funded, idol-worshipping philanderer.

The only reason Yash had been able to pull off the win was because he'd convinced the people of California that he could make law and order work without compromising social justice. Yash had brought the leaders of the Black justice movement and the police union leaders to the negotiating table. A meeting Vansh had pulled together for Yash, thank you very much, because Vansh had been friends with the leader of the union from his Peace Corps days.

"Do you think they have something a little stronger? Or a lot stronger?" Naina asked, her always self-possessed voice slipping slightly as her eyes widened with disbelief.

Vansh followed her gaze to the couple who rounded the corner into the private alcove. It struck Vansh that Naina had probably also been looking for some privacy when she'd found her way here. Which was obviously precisely what his brother and his girlfriend were looking for as they came into view, hands all over each other, making out like horny teenagers, entirely unaware of Vansh and Naina tucked away out of their line of sight.

Desperate sounds of arousal escaped from them as they tugged at each other's clothes and hair.

Vansh almost cleared his throat—he probably should have—but he was frozen at the sight of this new version of Yash. India said something, and laughter shivered through the two of them in a way so intimate Vansh stepped in front of Naina to protect her from it.

It had been barely a few months since Yash had, very publicly, left Naina for India Dashwood just weeks before the election, effectively risking his lifelong dream of becoming the governor of California to be with India instead of Naina. A fact that Naina seemed to be reliving with every cell in her being given how hard she was trying to appear nonchalant.

With another possessive moan, Yash pushed India into the wall and she arched her body against his. This uninhibited, reckless Yash couldn't possibly be the tightlaced brother Vansh had grown up in the shadow of.

Taking care not to look at Naina, Vansh cleared his throat loudly enough to break through whatever pheromone-fueled idiocy had gripped the newly elected governor at this very well-attended party.

Yash and India jumped apart with all the force befitting two usually uptight people caught in the act of quasi-fornicating in public.

Pushing India behind him, Yash spun around to find Vansh trying to channel their mother and glare without glaring. If Naina had not been standing next to him, Vansh would have been rolling with laughter. This was the sort of thing comedic writers spent hours workshopping. Vansh had spent four months, years ago, working with a friend on his sitcom. It had sounded like much more fun than it had turned out to be, and they'd never come up with a situation nearly this ludicrous.

"Naina." India was the first to break the mortified silence. Flaming cheeks notwithstanding, her voice was calm and filled with warmth. This was not a surprise. India had the sort of Buddha vibe Vansh had seen monks in Dharamshala aspire to with little success. "Vansh. I hope you're both having a good time," she added, doubling down on the yogic vibe.

That made Yash press a cough-laugh into his fist. God, was this really his brother?

India threw what could only be called the fondest glare at Yash, who seemed to be tearing up with the effort of containing his mirth. To be perfectly honest, if Vansh met his brother's eyes they would both burst into laughter.

"Oh, we're having a great time," Naina said, with every bit of the elegant drollness Vansh associated with her.

"Although not nearly as much fun as we interrupted," Vansh said before he could stop himself and gave up on holding his laughter back. "What the hell, Yash? This is literally a political party thrown by your political party."

"We just needed a moment," India said, her blush deepening. "It's been a lot."

Yash sobered and slid a protective arm around her. "The worst of the circus is over," he said, his statesman shoulders widening with purpose. "Campaigns are the worst part. Now the press will shift its focus to my work. They'll leave you alone. I'll make sure of it."

The relief on India's face was palpable.

Naina's body stiffened infinitesimally. She covered it up with more of that determined breeziness and smiled kindly at India.

Before anyone could say more, another intertwined couple turned the corner into the private alcove that was turning out not to be so private after all.

"I've been waiting for you to use your gavel all evening, Your Honor."

God, please, no! Those were the last words on earth Vansh ever, *ever*, wanted to hear his oldest sister say to her judge husband. Ever.

Yash, who was generally not the sort of guy who snorted with laughter, snorted with laughter so violently that Nisha and Neel jumped apart like someone had fired a cannon.

Nisha's hands pressed into her face. "No. No. Nononono. What the hell are you all doing here?"

"Not waiting for Neel to use his gavel, that's for sure," Yash said, still howling like a hyena. Which, to be fair, Vansh was doing as well.

Nisha charged at Yash. Neel grabbed her around her waist. As a circuit court judge (with a gavel), Neel obviously saw enough crazy shit on a daily basis that he was entirely unfazed by any Raje family shenanigans.

He held Nisha in check while laughing into her hair, and in the end she broke down and started laughing too, embarrassed though the laughter was.

"If either one of you tells anyone, I'm going to chop you into little pieces and pass you through a mulch shredder," their sister threatened.

"Who let her watch *Fargo*?" Vansh asked, and Neel looked heavenward.

Ignoring the question, Nisha disengaged herself from her husband and threw her arms around India. "I'm so sorry you're stuck with my evil brother," she said with the kind of gleeful affection that indicated exactly how thrilled she actually was that India was stuck with their brother. Then she noticed that Naina was also there.

Until this moment Vansh had believed that Nisha had inherited their mother's talent for absolute discretion. Nisha had a veritable toolbox of expressions under which she hid anything she didn't want others to see. But a blast of such extreme discomfort and confusion at Naina's being here flitted across Nisha's face that she couldn't seem to identify exactly which mask-expression to use to cover it up.

Nonetheless, she made a valiant effort. "Naina," she said only the slightest bit late, and Vansh hoped Naina hadn't noticed.

Letting India go, Nisha turned to Naina, unable to decide how to get away with not hugging Naina now that she had greeted India so effusively. Nisha obviously did not feel the same way about their brother's ex as she did about their brother's current girlfriend. Most of the family blamed Naina for trapping Yash in a loveless relationship for ten years.

"Great to see you, Naina," Neel said, saving the day with his signature warmth and circuit-judge equanimity, and gave Naina a friendly hug. "I heard you've moved back to town permanently."

"Sure have." Naina returned Neel's hug and then let Nisha give her a quick, and hella awkward, one.

Before the awkwardness could settle on them in earnest, Vansh noticed a bottle in Neel's hand.

"Is that scotch in your gavel-wielding hands, Your Honor?" Vansh asked, raising a brow at their stickler-about-these-things sister. Nisha was the one who'd given strict instructions for a California-wine-and-California-bubbly-only party.

Nisha was about to charge at Vansh when more sounds drifted in from the corner of horny doom that his siblings had evidently withheld from Vansh his entire life.

Ashna and her boyfriend entered the alcove already in a lip-lock, which at least made it impossible to say something incriminating that the others could use to embarrass them for the rest of their lives.

"Does anyone have a glass?" Neel asked as though they were at a bar watching a game.

In what was now starting to feel like an overdone off-Broadway comedy, Ashna jumped away from Rico, who had his hands halfway up her very prim dress.

Vansh dumped out his remaining overpriced yet not nearly strong enough bubbly into the bushes and offered his glass to Neel, who poured a healthy serving from the bottle.

Naina was the only other person with a glass, and she chugged her wine and held it out for a fill.

"Hey, everyone," Rico said as though getting caught with his hands and his tongue all over his girlfriend with a large majority of her family watching was the most ordinary of things. This perfectly described Rico Silva.

Ashna was their cousin, but Vansh didn't ever remember thinking of her as anything but his sister. After Ashna's parents' separation, she'd pretty much grown up here, on Vansh's parents' estate in Woodside. Sometimes Vansh thought Ashna was more one of the siblings than he was.

Face flaming red, Ashna snatched the glass from Vansh and took a mighty gulp. "Where's Trisha?" she asked calmly enough.

Vansh's other sister, Trisha, was the only one who was missing from the now crowded alcove. All eyes turned to the corner, as though everyone expected Trisha and her boyfriend, DJ, to appear.

"I'm calling her," Nisha said. "She's probably running around trying to find us to keep the aunties and uncles from cornering her and DJ and asking when they're getting married and making babies."

A phone started ringing and they all looked down at their pockets and purses. Then everyone seemed to register that the ringing was coming from inside the pool house. Just as that realization sank in, the door pushed open and out stepped Trisha and DJ.

Trisha had obviously been unable to pat down her always-wild hair after whatever DJ and she had been doing in there. Next to her DJ looked as cool as any man trying his damnedest to appear cool could. He took the glass of scotch that was circulating around the crowd and drained it.

"Macallan eighteen has a tad bit too much smoke, if you ask me," DJ declared in his British-chef voice. He was one of those chefs who probably thought about flavors and hints of this and that in his sleep. Also, it was evidently what he fell back on when caught in a compromising situation with his girlfriend by her zero-boundaries family.

"So you've all been defiling the pool house all these years and no one bothered to tell me." Vansh filled the glass up again, and yes, he sounded sulky as hell at being left out. Vansh was a good five years younger than Ashna, who was the closest to him in age. Between the age gap and the fact that he had gone off to boarding school in India at sixteen, he should have been used to the feeling by now.

"Eeew," all his sisters said at once.

Nisha took the glass out of Vansh's hand again. "It's a good thing we let you drink when you're underage."

He was twenty-six and they all knew it.

"It's illegal in the state of California for children to have sex," Trisha said, ruffling Vansh's hair with complete disregard for how much he hated his hair being ruffled. It took a lot of effort to get it to look this good. "And we're the Rajes. You're not allowed to get frisky until you're thirty."

"How are you allowed to be thirty-two and call it 'getting

frisky'?" Vansh said, patting his hair back in place. "And for the record, I could teach you a thing or two about *getting frisky*."

Trisha made a gagging face and then smiled. "Of course, baby." She wrapped her arms around Vansh. "You could teach most of us a thing or two about most things. You're our worldly baby brother, the light of our lives."

"The apple of our eyes," Nisha said, joining the hug.

"Our pride and joy," Ashna said, completing the group hug.

"But we are going to have to punch you if you mention sex around us again," Trisha finished up.

As his sisters squeezed him and let him go, the sting of being left out of their nefarious pool house antics, and everything else they always thought he was too young for, died down.

Naina was standing a little apart from the circle, her cool smile daring anyone to question how little she cared that no one had noticed her. Taking Naina's glass from her, Vansh took a long sip.

The casual glass sharing, unfortunately, drew attention to her presence. His sisters looked at one another and pretended not to look at one another, and Naina took the glass back and drained the little Vansh had left in there in one gulp.

The undercurrents of shade could have sunk ships.

Yash picked up the bottle from the patio table and filled Naina's glass up again.

"It's great to have you back, brat," Yash-the-politician said, trying to distract from the rising tide of awkwardness. "Great job again on your help with the campaign. I couldn't have done this without you. Any of you."

They all hooted and clapped.

"You better save the speech for the stage, Mr. Governor," Nisha said, staring down at her phone. "Ma just texted the family group chat. She's freaking out because she can't find any of us."

"Duty calls." Yash dropped a kiss on India's head. "You ready to go back out there?"

"You bet," India said.

"To Yash." Neel raised the bottle.

"To Yash," everyone repeated, and took sips straight from the bottle before dispersing.

Naina and Vansh watched them leave and Naina downed what was left in her glass then eyed the empty bottle in Vansh's hand. It was hard to know how much scotch they'd consumed, except from the nice buzz Vansh had swimming between his ears.

"I believe you asked if there was anything stronger than the wine available," he said.

Laughing with far too much relief, Naina dropped into the patio swing. The reflection of the full moon broke and scattered across the pool's surface. "This is what I get for even suggesting there was a lack of booze on the Raje estate."

Vansh sat down next to her.

You okay? he wanted to ask, but nothing about her allowed that question. Her jet-black hair fell in sleek layers to her proudly held shoulders. Her high porcelain cheekbones showed not a line of emotion. Her legs were neatly crossed at the ankles. Her manicured hands were folded in her lap. She presented as self-possessed and unbreakable a picture as there could ever be.

"I'm perfectly fine," she answered anyway. "It's not like what Yash and I had was real." The glance she threw the moonlight dancing on the pool was almost bored.

"Your friendship was real." Naina and Yash had been best friends since they were in grade school.

"And it still is." She played absently with the whisper-thin gold chain hanging from her wrist. "But anyone can see that India is better for him than I would ever be. And, well"—looking up from the bracelet, she spun a hand around in a circle—"all this . . . *Rajeness*. It's a lot. And it's not really my cup of tea. Not having to deal with this level of drama on a day-to-day basis is a huge relief. Everyone is better off this way."

Vansh didn't agree. His family was perfect. This drama was what he missed when he was gone. But she was right, it wasn't for everyone.

"What about you?" she said. "What's the Baby Prince's next project? Which part of the world are you jetting off to next?"

For so long it had been the question Vansh had lived for. Now, sitting in this alcove, where peace shimmered in the air despite the throngs celebrating on the other side of the pool house, Vansh found that he wasn't sure. For the first time in his life the thought of leaving wasn't an irresistible pull.

"Not quite sure," he said.

"Really?" She studied him in that partly amused but fully focused way of hers.

"Maybe it has to do with being instrumental in Yash winning the election, but being here suddenly feels different. That success seems to have changed something inside me." He touched his heart, where satisfaction and pride filled him up.

"You can't be serious." Was she laughing at him? Her tone slid from amusement to scolding, their familiar pattern dancing between them again. "*Success*?"

"I sense a question mark at the end of that word. Do you doubt it was a success?"

Her dramatic eyebrows arched over wide, amber-flecked eyes. "Success implies endeavor, Vansh."

"How can you say that?" Sure, he sounded petulant, but only because he felt petulant. "The meeting between the police union and BLM leaders would never have happened without me."

She made the effort to soften her tone but not her words. "That meeting happened because both parties trusted Yash."

No one said she wasn't entitled to her opinion. Vansh gave her his most charming smile, making sure his dimples dug into his cheeks in a way that usually made people melt. Not Naina, of course. Naina had been immune to his dimples since she'd caught him sneaking out his father's car at fifteen when he'd backed it straight into hers. While mildly high.

Publicly she'd taken the blame, but privately she'd lectured him for days and then kept on him about safety for months. Her lectures always hit harder than he'd ever admit. He'd felt terrible. Two cars had been destroyed. The worst thing was that they'd ended up in landfills. As a punishment to himself, Vansh had never owned a car after that.

He'd been grateful that Naina had taken the blame and saved his ass. It hadn't been the only time either. Ma and Dad never got upset with Naina about anything. Like Yash, she was beyond reproach with his family. Or she had been until the deception with Yash had come out. Now she seemed to be persona non grata, and the unfairness of that stuck in Vansh's throat. But the patronizing look she was giving him helped him get over it.

"That meeting happened because I spent a year in Guatemala with the leader of the police union in the Peace Corps. I was the one he trusted."

The smile she gave him was tolerant, but Vansh saw it for what it was: an eye roll disguised as a smile. In her eyes the credit Yash gave him was just another bone his family threw him.

She was not wrong about his family's indulging him. Vansh enjoyed all the gifts of his older siblings without being encumbered by the weight of expectations they all dragged around.

Vansh had no interest in letting the weight of other people's expectations and definitions of ambition hold him down. He traveled light, let the wind carry him where he was most needed.

"True success doesn't need external validation," he said as loud cheering rose from the jubilant crowd thronging the grounds of his childhood home.

Naina's eyes narrowed, as though she saw something about him that he himself couldn't see. The fact that she'd just dismissed his contribution to his brother's victory meant she didn't see him at all.

Naina's approval, or anyone else's for that matter, was immaterial. The only approval he needed was his own. And that he had in spades.

A thought that had been nudging at the back of his mind suddenly pushed forward. "I do need a new project. I just don't think I need to go away to find it this time." Helping Yash had shown him something. "I think my country and my family need me, and I've been ignoring them and chasing butterflies for far too long."

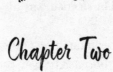

Chapter Two

Naina Kohli didn't like too many people. Liking people and being liked in return was a childish and shortsighted endeavor. It worked for those interested in transient happiness induced by dopamine hits and instant gratification. It had little to do with real life, which was a long, weary road.

Her parents, for instance, pretty much loathed each other.

Her father's loathing was more obvious, of course, because the patriarchy was a many-splendored thing. Men got to be honest. With their loathing for inferior spouses, with their disdain for their inferiorly gendered offspring. Men didn't have to fear loss, especially not the men who carefully constructed and inculcated dependency on them in their loathed ones.

"Naina beta!" Naina's mother threw a look over her shoulder, undoubtedly to make sure her husband wasn't watching, before rushing over to her only child across the throng of guests celebrating Yash's win on the Raje estate.

Naina and her father, the illustrious Dr. Kohli, were no longer on speaking terms after she'd told her parents that Yash was not interested in marrying her and that he was in love with someone else, who was not her.

So a yoga instructor with unknown parentage could trap him in a few months but you couldn't keep him after having ten years to do it?

Yes, Dr. Kohli was a delight. Not having to deal with him any longer was the most fortuitous thing that had ever happened to Naina.

The sheer enormity of the relief Naina felt at the fact that Vansh had gone off to mingle and she was blessedly alone when her mother found her should have been embarrassing, but Naina no longer let embarrassment and her mother mix in her mind.

Despite Naina's best efforts, her mother's presence, her smell, her voice—it all fell like precision cuts on the ice that usually covered her like impenetrable armor.

"You good, Mummy?" she said with a casualness that made her mother's hand tremble at her throat, where her string of solitaires caught every one of the million decorative lights brightening the Raje estate.

Naina had no doubt her father had ordered her mother to don the bling. *Wear your biggest diamonds . . . That thing you had made in India to replicate Tiffany.*

High-priced gems set to knock off even higher-priced gems was apparently the perfect way of announcing to the world that the Rajes had lost a precious alliance, while also making sure everyone knew that the Kohlis were just as good as the Rajes.

They weren't.

But Dr. Kohli would never know why.

He was a medical inventor, and each of his inventions might have changed millions of lives, but he had never felt the need to change the regressive ideology that had been grown inside his head in the sprawling, entitlement-filled *kothi* in the village in India he'd grown up in.

"I'm all fine," her mother said, eyes still darting around and taking note of who was watching her talking to her daughter while also making sure Dr. Kohli didn't show up and catch her in the act of consorting with the enemy. "I was not expecting to find you here."

If her mother had taught Naina anything, she'd taught her how to show up in uncomfortable situations. Every day.

"Whyever not?" The easy tone emerged from Naina's lips with barely any effort. "Yash is still my friend." He'd been her only friend, and if her being here months after her very public dumping made things easier for him by making him look a little less like a cheating jerk, then here she'd be.

"I don't understand you children," her mother said about her thirty-eight-year-old daughter who had never had a chance to be a child, and had spent her entire adult life trying to change the lives of women in the remotest, most neglected parts of the world.

"I know." Those words landed on her mother like a blow and Naina kicked herself. Casual indifference was the only way to not end up saying something hurtful to her mother. Hurting her mother was like kicking a puppy. For all her reputation for hardness, Naina would never kick a puppy.

Ask me about my foundation, Naina wanted to say. Her foundation had just received a multimillion-dollar endowment from Jignesh Mehta, the sixth-richest entrepreneur in the world. They were going to be able to bring sustainable economic independence to millions of women.

"That jacket looks so much pretty on you," her mother said instead, then, as though she couldn't help herself, she cupped Naina's cheek. The look she threw over her shoulder helped Naina keep the rush of warmth from sweeping her away. "You were always such beautiful girl," she added with exactly the same expression she wore while trying to resolve an irreconcilable loss on her household expenses spreadsheet.

Suddenly she took Naina's arm, and with another furtive glance combing the crowd, she dragged Naina to one of the powder rooms in the Raje mansion. Once they were inside, she locked them in. Despite all this caution, when she spoke her voice was a whisper, just in case someone had their ear pressed to the bathroom door in the middle of a party.

"It's not too late, beta. If you make marriage before Yash does, everyone will forget how sad they feel for you. Your Navdeep Mamu in Cincinnati called me yesterday. Our family is being so much supportive. They're all coming together with rishtas. Now that we're in forties with age criteria, mostly it's divorcés and widowers. But I put foot down. No men with children." Naina's mother never paused when she talked. It was as though she had to quickly deliver her speeches before she was interrupted and dismissed.

So, Naina had developed a mechanism for putting pauses in for her and tuning out the parts of the monologue that weren't relevant. Her mother said a few more entirely ridiculous things about *marriage criteria*.

The only marriage criterion I have is to never be in one, Mummy. Thanks for helping me keep it simple.

". . . Navdeep Mamu said there is surgeon who just joined his practice. Newly widowed. Very handsome. No children. Most dedicated to medicine and only medicine. No interest in politics and news and all those type things. Your mamu showed him your picture and he's very much flipped for you."

Oh, how Naina wished her mother had developed some skill for knowing what someone flipping for you actually involved. Then again, love was a figment of poets' imaginations that they subjected the world to because they couldn't stop dwelling in pain without making everyone else just as miserable as them.

An unwelcome montage of the Raje siblings climbing all over their significant others against a pool house wall did a dramatic dance in her head.

Well, no one said the Rajes weren't burdened with enough glorious luck to make everyone else look like the losers they were.

The Rajes weren't the norm and Naina wasn't stupid enough to believe that good fortune, or joy, rubbed off through contact. Spending a lifetime being friends with Yash had at least taught her that much.

"Remember how I always said I would only ever marry Yash? Just because he's in love with someone else doesn't mean I'll suddenly settle for someone else too." She squeezed her mother's shoulder, because Mummy looked like she needed something to keep her from collapsing under the weight of this revelation, which Naina had made at least fifty times since Yash's grand declaration of love for India Dashwood on national television. "I really appreciate how hard Navdeep Mamu and you have worked for me. I mean, a widowed doctor—with no children! How did your brother even find him?"

Her mother scowled. "Do you think I don't have enough people in my life treating me like stupid? Do you think I need my own child to do it too?"

"I'm sorry." She was. She was so deeply, deeply sorry for having hurt this woman. In ways that reached far beyond this conversation. "But I think that poor general surgeon deserves someone who knows how to do this." *How to be you.* "I know only one way to be happy, and that is by being alone and focusing on my work. I will never ever get married. Not if every surgeon in the world is widowed without children and not one of them will move on unless I agree to marry him." She met the abject disappointment in her mother's beautiful, tired eyes. "Never, Mummy, ever."

A sob escaped her mother, because sobs lived at her command. "What if Yash sees error of ways and takes you back?"

Naina had to laugh at that. Suddenly she saw how her mother had stayed with her father for forty years. It was this hope. This insatiable, entirely delusional ability to cheat herself into believing that the impossible could happen. That people could change how they saw things. That tomorrow was another day and all that crap.

She tried to enunciate the words without being rude, because Mummy had to understand this. "Yash is not going to do that. We never loved each other that way. We lied because my father wouldn't let me go to Nepal unless I got married. And pretending to be with Yash was the only way to change his mind. Yash was just helping me get around Dr. Kohli's ridiculous objections."

This wasn't the first time Naina was saying these words to her mother. She'd lost track of how many times she'd repeated them. Over and over and over. But there was that horrid hope that cut off her mother's hearing, willfully, stubbornly. Hope that had made her mother unable to hear Naina or to see Naina her entire life.

Which is why Naina couldn't say the other part. *If you had ever stood up for me, I wouldn't have had to turn to Yash.*

The parts Naina could say, she would say a hundred times if she had to. "I don't want to get married. To anyone. Not even if your Shivji himself came down from Mount Kailash. I am not made for marriage. I'm just not." And she wasn't going to apologize for it ever again.

With a shudder, her mother recoiled from her. "That is unnatural, beta. How you can say something so against nature, and society, and God? Your father is right. You are not normal." She looked like the very sight of Naina made her queasy with the enormity of her own failings. "What did I do to deserve child so abnormal?"

With not a word more, she unlocked the door and left, but not before she had peeked out to make sure she wasn't being watched.

Of all the questions her mother had asked today, Naina knew the answer to only that last one. She knew exactly what her mother had done to deserve a child so abnormal. She had created her, moment by moment, action by action, day by long day. It was a wonder that the question even needed to be asked.

Naina's mother had been the captain of her college basketball team. *A woman close to six feet tall is good for little else but sinking balls into baskets while barely seven people watch from the audience.* Naina had heard this a thousand times from her grandmother. Words Naina's father had repeated at least as many times over the years in one brilliant instance of gaslighting after another.

Needless to say, basketball was not something at the top of Dr. Kohli's list of things that made this daughter more acceptable.

Naina had been one of the taller girls in sixth grade. After that she had mostly stopped growing and ended up favoring her father's more average height genes. But until middle school she'd been tall enough that the basketball coach had asked her to come to tryouts.

She'd made the team with relative ease. But when she'd asked her father for the fifty dollars for team fees, he'd thrown one of his patented looks of utter disgust at her mother. The kind of look that had been responsible for teaching Naina the meaning of the word *fear* early in life. The kind of look that made her mother sob silently as she rolled rotis in the kitchen. The kind of look that had taught Naina exactly how useless tears were.

It was the look that had taught her she was not like the Raje children or like any of the other families in her parents' friend group. It was the look that made it seem like the floors of their home were lined with eggshells, and they were laid out with such skill that those who didn't live in their house never saw them.

Sometimes Naina saw the aunties study her for signs of something. Bruises? But her bruises were like the eggshells, invisible. Sometimes Naina thought people did see. But vision was like every other power: of no consequence unless you chose to use it.

When Naina had gone to her father with her request for the

basketball fees, he'd asked her how her grades were. They'd been all As. She'd always been too afraid to let her grades slip.

"You have one job," her father had once said to her mother. "To make sure your daughter does not end up stupid and uneducated like you. Luckily for you she has my genes." Dr. Kohli always directed his disappointment in his daughter at his wife, almost as though he knew that hurting her mother was far more potent than directly hurting Naina.

Many years later, when Naina had told him she was not taking the MCATs or going to medical school, the expression on his face had brought her the kind of indescribable satisfaction she'd never until that day experienced. The man who had toyed with her helplessness for sport her whole life had looked entirely helpless. It had been a day she'd been waiting for since what she had labeled the Basketball Incident.

The night her father had refused to pay the team fees, her mother had found Naina sobbing silently in bed.

"Maybe it's time for mother-daughter secret," Mummy had said, and slipped an envelope into her backpack.

Never before had Naina ever felt hope like that. Searing and sharp enough to hurt.

"Really?" Her excitement had made her voice burst from her far too loudly.

"Shh!" Her mother's smile had made her look like other mothers. "When you're being brave you have to be very very afraid that no one find out."

Naina had gone to bed smiling.

At her first practice, Mummy had shown up in a baby-pink tracksuit. One that made her look like one of the cool moms. Instead of the long braid hanging down her back, she had pinned her hair into a bun at her nape. When Naina had missed her shot, she'd come down from the bleachers and shown her how to make the perfect shot. Then she'd shown the other girls. She'd been firm and gentle, and magnificent. The girls on the team had followed her instructions like smitten fans. It was like having a whole different life.

After practice the coach had asked Mummy to be the team parent. Fear had flashed in Mummy's eyes, turning her back into the mother Naina had grown up with. In that moment, Naina had realized that she would never be able to bear having her old mother back. Never.

Her mother had seen those thoughts in Naina's eyes, because she'd agreed to become the team mom. Then she'd shown up for practice every day in her pink tracksuit with silver side stripes, and she'd worked the girls hard and made them laugh. The girls hadn't noticed her thick accent or cared that she pinched their cheeks when they did well. The girls just looked at Naina like she was the luckiest girl in the world. She'd even stitched them matching scrunchies from the fabric she always brought home from India. Team colors of green and yellow.

On the eighth day of practice, Naina and her mother came home to find her father waiting.

"How was basketball practice, Knightlina?" There was not a trace of emotion in his voice.

"Go to your room, beta," her mother said, a sob tearing her voice. "Now." That last word was in her coach's voice, and Naina knew that she would never hear that tone from her mother ever again.

The next morning, Naina came down to an empty kitchen and found a note on the island in her father's doctor's scrawl. "Disobedient girls go to school without breakfast."

Naina didn't care about breakfast. All she cared about was having her mother show up at practice. But, of course, she didn't. Instead Naina was met by the coach's sad eyes.

"Your mother was in an accident, Naina. You can be excused from practice today to go home early."

J-Auntie, Yash's housekeeper, had driven her home with Yash. Mina Auntie, Yash's mom, always stepped in to help when Mummy felt badly. Yash had held her hand through the entire twenty-minute drive as tears streamed from Naina's eyes. He'd known without her telling him that if he asked any questions she would die of shame.

"Do you think you can come help me with my chemistry project later?" he'd asked, his eyes so kind she'd felt like there was more to the world than what waited for her inside her house. "Ma will speak to your dad and J-Auntie will come get you."

Naina had nodded yes and walked inside by herself. She had no idea what she expected but it hadn't been her mother with her arm in a cast on a sling. One side of her face was swollen, and the skin squeezing her eye shut was dark purple.

Before that day Naina had been infuriated by her mother's cowering, by her pandering, by her jumping to do his bidding even before her father spoke. Now she felt shame. Her mother had known something she hadn't. Her mother had known and she'd made sure Naina never got to see this. Then Naina had put her in a position where the choice had been between something she wanted to show Naina and something she didn't want her to see.

Naina, even at twelve, had known without a doubt that there was no right choice for her mother to make. That's just what life was: a string of bad options to choose from.

God knew Naina had made her fair share of them. Sucking her best friend into a ten-year-long fake relationship was a pretty stellar example. Needing to give her father the finger at every available opportunity had been an irresistible and delicious motivator. She didn't need a therapist to tell her that.

Now, here she was, sitting on a five-thousand-dollar Japanese commode that knew how to keep her butt warm even when she was using it as a chair with the top down. In a house her father had spent most of Naina's life dreaming of her moving into as a daughter-in-law, because in his head that was how the world still worked. Your success lay in how well you married off your daughter. The fact that he'd never have that satisfaction made Naina positively light-headed.

At the ripe age of thirty-eight, Naina's revenge was complete. After stringing her father along with the dream of a son-in-law who was going to be the governor of California, getting to yank that dream right from beneath his feet had been vastly more satisfying than Yash's betrayal had been painful.

If the satisfaction of breaking her father's heart was the full-bodied jolt of a lightning strike, the pain of Yash's choosing someone else over her was a pinprick. One was the ocean, the other a raindrop.

So how could she be angry with Yash? And that girlfriend of his was just so hard to hate. Trying to hate India Dashwood was almost like peeing on a live wire. You'd burn yourself to a crisp and the darned thing wouldn't even get wet.

Standing up from the warm Raje throne, Naina washed her hands and touched up her lipstick. Kissed by Frost. She'd bought the shade for the name alone. It could easily be the title of her memoir.

Truth was, being back in California, all grown up and flush with redemption, wasn't a bad deal. The fact that her foundation had a gigantic endowment from a billionaire she had eating out of her hands wasn't a bad deal at all.

As for Mummy and the Rajes, Naina knew exactly how to keep them all where they belonged, at a nice safe distance where they couldn't hurt her.

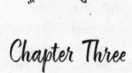

Chapter Three

*V*ansh watched Naina bestow one of her hard-to-win smiles on Jignesh Mehta. Like so many men before him, getting a laugh out of the untouchable Naina Kohli seemed to make the tech billionaire feel like the king of the world. Which he kind of was. Vansh wondered what they were talking about.

Clearly, Naina had her game face. The one no one could see through. She caught Vansh watching them and he winked at her, making her narrow her eyes. But the tight edges of her mouth loosened ever so slightly in the smallest of smiles. A real one, not a carefully manufactured one like she'd just given Mehta.

Vansh was about to start toward them, but she widened her eyes, a warning to stay exactly where he was. Which only made Vansh want to join them even more. But before he could decide if he wanted to needle Naina quite that much, Mehta caught sight of him and waved him over with the kind of excitement that didn't match up with the fact that Vansh had never met the man.

Vansh made his way over, ignoring the visual darts Naina shot his way. Mehta was a guest in his home, so there was no question of not going over to greet him when he'd been summoned so enthusiastically. Their mother had not raised someone that ill-mannered.

"You must be the younger Raje brother?" Mehta said excitedly. His voice was a little higher than Vansh had expected, and his tone was not exactly what Vansh would call entrepreneurial. He smiled perpetually but there was a restlessness in his eyes. The word *pugilist* came to mind—short and stocky with a clean-shaven head and a perfectly trimmed goatee.

Naina stood a head taller than Mehta in her heels. Which had to be a good five inches high because she almost matched up to Vansh's five feet ten in them. Which meant she could treat Vansh to her plentiful condescension eye to eye.

"This is Vansh Raje, Yash's brother," Naina said in her Dr. Kohli's Polite Daughter voice. "Vansh, this is Jignesh Mehta, CEO of Omnivore Systems."

"An honor," Vansh said.

"Cool!" Mehta said. "Cool," he repeated, just in case someone had missed it the first time. His tone reminded Vansh of high school boys from the nineties teen movies his mother loved. "And it's Jiggy. My friends call me Jiggy."

Naina quirked a brow. *Do not laugh.*

"I hear you're back from Zimbabwe, where you've been digging wells," Jiggy said. "Sounds like a blast."

Vansh had heard the mission described several different ways, but "a blast" was a first.

"It was a very satisfying project." Vansh refused to look at Naina, because not cracking a smile was now a matter of pride.

Jiggy turned to Naina. "All you rich kids running around the world trying to fix it."

This time Naina's brow rose less subtly. Vansh couldn't tell if she was offended that Mehta had put Vansh's work and hers in the same general category or if she was offended that he had dismissed them both as rich kids when he himself had a personal fortune of several billion dollars.

"Some rich kids run around the world doing the actual work,

while some let others do the legwork and buy the credit with their riches," Naina said, her tone so cold, Vansh didn't know how Mehta didn't freeze and crumble instantly.

Instead, getting a reaction out of Naina seemed to stoke Jiggy's smugness.

Truth was, if he wanted to use his wealth to purchase credit for good work that could use his money, then who were they to argue?

"Your foundation has been doing some amazing work," Vansh said. "And Naina's work is certainly a great choice for a flagship project."

"I know, right?" Mehta countered. "Glad you think so." He had one of those thick Western Indian accents overlaid with rolled American *R*s and lengthened *A*s.

"I know so." Vansh found himself getting into the nineties teen-movie banter.

"So, are you and Naina like close and all?"

That took Vansh by surprise. Naina too from the quick drawing together of her winged brows. Had the eyebrow game always been so strong with her?

"We've known each other our whole lives," Vansh said. Tone placating, because Naina looked like she was about to tell the Jiggster here exactly how much she didn't think any of this was his business.

"She was almost your sister-in-law," the man said, gossipy excitement making his beady eyes beadier.

"That would be true if Yash and I had ever had any intention of marrying." Naina grabbed a mimosa from a passing waiter and took a sip.

This fact-based rebuttal seemed to bore Mehta. He turned to Vansh. "You have a girlfriend, Vansh?"

Okay, so the man jumped topics like he was on a trampoline.

"Not currently."

"So where to next?"

"Haven't decided. I'm thinking about staying here for a while. Reconnecting with my roots and all that."

Mehta brightened. "Family is important. Are you and your brother close?"

Okay. "As close as two brothers can be."

This declaration seemed to make Jiggs happier than it should have made anyone who wasn't Vansh's brother. He bounced on his velvet Manolo Blahnik loafers.

"Will you be working with him?" So, they were in a full-fledged inquisition then.

"We're always involved in each other's work."

Mehta's face lit up like the gold embroidery on his thousand-dollar shoes. "Anything specific?"

"I've been traveling the globe looking to be useful," Vansh said, "but our country has quite a few of its own problems, does it not?"

"This is what I told Naina when I convinced her to move back here. But she insists on putting her focus on foreigners." This from a man who had famously scraped his way out of poverty on the streets of Mumbai before arriving in Silicon Valley with the proverbial six dollars in his pocket.

"Your money is very convincing, Jiggy," Naina said indifferently. But her eyes were alert. Obviously, this wasn't the gossip session Jiggy was selling it as.

"All I want is for it to be put to good use."

"Oh, money can always be put to good use. That's the general point of money," Vansh said.

Jiggy's bark of laughter was so loud that everyone within a ten-foot radius started. One of the aunties even pressed a hand to her chest.

Jignesh thumped Vansh's shoulder, all delighted bonhomie. "If you have any ideas—pet causes, if you will"—he gave a knowing wink that made as much sense as his general behavior—"I'd love to hear them. Naina's endowment is large enough that she could easily share it with another worthy cause."

Naina, who had been making the effort to look bored, snapped to attention, her focus suddenly fully trained on the two of them. "I didn't realize my endowment was available for the taking."

"Well, it is my money, and young Mr. Raje seems like the kind of person who knows how to help people." Something like anger flashed in Jiggy's eyes, even as he went on smiling.

Before Naina could respond to that vote of confidence, the crowd started clinking their glasses and everyone's focus shifted to Yash as he jogged up onto the stage that had been constructed on the back lawn.

Californicators, the college beatboxing band that had been performing as part of a long lineup of local bands, gave him an impressive vocal drumroll, and Yash shoulder-bumped each of the seven members and said something that made every one of them look like they had just kissed the Pope's ring.

Love for his brother swelled inside Vansh.

Finally Yash took the mic and cleared his throat, and the sea of guests who had coalesced from around the estate grounds to circle the stage burst into cheers.

"What a perfect Northern California night," Yash said, managing to sound victorious, earnest, and in awe of the very earth they lived on. "A night filled with hope."

Vansh hooted gleefully and the crowd joined in.

"A night I've dreamed of from the day I first tied my own shoelaces in kindergarten and my mother said, 'You did that like someone who will run a country someday.'" Deafening cheering. Yash's eyes glistened with tears. "Thanks, Ma!"

"Your mother is never wrong," their mother shouted from the front of the crowd, her voice strong and proud.

Yash gave her a smile that made every woman in the crowd melt into a puddle and press her hands into her womb.

"Yes, Ma, you are never wrong." He touched a hand to his heart. "Another thing my mother taught me was that actions are more important than rhetoric, so I'll keep this short. We just made something historic and important happen, and we did it without engaging in lies and slander. We did it by coming up with ideas. Ideas that will fix what we, not someone else, *we*, all of us together, have broken. Our state's future is bright."

More cheers.

"We do an amazing job generating wealth and keeping our job market buzzing enough to shore up our nation's economy. But we cannot leave our citizens, too many of them, who are struggling, behind. We're miles ahead of the rest of the country in protecting our natural resources, but we cannot let fires consume us and bring destruction closer and closer to our doorsteps. We need solutions. We are the land of innovation. I am counting on each and every one of you to put your heads together for solutions. My door is open, I'm still finalizing my team, and I will introduce them to you soon. But I assure you that every person who works for me will be hungry for your input and ideas. This is our shot, we're going to make it good."

After that he thanked their parents, their grandmother. Every one of the siblings and cousins. He waved up to the balcony, where their grandmother waved down to him. Their cousin Esha, who never left the suite on the top floor when strangers were present on the estate, might have been listening too, and he said a special thanks to her.

He thanked every person on his team by name, and finally he invited India onstage and kissed her. Which was so sweet that the hoots and cheers mixed with laughter and *aww*s. By the time he and India left the stage hand in hand, gazes locked like they couldn't believe the other existed, there wasn't a dry eye in the crowd.

Well, maybe there was one. Naina was glowering at Jiggy as

though she hadn't heard a word of the speech. Bummer, because during his speech Yash had mentioned that he wouldn't have won without Vansh's help with the historic meeting.

Jiggy offered Vansh a handkerchief, which he politely declined given that the billionaire had sniffled into it wholeheartedly through the entire speech.

"You lost a good man," Jiggy said to Naina. Either the man had no talent for reading his audience, or he didn't care.

Naina smiled. A smile that said *Screw you* as clearly as those words could be said. "I did. And now you want to take away my funding too." She was in no mood to pretend that she gave a shit about anything other than her funding. "Sharing the funding was not the deal, Jiggy."

"It's a huge endowment. And I want to know what Mr. Raje comes up with."

Oh. So the man was serious about hearing Vansh's ideas.

Obviously, Naina had grasped this before Vansh had. She opened her mouth to answer, but Mehta raised a hand to cut her off. "Let's give him a project so we can keep him around. Don't you want to keep him around, Naina?"

She kept her eyes on Jiggy. Vansh might as well have been invisible. "Not if it means sharing the money I need to do my work."

Why, thanks a lot, Knightlina!

"You did the work just fine without my money, now you'll figure out how to do it with a little less of it. Stop being such a grouch. Let's go get some cake." Grabbing Naina's arm, he dragged her away.

The glare she threw at Vansh over her shoulder as she mouthed, *Don't even think about it,* should have burned him to ash. It probably did, because suddenly Vansh couldn't feel his limbs, unless that was the adrenaline that was suddenly pumping through him.

Why would he not think about it? He didn't even have a project in mind yet and he already had someone interested in funding him. He did have a talent for this, no matter what Ms. Kohli thought.

"That was the best speech I've ever heard," someone said behind Vansh, voice cracking with emotion. "I would follow Yash to the ends of the earth. Is there anyone who wouldn't?"

Vansh turned and found that it was the data guy from Yash's campaign team. Vansh looked around to see who he was talking to, but he was sitting by himself and evidently talking to himself.

"Hi, Hari," Vansh said. Remembering names was one of his talents.

There were five empty flutes of mimosas at the table, and instead of answering Vansh's greeting, Hari downed the sixth, half-empty glass and dug into a gigantic slice of cake.

"Congratulations," Vansh said to him. Hari had worked hard on Yash's campaign. He was a genius with numbers and data, and he'd taken the information on demographics and voting behaviors and figured out exactly where to put campaign dollars and time, right down to neighborhoods and streets.

He'd worked mostly alone in one corner of the office by himself, just the way he was sitting by himself right now at a table tucked away from the crowd.

"Do you know what you're going to do now?" Vansh asked. He understood only too well the emptiness one felt after a successful project. He made it a point never to linger too long on any project. Satisfaction, but also loss. Because the postvictory flush didn't take up quite as much time as one would think.

Since the election, Nisha had accepted the position of communications director. She had managed Yash's political campaigns for the past decade. This was her chosen career, unlike with the rest of the Rajes, for whom Yash's ambitions were more of a pet pastime.

Rico, Ashna's boyfriend, who had handled the media for Yash's campaign, was moving on to work on a state senator's campaign.

One of the incumbent California senators was done with his term limit and the primary for that seat was going to be a bloodbath in two years. Maybe Hari could work with him.

Everyone seemed to be moving along, doing things, changing the world. Vansh had never had any interest in the rat race. He'd shrugged off that life years ago. He'd chosen to join the Peace Corps instead of going to college. He'd decided to see the world, work on real problems instead of toeing the expected path like everyone around him.

He had a gift, a gift for making positive change, and he had always been true to that. The trick was keeping his heart open. Also his eyes and ears.

Hari threw a shifty look at his cake and poked it with a fork. He wasn't exactly comfortable with eye contact.

Yash hadn't yet announced jobs in the administration, but there wasn't much for someone with Hari's skill set to do on a governor's staff, at least not until he was up for reelection. From what Vansh remembered from their interactions, Hari was painfully shy, to the point where it was usually impossible to get him to talk.

The guy probably just wanted Vansh to leave him alone.

"No plans," Hari said, his voice loud in the way of people who weren't used to talking to other people. Or people who'd had one too many mimosas.

Vansh looked at the six empty glasses.

"I like orange juice," Hari said.

Ah.

Vansh sat down next to him. "Was this the first time you worked on a political campaign? Are you interested in working on another campaign? I can talk to Rico Silva."

Hari's hands started shaking and he put the fork down with a clang. His mouth was full of cake that he chewed and gulped furiously. "No, no. That's all right!" He stood; the chair toppled over behind him. "I have to go." He tried to back away but stumbled over the chair.

Jumping to the rescue, Vansh grabbed his arm and kept him from going down with the chair. Then, setting the chair straight, he pushed Hari back into it. The man was shaking.

"I was just making conversation," Vansh said gently. "It's just that you did such a great job on the campaign I thought it might be something you might like working on. We don't have to talk about your plans."

Hari hiccupped and picked up a red carnation from the red, white, and blue floral centerpiece and smelled it. Then went on smelling it with great focus.

Vansh raised his chin at the empty glasses. "All these, um, glasses of orange juice. Did you—"

Hari burst into tears.

Okay. Vansh patted his shoulder. "It's fine, I wasn't . . ."

Hari buried his head into his elbow on the table and started sobbing so hard his shoulders bounced.

Vansh looked around. There was no one close enough to notice. For a few minutes, Hari just cried and Vansh just patted his arm and made reassuring sounds, trying to calm him down without embarrassing him.

Without warning, Hari sat up and threw an accusatory glare at the empty champagne flutes. "It's really good juice. I've never had juice this good ever. I think all that sugar is making me sick."

"Actually that's not . . . never mind, I'm glad you liked it. Did you drive here?"

Another sob spurted out of Hari. "I don't have a car." More hiccupping sobs. "Do you think they'll care if I get another glass?"

He tried to stand.

Vansh tugged him back as gently as he could. "That's probably not a great idea. And it's okay. I don't have a car either." Maybe he shouldn't have said that. Was that a terrible privileged-person thing to say, given that he had access to seven Teslas in his family alone? "I'm sorry," he said.

Hari slipped him a quick sideways glance, then looked away again. "You're so nice. You're even nicer than your brother, and I don't know anyone who's nicer than Yash."

"Same. I don't know anyone nicer than Yash either. Listen. Do you have a friend who can drive you home? Or I can arrange for something. That orange juice, it was—"

Hari started weeping again. He pressed his face back into his elbow. "No one can drive me home. I don't have a home." As soon as the words left his mouth he sprang upright and pressed a hand to his mouth and jumped out of his chair again.

And teetered on his feet. Again.

"Here, let me help you." Vansh grabbed his arm and walked him to the alcove behind the pool house, where he forced him to drink a bottle of water, which Hari promptly threw up into the bushes by the pool, hopefully also expelling some of the alcohol he had consumed.

"Am I sick?" the poor man asked miserably. "Am I going to die?"

"We're all going to die someday," Vansh mumbled, then said, "Actually, that orange juice . . . it wasn't just orange juice."

"But it tasted exactly like orange juice," Hari said with equal parts confusion and conviction.

"That's because there was orange juice in it. Along with champagne. Well, sparkling wine made in Sonoma."

Hari looked horrified. "But I don't drink."

Not what the puke in my bushes says, buddy.

"If I drink. If I drink . . . I . . . I . . ." The sobs started again.

Okay, time to get him to a bed. Vansh pushed him into one of the patio chairs and brought him more water.

"You are so nice." Hari sniffled as he drank.

Vansh patted his back. "You said you had no home. What did you mean by that?"

Hari did another jack-in-the-box jump and promptly face-dived toward the patio. Fortunately Vansh had the reflexes of someone who'd spent many an evening with drunken friends in various parts of the world. He caught the man before he hit the ground and put him back in the chair.

"Let's sit for a few minutes without jumping out of the chair, please. And keep drinking." He handed him the bottle of water. If he thought the mimosas were orange juice, that meant they had gone down fast.

He needed some food to soak up all that alcohol, but Vansh couldn't leave him alone. So he took him back to the corner table where he'd found him. "Don't move until I get back."

Then he went to the food tent and grabbed a couple of samosas and brought them back. Wasn't Hari the guy who'd always taken the leftover donuts and pizza home from Yash's campaign office? A faint memory of the rest of the team teasing him about it nudged at Vansh.

Thankfully, Hari hadn't moved. He sat there slouched and felled by mimosas. Well, time to fix mimosas with samosas. Vansh handed him the plate.

"I grew up in a big house," Hari said as though it hurt him to make the declaration. "In Bhopal. Now I live in a tent."

As the words left his mouth his eyes widened to saucers and he shoved the entire, rather large samosa into his mouth. And promptly started choking.

Vansh slammed his palm into Hari's back, making him expel the clump of potatoes and pastry congealing his mouth shut and cutting off his oxygen supply. Vansh was all set to perform the Heimlich, but Hari sucked in a huge slurp of air and color rushed back into his face.

"You saved my life," Hari said. Tears streamed from his eyes, this time probably because he'd just been choking.

Everyone knew how very much Vansh enjoyed saving lives,

but this situation was a little too absurd even for him. He handed Hari another bottle of water and looked around to see if he could find reinforcements to help with the situation, but everyone seemed otherwise engaged.

Naina and Mehta were deeply engrossed in their conversation, and they were the only other guests still left in this part of the yard. Everyone else seemed to be packed around the stage, mobbing Yash and listening to the band, which was really getting into it.

"It was just a very large bite of samosa. I didn't really do anything," Vansh said, making Hari let out another grateful sound.

"You followed me when I tried to leave. You cared. No one cares to follow someone like me." The tears were flowing in earnest now and Vansh wished he could do something to make the poor guy feel better.

"Of course I followed you. And what do you mean someone like you? You're every bit as worthy of being taken care of as anyone else."

"I didn't mean to say that," Hari said on another sob.

Vansh made a face that he hoped showed his confusion.

"The tent." Hari said the words the way one confesses to a crime.

"I don't mean to pry. But are you saying you live in a tent on a campsite? Or are you saying something else?" Was he saying he was homeless?

Hari nodded, which was somewhat confusing. Vansh had enough experience with the South Asian head nod, but those had accents too, and Hari's wasn't clear.

Two thoughts struck Vansh at once. One, that homelessness had been the first thing to occur to him, and that said horrifying things about the city Vansh loved. Two, that he didn't know what he would do if he found out that someone who'd worked on Yash's campaign had been—*was?*—homeless.

"If my family ever found out, the shame would kill them," Hari added through his tears.

Find what out? Vansh leaned forward. "Is your family in India or here?"

"In India," Hari said. "My father is an imminent doctor."

Vansh assumed the man meant *eminent,* unless he meant that his father was still in medical school. "My parents' friends and relatives have property all over Bhopal. If they found out that Dr. Samarth's son lives on the streets like a beggar, my parents would have nowhere to hide their faces."

Holy hell, he was right about Hari's being homeless.

Vansh must have looked horrified, because Hari looked horrified in response. "I'm sorry, I should never have told you. But you saved my life and I got emotional. It's an emotional day." Hari grabbed Vansh's hand. "You won't tell Yash, will you? Yash would be so disappointed in me if he found out. He would never have hired me if he'd known."

"That's not true. You should know that Yash wouldn't judge you based on where you live."

Instead of placating him, this just made Hari look even more distraught. "You cannot tell him. Please. Please! I couldn't bear it if he found out."

"Hari, it's okay. Calm down. I won't tell anyone anything you don't want them to know. But what are you saying exactly? Have you been living on the street the entire time you've worked on the campaign?" Now that Vansh thought about it, the salaries Yash had been able to pay his team were nowhere near enough to live in the city. Most of the team commuted.

How had Hari not told this to anyone? How had the media not picked up on it? "Didn't you give up your partnership in your social media marketing firm to work on Yash's campaign?"

Hari looked around to make sure no one could overhear.

"That's what I had planned to do. I heard Yash speaking last year and I knew I had to work for him. I had to do everything I could to make his plans for California a reality. You know, my grandfather was a freedom fighter in India and he used to tell me the stories of marching with Gandhiji and being hit on the head with batons by the British troops." He stopped and thought for a moment. "I'm not sure if my grandfather told me that or if I watched that in that Gandhi movie with that British guy playing Gandhi," Hari added. "I was really young when my grandfather used to tell me his stories. But I do remember how hearing him talk about freedom and justice and the rights of people made me feel. And Yash made me feel like that too.

"When I came to America to go to grad school, I thought it would be the land of freedom and equality. And in many ways it was. But in so many ways it was not. Everyone was just running after things and fighting each other over politics and religion, and no one cared about the fact that old people had to work in Walmart and that the Tenderloin was covered in homeless tents."

Vansh opened a bottle of water and took a sip. Why was drunk rambling always so damned insightful and true? "You're absolutely right," he said.

"I should never drink," Hari said suddenly. "I had promised my mother that I would never drink after I told my cousin that she looked like a cross between a horse and a rat at her wedding. Drinking makes me tell the truth. Someone handed me a glass and I thought it was orange juice. Who puts alcohol in orange juice? Why would anyone do something that devious?"

Vansh gave his shoulder another pat. "Never mind all that. Where are you living right now?"

Hari stood, a little more steady now. "I think the invitation said six to ten and it's already past eleven, so I have to leave. The Samarths never outstay their welcome."

"Sit down, Hari. You can't go back to the tent." Now that Vansh knew, he couldn't not do something. How was he not going to tell Yash this?

"But that's my home."

"No, it's the pavement. Can you not afford a hotel room with your paycheck?"

"I had to pay off my debts. I'm still paying off my debts. And I can't let my spot go. If I remove my tent, someone else will take it."

How had Vansh never wondered how homelessness actually worked? "Okay, well, I'm going to check you into a hotel tonight. We will figure this out in the morning." Pulling out his phone, Vansh started looking for availability at hotels in the area.

Hari's hands started shaking. "That's very kind of you, but they won't let me stay in a hotel."

God, he was afraid to ask. "Why?"

"Because they need ID."

"You don't have a driver's license?"

"My backpack was stolen. My passport, my wallet, everything was in there."

Of course the man hadn't reported it.

How had Vansh never wondered how crime worked for the homeless? Did the cops cover the people who lived on the streets? Who protected them?

Vansh had so much to learn, but first he needed to figure out how to help Hari. Then he'd think about what all of this would mean to Yash if a journalist got their hands on this information.

No matter what, he could not let this poor man—who had made it possible for his brother to win the election—go back to living on the street. It was time to clean up the mess that was Hari's life. Good thing Vansh was good at cleaning up messes. Good thing he was ready for a new project.

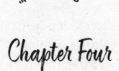

Chapter Four

Naina could not believe the brat was ignoring her phone calls. Sometimes she just hated the Rajes. Why the hell was she still stuck with them?

Because whether you like it or not, they are the only real family you've ever had.

Well, good thing she was used to living without family.

She still couldn't believe that bastard Mehta had offered up her funding to Vansh as though it were Halloween candy and Vansh and she were third graders, with Jignesh a teacher giving them lessons in how to share.

Naina's team in Nepal was already neck-deep in purchasing the land on which they would be building the clinics. The clinics were going to train local women to be midwives and employ doctors to provide prenatal and postnatal care. Right now the maternal mortality rate was nearly two hundred deaths per hundred thousand live births. Seventy-five percent of the deaths were avoidable by increasing accessibility to medical care. It was already too late to pull back on the number of clinics they had committed to.

They intended to use the Mehta endowment only to build. The maintenance and the running were going to be self-sustaining and paid for by the community and gramin banks. Naina had been working on the details of the microfinancing plan with the community leaders for the past six months. Everything was already in motion.

Vansh, with his cause célèbre bleeding heart, couldn't just walk in here and take clinics away from these women. Not when Naina had been waiting for ten years to find a way to pull her grand plan off.

Call me right now. Because I know where to find you, she texted Vansh.

Her phone rang almost immediately. It was a FaceTime call. She was at her desk, working, so she had to run to the hallway and check herself in the mirror. She pulled off the crab clip holding back her hair and fluffed it. Her hair hadn't grown back after the disastrous Haircut to Save Yash that had proved to the entire world what a fool she was.

God, she hated video calls.

"Well, good morning to you too!" the brat said as soon as she answered, tone all sunny, as though he were not trying to steal her endowment.

Wait, was he shirtless? "What do you think you're doing?"

"At this very moment, eating chocolate. Eighty-nine percent cacao." He chewed. Dear God, he was eating chocolate shirtless in bed.

"You're in bed. Eating chocolate." When tongue-tied, say the most obvious thing.

"I often eat chocolate after I brush my teeth. There's something about how the mint makes the chocolate taste." From the way his eyes got all dreamy it had to taste pretty darn good.

How was it okay for a man to have eyes like this? There were enough lashes lining the dark caramel brown that he probably needed to brush them a few times a day to take out the tangles.

They were even twisted together and flipping around in all directions. Like his hair.

This was why Naina never video-called people; the camera zoomed in on all sorts of details you didn't have to deal with when the whole person was present and not just their face ten inches from yours.

"There's something very wrong with you," she said, looking at the contrast between their faces on her screen. She didn't mean things like unfair lashes and shiny chocolate-stained lips that looked like they'd been pumped full of fillers. She meant her overworked scowl, which made her look like a frustrated witch, versus his self-indulgent smile, which made him look like a joyful angel. If that wasn't technology bastardizing facts, she didn't know what was.

"Can you please put a shirt on?" She hated that she sounded like a scolding auntie.

"Why?" He looked genuinely confused when he looked down at himself, which made the camera slide down his chest. And, well, what the hell? He was manscaped and glossy, and his muscles were cut in places where she'd never seen muscles cut before. At least not this close up and not outside of TV commercials and movies.

When had he gotten a tattoo? Did his mom know?

Okay, enough of this. *Enough.* "You've been ignoring my calls. And you're still in bed!"

He stopped studying his own body and brought his eyes back to the camera. "Did we have an appointment? Were we supposed to meet this morning?" He scratched the back of his head, which made his biceps, triceps, shoulders, *and* pecs flex in one choreographed swoop, *and* it made his tousled bedhead worse.

Who actually scratched the back of their head when they thought hard? Bad actors, that's who.

Put on a damn shirt!

She could not—*would* not!—be auntie enough to say it again. "First, it's past noon. So, if we were supposed to meet this morning, it's already too late. Second, responsible adults don't wake up in the middle of the day. Third, responsible adults don't smear chocolate into their teeth after they've cleaned them. It kind of defeats the purpose of the act of teeth brushing." They also don't call women while shirtless. Unless of course they thought of the women as not being women. "And finally, you don't steal a friend's work. It's just not something you do."

"Oof," he said, his tone miffed. "Say less."

"Can we not speak Gen Z please? I don't know what that means."

He laughed in the most self-satisfied way. "You're so intense in the morning, Knightlina. Which side of the bed did you wake up on?"

"I don't remember. It was seven hours ago!" She made every effort not to raise her voice. "Because it's a Monday morning and I have a job." That involved bettering thousands of lives.

Instead of getting out of bed, he sank back into his fluffy white pillows. "You sound bitter. It's not a good look."

"Wow, are you about to ask me to smile more?"

He reached over—making all sorts of parts flex and stretch beneath glossy skin again—and he must've pressed a button to raise the blinds, because when he settled back into those bright white pillows, columns of sunshine fell across his still-in-bed face and made the stubble on his perfectly square jaw glisten. Of course even his facial hair would grow out shiny.

"As a committed feminist, I resent that accusation," he said lazily. "It's a gorgeous thing when you smile, but you should smile only when you damn well feel like it. What I meant was you're the smartest, most selfless person I know, and bitterness is at odds with your true nature." He sounded like India Dashwood and it got on Naina's last nerve.

"Stop trying to be charming. I've known you since you were in diapers. The point is: I will not let you steal my funding. Not when I've worked decades for it. Not when you don't even have a project to fund."

"I wish you'd stop calling it stealing. That's seriously offensive. I've never stolen a thing in my life." He grinned, and the lighting combined with his unshaven jaw multiplied his dimples manifold. Good thing she knew exactly how much he weaponized those dimples. She remembered his unleashing them on all the aunties and melting them into puddles to get away with everything from getting extra cake at parties to getting them to double their donations to his school fundraisers. "Although, it is true that I have been accused of stealing many a heart."

She made a growling sound, and it made her feel like she was in a theatrical farce—one populated entirely by bitter old ladies. Why was it that every interaction with him these days felt like an off-Broadway production? Up until now he had been the Raje she'd had the easiest camaraderie with. "What's offensive is that you didn't say to Mehta: 'I appreciate your social-ladder-climbing, name-dropping need to work with me, but Naina actually does important, life-changing work and I would rather die than take even a penny away from it.'"

For the first time, his lazy demeanor slipped, and he sat up a little bit straighter. "You think the only reason Mehta wants to work with me is because of my last name?"

For the first time, she was glad this was a video call, because she didn't have to answer. She just had to raise a brow.

He looked wounded, but she didn't buy it, not for a second. "If that's true, then what does that say about why you got the funding last year, Knightlina, and not the year before that?"

How dare he? "Don't even think about saying what you're about to say next," she warned.

He ignored her warning. "So you're allowed to dismiss me and insult me, but I'm supposed to let you be an ostrich at my expense?"

"I'm not being an ostrich. I hear you loud and clear. You just suggested that I only got the funding because Yash was leading in the polls and I was with him." Did he have any idea how long and hard she had worked on this? Her entire adult life had revolved around her work.

"Only to disprove your theory that Jiggy-wiggy is offering me the funding because Yash is my brother." He sounded placating, and for some reason that made Naina even angrier. Must be nice to be this clueless.

"Do you genuinely believe that those two things have any sort of equivalency?"

"Of course they do. I'm not saying it's fair. But if you want to claim that one is true, then the other has to be." He had the gall to look like it hurt him to say it.

"Vansh, I'm not doing this with you right now. All I need from you is for you to call Mehta and tell him that you are not interested." Surely he couldn't be arrogant enough to think she'd let him get away with anything else.

"I can't do that. Aren't you at least going to ask me why I'm still in bed?"

"Do you ever get out of bed before noon?"

"I'm not dignifying that with an answer. But I was checking Hari into a hotel—"

"Your sex life is none of my concern and it only makes things worse."

"Wow, you really have no respect for me, do you? You're right, my sex life is not your concern. If it were, you'd know it never makes anything worse." Of course he had to grin at that. "Hari is one of the guys who worked on Yash's campaign, and I was checking him into a hotel."

"What? Are you talking about Yash's statistics guy? Why were you checking him into a hotel?" Had she missed that Vansh was gay?

"You're totally trying to figure out my sexuality right now, aren't you? Naina, Naina, Naina. Well, you can continue to objectify me freely. I am fairly certain I'm heterosexual."

She would not groan again. "Shut up. What were you doing with Yash's statistics guy?"

"Ah. So now you're interested."

"No, I'm really not." She had less than zero interest in anything to do with Yash's campaign. "But if it will get you to the point where you call Jiggy and refuse his offer because you don't need it faster, then let's get on with it."

He was sitting up now and getting out of bed, and she really wished he would put on some damn clothes, because he'd propped the phone on his nightstand and she could now see all the way down to his low-slung pajamas. Which were red with white polka dots. And the muscle-cuts-on-muscle-cuts situation was not restricted to the upper half of his torso.

"Vansh!"

He turned to the phone. And it was like one of those DaVinci Vitruvian Man animations of muscles in motion.

"Naina! I am not going to refuse the funding, because you just gave me an idea. Thank you!"

The urge to sink her face into her hands warred with the urge to shake him. "I'm shuddering here."

"Dirty girl, you're making me feel naked." Since when was it okay for him to talk to her as though she were one of his revolving-door girlfriends?

"You *are* naked, but I'm shuddering in fear of your idea."

He grinned with such self-satisfaction she couldn't tell if it was because he'd made her explain herself like a flustered girl or because he was just thrilled with himself in general. "I thought you'd be happy that I'm agreeing with you. It would be totes wrong for me to take the funding without a project. But I do have a project."

"Well . . . spit it out. I don't have all day."

His brows drew together and his lips pursed, making his dimples dig deep. "Why would I tell you if you're already dismissing it? Actually, even you couldn't dismiss this. Even you have to agree that homelessness is one of our greatest challenges in California."

Her groan came from her toes and burst forth with all the force of someone who really needed a break. Please, could she please catch a break? "What does Hari have to do with homelessness?"

"Well, I'm not at liberty to tell you. Actually, I need you to promise not to tell anyone about this conversation."

Who did he think she was close enough to that she could tell them she'd talked to Vansh—while he was half-naked—about that asswipe Mehta holding her funding over her head like a bone for a dog? It was too humiliating to share even with herself.

"I'm hardly going to run around telling people you were able to steal my endowment so easily. Do you have any idea how infuriating this is? Not to mention humiliating."

"Do you have any idea how condescending you're being right now? You're treating me like a child and I don't appreciate it."

He was a damn child. "Have you heard of *Emma*?"

"DJ's sister Emma Caine? The hot artist?" He disappeared for a second, then came back with jeans on and finished zipping them up. Why on earth did he think their relationship was close enough for him to be pulling on clothes in front of her?

"No, it's a book. The one DJ's sister was named after." Trisha's boyfriend DJ's name was Darcy James. And his sister's name was

Emma. Evidently their mother had been a big Jane Austen fan. "By Jane Austen."

"Right, I remember Emma mentioning that. Isn't Jane Austen that Darcy chick? Isn't he the one that Brit actor played who all the aunties were gaga over? Colin Farrell?"

Naina did it: she rubbed her hand across her face like someone who needed to erase this entire conversation from existence. "So . . . in the book *Emma*—which has nothing to do with Darcy, who is from *Pride and Prejudice*—Emma is an overindulged, albeit well-meaning, brat who is looking for matchmaking projects so she can feel good about herself while filling all that empty time she has on her overprivileged hands."

He pressed a fist against whatever tattoo was emblazoned across his left pec. Naina refused to stare at his pecs long enough to figure out what it was. "Young lady, are you accusing me of matchmaking?" he said in a bad British accent, sotto voce.

She should not smile, because this was not a joke. "No, I'm accusing you of looking for projects so you can feel good about yourself and relieve your boredom."

He picked the phone up from the nightstand and held it up. He was pouting and blinking vapidly, but his eyes shone with wounded anger. "Oh good gosh, I think you might have, like, had a breakthrough on my behalf or something." How had she found his habit of constantly doing voices amusing before this?

And why on earth did she feel like such a jerk? "All I'm saying is that my work is important to me, but it's also vital to a lot of women who need it."

"Mine is too. And you're wrong. This project is important."

"What project? This is not a game, Vansh."

"I know it's not. I need to figure out the details, but letting Mehta's millions help the homeless in our city seems important too."

"*Figure out the details?* Don't you see, what you're talking about is an Emma Project. It's vanity. It's looking for ways to play with people's lives out of ennui."

"No, it isn't." Now he looked really angry. "I can't believe this is what you think of me. You haven't even heard what it is."

"Fine. Tell me then."

A smile spread across his lips but his eyes stayed angry. He blinked, a slow, deliberately vapid blink. "Didn't you hear me? I think your Emma's going to, like, y'know, tackle homelessness in San Francisco." He used a high-pitched voice that was quite frankly offensive to every woman alive. With that he hung up, and Naina had not a clue how much of what he'd said was meant to be facetious and how much was going to screw up her life.

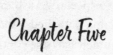

Chapter Five

Of all the emotions in the world, the one that Vansh disliked experiencing more than any other was anger. Rage killed brain cells. Well, he didn't know if that was true, but anger was simply unnecessary to accomplish anything. The world today put too much of a positive spin on rage. Rage was a form of hate. How could anything positive come from hate?

Naina had certainly made rage boil up inside him a few times. How dare she dismiss him this way? Vansh turned the speed up on the treadmill and lengthened his stride.

Jiggy Mehta had not offered to work with him because of his last name. Nor had he done it because Vansh was the governor-elect's brother. Mehta was simply aware of the fact that Vansh had spent his life understanding problems and working to solve them hands-on, at ground level.

Emma Project, indeed!

He'd show her exactly how much this was not an Emma Project.

He had gone to bed at seven that morning. Not because he was out drinking like other twenty-six-year-olds, but because he had spent the night trying to convince Hari that Vansh was going to get him safely off the street and then making it happen. This involved packing up and safely storing Hari's belongings—which, naturally, Hari was very possessive about—and finding a hotel and then staying with him until Hari stopped crying and self-flagellating about how he had messed up.

Hari had made Vansh promise over and over again that he would not tell anyone—especially Yash and Nisha—that he was homeless. Holy shit, Naina had riled Vansh up enough that he'd let slip that Hari and homelessness were related. Naina was simply too smart to not suspect some sort of connection between the two. Vansh looked at his phone and wondered if he should text her to remind her that it was confidential information. No, that would just confirm her suspicions. He'd wait to tell her in person.

Poor Hari. Vansh would never forget the expression on his face when he'd become overwhelmed with emotion after Yash's speech. Sure, mistaking mimosas for orange juice was funny, but the man was more guileless than anyone Vansh had met in a very long time. There was not a trace of self-interest in him. Even on Vansh's missions around the world, the friends he made always had an agenda. Hari was just trying to exist and having such a hard time of it. If anyone needed a hand, Hari did.

Keeping this secret meant Vansh could not go to the family for help.

He upped the speed on the treadmill even more and spent another twenty minutes running too hard to think. Then he lifted for forty minutes. Fortunately the gym in his parents' house was down the corridor from his room. Even more fortunately, Ma was probably too tired after Yash's party to join Vansh. When he was home she liked to walk on the treadmill next to him and catch up with him. Usually he was grateful to have her. Today he was grateful to be alone. Working out helped him think. Today, not so much.

Shaving and showering made him feel a little better. He spent an extra-long time drying and styling his hair, but the angry churn inside him was being stubborn. He took the foyer stairs down to the kitchen. Sometimes the grandeur of his parents' house grounded him. Again, today something was different.

He went looking for J-Auntie, his parents' housekeeper, to see if she'd make him a sandwich. Only because she would act all wounded if he made one for himself. His stomach growled. He always lived at the Anchorage when he came back to California. Yes, his parents' estate had a name. Yes, he knew exactly how pretentious that sounded. Now that he had decided to stay in California for the foreseeable future, he had to figure out where he would live.

Oh, who was he kidding? Ma would go into full-blown Extra Ma mode if he suggested living anywhere but here. He knew Ma hated that they all had their own places now that they were adults. It used to be the Indian way to live with your parents until you were married, and even after that if you chose. His older siblings had moved out after college. They'd had that tangible threshold to cross. Vansh hadn't gone to college but he'd lived mostly out of the home since the age of sixteen.

Ma had worked hard to make their family home a sanctuary for them, and he was glad for it. The Anchorage was even more comfortable than the palace of his ancestors.

The Rajes had ruled the kingdom of Sripore for a century before the Europeans colonized India and the British took over Sripore. Growing up, their mother had dragged them to Sripore every summer, intent on keeping them acquainted with their royal Indian roots.

Sagar Mahal, the Sripore palace, was a magical place, especially for a little boy with more energy than anyone knew what to do with. Every summer there was something new to discover, a chamber no one knew about, a tower with a secret staircase, a trapdoor in the back of a closet. Being the youngest of his siblings, five years younger than Ashna, who was the closest to him in age, Vansh had been left mostly to his own devices.

He was also the only one of his siblings who wasn't obsessed with reading. He'd heard one of the nannies at the Sagar Mahal tell one of the servants that the Baby Prince was more energetic and harder to handle than the others because he didn't read.

Having a learning disability in a family where academic brilliance was taken for granted wasn't fun, but it had been a while since Vansh had felt the sting of it.

Naina was one of the few people who knew how much he'd struggled with dyslexia. She'd read textbooks to him before exams when she'd hung out at the Anchorage. She'd had a way of doing it without making him feel stupid. And yet she had brought up a book and used it to treat him like he was stupid *and* lazy. But no, anger was never the answer. It's just that it was Naina. For all her scolding and teasing, he'd never known her to be mean. Unlike his sisters, who could be brutal, Naina was careful about how she treated people.

Most people saw her as cold and prickly, but that was because she didn't know how not to be honest in her reactions to people and she was uncomfortable with exposing any kind of vulnerability. Then there was the fact that she thought she was always right. Truthfully, though, who among us didn't?

That was exactly the reason why when she'd treated him like he was stupid, it hurt. He knew being dyslexic didn't have anything to do with his intelligence. No matter how severe his dyslexia, it didn't reflect on his ability to process information. He had proved that over and over again his whole life.

Hadn't he?

As he passed the empty den, he stood outside the glass-paned French doors. This was where he'd been standing when he'd overheard his parents. He'd been in kindergarten. It had been years since he'd even thought about that day.

Trisha knew the periodic table by heart at four, his father had said, his voice too angry for those words.

You know Trisha is not regular, she's an exceptional child, his mother had said, her voice too sad for those words.

All the others were reading chapter books by kindergarten. He can't even read words. How can one of my children be stupid?

Vansh had heard that children who walked in on their parents having sex never forgot it, no matter how young they were. There was just something innocence altering about that experience that made it indelible. There were few other experiences like that. Experiences that involved being violated in some way. Experiences like hearing your father call you stupid with such finality.

Vansh remembered everything about it. Like a scene in a movie imprinted inside his brain. Clear and stark and sepia toned.

His parents had the kind of relationship that made their friends roll their eyes with envy. Vansh had seen this his whole life. Children noticed things. His parents were always gentle with each other. Much more so than any other couple he'd ever seen. But that day, Vansh remembered his mother stepping into his father's space, not a hint of gentleness in her. *He is not like the others. You can't have the same expectations for him as you do for the others. But if I ever hear you call one of my children that ugly word again, I will walk out of this house with all four of them and never look back.*

There had been no raised voices. His father had responded only with the softest, *Sorry.*

After that there had been endless special ed teachers, therapists, experts. Whatever form of dyslexia Vansh had, it had taught him one thing early on: the only cure was to not read. Through school, he had access to all materials on audio and visual aids. He always took all tests separately from other students. Every teacher was unerringly kind. Every principal, who always knew him by name, made sure of it.

At home the pressure on his older siblings to excel was brutal. The quiet silence in that space when it came to Vansh was palpable. The Raje children were universally acknowledged as gifted learners. So, strife over academic pressure was rare, but every once in a while there would be tears over grades, fights over how unfair this or that teacher was. None of these meltdowns ever happened with Vansh in the room.

He only overheard them because like all youngest siblings he was adept at the art of eavesdropping. Without exception, everyone in his family was only ever complimentary about his schoolwork. About everything he ever did, really.

The truth was that he could never explain quite how much work it took to process something everyone else took for granted, to memorize and work around words. To hide. Consequently the need to have anyone understand that part of him had died a long time ago.

In eleventh grade he had chosen to go to a boarding school all the way in Northern India that promised alternative learning. There were no tests there, and he'd been surrounded by artists and musicians. He'd learned that the pursuit of success was a hamster wheel he could choose not to get on.

After high school, when he said he wanted to take a gap year and travel the world, his family had nothing but encouragement for him. After the gap year, when he decided not to go home but to join the Peace Corps, everyone acted like it was the most brilliant idea ever. After that he decided to go to Sripore and work with his aunt on her foundation for a while, and everyone acted like it was the most selfless and admirable thing to do. He never brought college up again and no one else did either. There was just never any time as he raced from cause to cause, project to project.

For the first time in his life, the need to run seemed to have exhausted itself out of him. It was strange to have this realization hit him here, outside these glass-paned doors. He liked who he was. It no longer felt like that wasn't enough. Now that he'd helped Yash achieve something amazing here, his parents' home no longer felt like the place he had to leave to prove things. This corner of the world had always felt different from everywhere else. Now it felt less complicated, safe. Vansh wanted to follow the urge to see how long it lasted.

As for Naina Kohli's vision of him not matching his own, it was just a matter of plucking out the nail she'd hammered into his self-esteem. Good thing pulling nails from his self-esteem was one of his many talents.

"What are you mumbling to yourself about?" J-Auntie asked as Vansh made his way into the kitchen, which was the size of the last apartment he'd shared with two people.

She was arranging cucumber sandwiches on a platter. A steaming teapot of chai and teacups sat neatly on a service trolley.

Vansh picked up a sandwich and popped it whole into his mouth. If J-Auntie's cooking could be counted as evidence, then his parents' home was definitely the best place on earth. Picking up two more sandwiches, one in each hand, he proceeded to stuff his face.

"Delicious, Auntie! How do you make cucumber taste like this?" Paper-thin slices of cucumber, delicately spiced Greek yogurt spread, and pillowy whole-grain bread. This was the life.

"His Highness was looking for you earlier," she said instead of acknowledging his praise, expression flat and respectful, the way it always was when she brought up his father. When anyone brought up the venerable HRH. That's what Vansh and his siblings called their father, His Royal Highness Shree Hari Raje. Behind his back, of course. He was a prince, and nothing fit him better than HRH.

Vansh finished the rest of his sandwich in one bite. It was not usual for HRH to ever be looking for him.

"But then he had to leave," J-Auntie said.

Vansh tried not to heave a sigh of relief and threw another hungry look at the sandwiches.

She handed him the platter. "Why don't I warm up a bowl of chicken makhni and rice for you."

"Was Yash here for lunch?" Yash was scheduled to move into the governor's mansion in a couple of weeks. He had a condo in San Francisco, and India had partially moved in with him, although she still ran her family's yoga studio in Palo Alto. But if there was chicken makhni in the house, that could only mean that Yash had been over for a meal.

J-Auntie smiled fondly. Yash and Vansh were her favorite people on earth, much to their sisters' chagrin. "Yes, Yashu came over with Ms. India but he left with your parents for a meeting. Ms. India is upstairs helping your grandmother and Esha with some yoga. Nisha brought baby Ram over and she's with them."

"Ram's here?" Vansh couldn't keep the excitement from his voice. He grabbed the tea tray from the trolley. "I'll take this up for you. Oh, and, J-Auntie, can you toss me a salad instead of the chicken makhni, please? I think I just ate seven of these sandwiches."

If he could help it, Vansh preferred not to fill his body with chicken soaked in cream sauce like his brother, who had the eating habits of a portly Indian uncle. Or as their sisters put it, the appetite of a PMSing woman. Fortunately for Yash, he was as blessed in his metabolism as he was with everything else. Even more fortunately, he was in love with a yoga instructor who'd hopefully inspire him to better his eating habits so he didn't have a heart attack in his forties.

Vansh couldn't exactly complain about his own metabolism either, but what was the point of working out for hours every day if you didn't respect your body? Vansh liked looking the way he looked, and the governor-elect of California certainly did not have a body like this.

Taking the tray with him, Vansh ran up to the suite on the third floor where his oldest cousin, Esha, and their grandmother lived.

Esha had never left the estate since she'd first moved here when she was eight, more than thirty years ago and long before Vansh's birth. Her parents, HRH's older brother and his wife, had died in a plane crash along with every other passenger on board except Esha, who had miraculously survived. But after the accident, Esha had started to have seizures, accompanied by visions when she came in contact with any new person.

"Look! The Baby Prince has arisen from his slumber!" Nisha called as Vansh carried the tray into the open living room that led to his grandmother's and cousin's bedrooms.

"A mere servant, Princess. I come bearing your favorite sweetmeats."

Nisha shivered. She hated the word *sweetmeats*, for no good reason except that the staff at the Sripore palace used that word to describe mithai, or any dessert really, and Nisha hated thinking about meat in her dessert. Which was 100 percent Nisha.

She grabbed two sandwiches from the plate and blew Vansh a kiss with a thank-you. India and Esha took only one sandwich each like civilized humans.

"Nursing mother. Must make milk." Nisha pointed at her breasts with the sandwiches and Vansh rolled his eyes. No way was he reacting with embarrassment. First, his sisters had beaten any embarrassment about womanly things out of him young. Second, if he reacted, they'd lecture him about how breastfeeding was perfectly natural. It was. Even so, a lecture about it over cucumber sandwiches wasn't at the top of his list of fun conversations.

India Dashwood was kneeling on the floor beside his grandmother with her hands on Aji's knees. She was massaging above the kneecap with careful movements.

Vansh dropped a quick kiss on Aji's head.

"I haven't seen you since breakfast last morning," their grandmother said. It was her way. Aji always started every conversation with her grandchildren with when she'd seen them last. This usually involved tears when Vansh was away and talked to her on the phone, at least a few times a week. It was much more lighthearted when he lived in the same house as her.

"I had lunch with you up here yesterday, Aji," he said without much conviction because he knew what she was going to say in response.

"Well, scarfing down a salad in ten minutes and then running off does not count. How do you have these big muscles when you don't eat anything?"

Vansh scooped up his nephew from his baby carrier. Ram had come into the world on the day Yash won the election, and Vansh didn't think there was another being on earth he loved more than this guy. Maybe Mishka, Nisha and Neel's older daughter, who was nine going on nineteen. But it was close.

"Ram Raje Graff, you are unarguably the most beautiful baby ever born on God's green earth," he told his nephew, who listened with rapt interest, his lovely blue-gray eyes twinkling. "You have the legendary lashes of your Vansh Mama. Now, this isn't for the faint of heart. It brings with it far too much attention from women. But I will share my tricks for managing the adulation. And don't worry about the cheeks. They might be the chubbiest cheeks in existence, but they will give way to this finely chiseled jaw."

"Will he also grow into the obnoxious vanity?" Ram's mother asked, not looking in the least bit worried.

Ram grabbed Vansh's nose with his chubby fist, an act of

solidarity Vansh appreciated. He pulled away and blew into his nephew's pillowy stomach, making him giggle. "Already my man is holding his own amid all these scary women.

"'I'm not afraid of them,'" he added in baby Ram's voice. "'I have a gavel like my daddy.'"

India and Esha spurted laughter. Even their grandmother laughed. Nisha kicked Vansh without stopping in her chewing. "Look, Ram, your uncle is wearing one of your shirts."

They all thought that was terribly funny too and guffawed some more.

"Don't listen to them," he said to his nephew. "It's a muscle shirt. It's supposed to be fitted to your muscles. But old people don't know that."

He sat down next to Esha, crossed his legs, and settled Ram in his lap.

"You look well," Esha said. She always said that to him, and it made him happy because it seemed to make her so happy when she said it. Then she frowned, studying his face. "Whom did you fight with?" Did he mention Esha was clairvoyant?

"Disagreement over work with someone." It was always best to stick with the truth with Esha. Everyone in his family had a sixth sense about when he lied, but Esha's clairvoyance was foolproof.

"Work? Are you leaving again? So soon?" Nisha asked, not looking happy at the prospect. Usually, any attempt from the family to keep him from taking off made Vansh restless. Today, it felt nice.

"No, actually I'm thinking about staying for a bit."

Nisha studied his face, eyes brightening, then getting skeptical. "A bit? Like how much a bit?"

"I don't know. I haven't decided."

Nisha and Esha sat up excitedly.

"Vansh! That's amazing," Nisha said. "That's the best news ever!"

"It is," Esha said. "It is a really good choice."

Until Esha said it, Vansh hadn't realized that there had been a prickle of doubt nudging at him. Now he felt like this was exactly what he needed to do.

J-Auntie brought up Vansh's salad, and after some good-natured but still entirely too nosy ribbing about his "himbo" eating habits, he ate in peace as they watched Ram try to jam a precocious fist into his own mouth.

When India came back out after helping Aji to her room with her achy knees, Nisha asked when Siddhartha was getting in. India's brother, Siddhartha, was an award-winning wildlife photographer who had spent the past eight months in Papua New Guinea photographing birds. Vansh had never met him, but he felt an odd kinship with him. Two men with wanderlust and a higher purpose.

Siddhartha was supposed to have arrived a few days before the election in November, but he had developed a fever and had to delay his visit until he was healthy enough to travel. That must have been some fever if it had taken two months to recover.

"I was hoping to meet him at the victory celebration," Vansh said. He had been totally disappointed when Siddhartha had not shown up.

"It's pretty amazing that he's a finalist for the Goodall award," Nisha said.

"Isn't it? I can't believe he's a finalist again," India said proudly. "He was a finalist seven years in a row but never won. Then he stopped entering. This year a friend entered him and he's a finalist again. I'm not sure he's happy. I don't think he enjoys the attention and he doesn't believe he'll ever win. But I think this year is different. You have to see the picture that finaled. It's amazing."

India reached for her quilted backpack and took out a magazine. "He refuses to text or email his pictures. But he always remembers to mail us the magazines. We just have to wait for the mail, and these days that feels like the pony express."

Vansh had never imagined India Dashwood could sound so gushy. She sounded like his sisters sounded when they talked about Yash.

India started to flip through the magazine until she came to a page with an eagle-like bird. The joint breath of every person in the room drew in as one. It was magnificent.

The bird's plumage was almost bright red in the sun, and it made a stunning contrast with a head and breast of pure white. The thing that jumped off the page, though, was the obsidian, knowing depth of its eyes. When you looked closer you saw that it was perched on the rusted butt of an old cannon.

Even with that detail, it might have been just another well-taken photograph until you noticed a ring of dragonflies circling its proud head like a floating crown. Every one of them gasped at the sheer power of the captured moment.

Next to Vansh, Esha went utterly still. She reached for the magazine and took it from India, her face drained of color. Vansh had watched Esha have several seizures through his childhood. They were rarer now, and it had been a while since he'd witnessed one. She stood on unsteady legs, magazine clutched so tight it made her knuckles white, eyes glued to the page.

The moment hung on to itself.

No one moved.

Without a word, Esha turned and went into her room, magazine pressed to her chest, and shut the door behind her.

Nisha squeezed Vansh's hand.

"I hope it was okay that I took out the magazine like that. I'm so sorry," India said worriedly.

"Esha reads newspapers and magazines. So, it wasn't that," Nisha reassured her.

"Should I go in and check up on her?" India asked.

Nisha looked unsure. "Let's wait a little. She probably just needed a moment. Sometimes she needs that. She likes us to help only when she asks for help."

For the next few minutes they sat there in silence, staring at the door to Esha's room. The hands on the grandfather clock ticked in silent jerks. Ram had fallen asleep on Vansh's lap and was sucking on his fist. He'd finally figured out how to get it into his mouth, and small exhausted snores escaped him.

Finally Esha came back out, face as calm as ever. The magazine was no longer in her hand.

Ram gave another snore and Esha smiled, which made them all breathe again.

"You never told me who you fought with," she said to Vansh as though she hadn't left two minutes ago like someone who'd seen a ghost.

"Naina," Vansh said, because he had no idea how to lie to Esha.

Nisha opened her mouth, then shut it when she remembered that India was in the room.

Mad as Vansh was at Naina, he didn't like what he saw on Nisha's face. He'd never understood why his sisters were always so awkward around her. Admittedly Yash and Naina's relationship hadn't been conventional. They'd spent more time together when they'd been friends than they had after they had started "dating." Which made sense because it had turned out that it had been fake dating all along.

Vansh was sketchy on the details, mostly because, in true Raje fashion, only the part of the information necessary to move on from the problem had been shared. Yash behaved as though getting into a fake relationship with his best friend to avoid dating was a mere misstep. And Naina behaved as though using it as a workaround for her daddy issues was none of anyone else's business. Pretty much like everything else about her life. Her resting face was a giant fuck-you to the world.

Why it suddenly bothered Vansh so much when it was directed at him, he had no idea. But when Naina took an interest in him, there was no dishonesty to it, no pretense. Just like when she disapproved, she held nothing back. Which made her opinion hard to dismiss.

Obviously his sisters didn't feel the same way. Ever since the fake-dating secret had come out, they'd acted like she was the Wicked Witch of the West Coast.

For a long moment Esha studied him, her eyes flickering with understanding as though she could hear his thoughts.

"Naina," Esha said finally, picking up a cucumber sandwich and examining it as though it were an irreconcilable piece in a complex puzzle. "I don't think you should back down."

Chapter Six

Not a day went by when Esha Raje didn't have to let the accident that changed her life go. Every single day. The airplane shaking around her. The screams that sounded so far away she wasn't sure if she was straining to hear them or blocking them out, because even at eight she knew they were different. Wild. Final. Dying screams.

What Esha hadn't known then was that she'd hear them for the rest of her life. Clear as the day it happened.

Over thirty years now.

Every day she sorted through the wreckage.

Every day she sorted the good from the bad and held on. To Aie and Baba Saheb, her parents.

Her aie, who had been filled with stories, the starched folds of her saris wrapping up an endless supply. Yarns she spun and wove all through the day into Esha's ears.

"You really should write that book," Baba Saheb had said over and over.

After Aie was gone, her stories had been lost, mangled in the metal of the wreckage.

Every day Esha dug through the debris and shook out the stories. Picked out the shrapnel from the detritus.

The press of her parents' arms around her. *It's okay, Eshu. It's okay, beta. It's okay. We're here . . .* , an echo in two voices, one in each ear. Arms wrapped around her, tight, so tight that for those last minutes they'd left no breath inside her.

Just bruises from their grip on her arms, their names on her tongue, their voices deep inside her ears.

Every day she tried to remember. Every day she tried to forget.

"I'm bored, Aie." They'd barely been in the air for an hour, but plane rides were the most boring things on earth.

Aie threw a glance around their private jet. A few friends had joined them on the trip. They were stretched out on the plush brocade seats, reading, listening to music, watching movies on giant personal screens. Brightly colored drinks sat in glasses next to them, with those sweet pink cherries Esha's nanny always let her have in her lemonade when the adults had drinks. The staff traveling with them were in the back.

"Aie, I'm bored," Esha repeated.

"Aie Saheb," her mother corrected gently. "Remember what your aji says. In public we say Aie Saheb. Protocol is important to your grandmother. Tradition is how we hold on to our ancestors."

"Leave her be," Baba Saheb said. "She's on holiday. I'm already taking this holiday because Ma Saheb has been on my case. Now let the child do as she pleases while she's away from the palace."

"As if you don't let her do as she pleases when she's in the palace." Esha loved to hear her parents bicker. Scolding and teasing, with that sparkle in their eyes that Esha only ever saw them get when they talked to each other.

"As if you don't either."

They were both right. There wasn't anything Esha wanted to do that she couldn't.

"Why do we need to hold on to our ancestors? Don't people die when they're ready to go away?" Esha asked, playing with the gold bangles on her mother's wrist. "Aji says if we hold on too tight we keep our people from moving on to the next life."

Aie had laughed at that, and Baba Saheb had shaken his head. "This is the result of filling our daughter's head with stories all the time."

Speaking of stories . . . Esha bounced in her seat. "Story, Aie, I'm bored."

"Tell her that one." Baba Saheb leaned back in his seat, the gold upholstery pushing out around his head like the sun halo on Lord Vishnu's crown. "The story you told me to get me to fall in love with you."

"I thought you fell in love with Aie—Aie Saheb—when she dropped the teacup and spilled hot tea in your lap," Esha said.

Her parents looked at each other in that way again, that way that made Esha feel hugged even when they weren't hugging her.

"I have the burn scars to prove it," Baba Saheb mumbled. "Inconveniently located too."

Aie's face went red and Baba Saheb reached across Esha to stroke the color brightening her cheeks. For a moment Esha was filled up with so much happiness she thought she'd burst. Her parents were the best parents in the world and someday she would marry a man exactly like Baba Saheb. Powerful, regal, kind. And she'd be a wife exactly like her aie. Soft, clever, and full of blushes.

Smiling, Aie turned to Esha. "Do you know who Garuda is?" She always started all her stories that way. *Do you know who Ram is? Do you know who Krishna is? Do you know who Mahatma Gandhi is?*

Even though Esha pretty much knew who every single person on earth was, thanks to Aie's stories and Baba Saheb's library and the collection of biographies for children that her uncle Shree had bought her for her first birthday. She was her uncle's favorite person on earth, as he always told her, but even he hadn't expected her to read at one.

"Dear Mahesh Dada, This is so you remember to pause in your politics to read to my niece. Love, Shree." It was the note her father used as a bookmark when he did read to Esha from the collection every night that he was home.

Everyone was always telling Baba Saheb to slow down, to take a breath. But Esha liked how he was always in motion, like the ocean waves outside Esha's window at the Sagar Mahal. Crashing and retreating and pushing and pulling and never stopping.

They were on that plane headed to Seychelles because her grandmother had given her son an ultimatum. "I'm not speaking at your rally for the next election if you don't take your wife and daughter on a holiday."

"Thank you for this," Esha had heard her aie say to him before they left for the airport as she attached his gold chain buttons to his kurta. Then she'd smiled in that way that made Esha think her aie knew everything, saw everything. "Even the fact that there's an environmental conference in Seychelles doesn't keep this from being special."

Her father had turned utterly serious. "You and Esha are the only thing in the world that matters. You know that, right?" he'd asked. "I'd give everything up for the two of you if you asked."

Esha had to shake all of this out of her head every day. Because in the end it all led to the story. "Do you know who Garuda is?"

Esha nodded, ready as she always was for the story.

"Once upon a time," Aie started in her storyteller's voice, "in the time of the Vedas, high in the Himalayas, two sisters, Vinata and Kadru, were married to the sage Kashyapa. One day, a celestial white horse flew past them in the sky. The sisters were struck by its beauty, but as always, they got into an argument. This time over the color of the horse's tail. Vinata believed it to be white like the rest of the horse. Kadru insisted that the white horse had a black tail.

"Stubborn in their beliefs, they entered into a wager. The loser of the bet would spend her life in servitude to the other sibling after they inspected the horse up close the next day.

"Kadru was the mother of a thousand snakes, and she ordered her sons to find the horse and attach themselves to its tail so that it would appear black during inspection. When the tail was found to be black, Vinata accepted defeat. So began her lifelong servitude to her sister.

"A few years later, Vinata bore a winged son, a boon from the gods for her service. Garuda was the strongest of all birds, and his snake half brothers would task him perpetually with chores that tested his strength. Being his mother's son, he too was automatically bound into servitude.

"When he was old enough to know about the lost wager, he vowed to earn their freedom back and asked the snakes what it would take. They asked him to acquire amrit, the nectar of immortality, from the gods.

"Garuda set off on the quest. Along the way, he fought a tribe of fishermen, then a monstrous elephant and tortoise, and saved a group of Valakhilya falling from the branches of a banyan tree. Finally he made it to the chamber where the nectar of immortality was guarded by the gods. The fiercest battle ensued, but Garuda vanquished the gods and claimed the nectar.

"More quests awaited him on his way home, but he made it through each. Finally, the king of the gods, Indra, tried to win the nectar back, but Garuda's courage and strength impressed him and the two became friends. Garuda told Indra that after he had delivered the nectar and earned his freedom, Indra could immediately steal it back from the snake broth—"

The plane gave a violent jerk, cutting Aie off. A few startled screams rose, then died down amid shocked laughter. Before Esha's heartbeat could return to normal, another violent bounce followed and the plane started to drop. Right out of the sky. This time the screams filled the plane and didn't stop. Esha's parents' arms wrapped around her.

"Stay calm, everyone. Stay in your seats." Baba Saheb's voice was lost in the screams.

"Think about the story," her mother said. "Don't be afraid. Focus on the story."

"What happened next?" Esha asked as the plane bounced and slipped and heat rose around them. "What happened to Garuda?"

"Garuda . . ." The word flew from Aie, slicing the air as the plane blew apart around them. For a second Esha was suspended, her parents' arms flying from around her. But only for a second. Then she was wrapped in warmth, a thousand feathers enfolding her as she spun down to earth, leaving flames in the sky.

The next thing Esha remembered was waking up tangled in tree branches. Rain falling from the heavens in sheets. The sound of voices rose from the earth below. Great beams of light cut through the night.

"Aie . . . Baba Saheb . . ." She tried to say their names but her voice wouldn't come out as more than a whisper. The voices on the ground continued to blast through the air, but Esha couldn't make out their words.

That's when she heard a sound. Much closer. The flapping of wings. It was hard to see in the darkness, but she squinted, and it spread its wings, the span wider than Esha's own spindly arms, the head a stark white. Eyes like two moons ringed in light.

"Garuda?" she whispered, and the word gave her back her voice.

"Say it louder," the bird seemed to say to her. "Say it louder."

She screamed it. "Garuda!" Her voice got louder with every scream. "Garuda! Garuda! Garuda! . . ."

"It sounds like there's a voice coming from up there," someone said on the ground. The beams of light poked upward, slashing through the branches she was tangled in.

"I'm here!" she screamed. "Help me! I'm here!"

Garuda watched her, moonlight eyes encouraging her.

So she went on screaming.

"We're here. You're safe," a voice said from the ground. "You're safe. Just wait. We'll get you down."

It was the last thing she heard before everything was gone again, swallowed up by the darkness.

When Esha woke up in the hospital, her grandmother was holding her hand.

That's when the first vision had come. Her grandmother finding out that her oldest child was dead. The pain of it had seared Esha's insides, alive, immediate. The moment, the place where Aji had found out, all of it inside Esha. All at once. Aji's pain, Esha's own pain, it had grown so large so fast that Esha had convulsed with it, then passed out.

Not one other person on the plane had survived. Just her.

For weeks, she was sure she was dead. She had to be. This new person wasn't her. This person was filled with screams, her brain a screen with endless flashing light. Scenes, scrolling and scrolling and scrolling with ugliness and terror like knives hacking at it without slashing through it. An impossible-to-unravel snarl of thoughts and pain and death. Every person at the palace was inside her head, all their feelings, all their actions, all these places Esha had never seen, churning inside her, wanting to burst out of her head. She'd rolled up in a ball and rocked and rocked, and when she stopped, the convulsing would start again.

They'd taken her to hospitals. There everything only got worse. The doctors and nurses and patients and their families, more places, more thoughts, more knives hacking at her.

"I want to go home!" she had screamed. "I want to go home!"

It was her uncle, Shree Kaka, who had listened.

He'd picked her up and taken her back to Sagar Mahal, even as her grandmother and the doctors and her aunt discussed what the right thing to do was.

Once they were at home, Shree Kaka had taken her into her room and closed all the doors and windows and warned everyone to stay away from her.

The noises had died down, but they hadn't gone away.

"Esha," Shree Kaka said, running a hand through his hair—hair that was exactly like Baba Saheb's, thick with silver streaks at the temples. "You want to tell me what's going on?"

She threw herself into his lap and cried. "Aie and Baba Saheb." It was the first time her mind wasn't flooded and she was able to miss her parents, to hurt because they were gone.

"I'm so sorry, beta." He cried too.

"You loved Baba Saheb." She knew how much. She knew and now she *knew;* his love for her father was inside her.

"Your baba was the best person I knew. The best person I will ever know. And you were the best thing in his life. And in mine too. You were my first baby girl. You never have to be afraid. I will always protect you and take care of you."

Something about the way he said those words made her tell him, even though she wasn't sure he'd believe her. "I can't stop hearing voices. And feeling everything about everyone. I don't want it."

He had listened. His eyes, so much like Baba Saheb's, took in her words without a single doubt. "We'll figure out what to do. We'll find a way to make it stop."

J-Auntie came into the room. "Ma Saheb sent some juice," she said.

Colors crashed inside Esha's head. Red and blue and black. A high wailing sound burst from her. She felt herself fall back, through her mattress, through air. Her lungs filled, liquid closing around her. Then she saw him. J-Auntie's husband, Baba Saheb's estate manager, under a tractor outside the groundskeeper's cottage. His body crushed beyond recognition.

When she came back into herself, a shaking mess, her uncle was still there, sitting in a chair next to the bed. J-Auntie was gone. Shree Kaka asked Esha what had happened and she told him.

They found the body exactly where she'd told them they would. It had taken Shree Kaka and Mina Kaki three days after that to get Esha on a plane and bring her to Woodside.

From the first moment Esha arrived, something about the Anchorage had felt more contained than the palace. She had felt tightly wrapped up here. People didn't walk the halls all the time. Even so, it had taken Esha a few weeks to step out onto the balcony outside her room. Her first time being out in the open air. Garuda had been waiting for her.

Sometimes he just sat there and they spent time in silence, and sometimes she talked to him and he listened, white feathery head taking in the sky as though a threat might fall from it.

Today, Esha had been telling Garuda about Yash's speech at his victory party, which Esha had heard from her room.

Garuda listened from his perch on the marble railing, his stillness absorbing her words. That's when Esha heard the sound.

She spun around.

There was a man standing in front of her. A man she'd never before seen. A man with hair too long and unkempt, and skin sunburned and craggy. A man so regal and stormy the Sagar Mahal seemed to rise up around them.

"Was that a Brahminy kite?" he said, his voice gravelly. A voice that seemed used to long silences. He was standing on the outside ledge of her balcony. The very, very narrow ledge.

She turned to look over her shoulder; Garuda was gone. "You shouldn't be here."

"What's a Brahminy kite doing in California?" His words came out so forcefully that he swayed on the narrow ledge.

Without thinking about it, Esha reached out and grabbed his hand, keeping him from falling back and down three floors.

He held on to her, finding his balance. "Thank you." His hold on her hand tightened before he let her go. Then he grabbed the railing and hopped over it, landing on her balcony.

"What are you doing?"

"I'm not going to hurt you."

"I know."

"Then why do you look so scared?"

"I don't . . ." She, Esha Raje, was standing close to a man—a man she had never seen before—and there was no noise in her head. She stepped closer to him.

He stepped back. "What are you doing?" he asked this time, looking more confused than scared.

She reached out and touched him. Pressed her hand right into his chest.

"Okay," he said, dark eyes studying her. "What are we doing exactly?"

She leaned closer and closed her eyes. Nothing.

"Who are you?" There was wonder in her voice. She brought her other hand to his chest, touching him with both hands now and taking a careful breath.

"Okay," he said again, obviously unsure of what to do with the situation he found himself in. "Are you smelling me?"

A laugh burst from her, spurting spittle onto his shirt. It was white and plain and looked like it had been worn a million times. He also wore gray-green pants that came down to his calves and were covered in pockets. "Why would you think I'm smelling you?" A strange and completely unfamiliar feeling was coursing through her.

She didn't have the answer.

She needed to ask. She had no idea what he was feeling. Except from what showed in his eyes, she had no idea what was going on in his head.

No idea.

"Because you made a face." He closed his eyes and pushed his face into the space between them and sniffed.

He was right. It did look like he was smelling her.

She had the uncontrollable urge to laugh again. "I wasn't smelling you. But you smell fabulous," she said.

He smelled like the woods. The ones on the estate she liked to walk in.

"I wasn't smelling you either," he said firmly, as though it was important for him to understand what was going on but he was used to figuring things out in as much time as they took. "You smell fabulous too."

"I do?" No one had ever told her she smelled good. No one had ever told her anything about herself.

"I'm Sid," he said, thick arched brows still drawn together. "India Dashwood's brother. I didn't mean to intrude."

"I like India," Esha said, examining the surface of his white shirt because it was so close to her face. The material looked thick but relaxed, the white not stark, and yet soft and clean, like moonlight.

He scratched his bearded jaw. She'd confused him. The motion made that woodsy smell stronger.

Then he smiled, and she couldn't tell what that smile meant. She loved that. Really loved it. The not knowing. "Are you one of Yash's sisters?"

"Yes. Esha. The oldest," she said. She hadn't said her own name in a very long time. Is that why he had smiled? Because he had been waiting for her to tell him what her name was?

"Hi, Esha the Oldest. It's nice to meet you." He smiled again, but it was more his eyes than his lips, and she leaned back to get a better look at them.

They were dark. Very dark. And large. Very large. And creases emanated from their edges like cobwebs pressed into skin. His entire face was like that, crisscrossed by lines and planes. His jaw was angled and covered in thick stubble that wasn't quite a beard. A raised scar split his upper lip and flattened his Cupid's bow, forming a crevice in his stubble. It was a face from the classics she had read as a child, a face from her mother's stories, a face weathered by wind and rain.

He cleared his throat.

She blinked, not happy that he had interrupted her study.

"Do you always stand this close to people when you meet them for the first time?"

That made her laugh again, but she covered her mouth because she didn't want to make a habit of spraying him. Stepping away from him didn't feel great, but she did it anyway because she couldn't explain why she needed to stand close to him. What standing so close to him and feeling nothing had given her. She laughed again.

His eyes did that thing again, as though he were gauging her. It was a look she knew well. Her family always wore that look when they interacted with her. They never wore it when they talked to one another, but with her, it was always there, brightening their eyes. A look that wondered when she was going to collapse into a seizure.

His gauging was somehow different. Not rooted in knowledge that she was broken. He was examining her. Trying to figure out what she was.

Maybe he'd figure it out and then she'd know too.

"Why are you up here climbing my balcony?"

"I thought I saw a Brahminy kite sitting on the railing. I had to climb up and see if it really was."

"You could see him?" He'd seen Garuda? How was that possible?

No one had ever seen Garuda other than her. When he didn't respond, she looked around. "Are you sure you saw him?" Usually, when Esha left the house and walked on the estate, Garuda stayed close. Flying in the sky or perched on one of the redwood trees. When she was alone and on the balcony, he was always there.

She searched the sky and he wasn't there.

"I'm quite sure I saw you talking to him. And he was unusually large. Even for a Brahminy."

"I don't want to talk about the bird." She took another step back. His woodsy smell faded and she didn't like that.

"Okay. Is it a pet?"

"Do you always say 'okay' and then do what you want to anyway?"

He smiled. His smile was as different as everything else about him. It seemed to split his face in half. And it made his eyes disappear.

"What is the scar from?"

She'd just been thinking about how warm his eyes were, and they went suddenly and completely cold.

"Is it a bad memory?" She'd never had to ask anyone that question either. Usually she just felt the pain of what they were feeling.

"Do you usually just ask another question when someone refuses to answer the one you've already asked?"

"But you didn't refuse, you just didn't answer."

"I was born with a cleft palate."

She blinked. He was such a confusing person.

"It's a condition where the roof of my mouth wasn't fully developed before I was born."

"Did it develop after, then?"

He smiled again, his earlier irritation disappearing from his eyes. They were constantly changing even though there was something rock steady about them. His smile made his scar turn white against his deeply brown skin.

"Several surgeries."

"My uncle and sister are surgeons."

"I know."

Without knowing what she was doing, she pushed off the railing and stepped close to him again and touched it. His scar.

He froze. For a moment he stood there stiff and motionless, then he grabbed her wrist.

No one had grabbed her or treated her with anything other than kid gloves for so long that she squeezed her eyes shut, bracing herself for dropping into nothingness.

"What are you doing?" he asked, his breath on her face.

She kept her eyes closed. "I was trying to touch it to see what it feels like."

"I meant why are you looking like I'm going to hurt you?"

"No."

"No?"

"Not you. Me. I . . . I . . . You're holding my wrist." She still couldn't believe that he was touching her. How could it even be?

"To keep you from invading my space."

"Oh." She opened her eyes. "I didn't mean to invade your—"

His hand was still wrapped around her wrist. "What did you mean? Just now, when you said I wasn't the one you thought was going to hurt you. You were." His hand was warm, rough, not gentle exactly, but careful.

"I'm not like other people."

He laughed at that. "You don't say."

"Is that sarcasm?"

"It's facetiousness."

"So you think I'm weird." Somehow that stung. Although she had no idea why it would. She was weirder than everyone she knew, tiny as that pool was.

"You're nothing like anyone I've ever met. But *weird* isn't the word I'd use." He said it softly, his eyes dipping to his hand, still on her wrist, as though he couldn't believe he was still holding her. But he didn't let go.

"If you say *special,* I might have to punch you."

This time his smile was surprised. "*Extraordinary.*" The fact that he was still holding her added a certain something to how the word fell on her skin. "Extraordinary. That's the word I'd use."

"You have no idea how much," she mumbled. "I'm sorry I tried to touch your scar. It wasn't because I was being creepy. It was because . . ." How did you tell someone that you were used to feeling things when you touched people or came close to them?

He let her go, but not at once. His fingers loosened first, then slid against her skin. She pressed into it, trying to extend the contact, her own fingers lingering against his as they pulled apart.

"You can touch it." His voice was soft in a way it hadn't been until now. "You can touch my scar if you need to."

She swallowed and reached out. The dip above his lips was delicate, the thin line harder than she'd expected, the smooth surface of his lips softer. Her fingers traced the scar, then his lips. His breath kissed her skin. Brightness shimmered in the air around her. Sparks traveled down her arm, making her light-headed, and that made her knees go suddenly limp.

As she crumpled under her own lightness, he caught her. Strong arms going around her and lifting her up. She'd been carried like this a million times, but she'd never felt it before. It felt floaty, new, different from the many, many times she had lost control of her body because she'd lost control of her mind.

Now here she was, mind fully alert, entirely empty except for the sensation of his arms wrapped around her, pressing into the backs of her knees.

Something between happiness and terror made her squeeze her eyes shut.

"Is there someone I can call?" he said in the gentlest voice. It was also adorably confused, and that made her open her eyes again.

"No one can know you're here."

"Okay." There was this particular way in which he said that word. With acceptance, and curiosity, and humor.

There was a sound. Her aji had come back up.

"You have to leave."

"Okay."

"You'll have to put me down first."

"Okay."

"Sid?"

He shook his head. "I have to see you again."

"I have to see you again too. But I don't know how."

"I'm India's brother, she's Yash's girlfriend. Surely I can just walk in here."

"No!" That would make Esha's whole life a lie.

She had no idea how she would face that. She shook her head, stomach suddenly queasy. "You can't. You can't tell anyone. You have to go now."

He put her down, and that made the queasiness worse. "Does anyone hurt you?" he whispered, anger and the will to stay calm warring in his eyes. "Do you need help?"

Something filled her chest. She touched his face, stroking the line between stubble and skin. "Not at all." At least not the way he thought.

He touched her hand, pressing it against his face as though he couldn't quite believe what was happening. Unlike her, he seemed far too comfortable with the feeling.

"I'll find a way. I'll come see you soon. I promise." Pulling her hand to his lips, he dropped a kiss on her fingertips. Then, leaving a strange magic swirling from her fingers through her body, he jumped over the railing the way he had come.

Before she could stop him or worry that he might fall, he leapt onto the overhang of the floor below, then the one below that, as agile as a mountain goat. He knew exactly where to step next.

As he disappeared from sight, eyes returning to her again and again, Garuda swept back onto the railing post.

"How did he see you?" Esha said, and got nothing but silence from his moonlight eyes. "Why did you let him see you? Do you know why he was so interested in you?" Questions she used to avoid the real one.

All she got in response was a cocking of his white feathered head. Then he too was gone. As always, leaving her alone when her grandmother stepped out onto the balcony.

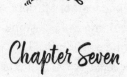

Chapter Seven

Naina made her way into the gigantic steel-and-glass lobby of the Omnivore Systems office building. For ten years now her workplaces had been in structures ranging from trailers to tents to barely plastered brick-and-mortar rooms.

The Omnivore steel-and-glass tower had an amusement park in the lobby. Yup, an amusement park, which meant the lobby took up the first twenty-odd floors. There was a Ferris wheel, a climbing wall, and a bungee-jumping cliff, built to look like an actual cliff. A bloodcurdling scream ripped the air as someone took a tethered leap.

Now that Naina had worked in this building for three months, the screams no longer made her jump out of her skin every time she entered the lobby.

She still had no idea why there was a pool under the bungee jump. Possibly to make the mess easier to clean when the bungee cord broke?

The glass capsule elevator in which she made her way up should've seemed a bit much for an office building, but there was an amusement park in the lobby. The elevator almost felt anticlimactic.

She got out on the fifty-second floor, where Jignesh had given her a suite of offices.

Mariel, her admin assistant, who made it a point to not crack a smile until at least two P.M. and four coffees, grinned widely at Naina. What on earth was that smile supposed to mean?

Naina thought she knew all of Mariel's smiles.

The "get your own damn coffee" smile. The "how much did that dress you're wearing cost" smile. The "you're taking the team out for lunch today because we've had a hard day" smile. Mariel wasn't exactly well versed in boundaries, but this smile gave boundaries a hearty shove.

"Good morning, boss." Mariel bounced in her baby-pink leather chair. Why Jiggy had given Naina an office decorated in every shade of pink, Naina didn't know. She had a lifelong hate-hate relationship with the color. "Or should I say good afternoon?" She wiggled her brows in a most inappropriately suggestive manner.

"Hi, Mariel. What's going on?"

Her assistant threw a glance over her shoulder and made a face one usually saved for girls' nights at Chippendales.

"Is Mr. Mehta here?" Naina asked.

Mariel, and the rest of Naina's team, had this way of getting weird when she had a meeting with Jignesh. During her first few weeks in the office, he had sent her extravagant flower arrangements every few days. Roses. Not your usual locally grown ones but some blue and pink variety from the Amazon—not the one you opened up on your laptop to order random things, but the rain forest that grew around the river in South America.

When Naina had told him to stop, he'd ordered birds of paradise from Hong Kong. She'd had to spell it out and ask him to stop giving her gifts and asking her out and showing any personal interest in her at all. How did the CEO of a company with over fifty thousand employees not understand the basics of workplace ethics and sexual harassment in the 2020s? Where was his legal department?

Finally, that was the question that had made him stop. Even though she'd had to phrase it as a joke.

The suggestive smiles from her team whenever she had a meeting with Mehta had become a permanent thing. She was pretty sure those smiles were ironic. These were . . . not.

"It's not Mr. Mehta," Mariel said, batting her false eyelashes in the most baffling manner.

Naina threw up her hands. "Have we got the résumés the doctors lined up?"

"Doctors?" Mariel said as though she were entirely unaware of the concept.

"Yes, doctors. The people who treat people when they're sick. In our case the people who will take care of pregnant women and their babies before, during, and after birth in Nepal. The thing we've been working for months on?" Naina hung her jacket up on the hot-pink coat tree.

The smell of musky, lemony cologne hit her before his voice did. For a moment Naina thought Yash was here, because the brothers wore the same scent. But their voices, or rather their tones, were as different as could be. This one was deep, droll, and terribly amused at the world.

"Is it employee training day? Will there be a quiz after?" He was standing in the doorway of her office, leaning into the frame, arms crossed for maximum biceps display, dimples out in full force.

"Vansh! What are you doing in my office?" She threw a glare at Mariel, whose pupils had dilated like someone watching an erotic scene in what she'd expected to be a family film.

Mariel's only response was to lick her lips and smile in Vansh's direction.

Sadiya, the economist grad student intern who was helping Naina with the administrative setup of the gramin banks in Nepal, came out into the lobby.

Did Sadiya just flip her hair?

Then Makayla, the international law expert who'd worked with Naina in Nepal for the past five years and had never been anything but immovably disinterested in any behavior she deemed frivolous, sauntered out of her office, pretending to be searching for something.

Did Makayla always sway her hips like that when she walked?

"Good afternoon, Naina," both women said to Naina in unusually breathy voices, bright (and super-creepy) smiles lighting up their faces.

"Coffee?" Makayla asked, eyes drifting to Vansh.

"No, thank you. Caffeine does a number on me. I'm more of a green tea guy," Vansh answered in a low-pitched fuckboy tone she'd never heard him use.

"I think Makayla was talking to me," Naina snapped.

"I'd be happy to get Mr. Raje green tea," her lawyer said. "Do we have any green tea in the office?" She threw the question at Naina, without looking away from Vansh.

Nice.

Mariel jumped out of her chair. "It's my job to get people tea," she tittered rather than spoke.

"I've never seen you get anyone tea before," Sadiya said.

"That's because none of you drink tea."

"When did you stop drinking tea? I thought it was all chai all the time," Vansh asked Naina with far too much familiarity, and the expressions on the faces of the three women turned to what could only be described as aggressive suspicion.

What was wrong with them? They were smart, competent women who spent their days cutting anyone who got in the way of their work down to size. Now they were standing here arguing over who would get Vansh tea?

"There's every color of tea in the kitchen down the hall. I'm pretty certain you can find the green kind too." She turned around and walked out of the pink suite without waiting for him to follow.

Naturally he followed, because suddenly it seemed like getting rid of him was not easy business.

Her three employees tried to follow too, but she glared at them and they went back to their desks.

"Grab a tea bag." She pointed at the tea box on the red quartz sideboard and picked up an Omnivore mug. Red with a black crow in flight, which looked a bit like a check mark if you asked her. But Jiggy had paid someone millions for a black crow in flight, so that's what it was.

Shoving the cup under the spout, she jabbed her finger into the annoyingly complicated drinks machine. It had taken her a week to figure out where the hot-water button was.

"That's a needlessly complicated coffee machine," Vansh said, looking through the tea and picking one, his body still telegraphing lazy nonchalance. "Ginger and lemongrass work for you?"

She thought about drinking a different tea just because she didn't want to admit he'd gotten that right. Satisfying as that would be, she needed her favorite tea right now more than she needed juvenile spite.

Handing him an empty mug, she snatched the ginger-lemongrass tea bag from him and dunked it into her cup of hot water. "You're in my office."

"Nice employees," he deadpanned far too smugly.

He was wearing a shirt that would have fit someone thirty-odd pounds lighter. Which made it perfectly clear that the shirt's job was to help one imagine what he looked like without it. Not that she had to imagine. Her brain cells were still trying to purge the vision of his bare chest with a tattoo she was proud she hadn't looked at.

"You're thinking about me without my shirt, aren't you?"

She scowled at him. "You have such a high opinion of yourself. What kind of person is so comfortable with his . . . his . . ."

"Body? Hotness?"

"Obnoxiousness."

"I was just objectified for . . ." He scratched the back of his head in that ridiculous thinking-hard gesture. "For standing there. And *I'm* obnoxious?"

"Well, you are wearing a shirt that you seem to have picked up in the kids' section, so . . ."

He dumped his used tea bag into a bright red trash can and blew into his mug, making steam rise around his face. "Did you just blame my clothing for the fact that those women were undressing me with their eyes?"

The bastard was smiling.

"Do you think sexual harassment of women is a joke, Vansh?" She took a sip and burned her tongue. And swallowed down a yelp of pain.

"Not even a little bit. But I'm not a fan of double standards either."

"You know there's a history of unbalanced power, lack of safety and consent, that makes it different when it happens to a woman, right?"

"I do know that, even though it's not that simple. I hope you're not planning to accuse me of encouraging them and asking for it."

"You were, as a matter of fact, encouraging it greatly." Before he could argue, she raised a hand to stop him. "It was still inappropriate, the way my team behaved. I apologize and will reprimand them."

"There's no need for that."

"I know. But I will anyway. But the next time you pretend to know what it feels like to be violated by the unwelcome attention of the opposite sex, I want you to know that if as a result of it there was any chance that you could get hurt in any way, you should absolutely feel free to put an end to it by letting them know that you aren't interested and that it makes you uncomfortable."

"I appreciate the advice." He took a sip of the tea. "Were you always this humorless, Knightlina?"

"Pretty much. Now, do you want to tell me what you're doing in my place of work, uninvited?"

"I'm not uninvited. Remember how our boss invited me to pitch some ideas for a project? The one that you so delightfully christened my Emma Project. I told you I have an idea and I'm here to share it with our boss."

"Will you please stop calling him that? He's not my boss. He is a donor. And he is most certainly not your boss."

Vansh shrugged. Which made his pecs pop. Possibly because the shirt was so tight that lifting his shoulders was a workout.

She started walking back to her office, again not waiting for him to follow. He followed.

"Tell me about the project," she said.

"No thank you."

"Excuse me?"

"Wow, does that stick get uncomfortable? The one that you have . . ." She narrowed her eyes at him and he thought better of finishing that sentence. "I'm yanking your chain. Jiggy wants us to go up to his office and I might as well lay it out for both of you together."

"Now?"

"In a half hour. Actually, since we have time, I can fill you in and you can help me come up with the details."

"Vansh!" She stopped in the middle of the corridor and he almost ran into her. "How can you show up at a meeting without a plan? And need I remind you, you're trying to steal my funding. What makes you think I'm going to help you come up with a plan? I'm not going to help you steal from me."

"That word is really ugly, you know that? Really, really ugly." She wanted to punch him. "What you're doing is ugly."

"Trying to solve—"

"If you say the words *solve homelessness* in my place of work, I will throw you out."

He grinned. Of all things.

"I'm immune to those dimples. Put them away."

He leaned into her, grinning even more widely, knowing exactly how to make the deep, deep dents sink into his cheeks over his smoothly shaven jaw.

"I have dimples?" he asked, and she'd be damned if he didn't do a very masculine version of batting his eyelashes at her, bountiful as they were. "I hadn't noticed. And I do know what my project is. I'm a little light on the details. You've done this fundraising thing for so long there's no one who's better at details than you are. I saw one of your proposals in Sripore. Incredible stuff. I was hoping that you'd help me."

What kind of person went to the person they were stealing from to ask how to steal from them? "You want me to help with the details?"

He blinked his pretty eyes at her again. Which part of *immune* was hard to get through his thick head?

"You do realize that what we do in this office is figure out how to build facilities that provide basic lifesaving healthcare to women with no access to any across two hundred villages serving seven hundred thousand women. Then we make sure that they are sustained on the money they generate so we no longer have to fund them. Then we plan to replicate that success in another two hundred villages and then another two hundred. And even with this funding, that's ambitious. If you take any part of our money it will essentially mean us having to start from scratch and figure everything out again."

He was watching her like he'd never seen her before. "You are one impressive woman, Knightlina."

"If you call me that again, I will dismember you."

He laughed out loud. A deep belly laugh that was just so . . . what was the word for it? Happy. She had to suppress a smile, and that made her frown.

She started walking toward her suite again.

He followed again.

Naina raised a hand when Mariel started to say something as they walked in.

It was going to be hard to live it down with her team, but she shut the door after Vansh followed her into her office.

"Okay, so maybe there is another option," he said. "We can work something out. I can't very well walk away from his offer." He threw a pointed look at her painfully pink office with its pink striped wallpaper and the dramatic, also pink, local artists' canvases. "The man literally has a Ferris wheel on the ground floor. Have you seen that?"

"Yes, Vansh, it's a giant Ferris wheel. It's a little hard to miss."

"Have you been on it, BTW?" He used letters instead of saying "by the way" like normal adults.

"Do you need me to answer that question?"

"I don't know, you're pretty badass. I can picture you slow-blinking and filing your nails on Space Mountain."

"Hah. That shows how well you know me. I would never file my nails in a public place." She extracted her laptop from her handbag and hooked it into her docking station.

"It's a figure of speech. Admit it, you're entirely unaffected by roller coasters."

How wrong he was. "I'm busy, Vansh. So if there's nothing else . . ." Sounding firm while settling into her glittery pink chair was hard, but she did it.

He strolled over and leaned a denim-clad hip into her desk as though he were planning on going nowhere. "What's that face? What did I say? Oh!"

"What?"

"You've never been on a roller coaster."

"My family wasn't exactly the amusement-park-visiting demographic." Her mother had asked to go once, but her father had deemed it frivolous. They'd gone to Yellowstone instead. Which was gorgeous, so she didn't care that she'd never been on a damned roller coaster.

"Not even Six Flags in Vallejo?"

She shrugged. When her father had refused to take them to Disneyland when Mummy asked, Naina had decided the joke was on him because it wasn't somewhere she wanted to go anyway.

"It just isn't something I've ever been interested in."

He opened his mouth and shut it. He'd probably just been about to tell her that his family had always had an annual pass to both Six Flags and Disneyland. Yash had asked her innumerable times to go when they were kids. Mina Auntie used to make him take Vansh actually, and Yash had always wanted the company. But Naina simply refused to ask her parents to let her go.

After the briefest knock, Mariel popped her head into Naina's office. "Mr. Mehta's here to see you." She said the words in a professional tone but widened her eyes at Naina, as if to say, *What is going on with you today? This was not on the calendar.*

Didn't Naina know it! She never deviated from her calendar. This was an important week. Her focus was on getting the interviews for the medical staff scheduled. Completely unexpectedly, they had almost fifty applications.

She shrugged at Mariel. Turning Mehta away was not part of her job description right now.

"Thank you, Mariel!" she said as Jiggy emerged from behind

her assistant in a lime-green golf shirt, black-and-white-striped slacks, and fluorescent-orange tennis shoes.

He started when he saw Vansh, then bounced over and pumped Vansh's hand with even more excitement than Naina's employees had displayed on seeing him. Must be nice to cause such a stir just by existing.

"So good to see you, Mr. Raje. What are you doing here?"

Something the tiniest bit embarrassed flitted across Vansh's face. Jiggy evidently had no memory of having invited him to the office to discuss anything. Unless he did and he was being his usual complicated agenda-ridden self.

"I thought I'd bring my project ideas to you."

"Project?" Someone like Jignesh running a multibillion-dollar company was one of life's great injustices.

The man's brain was capable of identifying obscure buried details amid the most complex of presentations, but Naina could swear she'd seen him change agendas midmeeting to throw people off more times than she could count, and she was quite sure he used not remembering his employees' names as a tool to keep them on their toes.

Every one of his actions was carefully orchestrated to manipulate people and situations to his benefit.

"I was just suggesting to Vansh that he reach out to the Dorsey-Masey Foundation to hear the proposal he's come up with." Why the hell had she just said that?

Both Vansh and Jiggy turned to her with sudden alert interest.

"Whyever would Mr. Raje take his proposal to anyone else when he has me? Didn't you promise you would work with me, Vansh?"

Naina was pretty certain Vansh had promised nothing of the sort.

"We talked about a possible opportunity at my brother's

victory celebration party," Vansh said, his emphasis on the words *my brother's victory* so subtle it was a thing of beauty. The glimmer of a smile he threw her way was barely discernible, but the gratefulness in it was unmistakable.

Only the stupidest person would let it warm her.

"I know. Didn't we have an appointment today?" Jiggy said.

Vansh's face didn't change, but his eyes brightened.

Just because she didn't enjoy Jiggy's using his power to mess with people—especially people he saw as privileged—didn't mean Naina was ready to share her funding with Vansh. No way in hell was she helping Vansh out with his pitch. The pitch he didn't have because he had no real project.

"Okay, so who are we helping out? AIDS patients in Africa? Vaccinations in Asia?"

"The homeless in San Francisco."

Mehta made a face. A disgusted face.

Vansh paid it no attention and went on. "There's eighteen thousand homeless people in the city of San Francisco right now. Stretched across fifty city blocks and growing. The city spends over one billion on them."

"They're all druggies," Jiggy said with disgust. "And mentally ill. And we can neither put them in prison nor get them treatment. Basically, our stupid lawmakers have made it impossible to touch them."

The struggle to stay unfazed made an angry flush tinge the tips of Vansh's ears. "Actually that's not true. Only about four thousand have addiction and mental health issues. That's the official number. Even if it's twice that, there are still thousands of people living on the streets who are there because of unemployment and housing issues."

"The government is already spending millions on putting them in housing. And it has not worked in the past."

"It doesn't work because most programs are giving them fish instead of tools for fishing."

"You want to teach the homeless to fish? I think a more worthy local cause might be to clean up the bay so that fish might actually thrive in there." Jiggy's laugh couldn't have been more self-satisfied if he'd actually implemented cleaning up the bay.

Vansh and Naina exchanged a glance. Jiggy did not look happy with the fact that they didn't laugh.

"What I'm trying to say is that several existing efforts focus on giving them a home, not the means to make a living so they can afford the home. Obviously, those are not the same thing," Vansh said.

The billionaire looked miffed. His face got all pinched and he pouted even as he remained smiling, and the result was not at all pleasant.

"You know, Vansh, I grew up on the streets of Mumbai, and it was not at all sexy."

Vansh threw Naina a confused glance. *Did he just say "sexy"?*

She looked at Jiggy. "I didn't realize we were going for sexy."

"This is Omnivore. If it's not sexy, it has no place here."

"But this isn't Omnivore, it's the Omnivore Foundation, giving back to the community and to the world," she parroted their tagline.

"You're not wrong," Jiggy said, studied alacrity returning to his voice. "All I'm saying is that optics are ninety percent of any business."

Which was why the corporate world was not for Naina.

"What did you have in mind to teach the homeless to fish, then?" he asked, turning to Vansh again.

Vansh's smile was too smug by half. "I'm working on something, but I need to look into a few things before I can present the idea."

Jiggy studied Vansh. "There's that same Yash Raje sincerity in you, isn't there?" He turned to Naina. "Blood is thicker, no?"

Naina had no response to that. Not that Jiggy had any interest in her response. He put a hand on Vansh's shoulder. "You know what's sexy in the world of charitable giving? Health stuff. Providing healthcare. Doctors Without Borders stuff. Women's stuff. Education rights. Malala-type things."

Vansh kept his face impassive, refusing to let Jiggy see that he was hurtling between disbelieving and outraged, but his eyes were more transparent than anyone's should be.

Welcome to my life, buddy. Yup, her fifteen million came with this. This branded version of giving.

"Isn't Naina doing exactly that kind of thing already?" Vansh said.

The biggest grin spread across Jiggy's face. He held out his fist and Vansh bumped it dutifully, not letting his confusion show and hanging on to his smile. Naina had to hand it to Vansh. It had taken her months to navigate Jiggy's unpredictable and—how could she put this delicately?—not at all logical behavior.

"Actually, you're right. Since your brother is governor, it makes sense. Fine. Fine. Do you like dandiya?"

"I'm sorry?" Even Mr. Charm himself was out of clues on how to keep up with Jiggy.

"You don't know what dandiya is? What kind of Indian are you?" Jiggy said, and Naina focused hard on figuring out what he was up to now.

"I do know what dandiya is." The way Vansh said it was telling. Naturally, dancing was something he enjoyed. He was just the kind of person who could lose himself in music and dance like no one was watching. "Some of my fondest memories from my years spent in India are of Navratri," he added with a nostalgic smile.

Good for him. For Naina, the Navratri festival, when her

mother dressed her to the nines and dragged her to dandiya parties every year, was an especially uncomfortable part of her generally uncomfortable childhood.

"I sponsor a ring-in-the-New-Year dandiya party. For charity, of course. Naina is coming. You should come too. It's next weekend. We'll make it a working party. You can tell me what you have in mind. But first you'll have to get this Naina to dance." He pointed his bejeweled hand at Naina.

Naina rolled her eyes.

"Get Naina to dance? You *are* ambitious, aren't you? Better men than us have tried and failed," Vansh said, and threw a wink at her.

"Come on, Mr. Raje. If you can't do that, how can I trust you to change the world?"

Naina didn't like the smile on Jiggy's face as he threw Vansh the challenge, as though she were a Frisbee in the game they were playing. She hadn't RSVPed, but who was she kidding? She'd have to go and hobnob with Mehta's guests. That didn't mean she was going to dance.

"It's a good thing getting people to dance is one of my favorite things," Vansh said, making her want to kick his shins.

"Good." Jiggy rubbed his hands together. "I love a man who loves challenges."

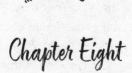

Chapter Eight

Vansh didn't have to take Naina a peace offering, but her apartment was on the way to the hotel Hari was staying at. He also had the odd urge to discuss the Hari situation with her. If he talked to her, if she met Hari, she'd know that her accusation that Vansh was acting out of ennui wasn't true.

There was a mild drizzle falling from a dreary sky. It was one of those magical San Francisco evenings, when all the good and the bad in the world fit on one inexhaustible canvas under a gray-blue sky, with the edges blurred like a watercolor.

As Vansh turned the corner onto the street where Naina's building was located, a man urinated onto the window of one of the ground-level units. He grinned at Vansh, and Vansh grinned back and looked away to afford him privacy. Before he could make his way to her building, his gaze fell on a familiar figure across the street, bent over next to a bundle of blankets.

Naina?

For a second he thought she might be fighting with the homeless person she seemed to be talking to. But her body was gentle, the lines soft. She came to standing with the umbrella that had been sheltering the man, who smiled at her from behind his thick beard. The umbrella had two spikes that poked out fabric-less.

She pulled something out of her humongous bag and started fidgeting with the broken umbrella.

Vansh stood there under the mist of the drizzle and watched as she stretched the fabric and secured it to the spikes and put the umbrella where it belonged. Then she ran across the street, damp hair escaping a messy ponytail and falling all over her face, black tights hugging her legs under a huge Berkeley sweatshirt.

It took her a moment to notice him.

"Vansh?" She'd always said his name like this, as though it were hers to say. The kind of ownership his family wielded over it.

It reminded him of the many times she'd found him off in a corner, too young and pesky for his siblings to include at parties, playing with the pets or bored with his Game Boy. All their parents' friends' children had been much older than him. It had never struck him before this that she'd always seemed on the outside too. Part of the gang without ever being on the inside.

As the grown-up kids did grown-up-kid things, Naina and he had played tic-tac-toe on pieces of paper or twenty questions about places they wanted to visit. She'd always asked questions. Never assumed everything about who he was the way everyone else did.

"A peace offering," he said, holding up the brown paper bag. "Aji's ladoos. Besan." Her favorite.

She looked over her shoulder at the homeless man dozing under the umbrella, then at the ladoos his grandmother made better than anyone else in the world. He hated that she was trying to figure out what his angle was. But she took them.

"I've missed these." As soon as it slipped out, she looked like she wanted to take the words back. "You just don't want to eat all that ghee and sugar and you don't know how to tell Aji."

"You got me." It was impossible to get his grandmother to stop feeding him high-sugar, high-fat foods. "This body takes work."

Her eye roll made the world perfect and familiar again. "Your loss. What are you doing in the city?"

"I'm here to see Hari."

Of course she stiffened.

"Can't you at least hear me out? I thought we could talk about things." They'd talked for hours about her work when he'd lived in Sripore and she'd visited his aunt there.

Part of him waited for her to lose her temper. But she seemed oddly vulnerable as they stood there in the drizzle with his grandmother's ladoos clutched to her chest. "We can. But I've worked really hard for this, Vansh."

There were shadows under her exhausted eyes. There always had been. He, like the rest of the world, tended to miss them under all the glamour, because Naina Kohli never let anyone see her like this, in a faded oversized sweatshirt with frayed edges.

I work hard too, he wanted to say. "I know," he said instead. "I would never let any harm come to your work. We can do both, right?"

Her eyes took him in as incisively as they always had, but there was a brightening of surprise there too. Something new. "Let's talk about it after Mehta's party," she said, and without inviting him up, she walked away, fuzzy boots splashing muddy water around those endless legs.

HARI LOOKED LIKE he hadn't moved in twenty-four hours. Hari, in fact, looked like he hadn't blinked since Vansh had left him rolled up in a ball on his bed, wide awake. Vansh threw the drapes open and sunshine streamed into the room at the Embassy Suites.

"Have you eaten anything?"

Hari pulled his knees tighter into himself and shook his head. "Did you tell Yash and Nisha?"

"I told you I wouldn't tell them. I don't break my word. You have to trust me. I'm not going to let anything bad happen to you."

Before Hari could say *you're so nice* again, Vansh patted his leg. "Why don't you get out of bed and take a shower and let's go out and get some food. I have some ideas I want to discuss with you."

"I can't afford to go out to eat."

"I don't want you to worry about that. I have a plan for how to fix that."

Hope flashed in Hari's eyes. It was then drowned out by the fear that perpetually widened them.

"Do you have a favorite place? A favorite food?"

"I love my mother's muli parathas."

Vansh loved those too, but finding the flaky flatbreads stuffed with spicy radish in San Francisco at such short notice might be a challenge even Vansh wasn't up for today. He'd get J-Auntie to make him some soon. "I'll tell you what, I'm going to bring you those the next time I come over. What about something local? Do you have a place you like to go to around here?"

"I like the center. They have meals for people like me."

"Great, we can go there, if you prefer."

Hari looked excited for the first time that day. "You'd do that?"

"I've eaten in messes and community kitchens in at least seven countries. I'll bet your community center is fancy compared to some of the places I've been."

Hari sat up. "I've never met anyone like you. I don't think I've ever met anyone who's lived in seven countries."

"Take a shower and I'll tell you all about it."

Half an hour later Vansh and Hari were walking down the three blocks to the community center against the chilly January wind. Vansh shrank deeper into his light jacket. At least Hari looked warm in his huge puffy jacket. It looked almost new.

Vansh rubbed his hands together; maybe they should have taken a car.

"You should get a better coat," Hari said, then started to unzip his. "Take this one. You don't feel the cold at all in it. Not even a little bit."

Something tightened in Vansh's chest. He stayed Hari's hand. "I'm fine. We're not that far. That's a great coat though. Thank you."

"Did you know they were called great coats in the olden days? I remember reading a Russian story about it back in school." Hari zipped back up. "That actor Ashton Kilmer handed these out last year to everyone on the street. He gave away thousands of coats last winter."

"That's awfully kind of him. I should call him and let him know you appreciate it."

"You know him?"

"His sister worked with Yash at the US Attorney's Office years ago, so we hung out a few times."

Hari looked impressed, and as they got closer to the community center, he got oddly more comfortable. When they got there, he brightened visibly. "You sure about this?" he asked Vansh.

"Of course. How's the food here?"

Hari grinned. "They have the best French fries," he said with the kind of excitement Vansh's adolescent niece displayed about fried potatoes. Come to think of it, Yash felt this way about fries too.

The center was full, probably because it was the North Pole outside. They were serving fried chicken, fried fish, fried mushrooms, *and* fries. Hari loaded up his plate.

"Hey there, Harry. How you been doing, man?" the server asked, and Hari blushed and nodded. "Who's your friend?"

"I work with *Hari*," Vansh said, emphasizing his name and pronouncing it "hurry" as it was supposed to be pronounced. But the server had already moved on to the next person in line.

They moved down the stations. "I had a big lunch, but these bagels look good." Vansh picked up a bagel and they carried their trays to a table in a corner.

Hari started scarfing down his food while eyeing Vansh's bagel with great amounts of sympathy.

"So, did you have a plan for what you were going to do now that the election is over?"

Hari's chewing took on renewed force. "Did you throw my tent away? If you did, I need to buy a new one." Hari's hands started to shake.

"Of course I didn't throw your tent away. I told you I wouldn't. I put it in storage at my parents' house, but you won't need it. You can't go on living on the street."

"I can live there for as long as I want. Mikhail has lived there for five years."

"You won't have to. We're going to make sure you don't go back there. We're going to find you a job that pays enough for you to rent a place."

Hari shoved an alarmingly large piece of fried chicken into his mouth. "Nobody will rent me a place without ID and credit history."

"Well, the first thing we're going to do is fix that. We'll get your passport reissued, and I can be a guarantor for your rent. There are ways for you to do that. There are government programs that will help you."

"No! They'll put me in jail. That's what Jim told me. They'll deport me and then the Indian police will throw me in jail. My mother will never survive the shame." He stood, the scrape of the metal chair on the tile loud in the silence. "I want to go back to my tent. Please."

Vansh held up his tray. There was still a substantial pile of fried food on it and Hari looked at it hungrily.

"Let's finish our meal?" he said gently.

Hari sat back down, and Vansh patted his hand and waited for it to stop shaking.

"No one is going to arrest you. You haven't done anything wrong."

Hari yanked his hand away, wrapped his arms around himself,

and started rocking. "They make you move out of the city. I don't know any place outside San Francisco. Other places scare me. Everyone looks at me funny if I sit on a park bench. One time they cleared out our tents. Mikhail knew they were going to do it and we took the Caltrain to Palo Alto. When I sat on a park bench someone called the cops and they came and chased us away."

"You won't have to sit on a park bench. We'll figure it out, okay? You're a genius. You see numbers and data like no one else can. Everyone needs numbers and data. We just have to figure out how to put your genius to use. Listen, I have a friend who wants to help you. He has a lot of money. He can help get you and Mikhail and all your friends off the street if we can just show him how to do it. How to put your skills to use."

Vansh had been part of programs that had done far harder things, in places with nowhere near the same resources. The way to get people out of poverty was to give them a sustainable means to generate income. It was basically a matter of seeding the income generation. There was more income to be had here in San Francisco than anywhere else in the world.

"You won't tell Yash and Nisha, will you?" Hari repeated, eyes skimming the room as though Vansh's siblings might pop out of the woodwork.

"Hari, they won't care. They won't judge you. They're not like that."

Hari started shaking again. Tears ran down his cheeks. "I can't have them think of me like that."

Vansh kicked himself. He couldn't bamboozle Hari into trusting anyone else before he earned his trust himself. "I'm sorry. Don't cry. We won't involve Yash and Nisha. Like I said, my friend Jiggy Mehta is on board with helping us."

"Is Jiggy Mehta the guy who runs Omnivore?" Hari said, eyes suddenly clear.

Vansh sat up. "Yes, do you know him?"

"My partner Jim, he wanted to sell our drill-down technology to Omnivore, but then Facebook changed something so our technology no longer worked with it." Apparently after graduating grad school, Hari and this Jim guy had started a company that ran analytics on social media platforms to identify consumer behavior.

"But you used that technology for Yash's campaign, right?"

Hari's eyes got shifty. "You can't tell anyone that."

"Why?"

"If Jim finds out, he'll sue me. The patent for my technology is in his name."

"Why?"

"Because he put his own name on the patent."

Vansh prided himself on never losing his temper, but rage rushed through him. "Okay, we have a lot of things we need to sort out. It's nothing a good lawyer can't do."

Yash would be the best person to go to. But of course even mentioning Yash would send Hari into panic again. When he'd met Makayla, the lawyer on Naina's team, she'd told him that she was particularly adept at making sure people weren't preyed upon in this exact way. Bingo. "I know someone who can help us."

"No. No one can help me. Jim told me no one can help me. He warned me against lawyers."

"We're going to take care of Jim, okay? Tell me what happened."

Turned out Hari had architected and created a tool that aggregated and analyzed people's social media data to predict their buying and voting behavior. As the company grew, Hari had become more and more depressed about the state of the world and what the social media data was telling him about it.

Then Jimbo—who seemed like a shark who'd brought nothing to the table and zeroed in on Hari as an easy target in the first place—had cheated Hari out of his part of the business and siphoned off all the company's money, saddling Hari with all the debt, leaving him hounded by collectors. In the end Hari had been evicted from his home and had ended up on the street.

He'd been living on the streets when he got a call back from Nisha about his application to work on Yash's campaign. He'd used the community showers and somehow gotten himself together for the interview because he'd become obsessed with Yash's speeches.

Hari's faith in him had spoken to Yash, not to mention his genius with numbers, and he'd gotten the job. But working on a political campaign didn't pay enough to afford rent for a place that was within walking distance from the campaign office in San Francisco, nor was it enough to pay rent somewhere else and then buy a car, with a nonexistent credit history. So Hari had worked on the campaign for nine months while living, literally, down the street.

The only shred of good news in this infuriating business was that Hari had spent most of the time he'd worked on the campaign sleeping at the office because he had worked almost around the clock. After Yash won, he'd been back on the street with no income.

A familiar fire was starting to burn inside Vansh. The injustice of it was sickening. Hari needed help. Thousands of others like him needed help.

"You still have a laptop, correct?" Vansh asked.

Hari nodded and squeezed his backpack with the kind of reverent affection one saved for one's firstborn child.

"Can you find every statistic you possibly can about homelessness in San Francisco? I need any data any organization might have gathered. All the current programs there are and how they're being funded. You take care of that while I figure out the rest."

Hari brightened. "You really think you can figure it out?" The faith that shone in his eyes despite his lack of faith in the world felt good. This was who Vansh was. He gave people hope.

The way Naina had dismissed him burned inside him. Her belief that things just fell into his lap was absolute. Sure, his looks and his name opened doors, but faith in his abilities never awaited him beyond those doors. That part he had to earn for himself after he'd reversed perceptions.

Purpose coursed through Vansh's veins. "I always figure things out. Finding solutions is what I live for. You'll see." And Naina and Jiggy Mehta would see too.

Chapter Nine

Naina was going to make a quick appearance at the party, make sure Mehta saw her face, and then quietly disappear. Fifteen minutes tops, that was the plan, and she wasn't deviating from it. Already being there dressed to the nines in a pale pink and blue ghagra choli was far more than she should have had to do for work.

Her mother had gotten the ghagra choli custom-made from a designer cousin in India. Which roughly translated to a cousin who knocked off designers in a tailoring workshop in the garage of her home. The outfit apparently replicated one that Deepika Padukone had worn in some Bollywood film, and that fact had made Mummy happier than Naina had ever seen her.

"I told my cousin that you had the same-to-same body and face as Deepika, don't even need measurement," Mummy had said tearfully when she'd given Naina the ghagra for what she thought was going to be Naina and Yash's engagement party.

The engagement had turned out to be as much of a pipe dream as the one Mummy had spun for her designer cousin. Not only did Naina look nothing like Deepika Padukone, but instead of putting a ring on her finger in a traditional Indian engagement ceremony, Yash had announced that he was in love with someone else. Consequently, the ghagra had sat in Naina's closet untouched along with Mummy's hopes and dreams.

As if those lies weren't enough, Naina was not, in fact, the same-to-same size as the Bollywood star. At least not anymore. When she'd tried to put on the damn choli blouse today, it had been too tight.

To be fair, the blouse had fit perfectly when her mother had given it to Naina. In the months after Yash's grand rejection of her, Naina had taken a little too much comfort in red wine and rocky road ice cream, even though she'd never seen herself as the rom-com heroine stereotype who dug straight into the ice-cream carton when faced with emotional devastation (slaughter?).

Now here she was, needing to rip the extra lines of stitching Indian tailors were always kind enough to leave on choli blouses, knowing that most women had these gorgeous tight-fitted garments made for occasions that they routinely starved themselves for.

Naina had prided herself on never fitting into any of those molds. She'd never thought about her body or how it looked in clothes. Her mother had been so obsessed with clothes and treating Naina as her personal mannequin that Naina had avoided thinking about fashion or her figure altogether.

Naina had, in fact, prided herself on not being anything like the women in books and movies. Projections of society rather than freethinking humans undefined by their gender.

Still, it hurt more than she wanted to admit to have to remove the baby-pink thread one stitch at a time. Well, not as much as it hurt that she was going to have to hang around at Mehta's party and watch him simper over whatever plan Vansh had come up with to chip away at her funding.

She was just so done with the Rajes. Every one of them with their smug smiles and the giant holier-than-thou chips on their shoulders.

The dancing had not yet started when Naina walked into the banquet hall, which was decorated with what had to be every red rose in North America *and* all the gold tulle in all the world.

"Whoa, are there any red roses left in the world?" There it was, the scent before the voice again. Did whichever cologne company they patronized know that these brothers kept it afloat?

At the sound of his voice, Naina spun, her heavily embroidered ghagra twirling around her, and caught him running up the wide entrance steps right toward her.

His eyes widened as he caught sight of her. He stumbled, tripped over his own toes, and fell with a thud to his knees.

"Vansh! What the hell? Are you okay?"

For a second he just stared up at her, mouth hanging open as he kneeled at her feet. The midnight blue and gold Jodhpur he was wearing combined with those starlit eyes turned him into an animated Disney prince brought to life.

Naina looked down at herself, making sure no wardrobe malfunction had occurred, and tried to keep her cheeks from warming.

A laugh huffed out of him. "What the hell, Knightlina? Give a man a heads-up. You can't just show up looking like that and knock people off their feet."

Giving him a hand, she pulled him up to standing. "Shut up. Stop blaming me for your clumsiness. You tripped. Are you hurt?"

He pressed his hand into his chest, her hand still in his. "Which warm-blooded human here is unhurt at the sight of you?"

She pulled away. "Not funny. Is anyone actually charmed by this stuff?"

"I believe so. But no one else tries this hard to hide it." He winked and they made their way through the red and gold hall. "All kidding aside, you look beautiful," he added only slightly more seriously.

She threw him a warning glare. "Thank you. I had to bring

my A-game. It's a matter of saving my funding," she said briskly, not adding that it was the only ghagra in her apartment and not in a box in her parents' house. And she'd sworn never to go back there.

Before Vansh could respond, Naina's mother hurried up to them, blood-red sari with a wide gold sequined border catching every bit of the too-bright lighting. "For a moment I thought Deepika was standing before me." She pressed a solitaire-studded hand into her chest.

"Hello, Mummy."

Her mother's brown eyes lined with dark kohl filled with doting tears. She swiped her pinkie finger against the kohl on her eyelid and pressed a black dot behind Naina's ear. She'd always done this whenever Naina dressed up. The black mark was supposed to ward off the evil eye by putting a blemish on perfection. The practice had always annoyed Naina, but today she felt like she needed all the luck she could get.

"I knew you would look most beautiful in this style."

"Mummy, please. Don't cry. It's just a ghagra."

"It was supposed to be your sagai ka joda."

As always, Naina had the urge to apologize. It was natural for any mother to have been excited about her daughter's engagement dress, but Mummy tended to process all her emotions through clothing. Naina should never have brought her so close to her dream of seeing Naina married off. Then again, if not for her mother, Naina never would have had to lie about being with Yash.

No! She would not blame Mummy for her father's faults. The world already did too much of that, blaming women for men's failings.

"Namaste, Auntieji," Vansh said, pressing his hands together and bowing his head and managing to not come across like a ham.

Naina always forgot how comfortable he was with Indian customs. He'd spent two years in boarding school in India and a few years working for his aunt in Sripore. Unlike his siblings, he spoke both Hindi and Marathi fluently. Also Spanish, Swahili, and French with some ease. A memory of his helping her out with Spanish in high school flashed in her mind out of nowhere.

Usually, she was the one who'd helped him with schoolwork. Mostly because he refused to go to anyone in his family with it, ever. But that day Yash was supposed to help her memorize a monologue, and he'd been busy. She'd been struggling with the grammar. Vansh, barely in school, and zipping around the Anchorage on his skates, had told her to focus on the story and not the words. It had worked. She'd gotten an A.

Vansh told her mother she looked beautiful as always in his unaccented Hindi, and Mummy blushed from head to toe.

Naina's own Hindi was all mixed up with Punjabi and English and barely recognizable. The rest of Vansh's siblings didn't speak but understood Marathi. Ashna and Esha had spent their early years in Sripore and spoke Marathi too.

"Hello hello, Vansh beta," Mummy said, tittering with delight. "Sorry, I got too swept up in how beautiful my Naina is looking. Very beautiful, no?"

Vansh grinned at Naina as if to say, *See!* Then, turning to Mummy again, he said, "You're right. She's exactly Deepika in *Yeh Jawaani Hai Deewani*. Same-to-same."

Naina stomped his toe, which was easy to do without her mother's noticing under her full floor-length ghagra. To his credit, he hid his wince well and treated her to the abundant force of his dimples.

She was immune. How many times did she have to tell him that? She was immune.

"That is what I am also thinking." Her mother plucked a piece of thread hanging from the short blouse on Naina's bare waist. A remnant of Naina's last-minute DIY alteration by ripping the too-tight blouse's seams open. "When you really do get engaged,

I will have another one made that will slap this one in face. It will, in fact, slap in face all ghagras all brides have ever worn." Mummy slid a meaningful look at Vansh. As though he were responsible for the fact that Naina's sagai ka joda had never made it to her sagai, completely ignoring the fact that Vansh had nothing to do with the engagement's never taking place.

Naina smoothed her hair even though there was enough product on it that not a strand had budged. She'd pulled it back into a French braid and tucked the short ends under. She missed her long hair and couldn't wait for it to grow back. How stupid was she that she'd thought cutting it to match India's and trying to pass as her in the pictures the paparazzi had taken of Yash and India kissing in public would help save Yash's campaign?

Before she could react to her mother's misplaced anger at Vansh, the prettiest young girl in the exact pink and blue ghagra Naina was wearing ran up to her with a "Naina Auntie! You look so beautiful!" Then she noticed Vansh and flew into his arms. "Vansh Mama! I didn't know you were going to be here! This is going to be so much more fun now!"

"Hey, Mishka. Look who's talking," Naina said as Vansh spun his niece around, then tucked her into his side. "You might be the most beautiful girl at the party."

Naina loved the child, but she wasn't ready for the crowd that had to be trailing her. Based on the way Mummy paled, they were all standing right behind Naina.

"Chandni, don't you look gorgeous! Is that Sabyasachi?" Mina Raje air-kissed her mother's cheek.

Having her sari complimented as a creation of her mother's most coveted Indian designer by none other than her most coveted social contact made Mummy's cheeks turn pink again.

"Always so graceful with the compliments giving, Mina!" Mummy said. "Is that one of the saris from royalty collection? It's very gorgeous." Mummy always pronounced it as George-us, no matter how many times Naina had corrected her as a child. She didn't correct her mother anymore, but the instinct to protect her from embarrassment still nudged inside Naina every time she said it.

Mina looked down at her purple and gold brocade sari. Like all of Mina Auntie's saris, this one had the look of an antique, rich with a deep history. "Yes, it's Shree's grandmother's. Part of Ma Saheb's mother-in-law's trousseau."

"Those are handed down from mother-in-law to daughter-in-law, are they not?" Mummy said.

Being Chandni Kohli's daughter meant having to deal with her saying the most inappropriate thing in any situation, and here it was. To make everything worse, her mother threw the saddest look Naina's way and teared up again.

"Well, I'm sure India will look lovely in it," Naina said, her voice so devoid of emotion she even impressed herself. She was tired of having to think about navigating this mess all the time. All the damn time. Yash had chosen India over her. No one in their right mind blamed him for it. End of story. Could they stop hitting her on the head with it for one damn second?

Her mother's nose turned red and teardrops slipped from her eyes. Mina handed her a tissue from her clutch bag and turned to Naina as though Mummy weren't embarrassing them all. "You look beautiful, Naina beta. It's good to see you."

"It's lovely to see you too, Mina Auntie." Her damn voice wobbled and she kicked herself.

It was no one's business how much Naina missed Mina. The best part of being with Yash had been getting to see Mina Auntie when Naina came home from Nepal. Naina had survived her childhood because of Mina, because she had given Naina something to aspire to. Not a family exactly—because no family was shiny enough for Naina to buy into that illusion—but Mina Raje had given her another kind of woman she could, maybe, someday be. Someday Naina wanted to tell Mina that without sounding like a simpering sycophant.

Where there was one Raje at a party, there would be others, and Nisha and Ashna were right behind Mina. They hugged Mummy and complimented her sari. Mummy in return complimented their ghagras, which were lovely but not quite as heavily embellished as Naina's. A fact that had to be getting her mother through the trauma of this meeting.

Finally, they turned to Naina, and there it was: that special awkward moment that Naina always experienced when she met Yash's sisters. A moment that seemed to stiffen their usually warm demeanors at the horrifying prospect of hugging her. Ever since Naina's dismissal from the role of their brother's girlfriend, they'd acted as though she'd suddenly contracted a communicable disease.

They reached out and touched Naina's arm, then did a half lean, half pull back, as though they'd suddenly forgotten quite how to manage a hug.

Oh for heaven's sake, she wanted to say. *Your brother is safe from me now, I'm not about to bite your arms off if you hug me.* But of course she didn't say it. Instead she returned the awkward arm-touch-pull-back maneuver.

"Vansh, you didn't tell us you were going to be here!" Nisha said, eyes sliding quickly to the lack of space between Naina and him. When had his arm gone around her?

Had he always stood so close to her? How had she never noticed? *Thanks for making it weird, Nisha.*

She took a step away and Vansh stepped closer again, almost automatically, as though he didn't even notice that he was doing it, and kept his hand on the small of her back.

"Naina and I are working on a project together for Jiggy Mehta, so I was issued a command to attend by the man himself."

That caused them all to drop into silence.

Total and utter fully loaded silence.

Naina hated being manipulated. It was the single thing she loathed more than anything else. Which was unforgivably naive, given the family she'd been born into. The *world* they'd been born into.

Somehow the fact that Vansh, someone she'd always felt safe around, was manipulating her made her blood boil. She turned to him, effectively dislodging his hand. In her three-inch heels he was barely a couple of inches taller than her. They were eye to eye and he seemed to pick out every bit of the anger she worked hard to keep hidden from the rest of their audience.

Gently, casually, he took the smallest step away, soft brown eyes filling with far too much understanding. This made her anger spike even more.

"Project?" Nisha said finally, but they might as well all have said it given the curiosity-laden gazes they focused on Vansh and her.

"It's all still hush-hush. We can't talk about it yet," Vansh said, dropping a kiss on his niece's head. "Do you know where the dandiya sticks are? I hope there's going to be more dandiya than garba." It wasn't the smoothest change of topic, but it worked.

"I hate garba," Mishka answered, bouncing on her heels. "Who wants to clap? I want to dance with the sticks. You'll be my partner, right?"

"I mean . . . yeah!" Niece and uncle fist-bumped.

Just as Naina was about to let out a relieved breath at the inquisition's ending, Nisha fixed her brother with one of her unamused glares. "How did you get involved in a project with Naina?" Did Nisha sound disgusted or was Naina being oversensitive?

"I got lucky, I guess." Vansh's tone was light, but he'd obviously heard the same thing Naina had in his sister's voice because there was a warning in there too. "Naina does the kind of work

I've been aspiring to for years now. Getting to learn from her is a huge opportunity." He slid Naina a look. "And an honor."

Naina's mother looked from one Raje face to another and her hand fluttered at her chest. "So nice of you to say, Vansh beta," she said. "He's grown up to be such good boy." She gave the compliment straight to Mina, who made the effort to smile but looked worried about her good boy.

"And so handsome also," Mummy added. "Same-to-same like you, Mina. How Bollywood has not snapped him up? All those star sons. You were such big star, he should be star-son-star too, no? He should have straight leg inside. Film magazines are always going nepotism, nepotism, nepotism. He's good candidate, no, for nepotism-nepotism?"

Something inside Naina snapped. "Evidently he's more interested in bettering the lives of people than dancing for the camera, Mummy," she said when she should not have reacted, but Nisha stiffened, and that was too satisfying by half.

"Vansh Mama dances better than any Bollywood star," Mishka said, gazing with adoration at her uncle.

"Damn straight," Mr. Modest said, bestowing another fist bump on his niece.

Everyone rolled their eyes. Some of the tension dissipated.

"They don't believe me, Mish-Mash!" Vansh pointed at Naina's face. "This person, she scoffs! We should show her."

As if on cue, the lights dimmed and the volume of the music rose. The crowd started to move toward the huge dance floor at the far end of the room. Mishka and Vansh looked absurdly delighted and grabbed Naina's arms, one on each side.

Wait, what?

No! Naina did not dance.

Before she could verbalize her protest, they started dragging her to the dance floor. Fighting them with this particular audience would have been mortifying, so Naina went, like a lamb to the slaughter.

Once on the large circular parquet floor, she threw a look over her shoulder. If the confusion on the faces they'd just left was the frying pan, Vansh and Mishka's clueless grins were fire.

She disengaged her arms from their holds. "Do you know what I hate more than coming to parties like this dolled up in clothes my mom gets made for me?" Naina hissed at Vansh as Mishka ran off to get them some *dandiya* sticks.

"I have a feeling you're about to tell me." Vansh made his look-at-me-I'm-disinterested face. Beneath all the charm, the scene they'd just left behind seemed to have disturbed something inside him.

"Dancing. I hate dancing."

"How can you be Punjabi and not like to dance?" He did a Punjabi accent and made an exaggeratedly confused face.

"How can you be Yash's brother and like to dance?" She made an even more exaggeratedly confused face.

"Touché. Have you noticed that you bring my brother into every conversation with me? I wonder what that's about."

She threw a glance at where they'd left the Raje peanut gallery across the room. That should have been explanation enough, but Vansh didn't seem to be in the mood for subtlety, so she added, "I was with him, Vansh, for ten years. He tends to come up in conversations. Plus, he's, you know, Yash."

He studied her, eyes turning unusually guarded. Fortunately the dance floor was starting to pack around them with dancers forming two concentric circles of partners facing each other. The only good part in all this was that there were now several bodies between them and their families, who were no doubt craning their necks to catch a glimpse of what was going on.

"What?" she asked.

"I can't figure out if that's hurt hurt, or *hurt*."

"Oh, that totally makes sense."

He smiled. His real smile, not his look-at-my-dimples-and-let-them-distract-you smile. "I mean you and Yash. What exactly happened?"

She flicked a piece of lint off her shoulder. "I'll forward the link. He explained it pretty well at the press conference, to the entire world."

Vansh's thick, perfectly arched brows drew together. Sympathy. A pretty standard reaction. One Naina was only too used to, but from him she hated it.

Mishka came back with the two-foot-long purple and gold sticks and handed a pair each to Vansh and Naina.

"Why don't I watch the two of you," Naina said. "We need to be in pairs, not threes."

Vansh took her hand and held her in place as she tried to make her escape. "This young man would love to dance with Mishka. Wouldn't you, sir?" he said to a young boy who was standing outside the circle by himself, dressed in the most adorable red and gold kurta.

The boy blushed. Mishka looked unsure.

"Here, you can be Mishka's partner," Naina said to Vansh. "And—what's your name, beta?"

"K . . . K . . . Kiran," the poor boy said, staring nervously at Mishka, who loomed a good head taller than him.

". . . And Kiran can be my partner. We'll get all mixed up when we start moving anyway."

They took their positions, Naina and Vansh next to each other facing Mishka and a blushing Kiran.

The music started to thump. "Are you ready?" the DJ boomed into the mic.

"Yeah!" everyone shouted in response, but none as excitedly as Vansh and Mishka.

As if his beaming smile wasn't enough, Vansh added hoots

and whistles, and the strangest sense of lightness bubbled in the pit of Naina's stomach.

And just like that, they were dancing. Stick against stick, then twirl, then again. At first she had to count the five-step movement, one and two and three and turn and five.

"Let go, Knightlina," he shouted in her ear. Not being his partner meant she stayed next to him as the circles moved. "It's just a dance."

He looked so ridiculously comfortable spinning on his toes and making eye contact with every person he passed that Naina felt the numbers leave her head and the music take hold.

For a couple of songs she forgot where she was, who she was. Then the music slowed and the circles dissipated for a break, and she was oddly disappointed.

"Impressive, Ms. Kohli," Vansh said. "I can't wait for the day I get you to let a bhangra loose on me."

"Never going to happen." But she was smiling when Mishka, Nisha, and Ashna walked up to them. Nisha and Ashna had also joined the dancing circles, and they were all glistening from their exertions. After grabbing bottles of water, they headed back to where the mothers were still standing.

"So this project?" Nisha said, tenacious as a dog with a blood-soaked rag. "Did you say it had to do with that grant you got from Jiggy before Yash's election?"

The rush of warmth that had been wrapped around Naina turned icy. Before she could answer, Jiggy Mehta jogged up to the DJ's platform and took the mic (gold, of course, a very, very bright gold). He was wearing a glittery magenta suit with sequins on the wide lapels and a golden bow tie.

Naina's gaze met Vansh's. His eyes danced with the laughter he was holding in.

Don't you dare make me laugh. She widened her eyes as Vansh adjusted his nonexistent bow tie.

"It's the new year," Jiggy said. "And I cannot thank you enough for getting those charitable receipts in on time for taxes." A smattering of polite laughter flitted through the crowd. "Dance the night away. And donate big because it's a new year with new deductions." More polite laughter. "Another wonderful thing about this new year is that we have a new governor!" This time the cheer that went through the crowd was loud and heartfelt.

Jiggy's smile showed exactly how much he enjoyed an adoring crowd. "Take a moment to stop and congratulate our new governor's family. They were gracious enough to attend today, even though Yash had to be in Sacramento working on the transition—which is exactly what we want him to be doing right now. No rest for the brave."

The crowd went crazy, and Jiggy held up his golden mic as though he were the one they were cheering for.

"That was not a name drop at all," Vansh said, and his mother and sisters slid him an amused glance even as they smiled for the cameras that surrounded them out of nowhere.

"Before I let you go, there was one more announcement I wanted to make," Jiggy said, looking like he was never letting that mic go. "As you know, the Omnivore Foundation has pledged to give away most of my personal wealth to the most deserving of causes around the world, much like Bill Bhai." He grinned. "That's Bill Gates."

He paused to let that settle into the crowd, then a new purpose entered his eyes. "As you also know, I am the perfect example of charitable causes creating opportunity for those with no opportunities. This year the Omnivore Foundation was fortunate enough to recruit a very strong young voice in activism and charitable giving into our fold."

Dear Lord, was he going to embarrass her in front of all these people by calling on her? Naina felt her cheeks warm, her heartbeat sped up.

Vansh smiled at her, eyes dancing with excitement. *Go, Naina,* he mouthed.

Shut up, she mouthed back.

"This person has spent the past decade trying to understand complex problems around the world and is in the perfect position to help us put our dollars where the greatest need is." His grin was smug, the crowd breathless with anticipation. "Please join me in welcoming Vansh Raje to the Omnivore Foundation."

Vansh hooted and started clapping as applause broke around them, his eyes still on Naina.

For a moment Naina almost moved as Vansh raised his hands and clapped in her direction. Then they both grasped—at the exact same moment—what Jiggy had said.

Naina froze.

Vansh froze.

"Vansh, brother, come on, get up here!" Jiggy boomed into the mic, gesturing wildly.

A smile spread across Naina's face. Some invisible force had to have taken her cheeks and physically pushed them up. Her hand moved of its own free will and she pushed Vansh forward, smiling and smiling, clapping and clapping.

For a second he studied her so intently that she thought he'd be stupid enough to say something. Then he smiled too, dimples digging deep, so impossibly deep they seemed hypnotic and 100 percent unreal. Then, with a look that she would not let slice her in half, he ran toward the stage and took the mic Jiggy handed him.

The ringing in Naina's ears was too loud. She forced herself to focus on Vansh's voice as he thanked Jiggy, dimples digging and digging. He was blushing, modesty and gratefulness flowing from him in big rolling waves. Every woman in the audience pressed a hand into her chest and body-surfed his boundless charm.

If his family was watching her, she didn't know. Her vision was tunneled to the stage and her cheeks burned from smiling. How she hated these men. They beamed at the crowd as though they'd won one war and were off to another. They sang each other's praises as though this was their wedding and they'd spent the past month obsessing over penning personalized vows that sounded exactly like the vows at every other wedding. Then they followed it up with chest bumping and back slapping and every form of male congratulatory ritual ever created on God's green earth.

"It's such an honor to have access to Omnivore's money," Vansh said with enough cheekiness that the laughter rippling through the cavernous hall turned delighted. Then he found Naina across the crowd and his voice turned just a slightest bit more somber. "The real honor, though, is getting to work with Naina Kohli and to learn from her. Mr. Mehta's generosity might be the Omnivore Foundation's soul, but Ms. Kohli's vision and organizational genius is its brain, muscle, and heart, pumping blood and distributing oxygen and making sure it all works."

Mishka let out a loud woot and the crowd followed suit.

"To Naina Kohli." Vansh lifted the glass Jiggy handed him in a toast as waiters rushed around the room distributing sparkling champagne.

"To new alliances!" Jiggy Mehta clinked his glass with Vansh's, beady eyes shining knowingly at Naina, telling her he had her exactly where he wanted her. Telling her this was his game and she was nothing more than a pawn.

The bastards.

Naina smiled at them and downed the entire glass in one gulp, bubbles hitting her brain like the realization of her own insignificance.

Mina Auntie hugged her with a "Congratulations, beta," but there were too many questions in her eyes. Questions that Naina would find reflected in Nisha's and Ashna's eyes too, no doubt, if she had the stomach to look at them. Her mother's hands fluttered at her chest and the rage inside Naina morphed into frustration. The kind of frustration that turned her back into the child she'd been. Powerless. Entirely and impotently powerless.

No, she was not that child anymore. She might not have power, but if they thought she was going down without a fight, they needed to think again. They didn't know her, and that was her power. She was unbreakable and she wasn't going to give up her project no matter how hard they made it.

"Excuse me," she threw at the Rajes surrounding her and at her mother. Then, grabbing another glass of champagne from a passing waiter, she emptied it down her throat and left to find a restroom.

Much as she wanted to, she couldn't leave yet. Her fifteen million dollars were at stake. The seven hundred thousand lives that would benefit from that money were at stake. The two men who were dangling her life's work over her head like a dick-shaped carrot were still onstage, surrounded by a worshipping crowd. Vansh did catch her eye for a second. If there was an apology there she couldn't have cared less about it. Fuck him.

He looked like he wanted to come to her, but he was mobbed. A celebrity no one could get enough of. Good. Finally, a break. A small one, but she'd take it.

On her way to the restroom she picked up two more glasses of champagne from a passing server, and, yes, she gulped them down because that bastard Mehta's booze was fucking delicious.

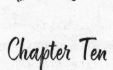

Chapter Ten

Vansh had been on that stage less than five minutes, but it felt like a lifetime. A lifetime in which he'd lost Naina. Where was she? Vansh needed her to be present when he had this conversation with Mehta. One moment she'd stood there looking like someone had stabbed her in the back. Fine, not someone, him. Then she'd disappeared without a trace.

He texted her. *Talking to Jiggywiggy about funding. You need to be here.*

He got that she was angry, but they could make this work for both of them. He hadn't caused this. He did, however, have an idea to make the situation work out for her as well. If she would only let him explain.

"I think we should give Naina another moment," Vansh said to Jiggy, who studied him with all the amusement of someone who didn't give a shit about what anyone thought. "She needs to be here for this conversation. It's her project."

"Well, she knows we're having it and she's choosing not to be here. I'm the host, I need to be on that dance floor with my guests." He flashed his eerily white veneers, a smile that didn't even make it to the general vicinity of his eyes. "Do you know why this is a dandiya night? It's the New Year, not Navratri. Why do you think I've gone through all this trouble to do more than gather people to eat miniaturized fancy food?"

"I don't know." Vansh threw another look at his phone. *Come on, Knightlina!*

"Because I like to dance. And no dancing is more fun than dandiya! I know you like to dance too. I saw you on the floor. No one moves like that unless they love it."

"I do like to dance." Vansh threw a glance around the floor, where the concentric circles of dancers had formed again and the DJ was about ready to send everyone off into spins. "This is such a great idea, by the way. Did you grow up with Navratri being a big deal?" Maybe he could distract Mehta for a bit and Naina would get his messages and turn up.

Mehta threw him a look he'd have thrown at a pathetic puppy who'd had a bad idea and was about to get kicked for it.

"Growing up I wasn't allowed into the Navratri venues except to make sure the toilets were clean enough to not stink up the place." He smiled as he said it, eyes angry, and Vansh's gut twisted in that way it did when the unfairness of the world made itself evident.

The way Mehta's eyes narrowed, it was clear what he thought Vansh could do with his sympathy. "So now, when I can enjoy a dandiya night because I made it happen, I don't appreciate my time being disrespected. Let's get this over with. We don't need Naina for the meeting. It's my money, not hers."

Good thing Mehta made it hard to sympathize with him for too long. "Actually you've already pledged the money to Naina's project, so technically it is her money, or at least her project's money."

"I love how noble you rich people think you are."

You're literally rich enough to buy everything my family owns a few times over, Vansh wanted to say, but he smiled.

Without waiting for a response, Jiggy turned and started walking. "You can fill Naina in later. If you can't calm a woman down with that face, what good is it?"

With another desperate look at his phone, Vansh followed Mehta. Why wasn't she here? He'd sent her twenty texts.

Jiggy stopped at the bar, picked up two glasses of scotch, and took them to a tall table all the way in a far corner where they had a view of the dance floor but were far enough to also have some privacy. Jiggy handed Vansh a glass. "I'm all ears. Tell me about this project you have in mind."

Vansh took a sip. Fine, he'd just have to fill Naina in later. He'd spent the past couple of days poring over the data Hari had collected. They didn't have an exact plan yet, but it seemed like focusing on people like Hari, who were employable but knocked down by bad decisions and worse luck, was a good place to start. Finding them employment seemed like a manageable piece of this gargantuan challenge.

Jiggy watched him.

Vansh opened his mouth. But he couldn't do it. He couldn't do this behind Naina's back. "You know what, you were right. You should be enjoying your party. Let's talk about this at your office."

Jiggy gave another one of his shark smiles, all teeth and bloodthirsty eyes. "Let me make this easier for you, Vansh. You know who's important in all this?"

Vansh had no doubt Jiggy was about to enlighten him.

"Yash," Jiggy said in a tone he might have used had he been saying *the Lord almighty*. "The Raje name. As you can imagine, Naina's work is meaningless to me, but being associated with the governor's girlfriend was a good look for the Omnivore Foundation. Doors open up. That's how the world works, as you well know."

Something cold curled around Vansh. He'd known this, of course, but having it declared like this as though it weren't wrong made it vastly more so.

Jiggy wasn't done. "You know who will always be related to the Rajes?"

As a matter of fact, Vansh did know. But he refused to jump at Jiggy's laser pointer like a frolicking kitten. He waited.

Jiggy took a sip of his drink. An auntie dressed like she was at a wedding waved at Jiggy from across the room. Then again, they were all dressed like that. This auntie just really loved her gold jewelry. The billionaire signaled at her to give him a minute.

"Listen, Vansh," he said, eyes on the dance floor. "I like you. I feel like you're my little brother. Except, if you were, I'd hate you for getting all the looks in the family." He laughed as though he'd made the funniest joke. "So I'm going to do something I never do. I'm going to let you follow your gut. Whatever project you have in mind, I've decided to be open to it. The only thing you have to do is convince Naina. You know how women like that are. Barracudas. Look how she couldn't hold on to Yash." He wiggled his brows. "But it looks to me like you could handle her." Another grin. "Honestly, looks to me like you could handle most women just by smiling." He poked two fingers into his own cheeks, digging finger dimples into them, and gave another self-congratulatory laugh. "So, handle her."

Vansh ran a hand over his hair. It was slicked back and stiff against his palm. "What am I convincing her of exactly?"

"I love that about you. That you're a straight shooter. All the cards on the table." He slammed his buffed and manicured hands down, rings with various precious stones on each finger clinking against the wood. "I'm saying I like your idea. You are right, homelessness is a stain on San Francisco. What a great city, no? The way Bombay was in my childhood, a little beautiful and a little ugly. Now Bombay has nothing beautiful left. We don't want that here, no? I'm saying you can have as much as you want out of the funding. I just don't want Naina making trouble. No female *chik-chik*, you get me? These activist types think making noise gets them whatever they want. The funding is yours, whatever part of it you want. What's left is Naina's if she still wants it."

You can't do that, Vansh wanted to say. But he could. "The work Naina is doing is important. Let's talk about this."

"I know it's important! That's why I took her on. I convinced her to move back to San Francisco and run the foundation. Just like I convinced you to move back too. There's nothing more to talk about."

Vansh hadn't exactly moved back, but this wasn't the time to split those particular hairs. This conversation already wasn't going where Vansh wanted it to go. "But Naina's funds are earmarked already."

"That would be relevant if the funds were hers. They're mine. And she can still use them, so long as you're on the project and you get to do your homelessness thing."

Before Vansh could respond, Jiggy pushed away from the table just as a new song started up. "That's my favorite song. The only Amitabh Bachchan dandiya song, did you know? Come on!" With that he dragged Vansh with him to the dance floor.

The circle of fast-moving dancers who were twirling and clinking the dandiya sticks to the five-step dance opened up for them.

Jiggy threw up his sticks and caught them on a spin, his shark grin challenging Vansh to a dandiya duel. *Really?* He was a lightweight, at least here on the dance floor. Vansh let loose some flashy moves, spinning and twirling his sticks in the air like batons. Jiggy's angry laugh was the last thing Vansh saw before Jiggy spun away. Vansh threw himself into the dance. He needed the motion, needed to fly faster than his thoughts.

Naina had been right all along. She was not going to take this well, and Vansh couldn't think of a single way to make it better, not unless he got Mehta to backtrack. And that seemed impossible without risking Naina's work *and* breaking his promise to Hari.

As he spun through the air, Mishka found him, and he did some comical moves for her. Making his niece laugh made him feel better. He always found a way. Why would this be different?

A few songs after Nisha's last glare telling Mishka it was time to leave, Vansh dragged Mishka off the dance floor. The press of bodies was thick and sweaty and euphoric.

"There's mango kulfi with fresh mangoes," his niece said, puppy-dog eyes out on powerful display. "Please. If you get some with me, Mom can't yell at me about it. She'll yell at you. In any case why does she have to drag me home now, when there's still dancing? Tomorrow is Sunday! Can you tell her to let me stay and you can take me home later?"

"I already got your mom to let you stay this late. Ice cream quickly, then off you go or she'll have my head. She just texted that they're already headed to the car."

"Fine," Mishka said, linking arms with him. "But what did you do for Mom to get so mad at you? I've never seen her glare at you like that."

"It seems like everyone's mad at me these days." He mumbled it, hoping the music would drown out his words. But his niece's hearing was as sharp as her brain.

"Do you mean Naina Auntie? I didn't know you two were *friends*." Did his nine-year-old niece just stress the word *friends* in a most adult way?

"When did you stop being a baby and turn into a nosy auntie?"

"I thought she was too beautiful for Yash Mama anyway. You two look much better together."

"Mish-Mash! Don't be absurd. We've been friends since I was younger than you. Now we're colleagues. Just for a short time, so save your sleuthing for your stories, okay?" Mishka wrote mystery stories that only Vansh was allowed to read.

She looked over her shoulder. "Shhh. You're not supposed to say that out loud."

He tucked a brown curl behind her ear. Evidently, the Raje penchant for secrets was a genetic gift.

"Sorry." He patted the hand she'd hooked into his elbow. "But listen, I want you to remember something. It's not always about looks."

"Only people who look like you can say that," she said lightly, but her eyes were sharp. She was listening.

"Well, people who look like *us* should know that better than anyone else then."

She sighed. "Fine."

They got the promised ice cream to go and he walked her outside. After giving him the tightest, lankiest hug, she went skipping down the colonnaded portico steps to the waiting car. Vansh quickly waved to his mother and sisters before going back inside. He didn't have the stomach to deal with their acting like he was cavorting with the enemy. Because truly, what was wrong with them? Hadn't Naina been a part of their family forever?

There was only one person who had the right to be angry at him right now, and he had no idea why that was making him sick to his stomach.

As he went back inside, a pink and blue ghagra flashed across the room. Finally. Where had she been this entire time? He shouldered his way through the crowd, refusing to lose sight of her. Was she weaving on her feet as she walked toward the bar? Yup. Definitely weaving.

She stumbled as she tried to get on a bar stool, but then she gripped the bar and found her balance. That was Naina Kohli for you, relying on herself even when felled by alcohol.

A man with a red beard who looked like he'd descended from the Scottish Highlands approached her. He seemed to have exchanged his kilt for a tux.

In response to the smile he gave her, Naina threw a glance over both shoulders. The classic Naina Kohli *Stay the hell away* scowl was so fierce that Vansh was impressed the man did not back away immediately. *Do it, buddy. Leave.*

Any minute now she was going to do something like flip him the bird, if not punch his nose. Breaking into a jog, Vansh pushed past the crowd, which was thickest around the dance floor but thinned out toward the bar, thank God. Only at a dandiya party could there be more interest in dancing than alcohol.

"I never fuck men with beards," Naina said sweetly. She was slurring.

Redbeard looked unfazed. "There's always a first time. Don't knock it till you've tried it." He was also slurring. Great.

Vansh inserted himself between the man and Naina and faced him. "Nice party, huh? You having fun?"

He didn't look like someone who appreciated being interrupted. "I was about to, then you showed up." Two pissed-off drunks and one of them was horny. It was a situation waiting to blow up in their inebriated faces.

"Ouch. That was needlessly hurtful, man. I appreciate honesty as much as the next guy. But you heard her. She's not interested." He pointed at the beard. "Maybe if you shaved."

"Rod! There you are. I've been searching for you everywhere." An Indian man with a ponytail, and with stubble that might be construed as a beard, walked up to the Highlander and wrapped an arm around him.

It seemed Naina was not the only sloshed person here being rescued by a friend.

"Excuse me," the new addition to their party said to Vansh as though he were interrupting friends having dinner and not trying to avert a scene. "Do you mind if I steal my friend away for a moment?"

"Can you steal him away forever?" Naina slurred behind Vansh, then placed her chin on his shoulder and watched. Was she humming?

The ponytailed man smiled.

His redheaded friend did not. The expression on his face was as opposite of a smile as an expression could get. "What the bloody hell?" he spat out. He did have a Scottish accent, which made Vansh want to laugh. "I don't fucking need this." Then, flipping Naina the bird and disengaging himself from his friend, he stumbled away.

"I think your Highlander's leaving," Naina said, spraying spittle into Vansh's ear. "I hope it's not to shave off his beard. I don't think I'd be interested even without the beard."

"I'm sorry. Rod's usually a gentleman. It's the jet lag," Rod's keeper said.

"And too much booze," Naina added helpfully.

The man nodded, a smile slipping. "I'm Siddhartha, by the way."

"Siddharthabytheway . . . ," Naina mumbled. "That's an interesting name. Where are you from?" She lifted her chin off Vansh's shoulder and reached for a glass of champagne the bartender had just set on the bar.

Vansh moved it out of her reach and signaled the bartender for a glass of water.

Siddhartha smiled. "Palo Alto."

"No, I mean . . . I mean . . ." She looked at Vansh, mimicking the look they were all more than familiar with. "Where are you *really* from," both Vansh and Naina said together, and the three of them laughed.

"Vansh." Vansh shook his hand.

"I know who you are. I'm India Dashwood's brother."

"Sid Dashwood! Of course. It's so great to finally meet you. This is Naina. Naina Kohli."

"Naina Kohli, the spurned ex," Naina announced grandly, and raised the glass of water the bartender handed her. "Spurned for the love of your sister. Yay, India!" She closed her eyes and made what could only be construed as a drunk person's attempt at the om sound. "Everyone's favorite yogi." Then she slurped down the water, spilling a goodly amount down her cleavage, which was on display because her dupatta had slipped down to her lap. "Welcome to the Raje web of intrigue, Siddharthabytheway not really from Palo Alto."

Sid smiled as though that spectacle hadn't just taken place, and Vansh knew they were going to be friends.

He threw Sid an apologetic look as Naina closed her eyes, put her chin back on Vansh's shoulder, and started making meditative sounds again.

"I've heard so much about you. That finalist picture in the Goodalls, it's brilliant," Vansh said.

The man blushed. "India showed you? Sisters! But thank you. Brahminys are such a part of mythology in that region, I've been chasing a shot like that for twenty years." He studied Vansh in a way Vansh couldn't quite understand.

"Well, amazing capture. I'd love to get together and talk about your work if you're going to be in town for a while."

This seemed to thrill Siddhartha. "Yes! Yes! Well, how about tomorrow? You're staying at your parents' place, I understand. I can come by."

"Sure. That's . . . Well, that's perfect. How about tomorrow afternoon?"

"Great. Sorry, I've got to go make sure my agent isn't off shaving his beard somewhere. Nice meeting you both. I'll see you tomorrow." Then he stopped and shot over his shoulder, "At your parents' house."

Vansh watched him walk away. He had the air of a man fully contained within himself, with not a care for anyone else's opinion. An island in a crowd. "Wow! He's great, isn't he?"

Naina lifted herself off Vansh's shoulder and Vansh turned to her.

"I wonder what he wanted from you," she said, and burped.

"What does that mean?" Vansh took the glass of champagne she'd picked up out of her hand.

"Give that back." She snatched the drink back, making it slosh over both their hands. "That means, it took him three seconds to want to be your best friend and invite himself to your house." She pinched Vansh's cheek. "Our Baby Prince. Everyone falls instantly in love with him. So . . . so . . . lovebialable . . . So . . . loveveeablible." She stuck out her tongue and squinted down at it, trying to figure out why it wasn't doing what she wanted it to.

"He's India's brother. He's family and I've been an admirer of his work for years."

Disinterested in his explanation, Naina stuck her mouth into the glass in Vansh's hand and tried to take a sip before he could pull it away again without letting his grip on her arm go because he didn't want her hitting the floor.

In his whole life Vansh had never thought he'd see Naina make that slurping sound.

"I think that's enough champagne for one evening."

"Are you calling me drunk? I've never been drunk. Ever." Another burp.

"Probably a good choice, given how hot you are when you're drunk."

His sarcasm was lost on her and she pinched his cheeks again. "You think I'm hot? Vansh, are you hitting on your brother's ex-fiancée?"

"Fake ex-fiancée."

"Fake." The word made her giggle, then hiccup.

Vansh needed to get her out of here and home ASAP.

"Your face is awfully close to mine," she said, breath sweet and sour with champagne.

"I know." He pulled her hand off his face and put a little distance between them.

She stuck one finger in his face and counted off. "I've never been drunk around anyone." Then another finger. "I've never danced with anyone. You're a very special boy, Vansh Raje!"

"So I've been told."

"You know who hates that I don't dance?" She patted his face and slumped close again. "Mummy." The smile she gave him could only be described as heartbreaking. "'I don't understand why young person like you not dance,'" she said in her mother's voice. "Well, I'll tell you why, Mummy. Because dancing is just . . . it's just such . . ."

"Fun?"

"Public embarrassment." She started to slide off the bar stool, and Vansh caught her and held her up. "But you're right. Corrrrect. Vansh is correct. It should've been fun. It could've been fun. It . . ." She waited for him to join her in saying the next part ". . . would've been fun. But then it turned into a public embarrassment." She tried to sit up again and push herself off him. "That pretty much sums up my life."

He made her drink another glass of water and she didn't fight him. "I'll tell you what. Let's go home and you can tell me all about it in the car."

She looked at him like he hadn't spoken. "Does it ever get old?" Again she waited for a response without really wanting one. "The adulation without doing one damn thing for it?" She was about to pinch his cheek again, but he held her hand.

She was drunk and hurt by Mehta's stunt, and she didn't even know the half of it. The fear of losing her friendship twisted inside him, along with how much he hated being dismissed by her this way.

"I do more than one damn thing for it," he said when he shouldn't have. There was a time and place for everything, and this was not the time for this conversation. "I'm sorry about what Mehta did."

She burst into laughter. And went on laughing until her breath caught and people started to turn and stare. Then she gagged and jumped off the bar stool on unsteady feet. "Shit. I'm going to be sick."

He helped her to the bathroom.

If there was an outfit that was not designed to throw up in, it was the ghagra choli. Vansh held back her dupatta, which was so heavy with beadwork it kept falling forward as she heaved and spurted into the commode. Hair came loose from her braid and he pushed it off her face. Tears streamed from her eyes. She brought up her guts one painful retch after another after another.

Finally, when there couldn't possibly have been anything more left inside her, she took a tentative breath and sat back on the floor of the bathroom stall.

He sat down across from her and flushed away the vomit, but the acrid stench still hung in the air. She watched him with wet, exhausted eyes. Liner and mascara and whatever else women used to make their eyes look this lovely were smudged into black streaks like the mask of Zorro.

Her nose ran and her hair had come completely askew. Raising his hand over his head, he pulled toilet paper out of the roll. Then, throwing away the ends, he handed it to her.

It took her a few moments to lift her arms and take the offering. She blew her nose and wiped her face. The sadness in her eyes made something scrape like nails inside his chest. Every bit of drunken recklessness was gone from her. She looked empty.

"Can you stand?" he asked, and she squeezed her eyes shut and nodded. But she didn't move, so he stood and took her hand and pulled her up.

She stood on shaking legs and leaned on him, and the nails inside him sharpened. Having known her his whole life, he knew how hard this was for her. This loss of control. Without a single shred of doubt, he knew that no one had seen her like this, ever.

On the floor next to the commode was a pink and silver purse, one of those sleek little things that looked like a silk-bound diary. It was splattered with throw-up. She looked at it and a bitter laugh escaped her. "Fabulous."

Careful to hold the unsoiled part, he picked it up. Then, wrapping an arm around Naina's waist, he took her out of the stall and into the fortuitously empty restroom. There he helped her wash her hands and splash her face. Then he propped her against the countertop and waited for her to get her balance. The fact that she let him was telling. Keeping from throwing up again had to be taking up all her focus.

Once he knew she could stand with the support of the sink, he emptied the purse of her phone and a single lipstick and held the beaded silky thing under the water as she watched with half-closed eyes. Just as he was done, she swayed on her feet and he grabbed her again.

Her body sagged with the relief of not having to hold itself up, which made those nails draw blood inside him. Head on his shoulder, she closed her eyes as he pushed the purse under the hand dryer and called a car. The fact that she let him set her dupatta straight and tuck her hair behind her ear with nothing more than a jaw clench—possibly to keep from throwing up again—made him want to damn it all and carry her out. But she'd never forgive him for that.

They were eerily quiet as they stepped out of the restroom

and headed to the exit, his arm around her waist holding her up, every piece of resistance inside her given up.

And then the last person on earth she'd want to see right now turned into the passageway. Vansh spun her around before she caught sight of her father and whisked her away to the back door and out into the night.

Please don't follow us, Dr. Kohli.

Dr. Kohli was the only one of his parents' friends who had always made Vansh's skin crawl. He'd never been able to put a finger on why, but he knew that his seeing Naina like this with Vansh would be a disaster of epic proportions.

He didn't follow them out into the chilly night and Vansh sent up a grateful prayer.

Had Naina been wearing a coat? She had to have, because her arms, her waist, everything was bare, and it must have been forty degrees.

The car was waiting. Vansh helped her in as she shivered. He asked the driver to raise the temperature and removed the Jodhpur coat he was wearing and placed it over her. All the dancing had overheated him anyway, and the cold catching his damp inner shirt felt good.

She barely budged, burrowed into his coat, and pressed herself into the car door. For the entire drive she kept her eyes closed and didn't say a single word. He didn't either. A first for them.

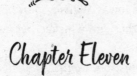

Chapter Eleven

*H*ow Naina had put herself in a situation where she was being carried into her own bedroom like a baby, she had no idea. The moment Vansh put her down on her bed, her stomach cartwheeled again. Hand pressed to her mouth, she ran to the bathroom.

God, not again. Why was it happening again? What was even left inside her? Her head spun even as it felt like it was in a vise. Her insides swam up her throat and spurted out her nose. Exhaustion gripped every inch of her. *Please, please, can it be over?*

His hands on her hair, on her back, they filled her with shame, but they were also the only thing that made sense. They anchored her and she held on to the feel of them.

Again her guts spurted up. Again he held her. This time it was so violent that when there was nothing left she sank back into him and shook, drained beyond bearing. Why had she been so stupid? Recklessness was not for her. Letting her guard down was not for her. More glasses of champagne than she'd counted going down was not for her.

"It's okay," he kept saying, breath warming the crown of her head. "It will pass. Let it out. Stop fighting it. It's going to be over soon. You're going to be fine."

"Not if I die first," she said, making him blow a puff of laughter behind her ear.

After that last emptying, the swirling in her stomach slowed. Her head still felt like it was floating over her neck. Her body still felt like a stacking puzzle with pieces not quite fitting together.

"I think I'm okay." It was time to try to sit up by herself. *Attagirl, you can do it.* When she didn't immediately hurl again, she felt emboldened to hope that he was right and that it might actually pass without taking her with it.

He let her go, but the way he held his body, she knew he was studying her as they sat there on her bathroom floor. She couldn't bring herself to look him in the eye. Couldn't bring herself to be the person he was looking at like that. A sorority girl bent over the commode at his frat house.

And yet, neither had she ever been a sorority girl, nor had he ever been a frat boy. Well, at least now they knew how it felt.

Suddenly she was angry. Why the hell had they never been able to be that? She was as cool as any sorority girl, damn it!

"Why the hell can't I?" she said, throat raw but body suddenly alight with indignation. "Why can't I be cool?"

"Okay," he said, taking that as his cue to stand, giving her a hand and holding her elbows as though he knew that her legs felt like they didn't know yet that she was fine.

He had beautiful hands, strong and warm and, like the rest of him, unmarred by a single imperfection. How had she never noticed his hands before?

"You have beautiful hands. Why have I never noticed that before?" Why was everything she was thinking flying out of her mouth? "Why is everything I'm—" She pressed a hand into her mouth.

He turned on the faucet—was he smiling?—and walked her to the sink. It was like they were stuck in an endless loop of his walking her to sinks all over the world. One sink, then another, then another.

"Where do you keep your pajamas?"

She met his eyes in the mirror. They were definitely smiling even though he was fighting hard to keep them blank, stoically putting his entire energy into not embarrassing her. Well, hah! "With those eyes, good luck hiding anything, baby!"

The way his eyes widened, she had to have said that out loud too.

Stop it!

What was wrong with her?

Her bathroom spun around her head, answering her question rather succinctly. A giggle flew out of her.

"I can't feel my own head." She let it drop from side to side like a bobblehead. "I'm so fucking drunk."

This time his smile was open and teasing. "No! Really?" Leaning her into the vanity to make sure she didn't face-plant, he went back into her room.

She splashed her face some more and rinsed her mouth and tried to keep from diving into the sink because it felt like a swimming pool. Was it a swimming pool?

Strong hands pulled her out of the sink. Straightening up felt like falling backward, and it made her giggle some more.

She sagged into him. So solid. He was so solid. An arm came up in front of her face and held a nightshirt up. "Do you need help getting out of—"

She spun around, stumbled again. He held her up. Again.

"He wants to undress me," she announced to her all-white bathroom and patted his cheek. "Sweet boy." She pushed him away. The vanity was digging into her butt, but it kept her from sliding to the ground. She reached behind her. "Do you have any idea how hard it is?"

He made one of his speaking faces: *I know. But I'm not sure which hardship you're referring to right now.* No one else she knew did this: talked without talking.

She patted his cheek again; his dimples felt loud against her palm, exaggerated dips and curves, textured patterns of sensation. "Have you ever tried to get a choli off?"

"Can't say that I have." His dimples dug deeper and she stroked one with a finger.

"Are these real?"

He removed her hand from his face. "No. Your brain is making them up."

Pulling her hands from his, she reached behind her again. The damn choli was squeezing the life out of her. Why the hell were these things designed like push-up bras and corsets had babies together after violent sex? The kind that involved restraints and things. "BDSM."

His eyebrows shot up, but she had no idea what part of that thought she'd spoken out loud. The beads were digging into her skin. She hated clothes.

"I hate clothes." Her hands wouldn't reach the hooks in the back. "What kind of asshole puts hooks where you can't reach them unless you're an acrobat? Or one of those people without joints? Those people who pop . . . poping . . . pooper . . . poo . . ." Her hands struggled to reach the clasps.

"I got it." Reaching around her, he found the hooks.

It was such a relief, she dropped her arms and pressed her forehead to his jaw, and smelled him.

"The entire cologne company." To hell with it, she didn't care what popped out of her mouth. *Just don't give in to the unbearable urge to lick his neck.* He smelled yummy. Like lemon bars and sex.

The laugh in his throat vibrated against her nose just as the tightness around her breasts from the choli released, setting her free.

She wanted to throw it off. Throw everything off.

"Lemon bars . . ." *Don't say the rest.* "And sex." She smelled him again.

He pulled her off him, eyes locked on hers. *Focus.* He spoke without speaking and pressed the nightshirt at her, using it to keep the choli blouse, which had started descending from her shoulders, in place. "I'll be waiting outside, try not to fall and hurt yourself." With those gentle, stern words, he left.

Easy for him to say. The choli dropped to the ground but the hook on her ghagra skirt fought her. "Get off me!" Yes, she screamed at it.

"Naina?" he said from the other side of the door.

"Haven't fallen. Still standing."

"Good girl."

Finally she got the blasted thing off and pulled on the white nightshirt he'd found. It said, *I'm My Sugar Daddy.*

The trip from the bathroom to her bed was a blur. Before she knew what was happening she was sprawled facedown, arms out, on top of her comforter. Flying like a bird.

Someone started to move her body parts around. The unstackable puzzle spilled everywhere. Flip, turn, roll. She was on a boat, pitching and twisting. A puzzle on a boat.

When it ended, she was beneath her sheets, comforter tucked to her nose. It was nice.

"I know you!" She opened her eyes.

His smile was the best thing in the world. Like frozen custard with crushed-up chocolate and strawberries folded in. Smooth and sweet and crunchy. He was decadent and irresistible. Like sex.

Stop thinking that word.

Sex sex sex.

"Does champagne make you horny?" Yup, that was her voice.

Raising those very sexy eyebrows, he pointed at a cup on her nightstand. "Can you drink some tea? It will settle your stomach and keep your throat from hurting tomorrow."

"Will it stop me from thinking the word—" She scooted up to sitting and tried to reach for the cup, and toppled over.

Naturally, he caught her. Because he was her hero. And now they were both laughing and she was draped all over him and his body was warmer and harder than anything she'd ever held in her arms. And it was pressed against hers. And champagne had to make you horny.

Her nipples beaded against the thick muscle of his chest. Heat shivered through her, dotting her skin with goose bumps. Cotton rubbed against cotton, and the friction made her want to press harder. Something strained between her legs.

Pull away.

Pull. Away.

She dragged the painfully hardened peaks against him and a moan escaped her.

It had been years, years since she'd touched anyone like this. All Yash had ever done was pull away. She shoved at the sting of rejection. Shoved at it with all her might.

It had never been like this. Like *this*. Like heat and hunger. An age had passed since someone had touched her. Since her breasts had touched skin other than her own hand. Since her clit had throbbed between her legs, starved for human friction, pulsing with need. She pressed herself into him.

The relief was like a fever. Like rage. Like a spasming muscle releasing, then cramping tighter, harder.

She should have been mortified, but her brain seemed to have given up registering anything but how hard his body was, how hot, a furnace. How it felt against hers. She couldn't tell if he was frozen or if he was pressing against her too. His breath was heavy in her ear. His body pulsed with something. Too afraid to move. Too afraid to let her go.

Please don't let me go.

He didn't.

Taking him down with her felt like the only possible thing to do. Pulling away from him felt inconceivable.

Please don't leave me.

She was long past knowing which words she was speaking and which words screamed inside her head.

Then she heard her name on his lips.

Naina. Let's think about this.

No. She wanted to scream it.

Stop talking.

Don't push me away. Please.

Their tangled bodies sprawled across her bed, across each other, skin to skin, heat to heat.

He didn't push her away.

"Your thigh is between my legs." She was clutching it with her entire being, as though her existence depended on it. It was heavy and hard and ridged even through the silk of his pants. The press of it against her clit was more pleasure than she'd ever experienced in her life.

All Yash had wanted was to get it over with. All she'd wanted was to get it over with too.

She didn't want this to be over.

Vansh. His name made every muscle in her body clench with need, and pleasure. And freedom.

He didn't reply, but his body responded. It hardened even as she felt him swallow a gasp.

Her face pressed into his shoulder, seeking out that smell, that warm touch of his skin. Her hips moved. The groan that shuddered in his chest was her name ripped up and scattered into breath. He didn't move, not away, not closer. Didn't make it easier. Not harder. Tremors traveled through him, taut muscles tightening, his body hardening impossibly against hers.

Naina. He pushed out the word.

Please don't stop me. Don't stop this.

Her hips took on a rhythm, thrusting back and forth, undulating against him with a languid force that gripped her core and fused it against him, pressing, then dragging, pressing, then dragging. Breath shuddered from her, her moans shameless, loud, and wretched as they broke free from her lungs.

Everything turned to one thing: him and her and the place where their bodies fused together. The place where their flesh kissed and rubbed. Friction building and building too fast. The explosion came faster than she wanted, not fast enough, and when it peaked and crashed it splintered her, the convulsion so violent and sharp she choked on her own gasp, trembled from it, toes curling, nails digging, lip bitten so hard she tasted her own blood.

Tears streamed from her eyes, saliva wet her lips, throbbing slickness gathered in the aching space between her legs. She was drenched, soaked to her bones. Liquid. Sweat and joy and shame. She didn't care. Couldn't care. Her release was too great, her body too satisfied, and it knocked everything else askew.

Somewhere outside her, he said her name again.

Somewhere inside her a voice tried to tell her something, but she couldn't hear it. Not when satisfaction screamed in her ears. Not when her heartbeat pounded through her limbs. Clutching the cotton of his shirt in her fingers, the silk of his pants between her bare thighs, she let herself fall, deep into the release that continued to convulse through her in quivering aftershocks.

When oblivion followed, she gave herself up to it, claiming what felt like the first breath of peace she'd ever known.

Chapter Twelve

Vansh was going to spend all of today—forever to be remembered as the Day After the Thigh Incident—trying not to look at his phone every two seconds.

Naina was not going to call or text. She was probably never going to speak to him again. Ever. The thought made him want to shake out his arms.

Maybe it hadn't been a great idea to let himself out of her apartment in the middle of the night. Fine, he'd stayed until morning, but she didn't know that because he had left before she woke up.

He leaned back in his chair, away from the desk of his childhood. Painted by an artist in shapes and swirls to keep from looking like a place of study. One of the recommendations from a therapist to counter the ugly feelings he associated with schoolwork. It still made him a bit queasy to sit here. He yanked off his headphones and stood. In the end, text-to-speech was the real savior. And his memory, which could give an elephant a run for its money.

That didn't mean all of it wasn't exhausting.

Hari had been sending him every piece of demographic data

he could find and compute about the homeless in the city. There was some information about education and past employment but not nearly enough. The segments with mental illness and addictions were the best documented. Yet again it struck Vansh how complex the problem was. Too many pieces to track and connect. History, economics, politicians treating people like pawns, people treating each other like nothing more than the money they could generate. But that wasn't different from any other problem in the world.

His wallet sat on his nightstand. Flipping it open, he dug out a folded piece of paper. The words were faded, as though his superhuman dyslexic memory had soaked them right off the paper.

Do not be daunted by the enormity of the world's grief. Do justly now, love mercy now, walk humbly now. You are not obligated to complete the work, but neither are you free to abandon it.

His friend Amara had slipped him the note one night after a gas explosion had killed fifteen people in their camp in Cambodia. A paraphrase of one of the teachings from her Jewish faith.

It had been a lantern in many a dark night.

As he always did when he thought of the note, he dropped Amara a text checking in on her. She was a young mother *and* the CIO of some hot tech start-up in Tel Aviv now, but she'd answer within seconds.

Thank you, my Indian prince.

Yup.

He sent her a broken-heart emoji. Then an eggplant, just because it had always made her laugh.

Another email chimed on his laptop, from Hari. He was work-ing on a Sunday morning too. Having a task that involved num-bers had already given Hari purpose and relief. Vansh couldn't abandon him any more than he could destroy Naina's project.

He dictated another text into his phone. This one to Jiggy, telling him they needed to talk some more about the terms of his coming on board at the Omnivore Foundation.

You know what the terms are, young Raje, Jiggy shot back. *Naina is good at moving things around and adjusting. She stays if you stay. I have to think about the foundation first.*

Vansh threw his phone across his bed. Physical rage was not his way. Any rage was not his way. Why had he even gotten out of bed that morning?

Well, he'd done it for obvious reasons. To run away from Naina's wrath and regret, for one.

How could he not have left? It had seemed like the only way to save them, whatever that meant. Dear God, she was going to be livid. He could feel her wrath in his very gut. At herself, at him, at the whole wide world. Letting her work through that without an audience had seemed like the only way to do this without . . . without . . . losing everything. Thank you, Jiggy fucking Mehta!

How the hell had Vansh let this happen? In one fell swoop, Jiggy had slid a noose of Naina's life's work around Vansh's neck. And the chair he was standing on was the promise he'd made to Hari.

Dramatic. He knew.

But too damned true.

Hari was in a hotel room waiting for something to help change the trajectory of his life. Sending him back to the street was not an option.

Seven hundred thousand women in Nepal were waiting for their lives to change.

Shit shit shit.

Call him a coward, but facing Naina in the morning was out of the question. What would they even have said to each other after . . . after . . . that? The fact that she had to have woken up with a hangover for the ages would not have helped the situation. Vansh was certain that finding him in her home was the last thing she'd want when she woke up.

Had she really clenched his thigh between her legs? Had he really watched her come apart? Naina, who never let go?

For all the vividness of the memory, Vansh had no idea how it had happened. How they'd ended up pressed against each other. He might have tried to stop her, but it was the *Don't push me away. Please*, that had done it. He wouldn't have pushed her away for anything. He didn't know if it was right or wrong. All he knew was that he had never experienced anything like it in his entire life.

Shit.

He could not lose their friendship.

The thought burst inside him like one of those slo-mo replays of a nuclear explosion.

He could not lose Naina. The comfort of someone seeing him so clearly. The discomfort of someone not avoiding the things she thought were wrong with him. Their love of the work that was their life, even though she wouldn't admit yet that their passion was one and the same.

Vansh was already in his workout clothes. He pulled on his shoes and made his way to the gym.

Forty minutes of lifting and her face as she fell apart wouldn't leave his brain.

He jumped on the treadmill, raising the speed to the point where he was almost flying off the belt. It was the only way to outrun this feeling, and his embarrassment. He couldn't remember the last time he'd ejaculated all over himself, inside his clothes, without anyone even touching his dick.

The idea of never seeing her again made Vansh raise the speed even higher. The idea of never having her fix him with that disapproving gaze while her incisive eyes saw all the way inside him—it was inconceivable. She held him to high standards. He liked that. She didn't give him a free pass. He'd never thought about how badly he'd missed that.

What the hell, Vansh!

This was Naina Kohli.

That was the thing. This was Naina Kohli. Miles out of his league, miles out of everyone's league. The most beautiful, the smartest, but also the most selfless and hardworking person he'd ever met. Also, the one person in the world who had no interest at all in a relationship. With anyone. Ever.

He knew this. He understood this.

Because he felt exactly the same way.

He always had.

Then why did he feel so fucked?

So. Fucked.

If he didn't slow down and get off the treadmill, he might go into cardiac arrest, and he wasn't ready to die. There were too many messes he'd made that he needed to fix. Step one: get Hari ready to meet Naina tomorrow. Walking into her office with Hari in tow might seem cowardly upon first consideration, but walking in there with Hari *and* a solution to their funding problem was the only answer to this mess. Vansh just had to make sure she listened before freezing him out.

He punched his finger into the controls and dropped the speed to a cool-down. By the time he hopped off the treadmill, every inch of his legs cramped. His shoulders and arms had been in agony before he'd even climbed on the treadmill because he'd lifted to the very limit of their capacity. He was drenched in sweat, hair plastered to his forehead and neck, shirt and shorts dripping.

Usually he'd be buzzing with satisfaction and adrenaline, but his limbs dragged with an odd weight. Even the act of downing half a gallon of water felt like work.

A hot shower called to him like a foghorn, and he marched toward it like a man only an act of God could stop.

One step out of the gym and J-Auntie found him, stack of washed towels balanced in her arms, her black-shirt-on-black-trousers uniform crisp as ever. "Your friend's here."

"My friend?" Naina was here? Why would she show up here? Maybe she'd decided to forgive him. Or maybe she was just hunting him down to kill him.

Before he could respond or break into a run to see her, J-Auntie looked at him funny. "He said you had an appointment. You don't look ready for an appointment."

"He?"

"Of course. India's brother can hardly be a she."

"India's brother?"

She fixed him with a worried look, one that said maybe he shouldn't work out enough to cut off the oxygen supply to his brain. "It's not like you to be so confused. Everything all right, beta?"

"I'm fine. Are you talking about Sid? He's the one here?"

"Who else would I be talking about? Does Ms. India have another brother I don't know about?"

A smile nudged at Vansh's lips. If he weren't a sweaty mess, he'd have hugged her.

She held up a hand. "Don't even think about it. I do not have the time for a shower."

"Come on!" But he wasn't ten and she'd endured enough sweaty, muddy hugs from him when he was a boy, so with a "You're the best, J-Auntie, thank you," he was about to head off to find Sid when she stopped him again.

"Oh, and His Highness was looking for you again." Her voice was as flat as it always was, but that thing Vansh hated flashed in her eyes. Sympathy.

"Thanks."

"Beta . . . ," she said, stopping him in his tracks once again. "He waited for lunch for you yesterday too."

"I was busy." Vansh wasn't consciously avoiding HRH.

The man was busy. Vansh was busy. It was just hard to get their schedules to match. The fact that Vansh couldn't remember the last time he'd been alone in a room with his father was immaterial. It also didn't matter because they had very little to talk about one-on-one. It wasn't like Vansh avoided him at family gatherings or anything.

J-Auntie knew better than to push, and with no more than a nod, she hurried off.

Vansh found Sid studying the Raje ancestral portraits in the living room. His hair was down today and not in a ponytail. It hit the base of his neck in waves, all at one length, not the expensively layered long hair some of Vansh's friends had sported over the years, but something one might chop off oneself. It made him look every bit the world-renowned wildlife photographer he was.

"These are amazing," Sid said, without taking his eyes off the painting he was currently studying.

It had been a while since Vansh had stopped to study the portraits or to think about his ancestors. Their presence was much more tangible in the Sagar Mahal. Here at the Anchorage, it was somewhat more muted, as though the spirits weren't entirely committed to making the journey their descendants had made, and they were out of their depth in this new world.

"Thank you," Vansh said simply. "I think this one was done by Diego Rivera. I'm told he traveled in secret to Sripore at my uncle's request. I believe they were friends."

If Sid had looked absorbed before, now he looked awestruck.

An expression that felt as out of place on his face as Vansh's ancestors would have felt here in California.

Sid twisted his body to meet Vansh's eyes, obviously having a hard time looking away from the painting. "India told me your family ruled Sripore for a few generations before the British came."

"Yes, they trace back to the fourteen hundreds. Most of it was a bloodbath, though. First the Moguls, then the Europeans. But this portrait is a modern one." Vansh turned to the painting Sid was standing in front of.

A portrait of his father's oldest brother, His Royal Highness Maheshwar Ramchandra Raje. Aji's firstborn and Esha's father. "That's my oldest uncle, my aunt, and that's their daughter, my cousin Esha."

Sid continued to stare unblinkingly at the painting. His eyes were the kind of dark that was at once flat and bottomless. Vansh had rarely seen a man with less readable eyes. "Do they live in Sripore?"

"They died. In an air crash. Some thirty years ago." Vansh had never met his aunt and uncle, but they'd always been a presence in his life, with their death anniversaries every summer in Sripore, and the pain in Aji's and HRH's eyes every time they reminisced. Then there was Esha . . .

"All three of them?" Sid asked, his voice barely a whisper.

"No, not my cousin. Esha, she's . . . she's very much alive. Thank God." Like his grandmother, he had the urge to touch wood to ensure Esha's long life.

"Esha," Sid said as though it were the strangest name to give a person. Well, his sisters were named India and China, so his tone made Vansh smile. "I'm not sure," Sid added, "but I think India has mentioned her."

Vansh let out a laugh. "Yup, there's a lot of us. It's a lot to keep track of."

Sid turned to him, his attention pulling away from the portrait for the first time. "That's not what I meant. There are a lot of you—which had to have been fun growing up—but you're all very unique and not at all difficult to remember."

Vansh liked this guy. "And like it or not, you're family now, so you have no escape from us." He looked down at himself. "I'm so sorry I'm not dressed. I didn't realize we'd set a time. I should have managed my morning better." He really wanted to stay and talk to Sid some more, but he had promised to take Hari shopping and they had a few things to figure out before they saw Naina tomorrow. Well, more than a few things if Vansh were to have a chance at surviving that meeting.

"Oh, that's perfectly fine. We didn't set a time. I was just in the area and you were generous enough to want to meet, so I thought I'd drop by. I'm not great with texting and calling. It annoys the hell out of my sisters, but I hate this sense of being tethered to a piece of electronic metal. Where's the serendipity in that?" His eyes slid to the painting again and lingered.

"You're exactly right. When I'm not stateside, it's like things are so much more organic. You meet people without warning them, you drop by. A lot of that is changing everywhere else too, but here in the US it's like you have to announce every move before you make it. I'm glad you stopped by. I hope you will again soon. But my mother would kill me if you left without eating or drinking something. Can I get you something?"

Sid pointed to an empty cup on the coffee table next to a plate of biscuits.

"Mrs. Junjunwala already took care of it when I got here." Vansh hadn't heard J-Auntie called by her real name in a long time. Of course she'd taken care of it. This also meant Sid had been waiting awhile.

"I'm really sorry. I promised to help a friend with something."

Sid waved away his apology. "Please. Go ahead with your plans. I will take a rain check though."

Vansh walked him to the front door. "Why don't you come back for dinner later this week? I'm sure my parents would love to meet you. They're off doing something with their grandkids right now. Our family currently revolves around the newest addition."

The smile that split Sid's face was completely different. "Oh, Ram is adorable. India and Yash are totally in love with him."

"We're all smitten. Thankfully Nisha drops him off with our grandmother on weekdays while she works. That way we get our daily Ram fix."

Sid threw a look over Vansh's shoulder. "I've never met your grandmother."

"That takes care of it then, let me check my mother's schedule and you're coming over. You can meet Aji then. She's a bit reclusive. She needs notice." Aji would want to meet India's brother, but to arrange a meeting with Aji, they'd have to make sure Esha was warned to stay away. None of which Vansh had time for today.

"I'd love that. And I look forward to meeting your cousin Esha. You said she lives here too?"

Vansh hadn't mentioned that. The family was well trained in the art of not sharing information about Esha and not encouraging questions about her. India was the one who had probably told Sid that Esha lived with them. Vansh pushed away the discomfort that nudged at him at the mention of Esha by a stranger.

"I'll text you about the day that works for dinner," Vansh said.

"I look forward to it. Maybe I can get the grand tour then too? The house is beautiful. And the grounds . . . Yash tells me you have quite a collection of birds."

Vansh opened the front door and spotless sunshine hit them along with the perfectly timed chirping of birds. "Yes! Did Yash tell you there's a family of scrub jays that just had babies? Our gardener's been keeping an eye out for them and he told me the other day they'd hatched."

Sid looked truly excited for the first time since Vansh had met him. "Would you mind very much if I got a few shots?" He pulled his phone out of his cargo capris, a fashion choice that seemed perfectly natural on him.

Vansh smiled. "Really? Would you be interested in anything as pedestrian as a scrub jay?"

"There's nothing pedestrian about a scrub jay. I take offense on behalf of all jays." His excitement made him look suddenly young. "If there's been hatchlings, I really don't want to miss it. It's the most life-affirming of things."

"Of course." Vansh didn't want to be rude, but he didn't have the time to take Sid on a tour.

"I know I've kept you too long. I can find the nest myself if that's okay, and then see myself out when I'm done." It was funny to see someone with such inherent gravitas being so enthusiastic about scrub jays.

"You sure you don't mind?"

"Mind? I'm a man who loves my solitude. Don't ever get my sisters started on how much."

Vansh laughed, because he could imagine India and China's views on the matter. "So, what you're saying is that you're actually thrilled I'm too busy to hang out with you?"

"Phew." Sid made an exaggerated relieved expression. Vansh liked this guy more and more with every passing minute. "Seriously, just point me in the general direction of the nest and I'll be on my way."

"Of course. It would be totally clueless of me to offer to show someone like you where to find a bird's nest."

Sid shrugged, but he didn't argue. Just waited with that gleam in his eye that seemed to have gripped him since Vansh had mentioned the hatchlings.

So Vansh told him to go around to the back of the house to

the redwood behind the pool with the hammock swing hanging by it.

"Perfect. Thank you." Sid was gone so fast Vansh wondered what having such a raging desire to see some newly hatched birds must feel like.

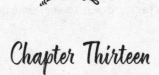

Chapter Thirteen

"Where are you?" Esha whispered the words into the air. They seemed to stay suspended there, not knowing quite where to go. Just like she didn't quite know whom she'd addressed them to.

It had been a few days since she'd seen Garuda. She'd come out onto the balcony more than usual and he hadn't come to see her. She'd walked around the estate a few times, but if he'd been circling above her head the way he usually did, he was too far up in the sky.

"Why haven't you come to see me?" she repeated, an unusual frustration nudging at her.

"I've tried my best. It isn't easy." The voice came from behind her, beyond the balcony's ledge.

Spinning around, Esha ran to the railing and leaned over. "Sid! It's you? You came back!"

"Whom were you talking to? Who else comes to see you like this?" He pulled himself up to the balcony's very narrow overhang and squinted up at her.

His hair was loose today and the wind blew it around his head. The sun caught the dark depths of his eyes as they took her in. She'd never seen a person lit up by the sun like this, and for a moment the world seemed to narrow down to her view: a man on her balcony's ledge staring up at her.

"Esha?" She loved how he said her name. As though it were a question tilted up at the end, a nudge.

"No! No one else comes to see me." That seemed to satisfy him, but saying those words made her think about how strange all this was. "I'm not sure you should either."

"I thought you wanted me to come see you."

She had. In fact it was all she'd been able to think about since he'd scaled the walls of her home like an acrobat. Or a very skilled thief.

"Please say something. Do you want me to leave?"

"No! Please don't leave."

His relief was a beautiful thing. Needing to study his reactions to know what he was thinking was a beautiful thing. All the wonder and excitement and disorientation she'd felt when she'd met him for the first time returned in a flood, and she stepped away from the railing and closed her eyes.

She heard him land next to her on the balcony and something flooded her, a strange warmth. A rightness. Curiosity. It was the curiosity that was the most exciting thing, the thing she didn't remember ever experiencing.

How had she never thought about how much she missed not knowing? How wondrous it was to meet someone new and to get to process them as a clean slate? From a place of utter and beautiful ignorance.

All she'd done her whole life was push away information about people as it bombarded her. The act of deciphering people was the heart of being human, but she'd never experienced it. Not in as long as she could remember.

"Esha?" he said again. He was next to her now. "You okay, sweetheart?"

"You called me sweetheart." She didn't open her eyes. She

couldn't. She wanted to gauge everything from his voice, his words, how they fell on her. She wanted to narrow down the points of intersection between them, feel every strand of connection as a separate thing.

"I'm sorry. It was a reflex. I'll be careful if you don't like it."

"I like it. I like it very much." She wanted him to call her sweetheart again. "Sid?"

"Yes?" If he thought it was strange that she had her eyes closed, his voice didn't show it.

"Will you tell me something about yourself?"

Okay. She opened her eyes and caught the word in his. It was an indescribably wonderful feeling to catch unsaid words in his eyes. Now that she had opened her own, she wanted to go on looking at him.

For the longest time, she did. And he looked at her in return. Just watched her as she watched him, the afternoon sun haloing around them.

She wanted to touch him again. Touch him and feel nothing. Well, she'd felt things, but those things were inside herself. Not inside him. She wanted to feel those again. Just those.

"What do you want to know?" he asked.

"Tell me something no one else knows about you."

He shoved his hands into his pockets without moving his gaze from hers. "You first. Tell me something no one knows about you."

That made Esha want to laugh, and cry. Everyone who knew her, a sum total of fifteen people, was always too afraid to ask her about herself.

"You," she whispered, studying his eyes for those precious reactions, trying not to be distracted by the beautiful lines that radiated out from their edges in a perfect fan.

She could tell he'd misunderstood what she meant.

"No, you first. Please," he said.

"I did go first. That was my answer. *You.* No one knows that

I've met you." If only she could explain what she meant by that. What it meant. *No one knows that I can't feel anything from you. Nothing.*

"Touché." He laughed. A lovely low chuckle that rumbled in his chest. "I meant tell me something about you that's about *you.*"

She couldn't not join in his laughter. *You have no idea.* "You should have specified that before. Now it's your turn." He was about to answer but she stopped him. "And you can't use the same answer I did. That's cheating."

His smile told her he'd been about to do just that. Having guessed it made her ecstatic. *I had to guess!* she wanted to scream, but already he had to think she was strange. She didn't want to make it worse.

"Fine," he said, tone sulky, but she was almost sure he was pretending it. Fine, not almost. She was sure he wasn't feeling sulky. He was feeling what she was feeling, excited that a stranger saw things he was thinking.

Only in Esha's case, it was a first. She was seeing—processing—his thoughts like other people did, like a normal person.

"I don't know my birthday." As soon as the words left him, he blinked in shock. A dark pain widened his irises.

Turning away from her, he leaned his elbows on the railing. There was something about the way he was breathing that was different.

"Sid? Are you okay?" She'd never had to ask anyone that question before and the words felt alien in her mouth, but the worry that something had just happened inside him that caused him pain, that was worse. Usually she had to push other people's pain away. Compartmentalize it and tuck it someplace where it was bearable.

Now she felt an urge to reach into the hurt that had tightened his body, pull it into herself and away from him.

Elbows still on the railing, he turned to her as though seeing her for the first time. "I've never told that to anyone before. I don't know why I told you."

"You've never told anyone?" It seemed like a very big thing for no one to know about a person. Especially a person who had a family she knew doted on him.

He seemed surprised at himself for having told her, then even more surprised when he kept going. "I was left at an orphanage in Goa in India when I was a baby. They weren't exactly sure how old I was. The orphanage doctor guessed I was between nine months and eighteen months." A sheen of sweat had broken out across his forehead as he spoke, and he wiped it on his shoulder. She thought he might stop, but he went on. "The headmistress put a random date on my birth certificate." His finger pressed against his upper lip, where the scar left a wide gap in his stubble and lifted his lip up. India Dashwood had the scar too, but hers was more subtle than Sid's.

"India has it too," she said. "The scar."

He made a grunting sound. "My sister China does too. Our mother adopted all three of us and we were all born with cleft lips. India and China were babies and their surgeries happened when they were young. I'd had basic surgery as a baby, but Mom brought me here when I was six and then we had to redo some of the surgeries. They did a lot of grafts." This time when he looked up it was like he'd forgotten she was there.

She leaned into the railing next to him. "How did you know about the birth date?"

For a moment he seemed to have no idea what she was talking about, so lost was he in the pain of the memories, in the pain of his surgeries.

Esha had the urge to touch him, but he already looked like his space had been violated. Something about how he was holding himself, how he was looking at her, pricked at her. She couldn't quite put a finger on what about it bothered her.

"You said no one knows that you don't know your birth date," she explained, "and that the headmistress made one up. Did she tell you that?"

"No." A whisper. He looked so lost she almost told him it was okay to not answer. Then he cleared his throat and spoke again, his voice stronger. "I overheard the headmistress telling a teacher that she thought she might have picked a date that was unlucky for me."

Esha's confusion must have shown, because he explained himself. "Apparently, Mother Superior had a secret. She believed in numerology and tried to come up with birth dates for her orphans that gave them the luckiest chance at adoption. I wasn't adopted until I was six." He smiled as though the ugliness in the world was amusing. "She attributed it to bad luck. But with my face, her numerology had to have been magic, because Tara Dashwood was traveling through India in search of something and she found me."

Esha had to touch him. She cupped his jaw. Until now, when she touched him, all she'd been able to think about was how she couldn't feel anything other than the physical textures on her hands. Now she felt something else. A tug deep inside. A sensation she remembered experiencing a long time ago, before she'd learned to push away every feeling. A real feeling that belonged to her and her alone.

He pressed his hand over hers, a greedy pressure, sandwiching her hand between his palm and his skin. She could tell that he felt the tug too and he wanted more of it.

"Why didn't you tell anyone?" she asked.

The smile on his face shone like the sunlight that was bathing them from all sides. "Our mother loved to make a big deal of our birthdays and I just never felt like telling her that it really wasn't mine."

"I'm so glad your headmistress picked that birthday for you.

But it seems to me that it was luckiest for your mother." And for Esha. He wouldn't have been here if his mother hadn't found him.

"My mother would agree with you." His voice was barely a whisper. "Do you always know the exact right thing to say? The exact thing people want to hear?"

She pulled her hand away, suddenly needing to move. "Is that what I did?"

He took her hand again as though he wasn't ready for them to not be touching. "I didn't mean on purpose. I meant it's a skill to say the right thing. A skill I've never had. I don't do well with words. I . . . I've never told any of this to anyone."

Why did he keep repeating that? Esha's heart stuttered in the ugliest way. Was this a new form of her oddity? Instead of feeling someone's feelings, they just felt compelled to tell them to her? To pour out their secrets to her?

Pulling away from him, she went to the rattan couch and dropped into it and hugged her knees to her chest. He came to her and squatted down in front of her, brows drawn together. He was wearing those calf-length pocketed pants again. She'd never seen any other man wear anything like that. Even though her exposure to men was restricted to her cousins and their significant others, something made her certain it was not a thing many men wore or carried off like this.

"What did I say?" he asked, in that way he had of speaking to her that landed somewhere between feeling like he'd known her forever and feeling like he didn't know a single thing about her but wanted to. As badly as she wanted to know about him.

Her hand went to his face again, stroking the sharp-soft beard. Already, it didn't startle him the way it had the first time she'd done it. He looked almost as though he'd been expecting her to do it. The textures of his face filled her hand again, already familiar. Beard over jawbone, creases in warm skin.

Just that, nothing more. No emotions that didn't belong to her rolled through her like water filling her lungs. No memories she'd never experienced splattered across her senses like acid eating skin.

How was this possible? How was this happening? She glanced up at the sky. No winged presence glided through it.

The dark way in which her heart twisted amid these beautiful feelings made it hard to breathe.

"All those things you just told me. Did you really not want to tell me?" she asked.

"Of course I didn't," he said carefully, aware it wasn't a simple question. "I've never told anyone, because I've never wanted to. This is the second time in my life I'm meeting you. Why would I want to tell you?"

Sick panic, that's what that feeling was. She wrapped her arms tighter around herself. She wanted to fold over. "I . . . I didn't mean to . . ."

His face changed. How had she thought his face blank? It moved constantly, picking up every nuance of feeling that went through her. Reaching out, he wiped her cheeks, and she realized that she was crying. "I don't know why you're crying. Please, tell me what's wrong. I didn't mean to hurt you with that story. It was a long time ago. Those memories don't hurt anymore."

The ball of discomfort wobbled inside her. "I'm sorry I made you say something you didn't want to. I'm sorry I made you dig that up."

"You didn't make me say it. I mean you did, but not because . . ."

The tears were streaming now. She'd been so relieved, so sure that her condition didn't happen around him. But it only manifested differently. Instead of the visions, she just forced him to tell her things. That felt worse, even more intrusive.

"Hey . . . You didn't make me say it. It's just that something about you made me feel safe enough to share it. I hadn't realized how badly I needed to." He looked distraught in a way that she couldn't have imagined him looking five minutes ago. All his weathered and wild strength brought to its knees.

This was what she did to everyone, stripped them bare, all the way to the heart of their feelings, without their wanting it.

"I thought you were different," she said.

He smiled, scar stretching in the most beautiful way. "I'm told I am. Even though I have no idea what you mean. Did you want to know the rest of it? How Mom found me. How we met India and China. How beautiful they were. How wonderful my childhood was. Will that make it better?"

"No." She shook her head violently enough that he stood and took a step back. "Stop telling me things." She swiped a hand across her eyes. "I think you should leave."

"Okay." It was his favorite word. He did things with it that were entire conversations. She knew that now. She just didn't know why she knew. How she knew. "Is that really what you want?"

She was shaking, the trembling coming from deep inside her chest. "Of course that's not what I want. But if you don't leave you'll end up with no secrets from me, and I know you like to have secrets." She knew that too.

Was it the way she usually knew things? Or was it this new needing to guess? God, she was so tired. Other people's feelings always exhausted her. These were her own feelings and she was still exhausted. Even more than she'd been before. "I mean, I think you like keeping things to yourself. I didn't see that . . . I just meant that I get the feeling . . . I swear that's the only reason I know. Or at least that's what I think. You believe me, right?"

"Esha?" He was next to her again, voice gentle. "Are you saying you think you might have influenced me somehow into telling you all that?"

The tears were flowing too hard now. Esha didn't remember the last time she'd cried like this. She cried all the time because of emotions that were not her own. But these were and she couldn't understand them. She felt like she was in a blazing plane. She felt the scratch of branches against her limbs. She was hanging in a tree. It was the last time she had felt her own sadness, and it swept through her in a rush that made everything spin and go dark.

He was leaning over her on her bed when she opened her eyes again. She jumped up and ran to the door that connected her room to Aji's and made sure it was shut. Her grandmother was on her walk, but Esha had to make sure.

He was in her room. "You're in my room!"

"I'm sorry. You fainted, I was about to get someone."

"No! Don't do that. No one can know you're here." He was in her room! Wonder filled her. "You're in my room," she repeated.

He looked around. "It's probably the most beautiful room I've ever been in." It was white. Everything in the room was white. The furniture, the sheets. The walls. The floor. The only color was the floor-to-ceiling painting of her parents. Even that was muted. Painted in sepia tones.

"Everything is white." Did he look alarmed? How did he see her? An oddity. A freak. Which she was. She knew that. "You're wearing white. You were wearing white the last time I met you."

"You think I'm a freak."

"What? You're the least freakish person I've met in my life."

"You can't make me cry again." Because that liquid sensation in her chest was wobbling again. Different this time. Different. Different.

"Why did you faint? Are you . . . is there . . . are you ill, Esha?"

She felt light-headed again and sat down on her bed. "I'm just a little dizzy."

He sat down next to her, reached into one of the many pockets in his pants, pulled out a candy bar, and held it up.

"I can't eat that." She waited for the usual kick of nausea at the sight of something that might have a strong taste.

"Do you have diabetes? I'm sorry." He started to put it back and she snatched it from him.

Before he could ask her anything else, she pointed at his pants. "I've never seen pants like that. Why do you have so many pockets?"

"They're cargo pants." He pointed at the candy bar she was holding up. "They hold a lot of stuff. Mostly food. Band-Aids. Flares. Heat blankets. I tend to go places where I need those things. And now, I guess it's a security blanket to have them."

"A security blanket?"

"Yes. Like something you get used to that makes you feel safe."

Voices came in from outside her door, and she jumped up. "My grandmother's back. You have to leave."

He was up and out the door and on her balcony in a moment. "Will you be all right?" he said, touching her face the way she had touched his so many times. Mirroring. Reflecting everything inside her.

She nodded. "Will you come back?"

"How can I not? You didn't answer your half of the question. You still have to tell me something about yourself no one else knows." He jumped over the railing just as Aji called her name.

"How did you get on the estate today?" she called after him.

"Getting into places I'm not supposed to be in is my special talent. Wait for me."

He hadn't even landed on the ground yet, but she already was. She was already waiting for him to come back.

"I'll wait for you." It was a whisper.

Three floors below, he turned to her one last time before disappearing, and she knew he'd heard her.

Chapter Fourteen

Never in her life had Naina ever had such vivid, full-bodied dreams. She came awake with an ache in her womb and a spasm between her legs and a strange pressure in her chest.

Jerking awake from a drugged-like sleep, she sprang up to sitting. Almost instantly, the heavy pleasure of her memories turned into a pain in her head so intense that death had to be better. Grabbing her head, she fell back into bed.

At least Vansh wasn't here. The throbbing in her head kept her from calling out his name to check if he was still in her apartment. On her nightstand sat a giant cup of Philz darkest roast and two Tylenol. That's how she knew he was gone.

Gone from her home, gone from her bed, gone from between her legs, where she'd mortifyingly dreamed of his being all night. The imprint of thick heavy muscle was still pressed into the soft skin of her thighs. Her sheets still smelled of him, of that heady rich citrus scent mixed with the tang of his body. And sex.

Groan.

Had she actually done that? The memory of it was too strong, too tangible, for it to have been just a dream. Who cared? She was still denying it. After swallowing the Tylenol down with the world's best coffee, she reached for her phone. Shit. It was past noon. No texts from him. No calls. Not even an attempt at a shirtless FaceTime.

As she dug through the guts of her phone—for a sign of what, exactly, she didn't know—something gonged like temple bells. Only the temple was inside her head, and it was on fire.

She squeezed her eyes shut. How could her head hurt like this? Was pain like this even human? The bells gonged again. Was that the doorbell?

God, please, you cannot be cruel enough for Vansh to have come back. She could not face him. Not now when her head was made of pain.

Another gong.

She grabbed a kimono from the hook behind her door. No, she did not thank her stars for having picked up the gorgeous tie-dye garment from the streets of Kathmandu that made her feel like a goddess.

It was going to take more than clothing to do that today. Plus, goddesses did not such agony suffer.

She checked her face in the hallway mirror. No! Ugh. Her eyes were slits, with raccoonlike markings around them, a post-coital raccoon whose horniness had destroyed her. Plucking wet wipes from the bathroom, she wiped and wiped as she went to the door and pressed the buzzer.

"Mar te nai gai si kudi!"

Mummy?

She buzzed her mother in with a "No, Mummy, the *kudi* is not dead." Although, the girl did wish she was. Unless she was and this was hell.

At least it wasn't Vansh. That was a relief. Even if it came with another brutal frying-pan-and-fire situation.

"So he was right then." Her mother walked into the apartment the way she always did, one part discomfort, the other part disbelief that Naina lived here now. The hodgepodge of all the feelings between her mother and her, every one of them unspoken, unexamined, unresolved, walked in with her.

"Who was right about what?" Although with Chandni Kohli, Naina didn't need to ask the question. Only one *he* was right. Always. "Actually, forget I asked that."

Naina walked into her tiny kitchen, which was open to her tiny living room, and grabbed her biggest glass and filled it with water. If Mummy was here and she was invoking the most venerable *he* of all time, Naina couldn't afford to wallow in a hangover. Even though her head was feeling like a band of monkeys was scraping at her brain with overgrown claws.

How had she lost control of herself like that? She never lost control of herself. There simply was no one in the world she could trust enough to lose control around.

Gulping down the water, she forced her brain to focus.

"What are you doing here?" Even the sound of her own voice was too loud inside her head.

Her mother walked to the blinds. No! She was going to open them. That side of Naina's kitchen got blindingly bright at this time of day. "Mummy, please—" Nope, she was going to do it no matter Naina's protests.

All Naina could do was squeeze the counter behind her to keep the bright jabs of light from making her throw up. Despite the fact that she was almost breaking her fingers with the force of her grip, her belly churned. But she didn't throw up. Thanks to the extra-strength Tylenol Vansh had left on her nightstand with that giant cup of lifesaving nectar.

Who did that? Who left your home after you had embarrassed yourself in the worst possible way and then remembered your key code that you probably gave them under the influence of too much champagne and came back and left you things? Things essential to your survival?

Fuck you, Vansh Raje.

This was all his fault. If he thought a giant tumbler of Philz fixed anything, then he was as arrogantly delusional as he appeared. Also, she needed to change her code.

The man had stolen her work from under her nose. Was it a requirement for anyone she let into her life to stab her in the back? Was that a damned qualification they put on the form they used to apply for her trust?

Wow. Too much wallowing, Naina. Get over yourself.

She gulped down more water while Mummy struggled with the half-stuck blinds. Naturally Naina's having a hangover meant her mother really badly needed sunshine.

No more throwing up for you, missy. Your life's quota is done. Over.

Succeeding in her mission to let in every last bit of the sun god's bounty, her mother turned to the couch and commenced glaring at Naina's pillows as though they made her as nauseated as Naina felt. Her mother's hands fluttered at her silk-kurti-covered heart, then reached for the pillows, which had obviously done something to offend her, and came back to her heart to flutter some more.

Naina's parents' house could have been a model home on a tour of a pricey subdivision from a builder selling the American Dream to newcomers. An expensive premolded version of Americana for those who didn't carry the privilege of it in their blood but carried the means to purchase it with some fresh green.

Every single thing in their house had to meet one basic criterion: it had to appear expensive. *Polished.* A word her mother had chased with the fervor of someone who knew exactly what it was like to be on the other side of the class glass.

Unlike her mother, Naina had always been looked at as the It Girl, labels and perceived elegance obfuscating the person she was to the point where not even she knew what separated the two.

It had been a powerful shield, and then it had just become

second nature, a substitute for something else that she was too much of a coward to define. Self-worth?

"Why so much color?" her mother said, as she had done before, when she'd first seen the bright green and magenta embroidered, batiked, and tie-dyed cushions on Naina's yellow linen couch.

The couch was the first thing Naina had bought when she found this apartment. A space that was hers and only hers. She'd seen the sunflower-yellow sectional in a shop window in the Scandinavian furniture place on the first floor of her building, and she'd had to have it, because of how it made her *feel* and because she could imagine how the pillow covers she'd bought years ago in Kathmandu would look on it.

Mummy had winced when she'd seen the explosion of colors and textures and delightfully tacky embroidery and mirror work. Then, of course, she'd fluttered and asked if the couch could still be returned. Something about the fact that she thought returning the couch was a solution to the pillow problem struck Naina as too damn ironic.

Her mother had visited only once before today, to see if Naina needed any help "setting up"—which translated (even when it was not spoken in Punjabi) to making sure everything looked *polished*.

The day after her visit, Mummy had gray-gray, gray-blue, and gray-black silk cushion covers delivered to Naina's apartment to better match *that* couch.

"You didn't get chance to change cushion covers yet?" her mother said, oblivious to the possibility that Naina might not have wanted to. "Where did you put them? I can help you. So busy you keep yourself. How will house things ever get done if you're working-working always?"

Today? Really? Do I deserve this visit today? Granted, she shouldn't have guzzled every glass of champagne that crossed her line of sight. She should not have done that. She admitted it. She was sorry. But please, please, must she be punished for every bad decision?

"I can do it later, Mummy. Would you like some chai?" She put a pot of water on to boil, grated some ginger into it the way her mother liked, and added sugar, lots of it.

"I'm good at all these sorts of things. Quickly quickly I will get done." Mummy snapped her fingers to prove her own efficiency at these sorts of things. "Are they in bedroom?" She headed off to the bedroom.

Was she checking for something?

"Mummy," Naina called after her, her own voice still too loud in her ears. "Don't worry about it. Please." She followed her, praying that Vansh had not left any signs of his presence behind.

"It's matchbox size, no, this place?"

"There's only me, so it doesn't need to be any bigger. Plus it's easy to clean."

"So much money that man has given you. One cleaning lady would be okay, no?"

Naina loved cleaning her own home. Tidying up was relaxing for her. Everything in its place.

Her mother searched her room.

"What are you looking for?" Naina didn't remember putting her clothes away last night. She had to have left them on the bathroom floor. They were no longer there.

Bonus points to the Dimpled Boy for putting them away, because if Mummy had found those clothes on the bathroom floor she would have taken it as a personal insult. Her beloved clothes disrespected thusly would have been an affront inflicting immeasurable wounds. Naturally, she would have said nothing, just looked wrecked. Which was far better than a mother who yelled and pushed outright, right?

"I'm looking for the cushion covers I bought for you, of course."

That wounded look flooded her eyes as her gaze fell on the covers, still in their plastic packaging, on the floor of the closet.

Naina touched her shoulder. "Don't feel bad. They're beautiful—just too fancy for my apartment. I was going to take them into my office and use them there. The decor in my office is much nicer than my apartment. Very polished."

Mummy's eyes lit up. "Really? Silly girl. I will send another set for office. Let's get these ones on here. Everything will look tip-top and polished here also." She started to take the covers out of the packaging.

For a second Naina thought about stopping her, but the sheer volume of excitement on Mummy's face was too much to dash, so she helped. Yup, that was just the kind of invertebrate creature she was. There was so little pleasure she gave her mother that she had to indulge her where it was possible.

She could only manage one cushion before impotent rage took over and she left the rest to her mother. As Mummy pulled Naina's beloved covers off and replaced them with the soulless gray ones, Naina poured tea through the strainer into two cups.

"Last night you danced. Have you started enjoying all that dancing-shancing now?"

Handing her mother a cup and taking a giant gulp from her own to burn down the groan that rose up her throat, Naina smiled and nodded and was happy to have her urge to throttle Vansh restored. She'd known that dancing when her mother was present was not a good idea. Why had she allowed him to drag her onto the dance floor? The number of parties that involved some form of dancing that her mother could have her invited to was boggling. Naina would poke her eyes out if she had to go to even one.

She was going to kill Vansh.

"So much you used to dislike, no?" Mummy made a satisfied face at the tea, which would usually have made Naina irrationally pleased with herself, but not when her heart was thudding with the possibility of what this visit might actually be about. "That Vansh, he's very good on dance floors."

The thudding in Naina's heart sped up. Her mother's bottle-brown eyes studied her with all their usual transparency.

Naina didn't respond. She picked up a cushion her mother had left naked and shoved it inside a stiff gray cover.

"You never did dancing and all that with Yash." A disappointed brow was raised. "So much more serious person, no? So much different those two brothers are."

No kidding.

This was not the time to feel his muscled thigh between her legs. *Stop it.*

"Isn't that normal though, for all siblings to be different?" Sometimes Naina amazed herself with her ability to keep her voice from showing the things she was feeling. They should give Oscars out for real-life performances. She'd have more than Meryl Streep.

"But usually only little bit different." Her mother made a pinching gesture, then flew her arms apart. "These two brothers? Lots and lots different."

Dear God, her mother wanted to say something uncomfortable. Which meant she was going to go round and round in circles until she found a way to say it without saying it. "Oh, you know what? I forgot, your Navdeep Mamu sent another picture of the doctor. Oh ho, he's not doctor. Even better. He's surgeon. Like Shree. He's general."

"Is he a military doctor then? A general and a doctor. And with no kids?"

"Don't make fun of Mummy, Naina. That's not nice."

"Sorry. I told you, I'm not interested. Can we please stop this rishtas thing now?"

"What stop this? How stop this?" She looked around the

apartment. "This is all not joke, beta. If in natural time you don't marry, then all sorts of unnatural things are starting to happen. The body is human, no? And humans are animals, no?"

Naina could ask her mother what she was trying to say, but it was becoming increasingly clear.

"Your father is twelve years older than me." And the circling continued.

"I know that."

"Challenges are there. I never say out loud, but you know challenges are there."

If sadness hadn't gripped Naina's heart quite so tightly, she might have laughed out loud. *Challenges are there.* That could go on their family's crest.

Nonetheless what her mother was suggesting, what she was so terrified of verbalizing, was utterly absurd. Vansh and her together was a ridiculous idea.

Don't think it.

Do. Not. Think. It.

The thigh.

God, could you please not?

"There is nothing between me and anyone, Mummy. I promise. No one. I never want to be with anyone. You know my work is the love of my life."

Something between dejection and relief flashed in her mother's eyes. Even when she felt relief, something tainted it. "My poor girl. Everything will be good. Better man will come. Better for you. But you have to forget also. Move on. Don't circle back to same place for new thing. You know?"

Naina shoved the gray cushions into her couch, smashing them into the yellow linen. Then she started to fold the discarded covers, which were going right back on as soon as Mummy left.

Her mother eyed the care with which Naina was folding. "Don't waste time. I'll take to Salvation Army drop-off on my way."

Naina had to have glared at her, because she flinched. Naina hated to see her mother flinch.

She could navigate this without hurting her mother. She could. "Thing is, I want to keep them. I mean I don't want to donate them. One of the women I work with loves them. She wants them, so I'll just give them to her."

"Good good. Some people like all these types of things. Such a generous heart you have. Oh! You never asked: why Mummy is here?"

Actually, she had asked. But that mattered not the least bit, so she picked up the cups. "Why are you here, Mummy?"

"I'm taking you for lunch. To Dosa. Your favorite."

That sounded really good. A mango habanero masala dosa was something she might be tempted to kill for right about now. Maybe her mother and she could do this. Mother-daughter things. They had gone out for meals when Naina had visited. Everything had been easier because she had just been visiting.

Since Naina had moved back, they'd never done this. Probably because the breakup happened and Naina stopped talking to her father. Her mother had found that impossible to navigate and mostly ignored Naina.

In the time that it took Naina to shower and pull on a sweater over jeans, her mother had poured the gallon of milk she had in the fridge into a saucepan and turned it into paneer.

As Naina emerged, trying to twist her still-too-short hair into a crab clip, Mummy was straining the paneer into a sieve and putting a weight on it to drain the water. Her mother made the best paneer in the world. It was legendary. So loved was it that she made enough for all her friends, even though paneer could now be purchased in the cheese section of every grocery store across the Bay.

Nobody else loved it quite as much as Naina did. Yes, she was a Punjabi stereotype. She loved her paneer. Being her mother's daughter, she only ever wanted to eat her mother's.

How can you be Punjabi and not like to dance?

"Thank you. That was very kind of you." She broke off a chunk of fresh paneer from the edge of the sieve and put it in her mouth. "How do you make it taste like this?"

Her mother dusted off her hands as though it were the simplest of things, but her eyes twinkled. "What's the big thing in making paneer?"

"For you there's no big deal, but for those of us who get to taste yours, only yours will do. You ruin us for lesser paneer."

When they left the apartment and headed to Dosa, her mother was grinning from ear to ear. Thanks to that stupid Tylenol, Naina's headache had receded enough that it didn't make her want to fold in half. Mummy's conversation turned to her beloved fabrics and fashion. Naina's mind tuned out and floated along, forgetting to push away the hope that wrapped around them.

As always, the dosas were perfect, crisp and lacy, and the unusual chef's addition of the habanero chutney made Naina's mouth burn in the best way. She'd inherited her ability to tolerate spice from her mother. Dr. Kohli was something of a wimp in this department, and so, naturally Naina and her mother only ever ate the truly hot stuff when he wasn't around.

"Never make people feel bad when you're better at something than they are," her mother had said with an unfamiliar amount of glee one night at dinner when her husband had been on call and she'd made the potato bhujia with enough red chili powder to make even Naina and her break into a sweat.

Just as their dessert arrived—hot gajjar halwa with vanilla ice cream—a murmur rose across the restaurant. Before Naina could turn around and check what the buzz was about, her mother's eyes went wide enough that Naina knew it wasn't good.

She also knew that it had to have something to do with the Rajes.

Turns out, it had to do with the Raje most directly to blame for her daughter's downfall. Yash Raje and his lovely new girlfriend, everyone's darling, India Dashwood, had decided to walk into the restaurant. It really was Naina's lucky day.

Chandni Kohli's mood did a nosedive as she stared at Yash shaking hands and taking selfies with people who stopped him as he followed the host. Asking her mother not to stare would only make her feel worse, so Naina tried to drown her objections in the rather spectacular halwa. The carrots had been cooked to buttery perfection in enough cream and sugar to obliterate pain as pedestrian as this.

India was the one who noticed Naina first. The smile she gave Naina was open and warm, and happy as ever with the world around her.

Naina had behaved terribly toward India. When Yash had met India last year and fallen for her as though the rug had been yanked out from under him, Naina had believed that he'd lost his senses and tried to "save" him. Which meant Naina had tried to convince him of how stupid it would be to risk everything on what she believed to be an infatuation.

Turned out it hadn't been one. Turned out Naina's machinations hadn't been as selfless as she'd believed them to be. Turned out India was the kind of person who held no grudges. After putting Naina in her place, deservedly, she'd been unerringly kind to her once she and Yash had gone public with their relationship. To give Yash his fair share of credit in the entire business, he was so smitten by India that she'd have to be blind to feel even a little threatened by Naina.

The happiest couple in all of San Francisco made their gracious way to Naina and her mother, who was having a hard time with the flutters again.

Yash leaned over and hugged her mother. "Namaste, Chandni Auntie."

India did the same. Then Yash, who'd suddenly transformed

into this warm and fuzzy person, gave Naina a big bear hug, and she realized how very much she had missed her best friend. Even this strangely expressive new avatar of him.

"You look exhausted. Are you working yourself to death again, Naina Kohli?" Yash said, taking in her no doubt red and swollen eyes.

"I think she looks beautiful." This completely dishonest and mistimed vote of confidence came from Mummy, of course. Even better, she said it with enough defensiveness that Naina wanted to slide under the table.

Yash smiled. He was always wonderfully kind to Mummy. Even though she could exhaust the patience of anyone who hadn't seen close up what she lived with every day. "Of course, Auntie. Naina always looks lovely. I just meant she looks a little tired and wanted to make sure she isn't overworking. I should have phrased that better." He turned to Naina again. "You look tired, Nai, but as beautiful as ever."

"How you can say that?" Mummy slid an accusatory glance at India, who was even more self-possessed than Yash (how was that even possible?) and met Mummy's substantially angry eyes with the kind of gentleness worthy of the yoga guru she was. "If you think my Naina is beautiful then why . . . why . . ." A sob broke her voice.

Naina wanted to throw up in the gajjar halwa. The sweetness of the candied carrots turned sharp in her mouth.

"Mummy, please," she whispered, fighting to keep the embarrassment from coloring her face.

Her mother turned accusatory eyes on her. "I knew your work-work-work mentality would make you lose-lose-lose. Your father was right. Even he doesn't like your workaholic business." She pointed at Yash with the spoon.

India and Yash exchanged the most cautious of glances, but the look that passed between them screamed in Naina's head.

Who would've thought her mortification had space left to grow? Nonetheless it multiplied manifold.

"I have to make a stop in the restroom. I hope you don't mind. Lovely seeing you both," India said gently before she walked away as discreetly as it was possible for a human to.

"Do you mind if I join you for a second?" Yash eased himself into the empty chair at their table and put a hand on Mummy's.

Mummy's face lit up. *This is not him changing his mind, Mummy.* How was it that those words even needed to be said?

"Her father is so much upset. I did not raise her to be like this way, I swear. I'm sorry." Two fat tears spilled down her rouged cheeks.

"Auntie, please. I'm very proud of Naina's work. You raised her to be perfect."

"See you're feeling regret? You know, I learn in life that it's never too much late to make change when mistake. Once you marry, then it will be too much late. Then you can't make mistake correct."

"Mummy, please. He's not regretting anything. We were dishonest with you. We were never together. It was my fault." Naina had made him do it. Lie to everyone. Although he'd gone along quite happily. Or unhappily. It didn't matter anymore.

"Of course it was your fault," her mother said, determined hope taking root in her eyes. "So correct your mistake." She turned to Yash. "Please, beta. At least say you think about it."

Shame should have choked Naina. Pride should have made her get up and leave. Fortunately for all present, she'd had too much experience squashing both shame and pride when it came to her mother.

"He will not say that. I don't want him to think about it. I don't want him to." She couldn't look at Yash. Couldn't bear the unshakable understanding in his studiedly neutral face. The face that had always been there for her when she'd needed someone.

His mask of non-judgment had been the support she'd needed. It had made her lean on him, push him into doing terrible dishonest things.

"Go, Yash," she said. "Please. You cannot make this situation better." But he had tried to, and she didn't want to be grateful for that but she was.

He squeezed Naina's hand across the table and threw another gentle look at her mother. "See you soon, Auntie. Everything will be all right." Then he listened to Naina and left.

Naina waved at the waiter for the check. Maybe doing mother-daughter things wasn't for them after all.

"Why you keep sending him away?" her mother said, voice trembling as she took an angry bite of the halwa.

Because I have to keep doing what you didn't do for yourself. What you didn't do for me. "I'm not sending him away, Mummy. He was never with me." Then, no matter how hard she tried to stop herself, she met her mother's disappointed gaze, tried not to reflect it. "You cannot leave someone you were never with. But leaving someone you are with and you don't want to be with, that is not impossible."

Chandni Kohli was a master at only acknowledging conversations she could process. It wasn't in the least bit surprising that she looked away from her daughter as though she had no idea what she was saying.

"If you got him back, then your daddy would agree to talk to you again. I would convince him."

"You would convince him?" Naina probably should not have said that with such anger, because her mother put her spoon down when there was still some gajjar halwa left in the bowl and Naina felt like a piece of shit that someone had stepped in. "I'm sorry," she added. "It's best for everyone if Dr. Kohli and I don't talk." She attempted a smile. "His blood pressure is much better, I'm sure."

"Don't try to make jokes and make side distraction. What is this, Naina? A father and daughter not talking. It breaks my heart. I know you think I did all things wrong way. But all things I did I wanted only one thing. For you to have father. A girl has to have father. You don't know what it is for a girl to not have father."

More than anything, Naina wished she didn't know what it was like for a girl to not have a father.

"And, a woman has to have husband."

"No, Mummy, she doesn't. At least not this woman. This woman doesn't want a husband."

Her mother slammed a fist on the table, her anger getting the better of her. "Why? Because you want to do all immoral things with little boys?"

"Excuse me?"

"No, *you* excuse *me*! I'm looking other way for many many things. I'm making your father very angry with how I raise you. I don't know all things. But I know, I *know* that this is wrong way. Your father will not be okay with this. We will not." Anger, the kind of determined anger Naina had never seen there before, sparkled in her eyes.

She couldn't possibly mean what Naina was pretty certain she meant. "I have no idea what you're talking about."

Was her father spying on her? Was this about Vansh's being in her apartment last night? Asking was opening up a can of worms and Naina wasn't about to do that. In the Kohli family you kept all worms firmly in their cans.

"Dr. Kohli has nothing to worry about. You have nothing to worry about. Whatever information he thinks he has, he's mistaken. You're safe, Mummy."

He will not be throwing you out.

Her mother studied her, too afraid of the horror and public humiliation that would domino from the scandal if Naina was seen anywhere in the vicinity of Yash's younger brother. Thanks to Naina's public dumping, the Kohlis were already maxed out on shame in the social circle her parents valued so single-mindedly.

"I promise. It's a simple misunderstanding." Naina picked up the spoon and offered it to her mother. A Chandni Kohli who did not finish her dessert was a Chandni Kohli whose sadness had gone past the point where her daughter could bear it.

For a long time her mother searched Naina's face for signs of a lie. When she found none, she took the spoon and finished her favorite dessert.

Chapter Fifteen

After spending half of yesterday forcing Hari into stores to buy clothes and shoes and then getting him a haircut, Vansh was back at the Embassy Suites bright and early and ready to face the day. Well, and also to face the one person who could slay him with a single cutting look. If she even acknowledged him.

No, he still hadn't texted her.

Yeah, she hadn't texted him either.

An entire day had passed since a possibly accidental, definitely mind-melting orgasm without a single word being exchanged. Probably a very bad sign. What was the protocol on unplanned orgasms with a friend?

Hari had been in the shower for the past half hour while Vansh paced his room, which was so pristine it looked like no one had ever lived there, let alone been there for over a week now. Even the bed was untouched. Vansh pulled the plastic off the paper cups and set the coffee to brew.

Then he poured it into the tiny sink in the kitchenette because it tasted like something regurgitated after a digestive episode. Finally, Hari stepped out in his new navy golf shirt and khakis.

"Very spiffy," Vansh said, and a blush spread across Hari's round face, his newly shaved skin going blotchy with self-consciousness.

Hari bounced a hand against his freshly cut, spiked hair. The hairdresser had shown him how to use the gel she'd sold him, and he'd aggressively gone at it this morning with the spikes. Go, Hari!

"Do I look like a porcupine?" he said, studying himself in the mirror.

"It would have to be a very well-groomed porcupine. You look ready to take on the world."

That made panic tug Hari's mouth down in a frown, and Vansh knew he had said something triggering.

"I don't want to take on the world. My partner kept saying things like that." He patted down his hair with shaking hands, flattening the porcupine into a hedgehog.

"Don't do that. It looked good. No one is going to make you do something you don't want to. I promise. You're not signing anything over. We can do some real good here. Let's spike that up again." Vansh plucked at his hair. "Can you try to trust me, please?"

Hari took a breath, nodded, and went to the mirror and spiked his hair back up. Then, turning his nervous eyes on Vansh, he gave him what could only be called a worshipful look. "Of course I trust you. It's eight A.M. on a Monday. You drove all the way from Woodside to San Francisco. You could be sleeping in a mansion right now. Yesterday, you spent all day shopping with me and working on the project. You get nothing from this. You're selfless."

Vansh peeked in the open bathroom door. It looked like nothing had been used and everything was exactly in its place. "It's eight A.M.," he said a bit impatiently. "And you're up and ready to go to work and start something new too. Even when you're scared. You're being very brave."

"But I need to. You, on the other hand . . ."

"My entire family works," Vansh tried not to snap. "More hours than is probably healthy. What I'm doing, some people might call it the opposite of selfless. Some people believe that the need to feel better about myself is what drives me."

Hari looked horrified at the prospect of such an accusation ever being hurled at Vansh. "Who would say such a terrible thing about you?" He pulled the bathroom door shut when he noticed Vansh looking inside.

Well, you're going to meet her today. "Many people feel that way, and they're not entirely wrong. But hey, if it changes something even for one person, it's worth it, right?"

That made Hari sniffle. "I will never believe that you are anything but selfless. You're a true hero, Vansh sir, and I hope you know that."

Vansh tried to smile. "First, I've told you, please call me Vansh. I'm not knighted. And I loathe colonial monarchies, so even if someone tried to knight me, it would not work out. I'm not your teacher either. I was in fact every teacher's nightmare." He slid open the closet. It was empty. "Where's all your stuff, Hari? How did you even get the bathroom cleaned up this much? You don't have to clean the hotel room. They have housekeeping for that. What did you do with all your stuff?"

Hari threw a quick look at the bed with its generic floral comforter pulled tightly into corners sharp enough to put a professionally gift-wrapped box to shame. Vansh went to the dresser and opened a drawer. Nothing in there. "This is your hotel room. You can use the closet and the drawers for your stuff until we find you a more permanent place."

"I can't afford this. I can't afford a permanent place."

"You can't afford it now, but we're working on you being able to afford it. Not just you, but others like you will have access to places to live."

"You really think I can help make that happen?"

"You're a genius, Hari. If anyone can pull this off, you can. The plan for the app we started working on yesterday is brilliant. I have full faith in it."

The realization had been coming on slowly, but of course technology was the answer. They lived in the technological center of the universe. In today's world an app was always the answer. It also meant Vansh could go to Naina today with a solution and not just an apology for the betrayal Mehta had trapped him in.

Hari smiled. His eyes were still fearful, but it was an honest-to-goodness smile.

"Did you not sleep in the bed last night?" Vansh felt terrible pushing Hari about this, but it also felt unfair to let him keep believing whatever was going on inside his head.

Tears started streaming down Hari's face, making him look suddenly even younger. "I'm sorry."

"Why are you sorry? Don't cry. Do you not like this room? I'm sorry, maybe we should have looked at a few hotels before we settled on this one."

"No, no! It's a very good room. But, but.... I slept on the carpet. Are you angry with me? I don't want you to be angry with me."

"I'm not angry with you," Vansh said, maybe a little more angrily than he'd intended. Then much more calmly, he added, "Why would I be angry? And even if I were angry, you can tell me not to be. Are you uncomfortable on beds?"

Hari nodded, and even with a lifetime of exposure to the head nod of his people, Vansh could just never decipher what Hari's head nods meant.

"I'm not sure what that means." He pointed at Hari's head and shook his own.

"What if the bed gets spoiled?"

"Spoiled? Do you, are you . . ." Was he incontinent? That was not a question he was asking a grown man. "Do we need to get you something to help you? Medicine. Plastic sheets. Whatever it is, there's a solution. There's nothing to be embarrassed about."

Those words fell on Hari like he had never heard them before, never considered them. He pressed a hand into his forehead, looking completely flummoxed by them.

"I don't mean to suggest that you have a problem. All I'm saying is that if you do—"

"I don't wet the bed."

"Okay."

Hari's fingers squeezed his temples. "If I damage something, they'll make me pay for it."

"How would you damage a bed by sleeping in it?"

Hari's only response was to look ashamed.

Vansh put a hand on his shoulder and met his eyes, a sick feeling rolling inside him. He kept his voice even. "You're not dirty, Hari. You've had a stretch of bad luck. You've been screwed over by someone who claimed to be your friend. You're a survivor. You are educated and smarter than most people. You helped a good man win an election because you can do things other people cannot. You built a company. Even without any of those things, you are as worthy of respect and comfort as anyone else. Even without any of those things, you are not going to dirty a bed by sleeping on it."

Hari didn't respond. He was staring over Vansh's right ear. He tended to retreat behind a wall when Vansh tried to give him any sort of pep talk or vote of confidence. The only way to deal with Hari when he was in this sort of mood was with action, moving along and doing things.

"Listen. Let's get this project started and you'll get your confidence back. I promise. Maybe we'll see someone. Someone who can help you."

"I'm not crazy. You think I'm crazy."

"Let's not use that word. You've just had a rough time recently and there is help to be had. If you need it. Never mind. One step at a time. Let's focus on this. You remember what I told you, we're going to see my friend Naina. You're still okay with telling her your situation?"

Hari nodded, a clear "yes" nod. "She won't tell Yash?"

"She won't. But she needs to know because we need her for the project."

"You think she'll help us?"

Vansh channeled Hari's noncommittal nod. "Not a clue, my friend. But we're going to find out. You ready for this? Don't answer that. I'm ready. Let's go!"

The smile Hari gave him was still a little too lost, but at least he didn't look despondent, and that was a start.

As VANSH AND Hari made their way to the Omnivore building, the absurd mix of terror and excitement Vansh had been pushing away since he'd left Naina's apartment intensified. Maybe showing up in her office unannounced right now wasn't the best idea.

He could text her. But what would he say?

How are you?

She'd had an orgasm, not a concussion. Although it might be argued that the strength of the orgasm was pretty darned concussion worthy.

I'm coming over.

She would simply tell him not to. Also, he wasn't about to use the word *coming* with her right now.

Leaving her alone was not an option. He had no choice because Jiggy had texted him again telling him to hurry and "iron things out" with Naina. If by ironing things out the man meant getting into her creases . . . Okay. Stop it. She was going to be mortified enough to kill him, and he was in too much trouble to be making dirty jokes.

In his last burst of texts, Jiggy had also given Vansh a week to present the project in his office with all the *i*'s dotted and all the *t*'s crossed. Because he wanted to make a splashy announcement at the company's annual kickoff meeting.

So, yeah, staying out of Naina's way the way she'd obviously want him to was not an option.

Whoever said the first step was the hardest had never met Naina Kohli. The first step into her office brought him face-to-face with her receptionist, who shot Vansh a long-suffering glare worthy of someone trapped in the middle of a mortal war.

"She's asked me to tell you that she's too busy for casual visits," Mariel whispered, then cleared her throat. "I mean she's . . . um . . . she's . . . what did you do?"

Wow. After his last visit here, Vansh knew Naina didn't run the tightest ship. Which had both surprised him and not surprised him at all. This, however, was next-level boundary leaping. Under other circumstances, Vansh would have loved it. He might even have laughed.

Fine, it was hilarious and he did laugh. The older woman with lots of bright blue eye shadow watched him as though she could keep watching him for the rest of her life. Good, because she forgot about the intrusive question, and *I offered the use of my well-built thigh* was not an acceptable answer.

"That's good, because this isn't a casual visit," he said instead. "Could you tell her that Hari Samarth is here with me?"

Hari stared at his toes, twisted his trembling hands together, and refused to meet Mariel's eyes even when she said hello to him. This made her throw an accusatory look at Vansh. As though Vansh had dragged an innocent to the gallows that were Naina Kohli's office for his own benefit in whatever game Naina and he were playing.

She was a smart woman.

"Oh, and could you also tell Ms. Kohli that we need to speak with her before we head up to our meeting with Mr. Mehta?"

Naina stormed out of her office much like a nor'easter. So icy was her demeanor that she might have frozen off Vansh's extremities. He checked his fingers to make sure they hadn't fallen off.

"Mariel, can you inform Mr. Raje that we are aware that he is aware that Mr. Mehta is currently in New York. Also, please tell him that lying to get his way isn't going to work." Then her eyes met his and her cheeks went flaming red in the most un–Ms. Kohli way.

"It got you out here," Vansh said directly to her, even though he was tempted to keep playing the "Mariel, please tell Ms. Kohli . . ." game. It just felt a little too TV Land classics to stretch it further.

Naina gave him her *We are not amused* brow raise and looked away, cheeks still flaming. Then her eyes fell on Hari. One look at his lost and tortured face and she melted like a nor'easter hitting volcanic lava.

She went to Hari.

Hiding behind Hari had been a good call after all.

Hari's hands trembled as he patted his spiked hair.

"It's lovely to see you again, Hari. I'm Naina. You probably don't remember but we met during the campaign. I'm so sorry, I didn't mean to be rude to you." A quick sideways look proved exactly who she'd meant to be rude to.

Hari turned the color of steamed beetroot. "Everyone knows who you are, Ms. Kohli." Then he looked mortified because that could have meant any number of things, and honestly Vansh was surprised that Hari, who tended to be unaware of nuance, noticed that he might have said something wrong. "I'm so sorry." His chin trembled. "I meant . . . I meant that everyone who worked for Yash Raje knew who you were." That just made it worse, and he pressed a horrified hand to his mouth.

The smile she gave him was the kindest, gentlest thing Vansh had ever seen. The vibe she sent Vansh's way without even looking at him, on the other hand, was 100 percent *I'm going to chop you into little pieces and feed you to vultures.*

"Hari, listen." Naina plucked a tissue from a box on the coffee table. "It's fine. I know what you meant. You didn't say anything wrong. Mariel can get you a drink. Chai? Coffee? Soda? Why don't you step into my office."

Hari looked at Vansh. "Can Vansh come too?" He looked beseechingly at Vansh.

"Of course," Vansh said. "Actually, can you give me a minute with her first? Why don't you wait here with Mariel and catch your breath while I talk to Naina."

Hari looked relieved enough that even Naina couldn't argue with that. Without waiting for her reaction, he walked into her office, head held high. Channeling Naina seemed to be the best way to deal with Naina.

Enough was enough. They were grown-ass adults and what had happened between them was not a crime. Yup, it was time to pull this Band-Aid off.

She didn't follow him. Instead, very gently, she took Hari's hand and tugged him toward her office. "I believe the only person I want to have a conversation with right now is Hari."

Hari looked quite ready to go to the ends of the earth with her. In all fairness, what human wouldn't?

Naina's eyes flashed like lightning bolts across a dark sky, going from kind warmth to cold hellfire as she looked from Hari to Vansh.

The woman was a force of nature.

Her impossibly high cheekbones were bright with color. Her hair was mussed into one of those crab clips that made it stick out in every direction and exposed her endless neck in a perfectly cut beige dress, which also ruthlessly exposed the most perfect shoulders and arms in existence.

How had he never noticed her body before? *Had* he never noticed it? Why did he suddenly not remember anything from before?

"We really need to talk, Naina."

Something about his tone made her let go of Hari's hand and turn to Vansh.

"Fine. Talk." Without joining him in her office, she snapped her fingers at him across the doorway. "I don't have all day."

Vansh threw a look at Hari and Mariel, who were watching with rapt interest. The doors to the other two offices were closed, so either Sadiya and Makayla were listening at the doors or they were out today.

Vansh threw a glance at the open door between them. *Just come in and shut the door, you'll thank me later.*

Her eyes narrowed. *Fat chance I'll be thanking you for anything, and the door stays open.*

Fine, if Naina wanted to do this with an audience, he had no choice. "If we don't come up with a way to work together, you're going to lose your funding."

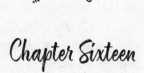

Chapter Sixteen

Naina had taken hits in her life. Really, she had. Waking up in her home every day had been like popping up in a game of whack-a-mole. Her father had never hit her. At least not that she remembered. Given how healthy her physical fear of him had been, it was possible that he'd hurt her when she was very young but she'd repressed the memory.

All her life she'd had dreams where she felt physical pain associated with him. Like her bones being crushed in a vise grip. The memories had never been clearer than that. So it might've been her physically taking on her mother's pain. She rarely had the dreams anymore.

In college she'd seen a therapist for a while, and she'd suggested hypnotherapy to dig into the memories. Naina had seen no value in knowing. She already knew all she needed to know: she hated her father, and that meant hating a small part of herself. Therapy had helped her be aware of this, and she worked every day to not let that part get big enough to consume her ability to live with herself.

It also meant never expecting anyone to take care of her and always expecting to be betrayed. Still, hearing those words coming from Vansh *hurt*. They hurt enough that she had to keep from wrapping her arms around herself.

He'd promised he wouldn't let harm come to her work. How had she been stupid enough to trust him?

Before she could react, Sadiya and Makayla rushed out of their offices. "We're losing our funding?" all three of her employees said together.

Naina turned back to the reception area and faced her team, their accusatory scowls falling on her as though she were the one who'd betrayed them. She couldn't bear to look at Vansh right now.

It wasn't easy to keep her tone confident. "We are not losing our funding." But she understood philanthropy and philanthropists enough to know that anything was possible based on the whims of those who bankrolled their work.

They did not look in the least bit placated.

"I'm going to figure this out. I don't want you to worry. I will not let it happen. You have to trust me." Finally she looked at Vansh, and he had the gall to look concerned. She held up a finger at him. "Get inside my office right now."

"I'm already in your—"

"Shut up." She stormed through the door, forcing him to back up, and turned to her gaping colleagues. "Can you give Hari the tour while I take care of this?"

Mariel nodded, and for once did not offer a conflicting opinion on the matter.

Naina shut the door with deliberate gentleness, because shattering doors by slamming them seemed far too tempting right now.

How could you stab me in the back? she wanted to scream. Instead she kept her voice steady. "I cannot believe you just did that in front of my team. This project is their life. My life!"

"I tried to tell you in private," he said too gently. "You're the one who insisted on having the conversation with everyone present."

She took a breath. She had to calm down. Why was her office so pink? Why was that fact irritating the shit out of her right now?

"Don't try this with me, Vansh. Don't think you can manipulate me just because . . . because . . ." She wanted to say *because we're friends.* But she had no idea what they were. It wasn't something she'd ever given a thought to.

Every single moment of their last encounter flashed in his eyes. Dear God, why had she done that? She was never drinking again. Not ever.

"I'm not manipulating you," he said as though she were a wild horse and he were some sort of animal whisperer.

He tried to take a step toward her, and she spun around, went to her desk, and dropped into the hot-pink chair. The desk was not nearly large enough to put enough distance between them.

"You are. You wanted your way. You wanted to barge in here, and you knew I wouldn't see you, so you dropped that bomb in front of everyone. That qualifies as pretty straightforward, garden-variety manipulation."

He crossed his arms. Even for a meeting like this he'd worn one of his undersized shirts. Solid navy, basic cotton, no logo, not even a pocket, and old-fashioned jeans that draped his hips in an adoring hug. Who dressed this carelessly when so much was at stake?

Someone who knew the power of the biceps that were bulging under the muscle shirt. That's who. Someone who didn't need to dress up to be taken seriously. That's who. Someone who didn't even need to be taken seriously to get what he wanted.

"Oh, and congratulations on being the new face of the Omnivore Foundation. Thanks for giving me a heads-up about Mehta making that announcement."

"You think I knew?" Up until now he'd been doing his usual

insouciant lounging thing and being all amused with the world. The spark of intensity shimmering beneath the surface that most people missed had been nicely tucked away. Now it flared, jumped to the surface in a hot blast. "Are you seriously accusing me of knowing that Jiggy was going to pull that stunt at the party? Is that who you think I am?" His hands shook and he shoved them into his pockets.

The fact that this was the thing that stripped him of his casualness stabbed at something inside her. Regret prickled when it had no business prickling. She couldn't trust him. He was like those large-eyed critters who looked harmless but tore off your flesh if you let them close. Only this was worse. She'd rather have her flesh torn off than lose her funding.

"How could you not have known? How can Jiggy have announced that you're working for his organization if you aren't? He's arrogant but he's not an idiot. And I'm not either. I've worked with the man for months and I've worked with more men like him than you can even begin to imagine." Calling attention to his youth and inexperience was unfair, but it was the crutch Naina needed. Everything felt shaky beneath her feet. Her work felt shaky, and she would never forgive him for that. "What has Mehta offered you?" Time to cut to the chase.

He let out another breath. "Let's calm down."

"Vansh. Stop scaring me."

"You were right. He's only interested in working with me because of my name." His face was unreadable, and she couldn't tell if he hated that or if he thought it was handy. He read the question in her eyes. "It's just what it is, Naina. But we can do something with it."

"I'm already doing what I need to do. What has he offered you?" She had a sick feeling that she already knew the answer, because his face changed. It gentled and got protective, the way it always did before he thought something was going to hurt her.

A look she'd never been able to identify on a single other face in her life.

"We have to work together. We have to make both our projects work with the money he's pledged."

That bastard Mehta. "That's impossible. And you don't even have a project."

"Actually, I have both a project and a plan to make sure you don't have a shortfall." He leaned a hip into her desk, eyes refusing to let her look away. He was done playing. "Listen, I have no intention of taking any money away from your work. At least not in the long run. Your project will take at least a few years, and not all the costs are up front. My project needs seed money. Once we build the app and the database, it should start to earn out and it will fund back into the endowment."

"There's an awful lot of ifs in there."

"Aren't there in everything? If you had let ifs stop you, we wouldn't be here." The glance he threw around her pink office was filled with respect. "We take a small part of the challenge and deal with only that. A large percentage of the homeless population is people who've had a spate of bad luck. What I'm about to tell you is confidential." He waited for her to acknowledge that and she nodded.

"Hari has been living on the street."

Her hand went to her face. "How?"

Vansh explained how Hari's business partner had cheated him and how he'd been homeless the entire time he'd worked on Yash's campaign. "There are a lot of others like him. People who've lost their homes because of not having a safety net. An illness, a lost job, an ill child. They have skills that local companies need. We identify them, identify opportunities, and then train each person based on their individual skills for a particular job. Like a match database. One person at a time."

"I have no doubt there are other agencies that do exactly that. How would this be any different?"

"The key is the software that's able to track and identify the skills of the homeless population in real time and an algorithm that matches that to local opportunities."

"An algorithm." She pushed her hand into her hair. The shorter-than-she-was-used-to strands had slid out of her clip and were falling all over her face. Her shortsightedness, not to mention hubris, in cutting it to save Yash's ass when it didn't need saving was just the reminder of her own stupidity that she needed.

"Yes. One that also tracks short-term and long-term jobs across local companies. It's like Tinder but for job hookups. We'll have to get companies to commit to hiring and training. But with the Omnivore Foundation's name, and the social justice cachet, that's doable. I already talked to the PR departments of a couple of the biggest employers here and they seem excited."

When had he put all this together?

Don't trust him. "And who's going to create this app?"

"It's what Hari does. Mehta's already excited."

"The app isn't what Mehta's excited about!" How could he not see this?

"When did you start seeing me as such a threat, Naina? I thought you were the one person I could trust to see me for who I am."

How could she not laugh at that? "That's precious. Literally everyone in your life sees you exactly as you want to be seen. You don't even have to do a single thing to deserve it."

Every bit of softness left his face. "And yet I do. I do everything I can to make sure I deserve it."

The sudden sharpness in his eyes said he believed that with all his heart. Fine. She wouldn't argue with that. Maybe she *couldn't* argue with that, but she was not feeling nearly generous enough to admit that.

Uncross your damn arms!

He did not pick up on her telepathic message and took a deep breath, which made his big, defined pecs push into his shirt and made the sudden stark press of his hard thigh come alive against her soft one.

She hated muscle memory. It was simply something human beings didn't need. What purpose did it serve? According to the theory of natural selection, the human body should have done away with it by now.

In response to her glare, he gave her his adorable flesh-eating-critter eyes. "Maybe the problem is that you think I don't deserve to be seen the way I want to be seen. You're acting like I don't deserve any of the things I have. You believe I haven't suffered enough for them. Isn't that a little judgmental, even for you?"

Was he seriously trying to turn this around and make it her fault? "I don't want you to suffer. I want you to not take what I've worked so hard for."

At least he uncrossed his arms, but then he threw them up in an incredulous gesture and it was like he was showing off again. "I'm trying to save what is yours."

She laughed. How were men so arrogant? "How did what is mine, what I worked so hard to build, become yours to save in the first place? Do you really not see how wrong this is?"

He stiffened as the truth in her words hit him. "I did not go after Jiggy. I did not go after your funding. You have to know that I would never do that."

"That only makes everything so much worse. It means it literally just fell into your lap without you even making an effort." She wanted to scream. She wanted to shake him.

He opened his mouth and she knew without a doubt that it was to suggest that Jiggy had given her the funding for the same connections that he had gone to Vansh for.

"You are wrong," she said. "I have done nothing but work to

get this endeavor funded for a decade now. I made progress with it penny by penny, dollar by dollar, long before Jiggy. For ten years I've worked with whatever funds I could find within the global philanthropic community."

She'd worked with Vansh's aunt to learn grassroots funding. Shobi Gaikwad Raje, Ashna's mother, ran one of the largest charitable organizations in Asia. She had taught Naina almost everything she knew about fundraising and dissemination. Maybe she should have stuck with that model. Big-ticket philanthropy came with too many caveats. Shobi Auntie had warned her that the bigger the charity dollars, the more pounds of flesh they demanded.

Naina had been naive to think that all Jiggy would want in return for his money was for her to stamp *Certified Philanthropist* across his forehead. Which she had done already. He'd been interviewed by every major media outlet about his giving. Already he was becoming a household name.

Vansh dropped down in the chair across from her. "Come on, Naina, it is not my fault that people as rich as God get to decide how we do the work we want to do."

Instead of tossing the Earth-shaped paperweight at his head like she wanted to, she spun a finger around his face. "Please stop with the 'we' business." She pointed—admittedly a little too dramatically—to her door, beyond which a terrified boy-man waited. "You had to find poor Hari and then create a project."

"Hold on a minute. We're talking about homelessness in San Francisco. Even you can't be angry enough to believe that I caused homelessness in a city with such a high Gini coefficient. Or that I caused Hari to end up in the situation he finds himself in."

"Oh, I'm angry enough for almost anything, but even I don't believe the great Vansh Raje capable of that."

"Thank you. That's a big concession. I feel positively coddled." His eyes were hurt, his dimples out to play, and the combination was deadly.

She had to have looked pathetic in her frustration, because his honey-brown eyes, so very much like his mother's, softened again. "I understand why you're angry. But you know my plan has merit. Let me show you the details. What we take from your funding will be temporary."

A blood vessel almost popped inside her head. "I am not going to let you touch even a penny of my money. It's all earmarked. I've spread it really thin so I could extend the network of clinics wider. We've already bought land and hired construction crews to start building."

"And none of that has to change. Will you stop being angry for one moment and listen to me? I'm trying to help you."

"You can't create a problem and then feel good about helping solve it. I know how your *help* works."

His eyes darkened. She hadn't exactly meant to draw parallels, but this was exactly why she'd ended up with him in her bed. He'd been the one responsible for her trying to wipe out the supply of champagne at Jiggy's party, and she did not need to be reminded of how he had *helped* her with that.

Was that a smile in his eyes? He put his elbows on her desk and leaned into them, into her. "Wow. Please tell me you haven't come up with a way to blame me for what happened that night."

Heat flushed across her skin. Suddenly her office was too small, and she leaned back in her chair, which only brought into focus the fact that he was leaning into her. "Sorry, I forgot. Nothing is ever your fault."

The smile in his eyes singed away, he straightened up again. "You're serious? You're suggesting that it is somehow my fault that you rage-fucked me? Actually, rage-fucked my thigh."

The temperature in the room shot up so fast, Naina thought she was experiencing her first hot flash. Did those happen at thirty-eight? She groaned, because that thought made her feel ancient as she stared into his stupid dewy young face. She was sure her own face had gone some mortified shade. The only good news was that for once Vansh's color rose too, just as fast and fierce.

Wait, had he just accused her of rage-fucking his thigh?

"You are the world's most infuriating person, you know that?" For a moment Naina thought she might choke on her own incredulousness and the fact that he was not lying. "What kind of person brings that sort of thing up when someone's life's work is at stake?"

"I was not the one who brought it up." He mirrored her finger-spinning action and made a circle around her face. "And don't make that face. You didn't say the words but you were thinking them. Never mind. I am actually not here to discuss our night together."

"There was no *night together*." She pressed her hands into her face and tried to breathe into an imaginary bag. If she didn't calm down she was not going to be able to get this conversation back on track, to say nothing of the fact that she was going to pass out from the heat in here. "You were gone before the morning and I am very grateful that you brought me home and helped me when I—"

"Got horny."

"Threw up."

They spoke simultaneously. Because the universe had decided to test how much humiliation it could stuff into one situation.

Great, now he was smiling again, and she wanted to shake him even more.

"Come on, Naina. Loosen up. It really wasn't that big of a deal."

Relief flooded through her. Thank God. Yes, it was not. She was so glad he thought so. "You're right, people drink too much and throw up all the time."

"Ah," he said as though he'd figured some great secret out.

She ignored his *ah*. *Ah*s like that deserved to be ignored.

"If that's how you want to play it. I'm fine with that."

How dare he pretend to be all generous. He didn't get to be all generous, after . . . after . . .

Had he just accused her of being horny?

"You're fine with *that*?" When had they both ended up leaning into the desk, their faces inches from each other? She'd never in her life been this angry with him. "What is *that* supposed to mean exactly?"

The man shrugged.

Pulling herself away, she stood. She needed to pull this conversation back too. "Forget I said that. I don't need to know what you meant. Let's talk about the real issue here."

He was still sitting, and he leaned back and got all super relaxed and stared up at her through that overgrown forest of untamable lashes. "The real issue? Fine. Do let's talk about the real issue. I'm assuming you've decided the real issue isn't the fact that you want to pretend that throwing up is all that happened that night. For future reference, if you want to use memory loss as an excuse and pretend not to remember what happened, maybe reacting the way you have isn't the best strategy."

Every light feeling inside her was replaced with a pulsing rage. "Strategy?"

He met her glare with a look that said, *You heard me.* "Yes, Naina. When you're trying to play the 'I don't remember' card, maybe don't act so cold and jumpy at the same time—maybe don't act as though someone rocked your world and you don't know what to do with it."

You know that thing they say about not knowing whether to laugh or cry? It was actually a thing, and Naina had never experienced it before. "You think you . . . oh God." How had she put herself in a situation like this with the world's most arrogant man? "Actually, never mind. Believe what you want to believe. I'm not engaging with your fantasies."

His eyes glittered at that, two bright stars twinkling in a galaxy of lewd thoughts. She raised a hand. "Stop it. That's not what I meant. Stop derailing this conversation."

"Is that what I'm doing? Derailing the conversation?" How did he make a word as simple, as functional, as *derailing* sound dirty?

"Vansh!"

"What?"

"There are important things we need to discuss."

He swallowed, and it was the first sign that he wasn't as unaffected as he was acting. "Fine. Let's discuss the important things then. Please remind me what those are."

"The fact that Hari is waiting outside. The fact that you've put my life's work at risk simply by—"

"Existing. I seem to be causing you quite a few dilemmas simply by existing."

He was not wrong but if she responded to that, they'd be back to his thigh between her legs, and all she wanted was to forget about that. Dear Lord, could she please please please forget about it?

He had the audacity to grin as though he'd heard her prayer.

"Can we just get to the point, Vansh?"

He stared at his hands, considering his options, and fortunately decided to focus on the right part of the conversation. "The point is we need to figure this project out."

"I don't have a choice, do I?" The amount of frustration she felt having to say those words made her want to storm out of there and throw Jiggy's money back in his face. But that was not how this gig worked. There were too many lives at stake. Too many parts already in motion.

"I did not intend for it to turn out this way. I promise I will do everything I can to not make you drop your budget."

"In the long run."

He shrugged. "I've got a business plan that will show you how little we need and how fast this can go live." Then he dimpled at her. So good was he at this dimpling business that she could no longer tell if it was real or not. "Let's please both take his money. Please."

As if she had a choice. "Fine."

"'Fine' as in I can call Hari in and you'll see what we've drawn up thus far?"

"Not just yet. I have conditions."

He was grinning from ear to ear. He thought he'd won. "Of course you do. May I guess them, please?" He wiggled his brows. Now that he'd gotten his way, he was back in full-blown playful mode. It was a miracle Serious Vansh had lasted this long.

"No. You may not. This is going to be strictly professional."

"You mean, no using my thigh for—"

"Vansh! No bringing that up. It was a mistake. I had too much to drink. Stop being a jerk about it." She hated the pleading note in her own voice, hated how vulnerable it felt to let it slip. Even more, she hated that he picked it up, saw right through her, then covered it up with a shit-eating grin, saving her from the mortification that flooded through her.

"Fine." He stretched the word out with all the petulance he could muster, but she saw through him too, saw how he did this, made things okay for her. She wanted to hate it, but she found herself suppressing a smile again, because his eyes were teasing again. "I won't bring it up. But, just so you know, you are really good at sucking the fun out of things, Knightlina!"

Chapter Seventeen

Vansh slipped the box of muli parathas J-Auntie had made for Hari into his backpack. As Vansh had predicted, Hari was doing better now that he had something solid to work on. Vansh loved being right. At first Naina had been skeptical about Hari's being up to the task. But she was slowly but surely coming on board.

There were currently two thousand tech companies in Silicon Valley. In the past week, Naina and Vansh had made contact with at least half of them. Naina may not have been entirely convinced that the app was going to generate the kind of interest and results Vansh believed it would, but she'd been willing to examine, albeit grudgingly, whether they were onto something.

Their strength would lie in which companies signed on. The tech industry was about reputation, and these days reputations for social consciousness were precious currency. Naina hadn't been able to argue with that. Truth be told, she'd been kind of impressed with him for it. As she should be.

Vansh needed to find a PR platform that would make the app attractive to the giants. Something splashy that got the media excited, went viral.

They were presenting the app concept to Jiggy today. Vansh shot a text to the team telling them he was bringing breakfast.

Yay, boiled eggs? Naina texted. Funny.

Before he could respond, Nisha walked into their parents' kitchen, Ram fast asleep in his baby carrier.

Vansh squatted in front of the love of his life, his perfect nephew, and reached for him. Nisha smacked his hand. "Don't you dare wake him up. If you wake him you take him."

Vansh scooped him up, and his guy, who smelled like vernal spring buds and milk, nuzzled into him. "Don't tempt me. I'll cancel work and take him, and a boy and his favorite uncle can paint the town red."

Nisha pretended to dab Ram's perfectly undrooly mouth with a washcloth. "So, this work thing . . . it's been a few weeks, right? Is it . . . um . . . are you seriously working with Naina?"

Vansh threw her a look. He didn't like her tone. "She doesn't think I'm working seriously enough."

Nisha frowned, maybe because he'd sounded far more fond than he'd meant to. "Did you want me to find you something to do in Yash's administration? If you're, you know, looking for work."

How much that question annoyed him wasn't something he could get into right now. "I'm quite capable of finding myself work. But thanks, Nisha."

"Of course you are, sweetheart. But you know Yash and I would love your help. And we're your family. And I know you value loyalty."

Wow! he almost said. But Nisha was obviously digging for information and he didn't have any intention of giving her an opening.

He rocked his nephew. "Speaking of family, is it my imagination or does this guy look exactly like his Vansh Mama? I mean, look at those lashes." The phone buzzed in his pocket and he had the intense urge to introduce his nephew to Naina.

Leaving Nisha mid–eye roll, he picked up the baby carrier and diaper bag and took them up the stairs for Ram's daily drop-off with Aji and Esha. Nisha followed.

After much oohing and aahing over his perfection—which he blissfully slept through—Ram was tucked into the cradle.

Vansh's phone buzzed again and he checked it. There were many LOLs about Naina's boiled-egg comment. Vansh smiled.

"Who's that?" Nisha asked, grabbing a croissant from the breakfast tray J-Auntie had laid out. Vansh picked up a boiled egg and popped it in his mouth, making it impossible for him to answer.

"How's the project going?" Esha asked. He had no doubt she saw right through his blatant attempt at avoiding Nisha's inquisition.

Before he could answer, Aji gave him one of her warmly reprimanding looks that he loved so much. "You've barely been home these past few weeks. I don't understand why you children work so hard."

Vansh could practically see Nisha's ears perk up. "If you haven't been home, where have you been?"

"The schedule on the project is very tight. We need to be able to demo the app in real time in a few months. Pulling that off will be a minor miracle."

"You really love this work?" Esha said, smiling. It wasn't one of her ethereal smiles. She was asking. Esha never asked.

"I do. I feel really invested in it."

"How is Naina?" Aji asked. "We haven't seen her in a very long time."

"Naturally she's not going to come and see you. Now that Yash is of no use to her," Nisha said. What was wrong with her? Nisha was direct and fiercely protective, but this was downright mean.

"That's unfair," Esha said. "Naina did not only come to see us because of Yash. Naina is much more than she seems."

Nisha scoffed and studied Vansh for a reaction.

Vansh wasn't sure what Nisha was trying. Her protective-big-sister personality was out in full force. Anything he said to defend Naina would be a dead giveaway. Of what, exactly, he didn't know. But it wasn't Nisha's business.

Naturally, Nisha picked up on the fact that Vansh wasn't going to take the bait no matter how hard she tried. Naturally, that made her try harder. "All I want is for you to be careful, Vansh!"

"Careful about what? We're working together. Naina is fabulous at what she does. She's family, Nisha!"

Nisha executed another scoff. "Family doesn't use one another. Doesn't hurt one another."

Before Vansh could react, Esha stood. She'd appeared much less fragile these past few months that he'd been home, but she still was unused to conflict.

"I'm sorry, Esha," Nisha and Vansh said together.

"Enough," their grandmother said.

"I'm fine," Esha snapped. Vansh had never heard her snap. "You're being unfair, Nisha."

Nisha looked like she'd been slapped.

Esha turned to Vansh. "You said you were working on a project to help homeless people in San Francisco?"

"Yes. We're trying to come up with a program that will help local companies find and train unemployed people within the city who live on the street."

"That's not usually Naina's sphere of interest. Why is she working with you on it?" Nisha asked, getting over her shock at being reprimanded by Esha far too fast.

"Because Jiggy Mehta has forced her to," Vansh said, then wished he hadn't, because Nisha made an I-told-you-so face.

Vansh mirrored her scoff, but already this conversation had gone on longer than he wanted it to.

"You know what would help a project like that?" Esha said, inserting herself between Nisha and Vansh. "International media coverage." It was an entirely un-Esha-like thing to say, and for a moment they all stared at her, everything else forgotten.

She seemed calm in the face of their balking, which was the first sign of the old Esha. "You should get some really hard-hitting photographs of your work. That will make it high-profile and make companies want to be part of it for the PR mileage."

Vansh stared at her. He should have been used to this, her knowing stuff, but it still threw him. "Photographs?"

"By some high-profile photographer who can capture the essence of the issue."

Sid Dashwood! Why hadn't he thought of that? Vansh hugged her. She didn't so much as flinch. "That's brilliant, Esha! I think I know just the photographer who might be interested."

Esha blinked up at him. "Who?"

"You know India's brother, Sid? He's in town and we've become friends." Vansh hadn't managed to have Sid over to the Anchorage to meet the family yet because he'd barely been home, but they'd been texting regularly. Sid had dropped by to photograph the scrub jays almost every day, and they'd spent some time talking about Vansh's project. "I'll bet I can talk him into it."

"Why would he do a project like this?" Esha asked, color tinging her usually pale cheeks.

"Because I think he likes me," Vansh said. The man's talent was exactly what they needed. The pictures of the hatchlings, tracing their growth, had been stunning. "Also, I think he might be a little bored."

"Well, his boredom would certainly work in your favor." Esha looked almost . . . Vansh wasn't sure how to apply this word to Esha, but he could think of no other word for it: *thrilled*. And Esha's sense about things was never wrong. "Even if it does seem out of his sphere of interest. Then again, you're working here in America and that's out of your sphere of interest, and Naina is too, so maybe this project is blessed."

Vansh dropped a kiss on Esha's head. She was the oldest but tiniest of the cousins. Five feet tall with the stature of a middle schooler. Usually, her demeanor was really young too, but suddenly she felt much more like an adult. "I'm going to give him a call. What do you think, will he do it?"

She closed her eyes and almost fell into a trance. "I could bet my life on it." Then she gave the strangest smile and Vansh thought that word again: *thrilled.*

"Thanks! I love you," he threw at the three of them, "but I'm terribly late." He picked up two more boiled eggs for the road and ran down the steps with Esha's smile and Nisha's glare boring into his back.

WHEN VANSH CALLED Sid, he was even more excited about the project than Vansh had expected. As Vansh had suspected, he was bored and looking for something meaningful. Now they had to figure out exactly what the photos would be. They decided to meet to discuss.

Vansh had spent a considerable amount of time over the past few weeks talking to people living on the street. Tina had lost her project management job when she'd been diagnosed with cancer, then she'd lost her home. Mac had lost his data networking job to a gambling habit that he was now in therapy for. Vansh had already brought Tina and Mac into interviews with Google and Oracle to be part of a training program.

"How about documenting those stories?" he asked Naina as he filled her in over tea at her desk.

She was in sunflower yellow today. A turtleneck sweater dress that showed off her shoulders. She only wore bright colors when she was struggling with something. Vansh knew some trouble had been brewing on one of the construction sites in Nepal. Naina didn't like to share problems that arose on her project. She seemed to think of it as a personal failure. But he also had a sense that she didn't want him getting involved in it, and why that bothered him so much he didn't know.

"Isn't Sid Dashwood famously reclusive? Didn't he refuse to take pictures of the president and First Lady once and cause a stir?" Naina asked. "Why would he want to photograph your project?"

"Honestly, he doesn't strike me as particularly reclusive. But then, reclusive people like me. I help them loosen up."

She made her most incredulous face.

"Look at you. Look at Hari."

"Sid's sister is dating your brother," Naina said. "And you think this has to do with you?"

He must've looked as hurt at that as he was, because she added, "Vansh, I'm not trying to be a killjoy here. But you have to be cognizant of why people hand you things. There are costs involved. You have to be aware of those."

"Really? Costs? What about Hari?"

"Come on."

"What?"

"You're Vansh Raje and you're acting like he's your best friend. Of course he's grateful and happy. Tread carefully, Vansh."

"Tread carefully? What do you think I'm going to do to him?"

"I'm not saying your intentions aren't always noble."

He hated when she did this, reduced him to being well-intentioned. "And you? What about you? What do you gain by spending time with me? By cracking yourself open to me when no one else can get close?"

Her laugh was bitter. Of course it was. Her *What am I going to do with you?* laugh threaded together with her *How dare you!* laugh.

"Laugh all you want. But you know you feel differently around me. It's who I am, but it's also someone I work hard to be. How can you refuse to acknowledge that?"

She pulled off the clip that was barely holding her hair together, then twisted and pinned it back up. "Fine, I acknowledge that people are drawn to you like moths to a flame because you offer up everything you come with without one thought to how dangerous that is." Her voice cracked, which mortified her so much her chin went up.

"Dangerous for whom?" he asked. For her? For him? For Hari?

Her laptop pinged and her eyes darkened with worry as she checked it.

"Is it Nepal? What's going on?"

She rubbed her temples but didn't answer and started typing out a response.

"It's stunning how little respect you have for me, Naina." What more did he have to do to prove himself?

She kept typing. "What am I supposed to respect exactly?"

Ouch. "I've worked on charitable missions from the age of eighteen, in the toughest parts of the world. That's eight years of trying not to live only for myself. That's not respect-worthy enough for you?"

She slammed a final key on her laptop and turned to him. "How many different charitable missions has it been in those eight years? Fifteen? Lightbulbs in Guatemala, digging wells in Zimbabwe, teaching English in Cambodia, saving gorillas in Tanzania, raising turtles in God knows where."

"It was chimpanzees, not gorillas, and I'm flattered that you have my résumé memorized. But all of that sounds very much like it's worthy of respect. Is that why you won't tell me what's going on in Nepal? Because you think I'm going to move on too fast?" He knew the issue was with one of her sites. A local gang lord demanding bribes. But she refused to get into it more than that. "Maybe I can help, Naina."

"This isn't just another project that you can move on from, that you have no skin in!"

"Let me get this straight, I can only help if I work on the same project for the rest of my life?"

"Maybe not the rest of your life, but long enough for it to matter."

This was about his leaving? "So timeframe is the measure of commitment? What happened to not turning acts of service into an extension of your ego? What happened to traveling light and touching as many lives as you can? Timeframe has nothing to do with level of involvement. Can't you see that you and I are not that different? The work we've done isn't that different. I can help with this. I know someone in Kathmandu."

Naturally that made her make an infuriated sound. She got up and started pacing. "I've worked my whole life for this. You and I are nothing like each other."

She kept saying that. But maybe she didn't sound so convinced anymore.

"You sure about that?"

"What is that supposed to mean?"

"It means I believe I've worked my whole life to change things that bother me, but you believe there's some ulterior motive of noblesse oblige and ennui and guilty privilege, or whatever Hollywood-archetype psychoanalysis you've performed on me. If that's true, it must mean there's something else going on with your obsession with wanting to change things too. I mean, isn't what's sauce for the goose sauce for the gander?"

"At least my sauce doesn't change with the changing seasons. I'm focused on something. Therefore the thing I'm focused on cannot easily be replaced with something else. This is about the lives of hundreds of thousands of women who can have a shot at basic healthcare and sustainable income. Your work is not lesser. It is just one thing today and another tomorrow." Her computer pinged and she seemed to fold inward as she turned to her screen. "Shit." Her fingers were shaking.

He went around the desk and put a hand on her shoulder. "Tell me what's going on, Naina. Let me help."

She pressed her face into her hands. For an endless moment she said nothing. Then she looked at him, letting him see what it took for her to put away all her fears and trust him. "A local gang attacked one of our sites and set fire to it. A caseworker is badly hurt." She opened up the email and read through the mayhem for him as silent tears slipped from her eyes.

Chapter Eighteen

It had taken Vansh precisely twenty minutes to get the home minister of Nepal on the phone. The home minister. On a video call, no less.

Turns out Vansh had roomed with the grandson of one of Nepal's longest-serving ministers, who had recently been elected a minister himself. Naturally they were the best of friends.

"Of course you are," Naina said, trying not to shake her head.

"Is it a crime to be well loved?" he asked as they waited on hold for Naman Thapa to join the call.

It wasn't a crime at all. Not even a little bit. What it was was a frickin' wonder, how Vansh could gather so many people so close, across the globe, across time. A smile slipped through the purpose on Vansh's face as Thapa appeared and they greeted each other like brothers, inside references flying fast between them. Evidently, the home minister and he had some smile-worthy memories together.

At this point, with her entire project at risk of imploding, Naina could not have been more grateful. Maybe she should have asked for his help sooner.

While they'd been waiting for the call to be set up, Vansh had filled her in on their history. Naman had been something of a genius in coming up with exact combinations of sativa and indica for maximum benefit. They'd spent many a night studying the constellations and working around their hopelessness about the state of the world. Naman had been on his last ultimatum from his grandfather to get his act together or be disowned.

The man had dropped out of Harvard, done a few years of med school in India, environmental science in Germany, art in Paris, philosophy somewhere else. Vansh didn't know anyone more terrifyingly brilliant.

One night Vansh had shared a note with him from his friend Amara that had changed Vansh's own life. Naman had laughed—as, Vansh said, he tended to do at everything in life. In the days that followed, Vansh had watched in disbelief as his friend went home and turned slowly and surely into a white-kurta-wearing, soft-spoken leader of the masses.

"I hope Ms. Kohli appreciates all the advantages that come with being your friend," Naman said as Vansh introduced Naina. His voice turned serious, all the brother-in-arms bonhomie evaporating as they turned to the business at hand. "Ms. Kohli, what a pleasure. I looked up the work you've done. It's impressive."

Naina filled him in on the situation at the clinic and watched his face barely move from its Buddha-esque sanguineness. He lifted his finger at someone off camera with a nod without taking his focus off her. "We've had a lot of trouble with this particular gang in that region. Thanks for bringing this incident to my notice. The locals haven't reported them, for obvious reasons. Fear is quite the silencer." Turned out this was the opening the authorities had been looking for to go after this extortion gang.

"Would it impact the project long-term if we went after these guys?" Vansh asked. "We can't have any more people working on the project hurt in the crossfire. Or get stuck in a battle with the local powers."

"That would be an issue if you were speaking to local law enforcement and not the home minister," Naman said with enough confidence to make up for the lack of modesty. "If we cut them off at their root, retaliation won't be a problem. But I need iron-clad witnesses and testimonies. No backing out once we start. I'll need your word on this, Vansh."

Vansh looked at Naina. Keeping a low profile and working around local powers was a strategy that had been painful but effective enough. Truth was, that was all Naina had thought possible.

"I can fly out today," Naina said. Latha, who headed up operations in Kathmandu, had asked her not to.

"I'd advise you not to do that. We don't need to add an angle where this could turn into an international incident."

"May I discuss it with my team there? I need their buy-in." She looked at Vansh.

"They're the ones on the ground," Vansh said. "They have to be the ones to decide."

"Of course." Naman looked between Vansh and her and cracked a smile for the first time since getting down to business. "My friend makes decisions from the heart, Ms. Kohli, and he's fearless with his. I'm glad someone's teaching him to worry about the darker side of the world."

The rest of the day was spent laying it all out with the team. The pros and cons and all the gray areas in between. They had to attack fast, before news that Naman was involved leaked out.

As soon as they'd made the decision, the arrests started. Thanks to the impeccable record keeping Naina had insisted on, they were able to keep their end of the bargain. After a few sleepless days when Naman's forces performed discreet surgical strikes, it looked like the project was back on track. Her caseworker was out of the hospital. The jubilation among the team was careful but palpable. Naina's relief was like a drug.

Vansh had kept up with his meetings with the PR and HR

departments of tech companies in between going over all the communications with Naman's office. They'd been spending so much time in the office, Naina felt like her butt had grown roots into the bright pink chairs in the conference room.

Today pizza boxes lay stacked on the table, three pizzas almost gone. Vansh had shaken his very judgmental head as the rest of them devoured it, as though they were monsters with no self-control whatsoever. He'd DoorDashed a grilled-chicken salad from his favorite deli for himself.

"You can stop glaring at the pizza now." Naina picked up another slice and bit into it.

No, she was not going to think about how his eyes studied her as the intense pleasure of thick yeasty crust and extra cheese sank into her very being.

"Feel free to put undeserving shit into your body whenever you please. Who am I to judge?" he said, voice all growly.

Sadiya wiggled her brows. "Word!"

"I'd like to put a deserving shit in my body one of these days. It's been too long," Makayla said, and everyone laughed.

Hari looked confused but happy. He'd become much more relaxed around them. Sadiya, Makayla, and Mariel had taken him into their hearts and under their wings. He'd even trusted Makayla enough to let her start the process of getting his lost paperwork back in order, and had started joining in conversations and offering opinions, even though he apologized profusely for it afterward.

"Why don't you like pizza, Vansh?" Hari asked in a voice that suggested he'd finally discovered a flaw in Vansh.

"I prefer to eat food that's good for me," Vansh said, although Naina had no doubt he'd rather lecture them about how one couldn't eat refined fat slathered on top of refined flour and look the way he did. She was glad he didn't say it, because the pizza was too good to be wasted on throwing at him.

She felt her own lips smiling as she chewed. "He also prefers to buy his clothes from the juniors section and he wouldn't be able to if he eats pizza."

The eyes he turned on her smoldered with the knowledge that she'd let escape that she was thinking about his body and the clothes he put on it. Maybe she shouldn't have gone there. But man, that thigh of his had not been junior sized, and his stupid gold-flecked eyes said he knew it.

"But pizza is so tasty," Hari said. "Do I have to give it up?"

"No!" Naina patted Hari's shoulder. "You eat as much pizza as you want and ignore Vansh. The rest of us do."

Hari grinned and looked at Naina the way the lamb from the nursery rhyme had to have looked at Mary when he followed her to school.

Then he gave Vansh an apologetic look, not wanting him to feel like he was being disloyal. "I would never ignore Vansh. Vansh saved my life," he said sincerely, picking up a slice.

"He did?" Makayla and Sadiya sat up and turned toward Vansh. They had moved past losing their good sense when he was in the room to taking great enjoyment in teasing him.

Color crested Vansh's cheeks even as his deep, deep dimples dived into them. "That's not exactly true. I merely assisted Hari while he was inebriated." He threw Naina another ruthless smolder. "That's something I'm good at."

"Did he also cause you to get drunk in the first place?" Naina asked sweetly.

"No!" Hari looked horrified. "I just didn't know that the orange juice wasn't *only* orange juice. Why would Vansh do such a thing?"

"Yes, Naina, why would I do such a thing? It's not like I can predict how people will act when they're drunk." He was all innocence, and it scrambled every bit of her own good sense.

How could eyes be this comforting? How could a face cause

so much pleasure? And that's why he was so dangerous. She'd do well to keep those large-eyed critters in mind.

"I was very badly behaved." Hari scarfed down his pizza in too-big bites.

"It's not badly behaved to be honest. You told me the truth." Vansh's eyes were in a tight lock with Naina's. "I was happy to be the person you turned to. I regret nothing."

"Such a giver," Naina said.

"Is that a bad thing?" Vansh said.

The phone on the table buzzed loudly, startling them both. Sadiya pressed the talk button. "Yes, Mariel?"

"Mr. Mehta is on his way inside."

Before Mariel had finished that sentence, there he was, Jiggy in a leopard-print tracksuit, smiling too widely at the gathering in the room. He'd given Vansh his hearty blessings on the app—of course he had—before jetting off to New York again. A respite that hadn't lasted long enough. Naina's body tightened involuntarily at the sight of him, the way one braces for a punch.

"Thought I'd check up on my army of do-gooders," Jiggy said. "How's our homeless friend?" His beady gaze landed on Hari.

Hari withdrew into himself.

Naina stood and got between Hari and Jiggy. "Hey, Jiggy. Welcome back. How was New York?"

"Best city in the world," Jiggy declared in his high-pitched voice. "Best city to have a wedding in." He'd been in New York City for his niece's wedding. A wedding he'd paid for, as anyone who read the news knew. "When you have an uncle with money, that is." He laughed as though there was nothing more fun than broadcasting your generosity.

"Exciting. Let's go to my office and you can tell us all about it." Naina tried to get to the door but it was hard to do while still trying to shield Hari, who looked ready to crawl under the table. Hari was terrified of Mehta. Vansh had introduced them before

Jiggy went off to New York, and Hari had told Naina that Jiggy reminded him of a shark and sharks were why Hari was terrified of oceans.

Vansh stood, helping Naina cut Hari off from Jiggy's view.

But Jiggy walked around them into the conference room. "Let's talk here. I like that everyone is here." He dropped into a chair between Sadiya and Makayla. "So what are we working on?"

Sadiya told him about their breakthrough with Naman Thapa. Jiggy waved it away. "Nepal is eight thousand miles away. What's happening with Yash's—sorry, I mean Vansh's . . . the brothers have such similar names!" He stopped to laugh. "We should just call it the Raje project to avoid confusion."

Naina sat down next to Hari. The muscle in Vansh's jaw clenched and released, but other than that he showed no sign of discomfort at the obviously deliberate slip.

"We've got twenty companies on board and we've gathered twenty-eight people who're interested in being part of the pilot," Vansh said, sitting down too.

"We've also been working with Siddhartha Dashwood to do photo biographies of some of the people in the pilot," Naina said. It was still annoying to her that Sid had become so involved in the project so fast, but she couldn't argue with how stunning his captures were, and how much mileage the app was going to get through them.

Jiggy looked from Vansh to Naina, a veritable calculator shining in his eyes. "I know, I know. I've heard all that. You made me drink all that Kool-Aid . . . if the homeless crisis is caused by the tech industry, then maybe the tech industry can do something to turn the crisis around." He repeated the words they'd presented to him last week and waved them away. Then he turned to Vansh. "Have you talked to your brother about this project?"

"I wasn't aware talking to Yash was part of the plan," Vansh said, that muscle in his jaw working again. Naina had tried not to think about the Rajes and how they were taking Vansh and her working together. From everything she'd seen, Vansh kept his work and, surprisingly, his life private. A task Naina would not have imagined possible. Every step Yash ever took seemed to be tangled up with the rest of them.

"No plan. No plan. I thought you were close and you'd talk, that's all." Mehta bounced in his chair. "Fine. Good. You're all working well together. This is very exciting." He threw another look between Vansh and Naina. "Let's demo the app to the board. Next month."

"Next month?" Vansh asked, unable to hide his surprise.

"Yes. Let's focus on this and put the Nepal project on hold."

Excuse her? Naina stood, wishing she could flip Jiggy's chair over, with him in it. "We're not putting the Nepal project on hold," she said so quietly every person in the room seemed to hold their breath while straining to hear her.

Jiggy's eyes skimmed their faces.

Before Jiggy could open his mouth again she added, "But we have a lot of things in motion, so we can certainly give some extra attention to this project. We can try to present to the board next month like you suggested."

Face saved, Jiggy stood. One month was not enough time to present the app to the board, and Jiggy knew that. He wanted a reaction from them. And Naina suspected he'd be thrilled with a reaction where Vansh and she fought over resources. She slid Vansh a glance. *Don't say anything.*

Jiggy walked up to Hari and looked down at him.

"You think you can pull this thing together in a month?"

Hari stuttered incoherently.

"We'll figure it out," Vansh said.

Jiggy spun to him, smile back on his face. "Good. I can't wait to see what your friend here comes up with."

"Me?" Hari said. It sounded like a hiccup.

"Yes. Vansh tells me you're the best and I trust Vansh. Don't you?"

Hari made a strangled sound.

With nothing more than a nod at Vansh and Vansh alone, Jiggy left the room.

"I can't present to the . . . to the . . ." Hari started rocking back and forth in his chair.

Naina squatted down in front of him and took his hands. "Hari, listen to me. That man is a bully. He can't hurt you. You don't have to present to him or to the board. Vansh and I will take care of that."

Vansh opened his mouth, but Naina put her hand up to stop him.

"I don't want to work on the app anymore," Hari said. "I want to work with Naina. On her project."

Vansh looked like he'd been kicked. He was quicksilver, a ripple-less pond one moment, rapids rushing toward a waterfall the next.

He squatted down next to Naina but no words came.

"This is my project now too, Hari," Naina said, and something trembled through Vansh's body next to her.

Don't jump to conclusions, she warned him with a sideways glance, and a smile returned to the edge of his mouth. A little too exhausted for Vansh, but a smile.

"We're a team," she said, looking at Sadiya and Makayla and, yes, at Vansh. "And wherever you feel most comfortable in that team is where you should work."

"Are you angry?" Hari asked Vansh.

"Not at all," Vansh said gently.

He didn't add how much was already riding on the app. He didn't push Hari, and the awareness of how very good he was at this whisperer business sparkled through her.

Then Vansh winked at her. "What matters is that Naina thinks we're a team." He stood and high-fived Hari. "You got us into the circle of trust, my friend!"

Hari beamed, when that hadn't felt like even a remote possibility minutes ago.

"Another slice of pizza?" Naina asked, and Hari's smile got wider as he took it.

"I do have only a little bit to go before the mock-up for the app is done. Maybe I'll finish that," he said.

Vansh whooped and jumped in the air. "Why don't we forget all this for the rest of the day and play hooky? Go ride that roller coaster? I know Naina's been dying to."

"That sounds like a fabulous idea," Sadiya said.

"I can't believe we've never done that," Makayla said.

"I've always wanted to ride the roller coaster," Hari said. "I didn't think I was allowed to."

"Why would you not be allowed to?" Naina said. "You work here and it's for all employees."

"All employees who aren't too chicken," Vansh said as he offered her a hand along with the challenge.

She took the hand—she wasn't interested in the challenge— and stood. "Guilty as charged. I'll watch."

His smile could lull even the most jaded. Yes, she was guilty as charged with that as well.

"She said we're a team, didn't she?" Vansh asked the others. "The team doesn't watch. It plays!"

They hooted, everyone including Hari, and filed out to tell Mariel the news of their spontaneous field trip.

"You can hold my hand, Knightlina," he said, standing a little too close. "I'll keep you safe."

She wanted to scoff, but looking into his eyes gave her the safest feeling she'd ever experienced in her life. Ever. She should probably step away from him, but she could count the golden flecks in his eyes. She shouldn't get used to the joy that emanated from him, but it sank into her the way his hypnotic dimples sank into his cheeks. Safety and joy braided together and squeezed her chest, but she couldn't bring herself to care that she could barely breathe around it.

Chapter Nineteen

*I*t had been two weeks since Naman had removed all their road-blocks with one authoritative wave of his hand. Vansh watched as Naina thanked Naman for the umpteenth time, something too fierce to name burning inside him. This was their last scheduled debriefing video conference.

"I'll admit I started out helping because of my brother here," Naman said. "I'd go to the ends of the earth for him, but getting to know you has been the real pleasure, Ms. Kohli."

Naina gave him her professional smile. Only she could turn a smile into a declaration of victory without sacrificing grace. "Likewise." Then she slid a sideways looks at Vansh. "I might have to record this to play back to Vansh."

A laugh spurted out of Naman. The past few weeks had been tense, but that laugh was the Naman Vansh knew. "I see Vansh hasn't changed at all," he said, slipping out of his minister-of-the-masses avatar for the first time.

Vansh shrugged and Naman started laughing in earnest. Naman had always had a problem putting the brakes on once he started laughing. To hear that laugh now made Vansh wonder if his friend's old habits had changed quite as much as he wanted everyone to believe, or if his new mellow gentility had to do with having adjusted his alchemical potions, so to speak.

Laughing so freely, he looked too young to be running any part of a country's government, but also earnest and unjaded enough to have a shot at actually doing it right.

He finally stopped laughing long enough to speak. "As a thank-you for the work you've done for my people, I would've liked to do you the favor of warning you against getting too attached to my friend here, but I know exactly how well those warnings work on women."

Naina stiffened next to Vansh, but her smile didn't slip. "That warning is entirely unnecessary, Mr. Thapa. I've known your friend since he was in diapers."

Seriously? she wrote on the Post-it pad they always used to carry out a side conversation during calls. Then she added a few question marks as she gave Naman her most dignified smile.

What? Vansh responded on the notepad, also decorating it with question marks. And a smiley face, because he knew it would fake-annoy her out of whatever was real-annoying her.

It was so much fun to be juvenile with her. Fortunately for Naman, it was only Naina and him on the call and not the rest of the team. She tended to be far too withdrawn with Vansh around them, and he hated it. Didn't she know that her stiffness around him was a dead giveaway of this thing that had taken to sparking in the air when they were near each other?

The more uptight she got, the goofier it made Vansh want to be. It made him want to make a complete ass of himself, if that would get her to crack a smile.

On the screen Naman lost his shit all over again at the mention of Vansh in diapers. "Lord, this is the most fun I've had in too long. Naina, Vansh, thank you." Finally they were done with the formality and down to first names. Then he got serious again, but only slightly. "And you know what? You have my full support on your project. Actually, let's do this: All permissions and licenses will go straight through my office. A fast track. Let's make this project such a success that it becomes a model for the rest of the world. My assistant will be in touch with the details." With that he hung up.

Wait, what? Had they just cut through twenty miles of red tape in one fell swoop? Had they just done that?

Naina let out an entirely un-Naina-like squeal and flew out of her seat and started jumping up and down, and Vansh was doing the same, and then she was hugging him and he was spinning her around.

Then they were standing there holding each other. Because keeping his hands off her this past week had felt . . . it had felt . . . wholly unnecessary.

"Did that really just happen?" she said, glowing like the full moon on a cloudless night, hair pulled back, tired eyes shining so bright their light burned through his body.

"Yes!"

She started jumping again and he spun her around again.

When he put her down, his arms still around her, she was shaking. It started in her shoulders, the tiniest sobs, then her eyes filled with it. Relief and bone-deep exhaustion, all the pressure of the past weeks, of years, trembling through her even as she struggled visibly to push it down. For all her effort, the swell of emotion seemed to overwhelm her so much she pressed her head into his chest, and lost herself to the silent sobs.

He stroked her back, his body registering how she felt in his arms before his mind did. Then his mind crashed into the information with an electric buzz that raced through him. These electric sparks had become his companions these past weeks.

How does this feel so damn good? his body and mind demanded together. In one voice. Flooding his blood.

She pulled away, face wet. "I'm so sorry. I . . . Oh God . . . I don't know why."

"Hey. It's okay. This is a pretty big deal." He dragged his thumb over her cheek, wiping at the wetness, and felt her velvet-soft skin push up in a lopsided smile under his fingers.

"It's been a lot." The gangster had caused so much havoc before Naman stepped in, threatening local doctors and activists who supported the project. The caseworker who had been badly hurt was recovering well, thank God, but it was entirely unfair that she'd had to go through that. Naina had been rock solid through it all, determined to not back down, but terrified of what it might cost.

Now she smiled. "This is going to change everything. It's going to happen, Vansh. The first clinic is going to go up, then the next. Then the next. No more roadblocks." Another sob filled with hope and relief escaped her. Another stroke of her cheek escaped him.

Tenderness wrapped around them. Their first victory, one they'd achieved together.

"Thank you," she said.

"No, don't thank me. You did this. You built up to this. I just knew a guy."

Her eyes softened. Her gaze caressed his face, dropping to his lips. Then, before he could absorb what that felt like, she went up on her toes and dropped a kiss on his lips.

A quick press, softer than anything. Fiercer than anything. Awareness flared through Vansh, fast and furious. On a sharp intake of breath, he cupped the back of her head and soaked her up. Everything he'd been waiting for.

Every inch of him waiting.

Every bit of him pressed into it now.

They stood there like that, time suspended around them. Soaking and reaching. Bathing in the feelings that held them in place, arousal tugging from every corner of his being.

Then a knock on the door to the conference room sounded. A boom in the silence. Naina jumped back like she'd been shot.

She dropped into a chair, chest heaving. "Come on in." She pushed her shaking hands under her, sitting on them.

The door flew open.

"What happened?" Makayla walked in, Hari close on her heels.

"What do you mean?" Naina sounded breathless, her eyes still dilated, as aroused as him.

"We heard squealing." Makayla looked between the two of them. Hari followed suit, head turning from Vansh to Naina. "You look like you jumped out of a plane."

Naina cleared her throat. "You're not going to believe this."

Vansh was still frozen in place.

"Naman Thapa just gave us an open channel into his office. He said he'd take care of all our paperwork. That's miles of red tape gone!" Saying those words erased everything else from her face but pure excited joy. She jumped out of her chair.

Now Makayla was jumping and squealing and throwing her arms around Naina. They held each other and jumped up and down.

Are you going to kiss her too? Of course Naina caught the question in his eyes. But she looked so happy he couldn't not get lost in it again. The imprint of her lips still danced like sparks on his.

"How did that happen?" Makayla asked, pulling away and high-fiving Vansh.

Naina filled them in as Hari settled into a chair in a corner, smiling. Makayla stuck her head out of the conference room and called Sadiya and Mariel in, and the jubilation started afresh and continued for a while.

Naina, who had been avoiding Vansh's eyes, finally looked at him as the others chattered on about the files they had to pull from various offices and submit again through Naman's office.

She beamed at him, finally losing her battle to stop herself from doing it.

He smiled back. "I believe I just proved that I'm not entirely useless to have around," he said, voice soft enough to not reach the others.

Something flared in her eyes, something fiery and consuming that made him forget there was anyone else in the room. "No one ever said you didn't have your uses."

He'd have bet anything that wasn't how she'd meant for it to come out, but he couldn't stop his smile from spreading wide.

Her eyes narrowed in response, face flaming. She threw a quick look at the others, still entirely absorbed in their victory. "Stop it. When are you ever going to let that go?"

Never.

"When is he going to let what go?" Mariel asked.

"Yes, Naina, let what go?" Vansh asked, making sure the most innocent of dimples dipped into his cheeks.

There was a way she had of pressing her lips together when she didn't want to smile but couldn't help it, and it made her eyes blaze to life.

"Nothing," she said, heat turning her dark brown eyes even darker. "I just want us to remember that our work's not done yet. We need to find a way to monetize the app so no rugs are pulled out from under our feet. Hari, let's see where we are on those designs. Makayla, let's look at the comps on what else is out there for our patent application."

With that, they were back in head-down work mode.

IT HAD TAKEN a week to get Hari back into the app after Jiggy had terrified him. Things were looking on track to present to the board. Naina had made it clear that Hari was not going to be part of the presentation.

Vansh didn't disagree, but he thought parts of the presentation coming from Hari would be exactly what they needed. They'd started with five people in the pilot program who were being trained. They'd found them spots in low-rent co-ops. Then Mac, one of the guys, had dropped out and disappeared.

This was going to be part of the program. They had hired a case manager to track everyone's progress and engaged therapists and career counselors. Sid's portraits of the pilot participants were magnificent. Now all they needed was for the right media outlet to pick them up.

"It's amazing what we've managed to do in such a short time," Naina said as Vansh walked her to her building. They'd spent the past six hours talking to more people so they could add to the pilot.

"Oh, are we allowed to say *we* now?" he teased, throwing her words back at her.

She stopped and turned to him. He hadn't meant to make her look like this. Apologetic.

"Yes. You were right," she said. That's it. Nothing more.

But it was enough. For now.

They were barely a block from her building. The sense of loss Vansh had taken to feeling every time he dropped her off outside the glass doors was back in his chest. How could he feel this way when he'd been spending twelve hours a day with her every day? Like something precious was about to be taken from him.

She threw him another sideways glance. "Hari told me again today that he doesn't want to present to the board."

Vansh didn't respond. He'd take care of Hari when the time was right.

A frustrated breath left Naina. "Vansh, we have to listen to Hari. You can't push him."

"Please don't tell me how to treat Hari. I care for him. I'm not going to hurt him. Why can't you trust me, Naina?" *What more do I have to do?*

Fierceness brightened her eyes. *How can you question my trust?*

As they stood there, unsaid words pushing at them, too many feelings pulling at them, a large raindrop plopped on Vansh's forehead. Then, before he'd registered that, the skies opened up.

They broke into a run. By the time they were standing in the tiny lobby of her building, they were both soaked to the bone, hearts beating fast.

A shiver went through her and she pulled her red peacoat tighter around herself. A raindrop trickled down the sharp ridge of her nose and slid off the tip.

He shoved his hand through his dripping hair to keep from wiping it across the wet sheen on her cheeks. "Go on up," he said. "I'll see you at the office tomorrow."

It was pouring outside, but he'd dropped her off at the glass doors often enough to know that she didn't want to invite him up. She'd drawn a line between them and she'd been determined not to cross it. For a few breaths they stood there, breathing through the effort that took.

"It doesn't look like it's going to stop," she said quietly, as though the line were pushing back at her.

"That's fine. I'm already wet." He turned to leave but she reached out and grabbed him, sending a spark shooting up his arm.

Her gaze dropped to her hand on his arm, where a magnetic force emanated, engulfing their bodies and sending shock waves through them both.

Instead of fighting it and pulling away, she let her hand stroke down his arm, leaving a trail of fire in its wake, and slid it into his hand. Her grip tightened. "Come on." It was a whisper, filled with all the things she didn't want to say.

"Are you sure?"

Their eyes met. What was he asking?

She nodded. *Yes.* What was she answering?

She didn't let his hand go as they waited for the elevator. Palm to palm. Fingers intertwined. For all the women Vansh had been with, had loved being with, he'd never held anyone's hand. Not like this. Not where it felt like his entire body was involved in the act. More than his body.

Blood rang in his ears.

He wanted to pull their joined hands to his heart, but it felt like a spell, magical, and he couldn't let himself break it with even the slightest movement.

In the elevator, nothing but their hands touched. Their bodies vibrated next to each other. Too close, but not close enough.

When they got to her door, she let his hand go. Her fingers shook on the keypad as she punched in the code to enter her apartment. Her hand rested on the doorknob, but she didn't push it open. Instead she pressed her forehead into the door.

For endless moments, she didn't move.

"You can change your mind. Do you want me to leave?" His voice was too soft, the need raging inside him too loud.

The wet-lavender smell of her hair soaked through the air, vibrated through his body, as she twisted around and reached for him.

She was in his arms. And then their lips were touching and she was devouring him like he was her last breath.

He fell into it.

The door swung open and he lifted her up, hands under her butt, tongue in her mouth. Hungry, so hungry. Ravenous. Their bodies flush, touching everywhere, her legs, her arms, everything wrapped around him. Turning around, he pressed her against the door, slamming it shut with the force of their joined bodies.

"Vansh," she said, and there was such wanting in her voice that it flooded through him. He'd never wanted anything more than he wanted to hear that voice again. Screaming his name.

"I want to make you scream." There, he said it even as she pressed herself into him. Legs wrapping tighter. Fingers digging into his hair. Everything she'd never said, he wanted her to scream it.

"I don't scream. Ever."

Shit. "That's it. You know better than to challenge me. Now I have to make you." He pressed his hips into hers, pushing into her heat. She moaned and the game was on.

Chapter Twenty

*I*t wasn't like Naina didn't know what an orgasm felt like. Riz, her vibrator, had some goodly miles on him. But when Vansh said he was going to make her scream, she was never again taking that lightly.

Her throat felt raw as she sagged against him like he'd wrung every last drop of pleasure from her, wrung every last scream and whimper from her.

Had she begged?

Yes, she'd begged.

He'd taken her by surprise. Yet, God, he hadn't.

He was panting between her legs like someone who'd sprinted up a hill. One of her knees was hooked over his shoulder. There was a thunderstorm inside her. Her entire wet body was throbbing and spasming like she'd turned into her vagina, all of her that one beautifully, blessedly pleasured organ.

The buzzing in her ears grew loud, loud enough to be clanging, like shrill metallic gongs resonating through her, slicing through the erotic fog wrapped tightly around them.

Shit.

It was her door.

Not the euphemistic one they'd thrown open with such abandon. The real one.

They disengaged slowly. She removed her leg from his shoulder and he rose up to standing. Her hand dug into his shoulder
to keep her body from sliding down her door, because her legs
hadn't reclaimed their strength yet. His eyes were disoriented,
like those of a man pulled from an abyss midfall.

This was the second time he'd left her satisfied and acted as
though he were the one buzzing with pleasure. She wanted to
touch his face. She wanted to touch other parts of him, know
what it was like when he came apart. She wanted to see that. Just
once in her life. Just once.

The bells went off again. Loud and clanging.

Body still pressed between the door and him, Naina raised
an arm and pushed her fingers into the keypad next to her head.

"Who is it?" She sounded breathy. Like her vocal cords had
just been blown out.

Well, duh.

"Why it always takes so much long to answer door?"

Every inch of Naina wilted. Actually wilted in his arms like
flowers left in a vase too long, and she could feel his body register
it. Every bit of it. She pushed off him, but he didn't let her go, his
hands lingering on her as though he didn't know how to.

"Mummy." She swallowed, hoping that the panic inside her
didn't show.

The way his eyes darkened meant it did. He saw. She did a
desperate wiggle and he released her. "Mummy! What are you
doing here?"

"What question is that? Why Mummy can't come over?" Her
mother sounded indignant. Indignation had replaced fluttering
as her favorite mode these days.

Vansh seemed to be trying to figure out how someone like

Chandni Kohli had created someone like Naina, and it made a horrible coldness spread inside Naina where pleasure had just warmed her.

"I'm . . ." He watched her struggle to tell her mother she was busy. She couldn't.

The nod he gave her said he understood her despair. How could he possibly understand with how close he was to his family? If Naina let herself think about how different their families were, she wouldn't be able to figure out what to do next. As it was, trying to process in her mother's presence what had just happened between them was going to be impossible.

It wasn't like he'd never seen her sadness before. Or her rage. Or every ugly feeling inside her. Nonetheless, she hated how clearly he saw it all now.

"It's okay, I'll go inside," he whispered, and she had that sense again, as though she wanted to touch his cheek, cling to his arm, hold on to him.

"Mummy doesn't have all day, Naina, only few minutes. Hurry, hurry. This is important. What for you're being such slowpoke?"

"Sorry, Mummy. I'm buzzing you in." She pressed the buzzer and they ran to the bedroom, which in her tiny apartment was ten steps away. It was a San Francisco apartment. There were no hiding places.

"Where will you hide?"

"In the bathroom?"

"She might be here because she needs to use the bathroom."

"Good point. The closet?" There was a knock on the door. "Don't worry. Just go. I won't let her find me. I promise." He kept promising her impossible things.

She turned to go, panic rising inside her. She kept believing his promises. Idiot. *Idiot.*

"Knightlina." The name he tended to use to cheer her up, spoken in a voice that said cheering her up was important to him.

She turned.

"Sneaking around turns me on."

A smile broke across her face. "Is there anything that doesn't turn you on?" Saying those words made her lady parts contract again. Or maybe it was the smile he gave her. All dimples and white teeth and simmering honey eyes.

Without waiting for an answer, she left, smile still tugging at her lips even as she tried to pry her mind away from things she could not be thinking when she opened the door for her mother.

"You all wet!" It was the first thing her mother said, and Naina almost burst out laughing. *Oh, Mummy! If only you knew.*

"I just got home after getting caught in the rain."

Her mother tut-tutted. "You should take umbrella!" She shook her own floral-print umbrella out and left it by the door. "You can keep."

"I have an umbrella, Mummy. You don't need to leave yours behind."

Her mother didn't argue, but Naina knew the umbrella wasn't leaving her apartment today. Mummy was also carrying a giant canvas bag that smelled like heaven. A food delivery. Naina wondered what she'd done to warrant a food delivery. She took it from her.

"I want you to stop eating all those unhealthy type things. So, I brought all healthy type food. Best diet. One-week supply. Next week, I bring again. Then in one month. Down to healthy weight. Slim and trim. Like Naina Kohli of before."

Everything made sense now. An intervention for Naina's "weight problem."

Naina wanted to groan, but the food did smell really, really good, and maybe eating healthy Mummy-made food instead of pizza and takeout was exactly what she needed. She put the bag on her kitchen counter and thanked her mother.

"Are you on your way somewhere?"

Mummy was wearing one of her silk zardozi kurtis. This one was printed with large purple and gold paisleys and embroidered in gold thread.

Her mother spun around to display her outfit. "Very beautiful, no? I can have made for you also. Maybe in less bright color for darker skin tone than Mummy."

Naina smiled, her mind sliding to the mind-bending orgasm she'd just had. That was the answer. That was what she needed to keep her mind on. A distraction from everything. Why had she not tried that before?

Because there was no Vansh before.

"Oh, and one more thing before I go to do lunch with Mina." She put an envelope on the countertop and patted it. "I did print-outs."

"You're having lunch with Mina Auntie?"

"We're doing lunches always once in while." For the first time that day her mother's hand fluttered near her chest. "Mina is worrying, I think."

Worried about what? But Naina didn't say it. She wasn't sure she wanted to open this particular Pandora's box her mother had taken to bringing to all their conversations. Especially not today.

"Any mummy will worry, no? If young boy is like that way."

Still not taking the bait.

Not that her mother needed responses to keep going.

"Yash and Vansh. So much difference in stress. One all settled. So stable. *Governor.* Can you believe?" Her voice crescendoed.

Yes, Mummy, I can believe. I was the one he threw off his wagon on his way to that goal. But, nope, not saying that.

"Then there's Vansh. Here today, there tomorrow, everywhere." Her hand made bouncing motions, and her voice reverberated with disappointment.

Naina knew she had accused Vansh of the same thing. Being fickle with his projects. That did not make him unstable, though. It did not make him undependable. Since Naina suspected she knew where this was going, standing up for Vansh would only tip the panic dominoes.

"People talk, you know." Her mother hadn't even made it all the way inside the apartment, but she'd already been down her list of talking points.

1. Weight problem.
2. Marriage problem.
3. Working-with-the-ex's-brother problem.

Only Naina wasn't just working with Vansh, was she? She was on orgasm number two.

To say nothing of the ones Riz had assisted her with. Or needed to barely assist with, thanks to Mr. Dimples and Pecs in her closet having taken residence in her dreams.

"You have to make response, Naina. That's why with Yash it not work out. You don't say, you keep inside." She patted her heart. "You keep all thoughts only on work things. If you don't keep up conversation, how you will talk to rishtas?"

That was an easy one. She wasn't going to be talking to any of these marriage prospects Mummy was intent on digging up from the far reaches of her extended family's network. "I don't know what you want me to say."

"Mina wants for you to stop work with Vansh."

That couldn't be true. Could it? "Did Mina Auntie say that to you?"

Mummy glared. "Not always one has to say in words. She doesn't like all such things either."

"All we're doing is working on a project to empower women

and provide support to homeless people. What such things?" And now she was a liar.

Not that their mothers would ever know that. As far as they were concerned, as far as anyone was concerned, there were no "all such things" between Vansh and Naina, and there were never going to be. Ever.

"Why you have to work with him? You know Dr. Kohli doesn't like either." And there it was, the real problem. Always Dr. Kohli.

"It's really cold in these wet clothes. I need to change. Do you want to stay and have tea while I change?"

Mummy looked at her Rolex (to "match Mina's same-to-same," except Mina Auntie's was probably an antique handed down the ancestral chain). "Cannot. Ten minutes only I have to be there. I will tell Mina you said you think about not working with Yash's brother."

"Please don't." But she shouldn't have said it, because her mother reddened.

"Why? Why you always have to make difficult, Naina? Why Mummy can't have peace? What I did to deserve no peace? Any time?"

Naina really was getting cold, all the way down to her bones. There was nowhere good this conversation could go. Her mother's peace was too tied up with things Naina couldn't give her.

"I'm sorry," Naina said. "We'll talk later, okay? I won't do anything that will embarrass you or Mina Auntie."

Her mother heaved a sigh of relief and squeezed Naina's arm. Why that made Naina feel so tied up in knots, she would never know.

"Look at pictures I brought for you. I know you don't look when I send on phone, so I make print. For you. For you, Naina. He very good boy. Promise me you look."

Naina nodded, and her mother patted her cheek and left.

When Naina opened the door to her closet, sadness was lodged inside her again.

The sight of Vansh on the floor of her closet tucked behind her clothes made a smile wobble in her heart, sunshine through clouds.

"I love these," he said as she pulled him to his feet, pointing to the cushion covers he'd been sitting on. The bright green and magenta ones her mother had stripped off her couch and replaced with her "polished" grays.

If Naina had been sad before, looking at those cushion covers cracked her in half. It didn't take much self-awareness to know that her reactions were outsized right now. Old wounds with their scabs plucked off. Her emotions would subside soon enough, settle the way they always did.

Without answering, she pulled out a T-shirt and joggers for herself and found a large-ish T-shirt from a fundraising run last year for Vansh.

"Sorry. You were probably cold in there." She handed him the shirt and a towel.

"I wouldn't describe how I'm feeling as cold," he said, picking up on her mood as he always did and trying yet again to shake her out of it.

She pushed past him into the bathroom and changed into dry clothes.

"What did your mother want?" he asked from outside her door as though they changed clothes around each other all the time.

Not that they were changing clothes around each other. Technically, there was a door between them. He hadn't seen her naked yet. He'd just had his tongue up in all parts of her. Her thighs squeezed together. *Stop it.*

Don't do all such things, her mother's voice said in her ear.

When she let herself out of the bathroom, he was drying his

hair with her towel, whilst shirtless. Whilst shirtless with that body. That body with cuts in places she'd never seen cuts before. Even through clothes it was hard and smooth, with ridges that filled her hands. Bare, it was just too much.

Turning as fast as she could, Naina made her escape into her kitchen, hands feeling bereft and emptier than they had ever felt in her life.

Chapter Twenty-One

Vansh followed Naina to the kitchen, pulling on the shirt she'd handed him as he went. It felt a little bit like he'd been dismissed. Or like he'd done something that touched her. He never seemed to know which it was with her these days.

Her kitchen was a wonderfully warm and tidy space that suddenly smelled like someone had spent days cooking for a feast. An oversized canvas bag sat on the countertop, emitting the most delicious aromas of fire-grilled tandoori chicken and naan.

"Your mother stopped by to bring you food? It smells amazing." His stomach let out a growl. It had been a while since he'd eaten. In fact, he'd worked out and then left to meet Naina and hadn't had time to eat.

"Are you hungry?" The nod she gave the food was too sad by half.

"Are you kidding me? I know what your mother's food tastes like. I'm starving."

"You haven't eaten anything all day, have you?"

"I just forgot."

"I can't believe I'm going to say this, but . . . Vansh, you look great." She said that as though it were news she was afraid to break to him.

He grinned. "I am aware."

She rolled her eyes. "I mean you don't have to starve yourself."

"I like looking good."

"No kidding." Finally a real smile. "My point is . . . What I'm trying to say is—" His grin grew wider and she shook her head. "God, you're totally going to take this the wrong way." He loved how she tried to control her reactions to him just so she wouldn't swell his head. He loved how she could never quite manage it. "But, well," she went on, "you'd still look good if your body wasn't this perfect."

"You think my body is perfect?" That heavy/light arousal was back in his limbs, tightening his gut.

It was a small kitchen, and somehow he was standing too close to her again. She raised her hand to push him away but then seemed to think better of touching him.

Turning to the canvas bag, she pulled out a foil package. The smoky, buttery smell of naan made the different types of hunger coursing inside him mix together.

"Does your mom actually make naan at home?"

She opened the packet and held it in front of his nose, and he picked one up and shoved it in his mouth and almost died on the spot from the chewy, yeasty deliciousness.

"Mummy's made it since before homemade naan was a trend. My parents have always had an old-fashioned tandoor oven in the house. Because Dr. Kohli needs his naan and kababs." The brightness sparkling in her eyes dimmed.

She grabbed a couple of plates—bright yellow hand-painted stoneware. Naina Kohli of the gray and beige couture loved bright colors.

"Do you want me to take the food out of the bag?" he asked.

"Thanks."

For a few moments the olfactory overload was almost too

much to bear. There were ten plastic and foil containers with all varieties of kababs. She'd even cut salads.

"All of this looks terribly healthy." Not at all the heavy food Vansh associated with Punjabi cuisine.

Naina smiled. He'd never met anyone who could hide quite so much anger and heartbreak in a smile. "It's a stereotype. Sure, Punjabis love their makhan and malai, but they can eat healthy too. Especially when they're trying to get their women to stay *slim and trim*."

She threw a look at the food and then at herself.

"I have no idea what that look is supposed to mean."

"You're very sweet, Vansh." This time her smile was genuine and touched, as though he'd melted her heart a little bit. He'd take it, even though he had no idea why it was being bestowed. "I've gained a little weight since the breakup, and Mummy thinks it's her job to help me get back 'into shape.'"

What was she talking about? "You're literally the hottest woman I've ever met."

She laughed. "It's good to know that horniness makes you blind."

That was the most ridiculous of all her accusations, but he couldn't argue about how much she turned him on. Before he could say more, she started popping the food in the microwave. Clearly, she didn't want to take that conversation any further. She was done with it.

"Mummy wasn't just dropping off the food. She was also dropping off pictures of 'boys.'"

"Boys?" He took the heated food to the breakfast bar. "Let me see." He searched the room and found an envelope.

They both lunged for it together. He reached it first, and her arms wrapped around him trying to pry it from his hands.

"Vansh!" She sounded desperately embarrassed even as she laughed. "Why do you want to see?"

Having her laugh in his arms was a sensation that scrambled his brain, and he let the envelope go. Sitting in a closet by himself had been enough to calm him down, but before that he'd almost spent in his jeans for the second time with her.

"Maybe I can help you choose."

"I should let you. So you can lose your appetite too and not finish all my food." She sat down on one of the two bar stools and piled kababs on their plates. "Do you think she brought food and the pictures together knowing I'd lose my appetite? 'New weight-loss idea!'" she said in her Chandni Auntie voice.

"Come on. They can't be that bad. And this smell is giving me a . . ." *Don't say hard-on.* He didn't say it, but he had a feeling she heard it nonetheless. He bit into a bright red tandoori drumstick and let out a moan. "Okay, definitely a hard-on."

She punched his arm and they ate in silence for a while, because . . . because what words could get in the way of this? They kept piling each other's plate with naan and chutney and perfectly seasoned melt-in-your-mouth pieces of goat and chicken. "This is food your mother brings you when she wants you to eat less?"

Her laugh seemed to come from the deepest part of her, and he felt like the king of the world.

When there wasn't an iota of space left inside him, he walked his fingers toward the envelope still sitting on the black granite.

"Fine." Naina shrugged. "At least someone is excited about those pictures."

Not waiting for her to change her mind, Vansh slid the pictures out of the envelope.

A man with intense eyes and a sharp blue Sikh turban smiled uncomfortably for the camera.

"He's kind of hot."

Naina spurted out a laugh and choked on the piece of cucumber in her mouth.

Leaning into her, he started rubbing her back. They both laughed until they teared up.

"Let me guess. Doctor?"

"Even better. 'Surgeon—the general one, like Shree . . .'" Again she used her mother's voice, and Vansh whistled. "'Widowed . . .'"

"Ooh, exciting!"

"'And the best part . . . . childless!'"

"No! Seriously? Where did she even find him?"

Despite her laughter, her shrug was sad. "No idea. I didn't even know childless widowed surgeons were still being manufactured." Her smile got weighed down with hurt, but not in a terrible way. She had so many shades of sad. "Almost makes me wish I was in the market," she added, voice light.

"You're not?"

She looked horrified. "God, no! Not ever. Not even a little bit."

He almost asked why she didn't tell her parents that, but he wasn't stupid. Of course she had. Probably multiple times.

For a while they sat there. Comfort, discomfort, anger, laughter, all of it strewn on that breakfast bar and mixed in with an embarrassingly small quantity of leftovers. They'd gone at the food like starving scavengers.

"Will you tell me something, Naina?"

She gave him no more than a lazy blink, but he could tell that she was wide open, loosened by food and laughter. Strangely filled up, if he could project his own feelings for a second.

"Why did you and Yash break up?"

A sip of water. An angry swallow. "Technically it wasn't a breakup. We ended our arrangement. And I answered that already when you asked me before. Watch the press conference. I'll send you the link."

"I've watched the press conference. I mean, what's the real story?"

Her eyes went round, over-the-top faux shock, because he was pushing a line. But it also meant she was letting him. "Are you accusing your brother of lying? I thought the word on the street was that Yash Raje never lies." She loud-whispered that last part.

He fucking loved it when she was like this, unguarded, light with her fearlessness, bright with it.

Sure, Naina was the ballsiest woman Vansh had ever met—which, given his family, was something—but she was a damn fortress when it came to her feelings or acknowledging emotions. More than anyone he knew.

Not right now though. Right now he knew she'd give him anything he asked for. What he wanted most, more than anything he'd ever wanted, struck him with a sudden powerful flash of clarity. The time to hold back was gone.

"Did he?" he said, meeting her eyes. "Did Yash lie? I'm asking for Naina Kohli's side of it."

Chapter Twenty-Two

Naina had to laugh at Vansh's question. He looked so sincere. She felt a prickle of something she couldn't identify. Sadness? Tenderness? She should probably have made the effort to hide it, but with how satisfied her body was with food and other things, she felt reckless.

"Wow. What game are you playing, bud? Didn't you know that Naina Kohli's side doesn't matter?"

He didn't smile, which made her smile fizzle out too.

"I'm asking, Naina. Tell me." His voice had a silken quality to it. His whisperer voice. He would have made a good vet. Able to soothe animals, lull them away from pain and panic before shoving killing serum into their veins when they were too sick to live.

That last one seemed more appealing than answering his question.

"Why are you asking, though? What difference does it make?"

He didn't answer that. He just looked at her as though the question were an insult. An insult to whom? she wondered.

For a while she said nothing. There wasn't much to say. Except that both she and his brother had lied, but also, neither of them had lied.

"What is it specifically that you want to know?"

"All of it."

How did you tell someone things you'd never spoken out loud? How did you tell someone that your parents had looked at you as a burden they needed to get off their hands for as long as you could remember? How did you tell someone what it felt like to never stand up for yourself because the person who was supposed to protect you knew the way to control you was to hurt someone you loved?

There he sat at her kitchen table, beautiful eyes filled with the need to understand. If she told him, would the way he saw her change? Suddenly she had to know if it would. That was possibly why she told him. All of it.

How the only way to push back with her father and to get him to let her do things she wanted to do was to use Yash. The excitement she had felt when she'd been accepted into the fellowship in Nepal. Ten people from over fifty thousand applicants around the world had been chosen. From the moment Naina heard about the program, that was where she'd wanted to do her doctoral work. It was all she had wanted. It had gripped her soul. Infested her dreams.

"*Absolutely not.*" Those were the words her father had said. "*You're twenty-eight. You've spent enough time on this rebellion against me. You will marry and then you and your husband can decide what you can and cannot do.*"

She hadn't expected pride or congratulations, she wasn't that reckless with her hope, but the absolute dismissal of her dreams—that had killed something inside her that day. Finally snuffed her out.

In its place had risen a girl who had looked her father straight in the eye and told him a bloodless lie. "*I will only ever marry Yash, and Yash doesn't want to marry until he's won his next election.*"

They had been at Nisha's wedding reception in Sripore. A time of joy, a time when the Rajes had virtually burst with love and laughter. Naina had watched as Shree Uncle held his daughters and teared up as Nisha did her bridal thing. Mina Auntie and Ashna's mother, Shobi Auntie, had lectured the girls about not losing their identities when they became wives. So much wisdom and support.

All the while Mummy had fluttered, terrified that Naina might tell her father to go to hell and then go to Nepal without his blessing, leaving her to consequences Naina had never been strong enough to ignore.

It had been a cruel joke that Naina had received the email accepting her into the program at that particular moment in time. Or maybe it had been her luckiest break. She'd made the announcement to her father without asking Yash, knowing he'd back her up. Knowing Yash had no interest in a relationship either.

Yash had always hated the way Naina's father treated her. He'd always been angry that she'd never had her family's support. Naina had believed that he shared her righteous anger enough to help her. Truth was she had never stopped to ask him if he would.

It had felt like a safe assumption that her impulsive declaration that Yash and she were in a relationship benefited them both. Yash had been in a terrible accident at fifteen when a car had crashed into his bike. It had left him in a wheelchair that doctors told him he'd never get out of. It had taken Yash all of a year to prove them wrong, but after that he'd only ever been interested in showing the world that nothing was going to get in the way of his ambitions. He had shown no interest in women or relationships since the accident. Things had only gotten worse when an intern who worked for him had drugged him and recorded them having sex. That had convinced him once and for all that he couldn't trust his own judgment when it came to women.

Naina had stood by him like a rock. Having her in his corner publicly had given Yash the optics he needed. It had helped his political career. She'd told herself she was helping a friend. In hindsight it was clear they'd both just used each other to get what they needed at the time.

For ten years their arrangement had worked. All the optics with none of the emotional labor of a real relationship. Then India Dashwood had come along, just when Jiggy Mehta had offered Naina the endowment. For the first time since they'd gotten into their arrangement, what they wanted had been at odds with each other and their lies. Yash had chosen India. Naina was pretty certain it had never even been a choice.

Her ego had been publicly shredded. Even though Yash had tried his best to be gentle, to stay her friend. Even when she hadn't shown him the same courtesy.

"Were you ever in love with Yash?" Vansh asked when she finished, his eyes intense as he hit at what he thought was the heart of it.

"That doesn't matter."

"What does that even mean?"

"It means I can't."

It was clear from his face that he had absolutely no idea what she was talking about. "Same question as before: what does that mean?" He truly had beautiful eyes. Perfectly shaped, wide with a slight uptilt at the edges like rotated commas. Even without that thick forest of lashes and the gold flecks in the amber irises, they were dramatically beautiful. But it was the deep caring in them, the ability to zero in on you and connect, that made them devastating.

"I'm not built to be in love."

"Ah."

She wanted to shake him and his cornucopia of *ah*s. "I know that's hard for people like you to wrap your head around, but love is not the real world to me. It's a fantasy. In the logical part of my brain, I get that it exists. I see your parents. I see your siblings. I get that they believe themselves in love. I just don't function that way. It's like vampires."

"Vampires," he repeated.

"I get what that word means. I totally understand it. But in that deep place where we know if things are fact or fantasy, I know that they aren't real."

His response was to continue to watch her. He knew she wasn't done and he was waiting, the gold in his eyes picking up the sunlight streaming into her kitchen.

"It's a matter of base beliefs," she explained. "Like God. That's the opposite of the vampire thing. I have no idea who God is. No one can tell you for sure what he, she, they are, tangibly. But deep inside I know something larger than me exists. To people like you, the concept of love is like the concept of God. Fundamentally possible. Even in the absence of proof. For people like me, the concept of love is like the concept of a vampire. Fundamentally fictitious. Even if someone were to present proof."

"Wow," he said finally. "You've given this a lot of thought."

She got off her stool and started to put away the leftovers.

He followed and started to help, taking the dishes to the sink and washing them. "So, what you're saying is that you were never actually in love with my brother."

The question got on her very last nerve. "I love Yash as much as I can love anyone."

Putting the dishes on the drying rack, he turned and leaned his hip on the sink, and met her eyes from beneath those lashes. "But you've never been moved to come against his thigh."

The plastic container slipped from Naina's hands, scattering slivered onions all over her floor. "Oh my God, Vansh! Are you ever going to stop bringing that up casually in conversation? What is wrong with you? I was inebriated."

He squatted and started picking up the onions. He did not remind her that what they'd just done against her door had happened while she was quite *un*-ebriated. But it was in his eyes.

"I wasn't exactly thinking." She wiped the floor as he picked up the last onion piece.

They were squatting face-to-face in her tiny kitchen, their knees almost touching, and there was something a little too intimate about it.

"Do you realize?" He leaned closer, as though sharing a secret. "That's actually a really good thing sometimes."

A groan escaped her. "Are we really having this conversation? You think just because—"

"You used my body to jack off," he offered helpfully.

Heat rose up her cheeks and she stood. "I don't think that's what it's called for women." She sounded quite unaffected, thank you very much.

"My fault. What is the right term?" He had the gall to scratch the back of his head, his thinking-hard pose. "Rub the nub? Diddling Ms. Daisy? *Ménage à moi?*"

She hated that she started laughing. Hard. "You're incorrigible." She punched his shoulder. "And your attempts at embarrassing me are terribly ignoble."

He stood too, body loose with laughter, and too close for comfort. "Quit using Old English to distract me. Also, you need to work on those tells, Knightlina."

"I'm terrified to ask."

"Well, Old English is your crutch when you're uncomfortable. But we digress."

She raised a brow, but she would not step back. "Conversely, you get crass when you enjoy someone's discomfort more than you should."

"Actually, I think it's fabulous that you're comfortable enough to . . . umm . . . jill off on my body."

"I'll bet." It had gotten hot in there, but she was still not step-ping back.

His eyes, that's where the heat was coming from. "Are you saying thinking about it doesn't make you want to do it again?"

She had no answer to that question. Truth was, she wasn't sure. Before she responded he raised a hand to stop her. "Don't bother to lie, it's simple enough to disprove."

That too she was aware of. He had disproved it very recently and thoroughly against her front door.

He tucked a loose lock behind her ear and the tenderness of it trembled down her body. "What I'm saying, Naina, is that I really liked doing that with you."

She stepped back and walked around the breakfast bar, put-ting a few feet of solid stone between them like she should have done before this conversation got so out of hand. "Vansh, we can never do that again."

He leaned into the bar, arm muscles popping—on purpose, she'd bet her life on it. "Or we can do it a few times more."

"You cannot be serious!"

"Hear me out, I'm perfectly serious. Look how comfortable we are with each other. Have you ever been this comfortable with someone and still been on fire like this?"

Her only response was a gulp that got stuck mid-swallow. He thought she was comfortable right now? How did *he* look so relaxed? No twenty-six-year-old had the right to look this comfortable in his skin. *Be* this comfortable in his—absurdly gorgeous—skin.

"We both enjoyed what's happened between us. We both want it again." He waited, as though giving her a chance to disagree, but she couldn't get words out. "So we enjoy it for a bit," he con-tinued, "and then we move on. Because look at us. We're talking about it. Two friends. Two adults. With no strings, no expecta-tions to mess things up."

Dear Lord, was he thinking about another arrangement? "The last time I got into an arrangement, I ended up publicly humiliated." *By your brother!*

He had the audacity to shrug. "That was because: One"—he started counting off on his fingers—"you dragged it out for ten years. Two, it was public. Three, you didn't spend any time with each other or communicate. Four, it wasn't about sex. Five—"

"Stop. Fine. God. Has anyone told you that you really know how to flog a dead horse?"

"You're doing it again. Because seriously, who says 'flog a dead horse' anymore?"

She harrumphed and felt like a rheumy old grandfather. "Anyone who is long enough past adolescence."

"Say less." He grinned, then rolled his eyes when she made a face. It was impossible to explain quite how differently an eye roll hit when one had a forest of lashes. "Fine. Let me speak Naina to you: may I lay this out?"

"Could I stop you even if I tried?"

"Nary a chance. So here's a plan for your . . . for your . . ."

"Perusal?"

"Yes! Peruse this: One, we'd put a time limit on it. I'm going to be ready to move on from California in . . . six months. One year tops. As you said, I don't commit to projects. I leave before I get any skin in the game."

"I didn't mean—"

"Stay with me, Knightlina. You were right. I'm agreeing with you here."

"Fine."

"Even if I decide to stay—"

"You're already contradicting yourself."

"No, I'm not. What I'm saying is even if I stay, we set a time limit and stop."

"Stop what exactly?" She couldn't believe they were having this conversation, but now that they were, the least she could do was find out exactly what he was proposing.

"One step at a time. We'll get to the details soon enough."

Waving her arms as if to say, *Do go on*, Naina went to her couch and dropped into it.

"Two, we tell no one. I mean, we literally have the nosiest families in all the universe, so we zip it and sneak around. Admit it, pushing me into the closet to hide me from your mom was exciting. Have you ever snuck around being bad? It's really fun."

"Sometimes I wonder at what manner of life you've been living, Baby Prince."

He sat down next to her. "Really? I didn't think I'd have to sell the secret thing."

"You don't. I'd rather poke my eyes out than watch your sisters bleed at the pain of their little brother being chewed up by the barracuda."

"Are they that bad?"

Worse. Until The Breakup, the Raje sisters had been lovely to her, albeit a bit distantly fawning. Since the breakup, she'd all but stopped existing. "It's natural for them to hate me, Vansh." Although, really, it wasn't.

"They do not hate you."

"Let's carry on."

His eyes lit up as though he'd already convinced her. He seriously needed to learn the fine art of not jumping the gun.

"Gladly." He stuck out his counting fingers again. "Three, you're easy to talk to, Knightlina. I like talking to you. Talking to you is as much fun as having my thigh jacked—sorry, jilled—off upon."

"Can I stop you there for one moment and mention that if you say 'jill off' one more time, I'm going to punch you?"

"See, you have no problem telling me exactly what you want. We communicate communicate communicate. Keep those channels open while we"—he wiggled his brows—"explore other channels."

"Vansh! I do not believe you just said that."

He blew on his knuckles. "I live to amuse you, m'lady. And the last one is the easiest. Four, sex is sex. We keep it separate from the rest of it."

"And how, pray tell, do we do that?"

"Easy. We stay focused. We admit how badly we want each other. I mean, we already know this is about us not wanting to keep our hands off each other." Their hands were inches apart on the bright yellow linen of the couch, and he was not wrong, the tug was a tidal force. "It's already out there in the open. Nothing to hide, nothing to prove."

Except nothing was ever that easy. How could anything possibly be as easy as it felt with him?

This was Vansh. *Vansh.*

"How old were you at Nisha's wedding?" Those were the first words that popped into her head. The only response that felt like it might derail him, shut off where her own brain was going.

It made her withdraw into herself and pull away from him.

His hand followed hers as she pulled away. *How does it matter?* That was the question in his eyes, but he didn't ask it. "Sixteen," he said simply.

I don't remember you at all, she wanted to say. Because she didn't. All she remembered from back then was anger. Rage. The constant sense that she wanted to break something but didn't know how to.

"I don't even remember being sixteen. Actually, that's a lie. I do remember. When I was sixteen my father sat me down and let me know that I was not permitted to date. Not ever. That no daughter of his would be a whore. That as soon as I had a degree,

I'd be getting married. That was the first time I told him I was only interested in Yash."

Every time she mentioned his brother, she had the urge to search his face. How could it feel this irrelevant that Yash was his brother? It wasn't irrelevant. It couldn't be.

All she saw in his face was openness as he waited for more. He was the ocean. Whatever piece of her pain she tossed at it disappeared into it like a pebble.

"I remember my father's eyes lighting up," she continued. "The loathing in his eyes when he'd warned me against being a whore turned to excitement when I mentioned Yash."

Over the years, Dr. Kohli had brought it up several times. "*I'll talk to Shree,*" he had said. "*We can set it all up.*"

Her response had always been panic. "*You know how ambitious Yash is. He doesn't even want to think about marriage yet,*" she'd told him year after year, the lies coming easy. Unsurprising, given that the very soul of their family was his lies.

"*It makes sense that he wants to establish himself in his work first.*" That's what he always said about Yash, while not affording Naina the same understanding.

She'd been twenty-eight when she'd gotten into the arrangement with Yash. That should have been old enough to be able to do whatever she wanted with her life. The fact that she'd been working for the Ford Foundation and doing postdoc work should have meant something to her father. It hadn't. Not even a little bit.

She was thirty-eight now. Too old to get into another arrangement. But Yash and she hadn't sat down face-to-face like this. They hadn't talked about it. That had never been an option.

She was thirty-eight. Too old to not know what to do when a man this beautiful was scooting closer to her because he knew how irresistible he was. Why should she resist him?

"This has nothing to do with your father. This is about nothing but us. Just you and me. And what we want," he said with a sincerity that made her want to forget that the world was not a safe place. "I can't stop thinking about—" He paused, as though it was important for him to get it right, to say the thing that would convince her, to not say the thing that would scare her away. "You against that door. You against my tongue. You against my thigh."

Her lips parted, and her breath came out heavy and hot. She hadn't stopped thinking about it either. It was an undercurrent, a substructure to all her thoughts since the moment it had happened. Which made it dangerous.

"You're never going to stop using that against me, are you?"

He was inches from her now, and she saw every dirty thought that flashed in his mind in his eyes. "The only thing I want to use against you is my thigh, and my tongue, and my hand. Again and again. It's beautiful to watch you come, Knightlina."

How she could speak right now, she didn't know. "Don't call me that."

"I won't if you don't like it. I won't do anything unless you like it."

How was it fair that someone who looked like him had such a filthy mouth? How was it fair how much she liked it?

"I don't like it." She hated that name. "Or I don't when . . ."

"When anyone else uses it. I get it. It's okay to like things when I do them. It's my gift. I'm impossible not to like."

"Oh my God, Vansh." He went from hot to silly like it was nothing, winding her up, then unfurling her. Heat and warmth. Laughter and more emotion than she could contain. "You know what your gift is? Arrogance." But she wanted to stroke the smile splitting his face.

"Damn straight I'm arrogant. How could I not be when someone like you finds it impossible to resist me?"

"I can resist you just fine."

"Why though? Who's asking you to? Aren't we adults?"

"I've seen you in diapers, Vansh!"

"I haven't been in diapers for a very long time, Naina."

"I was going to be your sister-in-law. Your family will kill me."

"I didn't say I wanted to fuck you when you were going to be my sister-in-law. I didn't even look at you when you were with Yash. Even though you were never with Yash. I didn't even think about you that way. I swear. This is about you and me. No one else."

"Mina Auntie will fillet me."

He cupped her cheek and her entire body sank into his touch. "Hey, Ma loves you. She always has."

She had to drop a kiss on his lips, because for all his dirty talk, he saw what mattered to her, what made her ache. The idea that Mina Auntie might not love her anymore killed her. Her fear shivered on her mouth and he sucked in her lower lip, soothing her. He dragged kisses along her jaw, whisper soft. He heated her blood even as he stroked her senses, calming her.

"What if I hurt you?" she whispered as he pulled her onto his lap and she straddled him, their bodies moving and fitting with the kind of ease that baffled her. "Mina Auntie would never forgive me if I hurt you. I can't have her hate me. She's . . . I just can't have her hate me." How was she even thinking about this with what was at stake?

"I'm a big boy, Knightlina." He dropped a kiss behind her ear on a spot that connected directly to a spot between her thighs, where she was already pressed close enough to know exactly how big of a boy he was.

He smiled against her lips and she knew he'd guessed her thoughts. He pushed himself into her, the thin cotton joggers doing nothing to keep the friction of him in his jeans from stroking her into a frenzy too fast. What was it about him?

"No one has to know." His thumb stroked her lips, which were trembling with arousal as she rocked against him. The friction of him, hard and rough against her soft and yielding center. It washed through her like a drug. "We're working together for a short time. We're horny as hell for each other. We're both not interested in anything long-term. How can you deny how good it is between us?"

She tried to come up with a way to deny it, but she couldn't. "What if you fall in love with me?"

"I thought love was a lie." He was rocking into her too. An erotic rhythm that dilated his eyes, made the dark centers huge. "I won't. I won't fall in love with you. I've never been in love. You're right. It's a lie." He was breathless and she was too close to splintering.

This wasn't happening again. Not this way. This wasn't going to be one-sided again. She wasn't going to be the only one screaming her pleasure this time.

"It's a deal," she breathed through a moan, getting off him and reaching for his zipper. "Any ideas for how we might seal the deal?"

Kicking off his jeans, he rolled over her. "I have some ideas, Knightlina," he said, deliciously winded, "and I think you might like them."

Chapter Twenty-Three

Is something going on between Vansh and Naina?" Sid asked as he and Esha made their way down her favorite trail on the estate.

Sid met her on the trail almost every day now. Vansh had invited him to roam the estate at will and photograph all the resident birds.

Esha threw a glance up at the sky. Still no Garuda.

"Not anymore. Yash is with India now. And his engagement with Naina wasn't real." She must have sounded absent or preoccupied again, because he smiled and followed her gaze. Much as she craved his visits, lived for them, she'd never get used to how she felt around him. How she'd taken to feeling even when he wasn't around. Her mind still, quiet, able to take in the world. It had happened slowly. Other people's voices and feelings fading away. It was disorienting.

But also wonderful.

He was the most observant person Esha had ever met. People studying her reactions was something she was more than used to, but there was a singular attentiveness to Sid, an alertness.

While everyone else was always only trying to make sure she

wasn't going to collapse into a convulsing heap, or trying to figure out what she saw inside them, Sid was constantly aware of what she might be feeling. What she might need. Curious about what thought might've flown through her mind. Or what reaction she might've had to something he said. Or how the beautiful sights they were passing might affect her.

"I do know that Yash was in some sort of relationship with Naina and that they've been best friends since forever," he said, amusement threading through his voice. "I'm talking about Vansh. The younger of your two brothers." She loved that he always said *brothers*, never *cousins*. He understood what her family was to her. "Vansh, whom I'm working with on the San Francisco project. I think he and Naina are more than just friends."

"Sorry, I thought you said Yash." Saying those words made her irrationally happy. Getting things wrong made her irrationally happy. "Really? Vansh and Naina? Is that weird?"

He shrugged. "They don't feel weird together. Just happy."

Having him tell her that also made her irrationally happy.

She looked up at the sky, feeling like she wanted to spin around. Out of habit she searched the cottony clouds for Garuda. But still no sign of him.

"You're distracted today. Why do you keep looking at the sky? Are you searching for the Brahminy kite?"

She stumbled and his grip on her hand tightened, keeping her from falling. She pulled her hand away and he let her go.

"Are you ever going to tell me what the deal is with that kite?" He didn't add that she had told him nothing about herself. None of the truths that suddenly felt like stories she'd made up. Not how much of a miracle this was, their walking on the estate together, her having so many thoughts.

With the thoughts of others gone from her mind, there was suddenly space inside her that she could fill with whatever she wanted. And sometimes she didn't like the thoughts that flooded in.

She started walking again. Discomfort flared in her chest. When they walked around the estate, one of Sid's favorite things to do was to name all the flora and fauna (his favorite phrase) on the trails. He loved to tell her the histories of where they had originated and how they had ended up in Northern California, or some myth or legend associated with each, or a personal experience.

For a person whose work involved being quiet forever and ever, he was full of stories. All his stories had to do with this thing he loved, that consumed him. Nature.

"Is it only about the kite?"

He didn't stop walking but he stiffened the slightest bit. It had become her favorite thing, studying his reactions, decoding the language of his body—gestures, expressions, modulations, all of it speaking to her, meaning something. A something that drew from an entire vocabulary of meanings, and she couldn't stop deciphering and deciphering him.

"This." She stopped and waved a hand around her. She'd never been a gesticulator, needing to keep her actions contained to keep everything from unraveling her. The action felt much less alien than it had felt at first. "The fact that you come to see me." The fact that he had climbed her balcony because he'd seen Garuda rolled over inside her. "Is *this*"—us—"only about finding a bird?"

Had she been an idiot? Had she trusted him, actually allowed herself to unravel because he was obsessed with his flora and fauna?

She started walking again, but it wasn't a walk, it was a run. It jolted her body, always used to care, with a strange live beat.

Reaching for her arm again, he stopped her. "Should you run?"

He thought she was sick. She was, though. She was sick. She'd been her whole life.

"Esha, if you say some of those things that are churning inside you, it might help you." His dark, brooding eyes were like a lake, bottomless with understanding. The kind of understanding he exhibited about every creature on earth.

"Is that a characteristic of the *Homo sapiens*?"

What? He didn't say the word. It was his eyes that did. He just waited. A scientist. A photographer. A renderer of nature.

"What have you found out about me? You've been studying me for a couple months. What am I?"

A blast of pain went through the onyx depths of his eyes. There was always a staidness to him, a quietness, but this was an explosion if she'd ever seen one. Violent.

His body pulled toward her, pulled away from her. Exactly mirroring what she'd been feeling. Maybe she should never have said what she'd said. Maybe this was not how adult humans communicated, verbalizing every thought that popped into their head.

An apology came to her lips, but she stuck out her jaw, something stopping her from spilling it only because she didn't want him to leave. He was going to leave anyway. She could see it in his eyes.

Then he blinked, as though he'd had a sudden realization. "Esha." A breath. Every word that ever left him was deliberate. He didn't have this human-communication thing down pat either. "You're like no one I've ever met."

How could she not laugh at that? Laughter spilled from her, a geyser erupting in harsh spurts.

That made him step closer, made him cup her jaw. When he touched her he always did it without hesitance. "Don't."

"Don't what?"

"Don't make it sound like there's something wrong with the way you are."

She wanted to laugh again. Where could she even begin with how much was wrong with her?

"You don't have to be like everyone else to be normal." He said it with more force than she'd ever heard him say anything.

"Isn't that the definition of normal? Being like the norm? That's what you spend your life searching for, right? The things that are different from other things. The things that make one thing, one being, one form of life itself?"

His mouth dropped open, only the slightest bit. She'd surprised him. Again.

"I've never thought about what I do that way." Of all the things he could have said, all the denials he could have made to make her feel better, this punched her in the chest. It made her want to stay, to verbalize the apology.

"I'm sorry. Sometimes I don't know what I am."

Silence settled on him again, but he was still standing close and his body absorbed her words instead of searching for ways to deny them.

"I think I do. I know who you are." The words were a whisper. It struck her that he might be the only person on earth who might figure it out.

Was that why she was with him? Here, outside the protection of her room and her family, trusting him to show her what she was?

"I can't articulate it, though. What I can articulate is that I don't know who I am when I'm with you. No, that's not true. I know I'm a version of myself that I had never considered before, and it's not only when you're near me. It's all the time now. You've made me new, Esha. I don't know what to do with that."

He'd made her new too. It was absurd how much. The urge to laugh gripped her again. He seemed to find the laughter in her eyes, study it with his usual care.

"I haven't seen him since I met you . . ." She took a breath. "Garuda." It was the first time since the accident that she was saying Garuda's name out loud to another human being.

A wave of something seemed to go through the air and resettle the atmosphere. Her gaze traveled to the sky again. His did too. The sky brightened and they both blinked together.

The sound of wings whispered in her ear. A soft kiss and then it was gone.

He watched her, and waited silently for her to go on.

"My aie was a storyteller," she said. Again, she was mentioning her mother for the first time in what seemed to be decades. The words pierced her tongue as they left her and sliced down the middle. *My aie.*

He took her hand and started walking again, and the words spilled from her. Easy and difficult. Slow, then fast. The way her mother had told her stories. The way she'd seemed to give a rhythm to them.

She told him about her childhood in Sripore. About Baba Saheb and how Aji used to be before the accident. Esha before the accident. Aie. She told him about the flight. About how those flashlights had looked in the darkness and rain as she hung from that tree.

Finding words should have been harder. Or easier. Or something. But they came, and she gave them to him. He wasn't the only one who needed to study unknowable things. She wanted to know too, and digging up buried things and speaking them seemed like a good first step. Essential.

She left out the part about Garuda. That seemed like a secret between her and those who were gone, and letting the secret go was too much like letting them go.

"Where does the Brahminy kite fit in?" He'd listened to all she'd had to say and then zeroed in on Garuda.

An icy wave rolled through her.

"When I tell you about him, will you leave?"

"Is that what you fear? That I've been coming to see you because I want a photograph?"

He'd told her how he'd sat on a rock for weeks, almost without moving, to photograph black-bellied sandgrouse that nested in the cliffs of Portugal.

Taking her hand, he pressed it to his heart. "I'm going to make you a promise." His intense eyes were on fire, the blaze steady. "No matter what happens, no matter what this—us—turns out to be, I will never photograph your Garuda. Not if he sits on your shoulder and speaks to me and tells me to do it. Not for anything on earth."

"Sid." She stepped closer to him and wrapped her arms around him, hugging him for the first time.

His arms went around her, as though he'd been waiting, breath whooshing out of him and tickling the top of her head.

Her body softened, relaxed. She let her head press into his chest, where his heartbeat skittered beneath her ear.

His chin rested on her head. "There is only one thing I'm here for, and it's not a bird."

"When I told you about the accident, there was something I left out," she said against his chest.

He made a hmm-ing sound.

Without meaning to, her arms tightened around him. His response was to stroke her back with his thumb. A lifetime of practicing grounding techniques, and just that tiny motion brought her back into herself and the remaining piece slipped from her lips.

She told him what she'd never told anyone but Shree Kaka in the hospital more than thirty years ago. She told him how the inside of her head had changed. How the visions had taken over her body.

"The day you landed on my balcony, it stopped. The fact that I'm touching you and I have not passed out from the pressure inside my head from your feelings, your past, your future, everything. I don't understand it. But you're my miracle."

"That explains so much." His words fell on the part in her hair. Simple. Easy.

An entirely unfamiliar warmth ran down the back of her neck

and traced her spine. It was a hunger she'd experienced through others but never for herself. Like so much she'd been feeling with him, she separated what she knew but wasn't hers, from what was only hers and tried to claim it.

He was watching her, eyes so dark she could barely distinguish his pupils from his irises. Her gaze slid down his face. The wide, strong ridge of his nose. His scar, which this close was a complicated constellation of star shapes. His wide, bright teeth. The hollows beneath his cheekbones. The inky darkness of his beard. And finally his generously lush lips.

The sensation that had slid down her spine pooled in her belly, warm and sharp. The world seemed to find its center in his mouth.

"Are you going to kiss me?" she asked, making a smile break across his face.

"Only if you want me to."

"Do you want to?"

"Very much. You?"

"I think so. But I'm also scared."

The thumb on her back started stroking again. He swallowed. "I am too."

"Why are you scared?"

"Honestly? I'm not sure. I've never discussed a kiss in such detail before doing it."

She started laughing. A strange feeling when your body was pressed flush against someone else.

He dropped a kiss on the corner of her mouth, and it made such a wild feeling rush through her that she pressed into it. Then his mouth slid across hers, until their lips were touching, fitting. Sensitive skin to sensitive skin. And then he was kissing her.

She'd expected to fall, to let consciousness go. The way her body had always reacted to stimulation. Instead something inside her reared up and roared to life. She lifted her arms and wrapped them around him, grabbing his head to find purchase, reaching up on her toes. Her mouth seemed to take over everything. Pushing and pushing and feeling.

He smiled into her lips.

"Why are you smiling?"

"You're doing it again."

"What?"

"Examining your own body's reactions against me."

"Sorry."

"No. Don't be. Tell me how you feel."

"Like I want to eat you up."

Now he was laughing. Having someone laugh into your lips was the most amazing feeling.

"What?" she asked.

"You have to open your mouth to eat."

"What?"

He pressed into her lips with his again. Warmth slid down her body again. He used his lips to part hers.

She gasped, the feel of the inside of his mouth completely taking her by surprise.

"Still okay?" He pulled away just enough to ask.

She yanked him back to her. She opened her mouth and let him in, feeling and feeling and feeling. Then she did it too, reaching and reaching, as deep as she could go. All the way, thick tongue and soft tissue and hard teeth and so much sensation sinking to all ends of her body.

He was laughing when she pulled away for a breath, even as something about him seemed different. His eyes had gone wild and heavy lidded. If she hadn't known better she'd have thought he was furious. Anger and arousal, two forms of giving over control.

"Is it normal to laugh when you kiss someone?"

He shook his head. "Not at all."

She stroked his lips with her thumb. "I didn't feel anything!"

His hand went to his chest. "Have mercy, woman." But he was smiling.

"I mean I *felt* a lot. But . . . but it was all mine." Wonder was a live thing inside her. "All my own feelings."

Another smile.

"Can I ask you for something, Sid?"

"Anything."

"Will you take me out? I want to leave the estate. But I don't want my family to know." She couldn't imagine their finding out and she didn't know why.

He smoothed her hair, stroked it. Her bun had unfurled and her hair hung down to her hips. "If you could go anywhere in the world, where would you want to go?"

"Sripore." She didn't even have to think about it. "But somewhere closer first."

"I think I know just the place," he said with such sincerity that she had to kiss him again.

Chapter Twenty-Four

I miss you," Vansh said, dictating a text to Naina. Then erased it. He felt like he was constantly walking the tightest rope between wanting to be with her all the time and scaring her away with one wrong word.

Are you sore? he texted instead, knowing she'd find that much easier to handle than an "I miss you." Turned out she was remarkably comfortable at keeping things physical.

Why would I be sore? It's been years since I worked out, she responded, even adding a confused emoji.

Liar. I have evidence to prove you've been working out, quite vigorously, every day this past week. A few times a day even.

Evidence? Yuck!

My dirty dirty girl, he texted back.

He slipped his phone into his pocket, grabbed his backpack, and headed for the door, and ran head-on into his father.

Actually running into him meant he couldn't change course to avoid him even though he really didn't have time to stay and talk to anyone.

"You seem in a hurry, son," HRH said, and they both straightened with the kind of awkwardness befitting a grown son running into a father full tilt. "I haven't seen you in weeks." He gave a gruff laugh. "Your mother assured me you were living here. But I was starting to doubt her."

Vansh studied him for a second, not sure how to respond, then realized he was joking and returned a dutiful laugh. "Did you need something? For Yash's transition?" Vansh had checked in with Yash a few days ago, and all had seemed well.

That made HRH's generally stiff demeanor stiffen some more. "Not at all, no. Yash is quite self-sufficient, as you well know." Pride shone in his eyes.

HRH and Ma had been in Sacramento every chance they got since the transition, making sure Yash had everything he needed. Suddenly HRH seemed to notice that Vansh was still there. "Not that your help during the election wasn't vital. Extremely vital. Extremely."

"Thanks."

"Umm. Son, I . . . did you want to come back in and grab a coffee or something?"

"Does someone else need something?" Vansh's mind ran over all his sisters. He'd not been speaking to them as much as he usually did. But they all seemed fine, if a little nosier than normal. "You can text me if you need something." He resisted the urge to look at his wrist to indicate that he was in a hurry, since he didn't wear a watch.

"No. I just haven't seen you in a while."

Well, he'd been right here. "I wish I could. But I'm late for a meeting."

His father stepped back, in the most HRH way ever. "Of course. I didn't mean to keep you. Things going well with . . . um . . . with . . ."

"Jiggy Mehta. Yes, everything's great. I really have to go." Vansh took off down the hall to the front door. Why had he never noticed how needlessly long that walk was?

"Vansh," HRH called behind him, and Vansh turned.

"Yes?"

"I see that . . . that you're working really hard. Um. I just . . . I'm proud of you too." He scratched a spot on his cheek. "Not too . . . I meant you, not you *too* . . . I'm proud of you."

"I know what you meant. Thanks, Dad." With that he made his way to Ma's old car, which he always used while he was home. He almost turned around again and asked what HRH was proud of exactly. It wasn't like he knew what Vansh was up to.

I'm proud of you too. Classic HRH.

Vansh was laughing when he drove out of the Anchorage gates. Because it was funny, actually. Hilarious.

NAINA AND VANSH had spent twelve hours at the office putting together the presentation for the board and interviewing caseworkers in Nepal over video. They'd made three job offers to doctors. As for the San Francisco project, with four of Silicon Valley's biggest employers on board, presenting to the board was going to be a cakewalk. Vansh felt certain he could even get the board to up the funding. But in this moment he couldn't have cared less.

Adrenaline ran through his system for a whole different reason.

"I told you sneaking around was exciting," he said as they stumbled into Naina's apartment, kissing breathlessly. Was there another way to kiss her? "Do you know how hard it is to not touch you just because someone else is there?"

Vansh didn't think he was going to make it to the bedroom.

"It's torture, Vansh," Naina said, pulling his shirt over his head and wrapping her legs around him. His jeans were already halfway down his legs, her underwear somewhere on the floor.

The back of the couch would have to do.

"Thank God you're so athletic," Naina said when they ended up tangled on the couch, after. Utterly satiated and thoroughly naked.

For a while they lay there boneless and panting.

"I take it that was good for you too?" he said when he could speak, dropping a kiss on the tip of her nose.

"Any better and I might be dead."

Those words, the way she said them, utterly happy in her skin, shook something inside him, reset it. Reset him. Just like that, a smile was nudging at his lips and his hand was cupping her breast again. "How are you so damn beautiful?" He could barely breathe from it.

Her eyes started to fill with something serious, but then his thumb strummed her puckered nipple and her eyes went fuzzy. She nipped at his lower lip, sending sparks through his body, which was so spent it shouldn't have felt anything.

"Much as I enjoy your worship, you're getting a little obsessed with my body." Her smile pushed into his lips, and Vansh decided it was his favorite sensation in the entire world.

His hand trailed down her belly to the soft mound that filled his hand perfectly. She wasn't always ready to be touched so soon after she'd had an orgasm. Tentatively, he stroked her, studying her response. She purred with pleasure.

"While your body is quite worthy of worship, I think I'm obsessed with your pleasure. I'll admit it, I'm obsessed with seeing you orgasm, Naina. It's a beautiful thing. I really love the way you come."

She pressed into his hand, a gentle rhythm. In no hurry. Filled with trust. "Doesn't everyone come pretty much the same way?"

That made him laugh. This woman, with all her worldly confidence, genuinely surprised him sometimes with how little thought she'd given to sex.

"No, Knightlina. Everyone comes just a little bit differently." He continued to stroke her with his thumb, placing two fingers at her entrance, just touching, nothing more. Her eyes went so wildly unfocused, it was like she'd taken a hit of something potent. "The way a person orgasms is a reflection of their personality. Them condensed down to that moment of complete freedom."

"How so?" It was a miracle she was still talking. But her words slurred, and that made him smile and slow his fingers even more.

"So, a shy woman will usually be disbelieving when she comes. She might even cry. An exuberant one will make sure you know exactly how exuberant she is. She comes harder when she gets to really show how much she's enjoying it. Then there are the 'in it to see if it's worth their while' women, and the 'I had no idea it could be like this' women. Those are the ones that imagine you proposing even as they come. Which kind of takes away from the entire thing."

She started to convulse on his fingers, slow, long pulses that sent seismic tremors through her body.

"And I?" It was a sob, a gasp, the most beautiful sound.

"Look at you, all needy for praise."

She squeezed his hand between her thighs, giving him every last bit of her release, stretching out under it, pushing herself into it. "Fine, don't tell me." Another shudder, then another. Her eyes fluttered closed as though nothing but what she was feeling mattered.

"See, *this* . . . for someone who is so focused on not caring at all, you come with care. You involve every single cell in your being. You give yourself over to it."

Without opening her eyes, she reached for him and moved just enough to slide him into her, one leg draped around his hip. It was exactly what he needed, all he'd ever wanted. There was no rush this time. No pounding hunger. They lay there side by side, their bodies facing each other, touching without overwhelming, without owning. Savoring. A balance of giving and taking. And yet when he was done, spent inside her, he knew there was nothing left of him. No him outside of her.

The power of what had just happened between them hung in the air like reverberations from a million gongs as they sat up and pulled on their clothes. This time the wordlessness was heavier. Something inside them had been wrung out.

"Do you think we can present in a week?" he said, because he knew that this silence would only make her fall into her thoughts, and he didn't want her going where he couldn't reach her.

Talking about work was the best way to bring her back to the moment, to keep her with him.

She started to search the couch for discarded clothing. "I don't think we should force Hari to present."

Not this again. But he didn't want to argue, so he didn't respond.

"He's not up for it." She found her underwear behind the uptight gray pillows on her couch and pulled it on, totally unselfconscious.

"Hari's doing great. Why would you say that? Did he say something to you?" Vansh pushed himself off the couch, limbs still insensate, and started tidying up the soulless cushions that were such a misfit on that happy couch.

"Yes, he has, and not just to me. He's said it to you too. He doesn't want to be in a boardroom in front of Jiggy and his yesmen. Don't you see? He can't do it."

"The man isn't as weak as you think. As weak as he thinks. How will he believe in himself if we don't believe in him?"

She gave him one of her fierce looks. The one that told him she wanted him to know he was being an idiot. Well, so much for the afterglow.

"You've created a narrative on Hari's behalf. One that makes him a victim. Cheated, innocent, screwed over and unable to handle it," she said.

"No, I have not. I *know* these things about him. They're all true. He was cheated, screwed over. He *is* innocent and brilliant."

Now she looked at him as though he were melting her heart with his naïveté. So, maybe there was some afterglow after all, just not enough for her to believe that he knew what he was doing.

"Yes," she said too gently, adjusting his T-shirt where it bunched over his jeans. "But being capable of existing in the corporate world takes more than just brilliance with numbers and coding. He has challenges. Debilitating social anxiety that has got in his way. Maybe other challenges that have gone untreated and are responsible for some of the things that have happened to him."

He adjusted a cushion that wouldn't sit right. "Please tell me you're not saying he deserves his misfortune. And please don't act like I don't understand what a person's challenges can take from them." She'd watched him on his headphones, memorizing every word on those slides. "Since when did you start believing that people deserve their misfortune? You of all people."

That took care of every remaining trace of afterglow. Good. He didn't want her coddling him.

"Whatever the hell that means, I'm going to ignore it right now. Because we're talking about Hari, not me. Or you. You've had help. He hasn't." If she thought the softness in her eyes made what she was saying any less harsh, and absurd, she was wrong. "Vansh, what I'm trying to say is that you are pushing Hari into a place where his struggles don't give him the tools to know how to handle things. You're being unfair, and arrogant in thinking that just because you think it can be done, he can do it. He can't. Not yet. Not until he's had help and he's ready." She'd been trying to get Hari to see a therapist to help with his anxiety, but he'd been stubborn in his refusal. "You know firsthand the difference help makes."

"This is not about me." He wasn't about to tell her that therapy was not a magic wand. It was just tools. In the end, he'd had to overcome his own challenges one step, one workaround at a time. And he'd been able to only because the people around him believed that he could. The best thing he could do for Hari right now was to trust that Hari could do anything. "Why does every conversation we have lead to this? You telling me that everything I have has been handed to me on a platter."

She came to him and wrapped her arms around him, and despite his best effort, his indignation melted. "I know a lot of people who've been handed everything on a platter. But I don't know anyone who's done better with it than you. I know it was your work to do, and you've done it in ways that make me so proud of you I don't even know what to do with it. But you're right, this is about Hari. He can't pull this off. Not with where he is right now. He's fragile. It's wrong to push him."

She was proud of him? His brain had stopped listening after that part. The urge to pick her up and swirl her around the room was strong, but she still looked serious and he resisted. But he couldn't stop a smile from spreading across his face. "Well, I disagree. Next week I'm going to prove you wrong. But first, about how proud you are of me . . ."

She smiled and shook her head. "You didn't hear a word I said after that, did you?"

"Nope. So, speaking of proud, how impressed are you with those pictures Sid Dashwood and I got?" Vansh was starving and his stomach let out a growl.

He went to the kitchen and started digging through her fridge. "Did Auntie bring you more 'diet' food?" Yup, she had. He pulled out a Tupperware container of shami kababs. "Want some?"

She nodded and he popped the food into the microwave. There was enough for an army platoon. Which meant he and Naina were going to annihilate it all in one sitting.

"I didn't realize you held Sid Dashwood's hand while he took the pictures."

"Ha ha. I did know the histories of the people he photographed, and I helped him get under the skin of the project. We discussed the concepts for days and came up with the stories we wanted to tell."

"That, you did do." As the kitchen filled with the aroma of spices, Naina's eyes filled with skepticism.

"And . . . ?" Vansh asked, knowing that look only too well.

"And I'm still unclear on why Sid helped us in the first place. He's a seven-time Goodall finalist. He's also not this friendly with the rest of your family as far as I know. He said the other day that he hadn't even met Mina Auntie and Shree Uncle or any of your siblings."

"And it's impossible that he took a liking to me? Given how much you like me, that should be easy for you to understand."

She grinned into her kababs, eyes all sparkly again. "I certainly hope you're not doing the same things with him you are with me to win his favor."

"Come to think of it, he is my type," he said. "Maybe it's our shared wanderlust." Saying that reminded him that he hadn't felt the need to leave in quite a while. She studied him, but he was going nowhere near that train of thought. "Or maybe this is about you. Maybe he's trying to make it up to you since his sister has your ex." He put more food on her plate.

She popped a luscious chicken patty into his mouth. "Fake ex."

He loved that phrase almost as much as the flavors exploding on his tongue. "Thank the good Lord for that. And for this. You haven't lost weight, have you? Because if Auntie stops sending this food, what are we going to do?"

She grinned as he slid a piece into her mouth. "I still think it doesn't add up. There's something else Sid wants out of this."

"Why do you think everyone is using me? I'm not some babe in the woods, Naina. I've lived by myself—quite successfully—since before I was even an adult."

She didn't answer immediately. They leaned into the countertop and continued to feed pieces of kabab into each other's mouth.

"Without ever having to make any money or support yourself," she said finally around a mouthful.

"And you've what, worn clothes from Target and paid your own way through college?" He picked a morsel from her lips and popped it into his own mouth.

"I do, as a matter of fact, have quite a few clothes from Target. They're quite nice. And yes, I did pay my own way through college. I had a full ride. And I worked to pay my rent."

"Is this a hit on me not having gone to college?"

She wiped the edge of his mouth with her thumb and dropped a quick kiss on his jaw. "No. This is me telling you, again, that you leave yourself wide open, that you have no fear, and that some people can interpret your generosity as weakness and feed off you like a damn carcass."

"I don't know if I should be livid or flattered."

Her smile turned up the giant floodlight that was perpetually burning inside him these days. "Being flattered would be most on brand."

She thought she was so funny. But he loved how they could talk like this without anger, something intangibly strong letting them push without fear. That didn't mean he wasn't getting a little tired of all these allusions to his cluelessness.

"I happen to like being this way. Trusting people, trusting myself, is a gift, and I'll keep it, thank you very much. It's so much better than being a cynical old crone."

She popped the last piece into his mouth. "Did you just call me old?" A teasing smile shone in her eyes. Another favorite.

He went to the sink and rinsed out the Tupperware. She followed him and pressed her face into his back, arms around his waist.

"No, I just called you cynical." He leaned back into her hug. "You have a serious problem with prioritizing criticism, you know that?"

"I do know that." Her easy laughter fell onto his back, filled his chest, filled every part of him.

It struck him again, with some force, that for the first time in his life he wanted time to stand still. He wanted to be nowhere but here. He wanted this moment to last forever.

Chapter Twenty-Five

Our project is in the *New York* fucking *Times*!" Jiggy Mehta said with his usual self-congratulatory air that made Naina want to drop him off his bungee cliff without a cord.

The pictures were truly brilliant, capturing the pain of falling through the cracks. With a human face and the possibility of a human solution. The hope of making it out with your self-respect intact. The hope that a society this capitalistic could also be responsible. Ideology that felt political and hollow in words took on inescapable impact with visuals as honest and raw as these. Vansh was right. Sid had been the perfect person for this. The exposure this piece offered had brought together twenty of the city's largest employers. Maybe that was all Sid had wanted, to be of service to his hometown.

In either case, what Vansh had put together in a matter of months was miraculous. Pride the likes of which she'd never known gripped her from head to toe as she watched him. And that brought home something she'd been pushing away. The sheer volume of something too close to happiness that she felt just looking at him. It was terrifying.

Vansh winked at her over Jiggy's back. There was just such

utter joy to him. It leaked into the air, seeped under her skin, pulsed inside her chest. It made her light-headed. Like the kind of person who laughs for no reason and skips. Anger at letting herself get to this point kept kindling inside her, but the irrational joy of his smile kept dousing it. Anger—which had been a powerful force all her life—felt oddly futile.

Tell me why you're so afraid of happiness. Vansh had said that to her a few days ago when they lay in each other's arms doing the one thing that was uncomplicated.

Why, indeed. Naina wasn't so much afraid of happiness as she believed it was fleeting. And she didn't give herself over to fleeting things.

He'd pressed her hand into his chest. *The happiness inside here when I'm with you, how does it matter if it's fleeting? I wouldn't give up even one second of it.*

"Aren't you happy?" Jiggy threw at her across the conference room table, his usually syrupy tone—especially in Vansh's presence—impatient.

"Sorry?" Her mind had wandered away from their old-boys' back-slapping. Please let her not have spoken her thoughts out loud.

"Aren't you happy that Vansh's work is in the *New York Times*?"

Naina wasn't sure if he'd stressed the words *Vansh's work* or if she'd imagined that, but it got on her last nerve. "Technically, Sid Dashwood's work is in the *New York Times*."

Vansh looked like she had knifed him. She shouldn't care. He should have corrected Jiggy himself. But her heart twisted, and that made the anger she'd been beckoning return.

"Technically," Vansh said, smiling at Jiggy, "it's not my project alone. It's ours, Naina's, mine, Hari's, Sadiya's, Makayla's, Mariel's, yours."

Automatically her chin went up. It had taken him too long to react. Fine, it had been seconds. All the same, she fixed Vansh with a glare that said this wasn't quite the group-hug moment he wanted to make it.

Jiggy clapped. A slow clap, as though this were the rehearsal for a theatrical farce and he the director. "Very lovely!" The nasty gleam in his eyes was anything but lovely. He reminded Naina of her mother's friends when their gossip was particularly vicious. "Sharing is caring." Jiggy wiggled his brows and Naina's skin crawled. "I love all the *caring* you two have been *sharing.*"

His laughter boomed through the room.

Every intimate moment between Naina and Vansh seemed to scatter across the mahogany table and lie there exposed as Jiggy voyeuristically lapped it up.

"Rich people, whole different code of ethics, no?" he threw at Hari, who had been trying to disappear into the corner.

Naina went to Hari. He had gone pale and was visibly trembling at all the undercurrents of tension. She sat down next to him and patted his hand.

"I have no idea what that's supposed to mean," Vansh said, letting annoyance slip past his usual charm. "But our code of ethics on this team is beyond reproach."

At that, another belly laugh burst from Jiggy. The man was really getting into the horror-movie-villain role today. "I'll tell you what. I have a board meeting in a half hour. Let's get your presentation in front of them today."

Hari made a sobbing sound.

"That's impossible," Naina said just as Vansh said, "That's a great idea."

This of course made the bastard's amusement explode with enough force to generate a mushroom cloud. "The *NYT* thing really helps us sell this to the board. Timing is everything in business." He wagged a finger at Vansh. "You're the man," he said. "You get it?"

Discomfort flitted across Vansh's face.

Jiggy wasn't done. "Get your guy presentable." He tossed the coldest of glances Hari's way. "There's no sniveling in board-rooms." With that he strode out of the room without waiting for agreement.

Hari started shaking.

Naina wrapped a gentle arm around him. "Listen, it's okay. You don't have to be there when we present."

Vansh sat down on Hari's other side, eyes filled with worry but also with determination. "Unless you want to be. What Naina means is that we will be there and we will help you every step of the way."

That was not at all what Naina meant. Not even a little bit. If Hari hadn't been shaking next to her, moments away from col-lapsing with panic, Naina would have pulled Vansh out of the room and bitten his head off for speaking for her. Instead, she tried to telepathically send her thoughts to him, without chang-ing her body language, as she calmed Hari down.

"I believe in you, Hari," Vansh added fiercely.

Hari looked at Vansh with such adoration, Naina could practi-cally see him steeling his spine to not disappoint him. "I can do it," he said, still shaking.

Naina had the urge to snap at Vansh, but Hari was making too much of an effort and she couldn't bring herself to. "Only if you want to." With a glare at Vansh, which he stubbornly ignored, she pressed the intercom and asked Mariel to bring in some hot chocolate.

Vansh took Hari's hand. "Naina is right. Only do it if you want to. But you've done such amazing work and I know you want to help your friends at the community center. Mikhail and Tina and—"

"Tim and Douglas," Hari added.

"They already have jobs thanks to you. You're a matchmaker, remember?" Vansh said. "You're stronger than you think."

Hari smiled, but it was so forced Naina wanted to shake Vansh.

Don't do this, she mouthed to Vansh.

Have some faith, he mouthed back. He took the hot chocolate from Mariel, and brought it to Hari. "Thanks, Mariel, that looks intensely chocolaty. Fit for a star who's going to kill his presentation."

"Vansh!" Naina snapped. Hari started shaking again and she kicked herself. "It's okay," she said much more calmly. "The hot chocolate does look delicious."

"Mr. Mehta just called to say you need to be upstairs," Mariel said, looking concerned. In the ten seconds she'd been there, even she could see that this was not good for Hari.

Vansh looked unsure for a minute, but then he stood, determined as ever. "I know you can do it. I'll do most of the talking and it will be over before you know it. This will help bolster your confidence. Trust me."

No it won't, Naina wanted to scream, but Hari was forcing a spring into his step, despite his obviously trembling legs.

"All you have to do is show them the mock-ups of the UI, which is slick and intuitive, and then walk them through the code that parses the data. You have everything in here." Vansh tapped the laptop and gathered the notes they'd been working on. "Naina and I will take care of everything else. We want them to see that this solution comes from a place of real experience."

By the time they had made their way up to the hundredth floor, the boardroom was full of seven very serious-looking men and two very serious-looking women, each one of them used to only ever having their way.

Hari watched them through the glass wall of the lobby. "I can do it," he said with such hope that Naina had to nod.

She plugged her headphones into his ears. "You know what helps me when I'm nervous? Music." She pulled up some bhangra numbers that she knew Hari loved on her phone. "It's Badshah.

You love this one." They'd listened to it on repeat as they'd worked around the clock these past few months.

As soon as the music started, Hari's shoulders loosened, though only a fraction and not nearly enough to indicate that taking him into that arena of lions was all right. They'd smell his nervousness and make sport out of him. Which was what Jiggy was looking for. Naina was sure of it.

Hari sank into a chair, head bobbing slightly to the music.

"We can't do this, Vansh," she hissed. "He can't. I've seen this my whole life." God, she hadn't meant to think of her mother, but here it was. People had limits.

"And you've always pandered to the bully. Don't you want to stand up for once?"

Naina's heart started to thud. She had known this . . . this mixing emotions with work—this arrangement—was going to spell disaster. Why had she still done it?

As soon as he said it, regret rushed into his eyes. His hand twitched as though he was thinking about touching her, but he didn't. Smart man. "Sorry, that was out of line."

"Damn straight."

"You have to trust me."

"I'm already seeing how stupid that is."

Naturally, that fell on him like a kick to his groin, which in turn made her so angry, she couldn't remember why she'd been having trouble with it before.

Before Vansh could answer, one of Jiggy's assistants stepped out of the boardroom and announced that they were ready for them.

Hari jumped up and gave Naina her phone. "Let's do this," he said.

Vansh studied her face. She'd expected smugness, but all she got was worry. *We okay?*

She didn't know.

The moment they stepped into the dark-paneled room, Hari's body seemed to seize up again, eyes widening and glazing with fear. Vansh squeezed his shoulder. The sense of impending doom bloated inside Naina.

Vansh plugged his laptop into the system, and the presentation they'd been working on popped up on the screen. Sadiya and Vansh had created a story so compelling and slick that just for a moment Naina felt hopeful, but then a squeak arose from Hari. His shaking turned frenzied.

Naina reached over and took his hand, a gesture of weakness not one of the suits missed.

Vansh introduced them, and as always everyone was instantly charmed. Naturally, they all knew who he was. He started with the statistics, figures of how many people lived on the streets in San Francisco. All his ease and charm were nothing compared to the passion and knowledge he projected. Every one of them sat up and hung on each word. No one would ever know that he had the entire thing memorized, that he wasn't reading the words on the screen, that he couldn't.

Watching how hard he worked around his dyslexia, how confidently he embraced the tools that helped him, how very much he gave to every single thing, the pride she felt in him came back in a rush, drowning out everything else.

He wasn't wearing a suit, but he had started to wear button-downs to the office in place of his muscle shirts. Not that he didn't make button-downs look like muscle shirts. Arm muscles pushed into his sleeves as he pointed at the screen.

"Why don't you let your programmer explain the architecture and the database structure to us?" Jiggy said. He'd been watching silently, but finally his hunger for blood and drama won out. He was up to something.

The room's collective attention turned to Hari, and he made a choking sound.

"Mr. Samarth isn't feeling great today," Naina said. "Maybe Mr. Raje and I can explain the technical details."

"Unlike you and Mr. Raje, Hari can give us ground-level insight into the project. He's actually been living on the street for some amount of time, has he not?" The bastard had the gall to smile.

Vansh started to respond but Hari jumped out of his seat, breath coming out of him in gasps. His hands were clasped around his stomach. His skin had gone an alarming shade of gray. Before Naina could do anything to help him, he made a horrid gurgling sound and projectile-vomited across the boardroom table.

Expletives and gasps filled the room with its perfect acoustics. Chairs scraped back. Everyone scrambled away from the hot-chocolate-colored wave.

Naina and Vansh both lunged toward Hari, trying to catch him, but his eyes rolled up in his head and he slid down to the floor struggling for breath as Jiggy screamed and screamed in the background.

Chapter Twenty-Six

"A panic attack can feel an awful lot like a real heart attack," Dr. Warsi, whom both Vansh and Naina had known their whole lives, said. "We've sedated Mr. Samarth. We'll keep him here at least for a day or until we come up with a treatment plan."

They thanked her and she told them that they could wait in her office if that was more comfortable than the waiting room, but that they didn't have to. It was late enough that Hari would hopefully sleep through the night. They could come back tomorrow.

"Will it be okay if I just stay here overnight?" Naina said. "We're the only family he has and he'll be scared if no one is here when he wakes up." Her nose was red from the tears she'd been holding back.

Vansh was gutted by guilt. The sight of Hari collapsing kept playing in an endless loop inside his head.

He reached out and took Naina's hand, terrified that she was too angry with him to let him. But she did, and his own eyes prickled with the tears he'd been holding back.

Dr. Warsi slid a glance at their joined hands. Her suddenly shrewd gaze seemed to zero in on exactly how much comfort they were taking in the contact. The doctor went from physician to auntie in one second flat.

Naina tried to disengage their hands, but Vansh was in hell with how guilty he was feeling and he couldn't let go. For a second, recklessness flashed in her eyes, as though she couldn't have cared less what anyone thought either. In the end she gave her hand another tug, and Vansh followed her eyes to Farah Auntie and let go.

"Well, it was wonderful to see you both again. One hasn't seen you stateside for a while, Vansh," Dr. Farah Warsi said over the awkwardness that settled around them.

"It's nice to be back. It's been over six months," he said. The longest he'd been home at a stretch since the age of sixteen. His gaze slid to Naina.

Farah Auntie let out a shaky laugh. "Mina must be so happy that you've decided to stay." She threw another baffled glance between Naina and him.

They thanked her again, because he had no idea how else to respond. When he'd first come home, Ma had been busy with helping Yash settle into the transition. Then Vansh had gotten so lost in his work with Naina, so lost in Naina, that he'd barely seen his family.

With another reassurance that Hari was going to be fine, Dr. Warsi hurried away looking very worried.

Naina and he made their way to the waiting room. If Naina had looked distraught before, now she looked exhausted beyond words.

Vansh had the urge to scream, but they were in a hospital. And he never screamed. Never lost it. Then again, he'd never caused someone to break down either.

"What are we doing, Vansh?" Naina said as soon as they were in the privacy of the waiting room. "What the hell are we doing?" She pressed her face into her hands. "My whole life is upside down. Hari's hospitalized. My work—I don't even know what Jiggy is going to pull next." She looked up and pointed to the door. "And my God, how did we ever think we'd be able to sneak around when people who've known us all our lives are everywhere? How did I let my life get this messed up?"

Vansh opened his mouth and she raised a hand to stop him. "Don't apologize again. It doesn't change anything."

"I know. I shouldn't have pushed Hari. I should have listened to you. I will do better. From now on Hari will only do what he's comfortable doing. We're going to get him the help he needs." Why hadn't he listened to her? He'd let his own experiences cloud his judgment. All his life he'd pushed himself, when the world's pushiest family refused to push him. He'd told himself it wasn't about them not believing in him. He'd told himself he didn't care. But it had been a hole, and he'd tried to fill it by doing for Hari what no one had done for him.

He'd been an idiot. And it had hurt someone he cared about.

A laugh huffed out of her. "How is it so easy for you to believe that everything can be fixed so simply?"

"Why are you laughing? Is it funny that I feel like such shit?"

He must've looked as wrecked as he felt, because she cupped his cheek. "No, I hate that you feel like shit. You feeling like shit hurts me more than I want it to. I know you never meant to hurt Hari. I know you were trying to be supportive. I think he knows that too. But I can't see us fixing this mess."

He pressed her hand into his cheek, letting all his need for her show. "Of course we'll fix it. I want you to trust me."

With another laugh, she pulled away. "I think the fact that you can get me to trust you so easily is the problem. You knew I'd trust you. Even before you asked, you knew. Because everyone does."

Wait, were they still talking about Hari? Or was this about them? "Are you seriously bringing our relationship into this? I should have listened to you about Hari. I should have listened to you about Mehta. I was wrong to push too hard and I admit that. But there is nothing nefarious about our arrangement. I've never asked for more than you wanted to give."

She swallowed. Anger darkened her beautiful eyes. Eyes he could read more and more clearly with each passing day. Eyes that were no longer sad all the time. He hated the turmoil in them now. Hated it.

"I had only recently gotten out of a relationship with a man who risked his life's work, a gubernatorial election, for another woman when you asked me to get into this thing with you. You think I'd even have considered it if you weren't so damn easy to trust?"

"I thought we were past this. You'd just gotten out of a *fake* relationship."

"Maybe that's not relevant."

It was his turn to laugh. "It's literally the only thing that's relevant." Their arrangement was not the same thing. "You didn't even want to be on the same continent as him. The only reason you even thought about turning it into something real was because your work brought you back here. Does that not tell you anything?"

"Of course it does. It tells me what I've told you before, that I'm not made for relationships, I'm not capable of love."

The way she said it made him want to hunt her parents down, hunt Yash down, hunt everyone in his family down for treating her like she was responsible. For reinforcing this shit she believed. Well, he knew they were wrong. She was wrong.

"What if I told you that's a lie? What if I told you that's the biggest lie I've ever heard anyone tell themselves? Ask me how I know."

Panic flashed in her eyes. She was terrified of what she saw in his eyes. He tucked a loose lock of hair behind her ear and her body softened instantly. "Fine, don't ask me. But being afraid to love is not the same as not loving. Everything you do, every action you take, there's more love there than I've ever witnessed."

"Then maybe I'm capable of it. Maybe I'm not worthy of it." Turning away from him, she started studying the bookshelf. A menagerie of books family members of patients had left behind, interspersed with children's books about loss and sadness and asking for help. Books that might have helped her a long time ago.

He stepped close to her, and her body loosened and tightened at the same time.

"Another lie," he said behind her. "You are worthy of love. Ask me how I know."

She spun around. "Vansh, listen. Please. I can't—"

"Don't look at me like that. I'm not asking for anything. I'm not." Was he? "All I'm saying is—"

"Why you not call Mummy?" Naina seemed to fold inward as her mother's voice cut Vansh off.

They spun as one toward the waiting room door.

"Why did you two not call us?" Ma was here too? What was happening?

Naina's arms went around herself as she looked from Chandni Auntie to Ma, who didn't even spare her a glance. Which was entirely unlike Ma.

"Thank God Farah called us," Ma said, while Naina's mother looked on with a hand fluttering at her chest.

"Thank God we were at yoga studio." As soon as the words left Chandni Auntie's mouth she slapped a hand across it. India Dashwood's yoga studio was minutes from the hospital.

Ma looked at Chandni Auntie as though she'd just revealed that they'd been conspiring to murder Naina in her sleep.

Naina looked like that was exactly what they'd been doing. How could her own mother be going to India's yoga studio? Uncontrollable rage rolled through Vansh. Did they think she was a damned punching bag?

Control yourself.

He never had to tell himself that. Ever.

Instead of her fiery glare, Naina threw him a pleading look. For the two mothers who didn't seem to notice any of her feelings, she manufactured a smile.

"You go to India Dashwood to learn yoga?" he said to Chandni Auntie, unable to hide his incredulousness. This was her mother!

"Vansh, please." Naina's voice was barely a whisper, but the way she said his name seemed to hit Ma and Chandni Auntie like a grenade.

"We were lucky to be close enough when Farah called us." Ma tried to sound imperious, but she knew how ridiculous this was. She had to.

"Why would Dr. Warsi call you?" Vansh said, with all the incredulousness he was feeling.

They all knew the answer, of course. Farah Warsi believed it was part of the Auntie Code. Friends kept an eye out for each other's children. Also known as the spy network that plagued desi kids across the world, and apparently didn't let up even after they weren't children anymore.

Ma doubled down on the imperiousness. "You're our children! And you didn't tell us you were at the hospital."

"We brought a friend to the hospital," Vansh said. Naina seemed to be having a hard time making words. "We are just fine. You didn't have to drop everything and run over."

"Yoga class was done," Chandni Auntie said. "Very hard to leave in middle. That teacher—you don't know her—make us leave phone out." If her words hadn't made Naina wilt like a plucked flower, Vansh might have thought it was funny. But this level of insensitivity wasn't funny. It was cruel.

"I know you were at India's studio, Mummy. It's okay. I don't care. I have nothing against India. You know that." She said that last part to Ma. Who still hadn't acknowledged her.

Her mother looked unsure, as though she wasn't exactly ready for Naina to forgive India. Which again was absurd given that she was patronizing India's business.

"It's truly okay, Mummy." Naina's words were flat. He'd never seen her this bloodless, this listless. "Maybe she can help fix your shoulder pain."

"So, is your friend well?" Ma directed the question at Vansh.

"Hari had a severe panic attack. They had to sedate him. They're keeping him overnight," Naina answered, struggling to keep her voice flat even as her eyes searched Ma for acknowledgment.

Ma nodded without looking at her, and Naina looked like she might cry.

Vansh stepped close to her. He almost reached for her, knowing he'd do anything to make her not look like this, like she was worthless and despised and okay with it. He'd have done anything to bring the Naina he knew back. For one blindingly bright moment she almost leaned into him, but her mother made a squeaking sound. Ma looked at Vansh like she didn't know who he was, and Naina stepped away from him.

A pulse started pounding in his head.

"Well, I'm glad Hari's okay," Ma said. "Panic attacks are fairly common. There seem to be a lot of those going around in our family recently. Dr. Warsi is the best. She'll take care of him."

Chandni Auntie laughed that uncomfortable laugh that people laughed when they were trying to avert oncoming disaster. She seemed to do this a lot. Every time she did, Naina seemed to get smaller.

Naina turned to Ma. "Thank you for stopping by. We . . . um . . . I really appreciate it." Her voice wobbled and she cleared her throat.

Ma didn't respond.

"Ma!" Vansh snapped.

His tone startled her and she threw a quick, formal smile at Naina. But a more distant smile Vansh had never seen her give anyone. Barely a second's worth of eye contact. Not even a hint of the warmth she'd always shown Naina. Even after she had found out about Yash and Naina's deception, she'd never held it against Naina. What was going on here?

"Well, Vansh seems to think stopping by wasn't necessary." Ma searched his face. "But since I am here, maybe I can give you a ride. I am headed home, and I've barely seen you in months."

Naina had frozen up. She looked pale and stiff, brittle enough to crack with one tap.

"Naina and I are staying here until Hari wakes up," Vansh said.

"No! That's not good idea," Chandni Auntie said, her pitch rising to match her horror. She looked like someone had dropped a mountain of evidence in her lap for a crime she'd suspected. "Naina must go to own place. I don't like all such things." The fluttering hand at her chest went crazy. "Dr. Kohli, he doesn't like all such things," she added, as though Dr. Kohli's opinion on the matter would hold sway where her own had not. "In Kohli family, girls don't stay all night out like this way."

Naina's hand flew to her mouth and something inside Vansh snapped.

"Naina has literally lived by herself for twenty years!" His mother turned a warning glare on him. Naina couldn't seem to move. "That's two entire decades that she's stayed out all night like this way!"

Finally Naina moved. The warning glare she threw at him had no force. She had no force.

Her mother seemed to gain bluster from having snuffed Naina out. "Her father will never allow all such things. He will disown. Throw her outside."

"That's outrageous," Vansh said to Chandni Auntie, and turned to Naina. *Why won't you say anything? Where are you?*

It was like she wasn't even in the room. "You're her mother," he said, disbelief making his voice harsh. "Don't you think you need to stop him? Keep him from doing something so cruel? She's at a hospital with a sick friend, for God's sake. You should be proud of her." He looked at his own mother. "You should all be so god-damned proud of her!"

"Vansh." Finally Naina spoke. It was barely a whisper. "Please stop." She was shaking.

"They're being unfair. Why won't you stand up to her?"

Chandni Auntie looked horrified. Her eyes filled with tears and with a loud sob she ran from the waiting room as though she and not Naina were the one who'd been hurt.

Naina ran after her and tried to grab her arm. "Mummy, please."

Her mother shoved her away with so much strength Naina stumbled back. Her eyes were dry, horribly dry.

"No, Naina. Don't come near Mummy." With that Chandni Kohli ran down the corridor with the nurses and the medics staring after her.

Ma followed her, tossing the most disappointed look over her shoulder at Vansh.

Naina stumbled back to the waiting room and dropped into a chair. Vansh squatted in front of her.

When he tried to touch her, she shook her head. Not touching her right now felt impossible, but he waited, let her gather herself.

Then she said the last thing he could ever have imagined her saying. "I'm sorry you had to see that." She sounded embarrassed. A teardrop slid from one eye and she squeezed her eyes shut.

"Naina, come on."

She didn't react. It was like he wasn't even there.

"Should I go after her?" Vansh asked.

That made her open her eyes. "God, no. Please. I think you've done enough." But she didn't sound angry with him. Not the way she'd been so many times.

"I'm sorry she reacted that way. But what was wrong with what I said? Shouldn't someone have said it by now?" He studied her face, genuinely lost in the face of this lifeless avatar of her. "Shouldn't you have?"

Naina's hand shook as she pressed it into her temples. "Shouldn't I have what?"

"Told her the way she treats you is unfair. The way she never stands up to your dad is unfair."

She smiled then and touched his cheek. He grabbed her hand, relief washing through him.

"Vansh, it's not like I can't see what she's doing. That's not why I don't say anything to her. Anyone with even the most minimal insight can tell how afraid she is and what she's afraid of. It's why no one ever says what you just did. Because they know why she's like this. She's terrified of her husband leaving her. She cannot imagine a life separate from him." She swallowed. "Even though he's a monster." She pulled her hand back. "She knows this. If she could change, she would. She doesn't have the capacity to change."

Capacity. The word hung between them. She'd tried so hard to tell him that Hari didn't have the capacity to do what Vansh had so stupidly pressured him into doing. The consequences of his actions had been horribly harmful to an innocent person. She'd told him over and over again she didn't have the capacity to love.

"You telling her to suddenly gather the courage to change because you're fucking her daughter is nonsensical. It's exactly why I knew this—us—was a bad idea."

Taking her hand again, he pressed it back into his cheek. "Naina. Please. Don't say that. I should have seen that. I'm sorry. But we're not a bad idea. I'm an idiot sometimes, but I'll do better,

I promise. I'll fix this, I promise." Promising to fix things he'd broken seemed like all he did these days. But what was wrong with that? He wanted to. He could.

Her eyes said she wanted to believe him. "You can't fix what you don't understand. My mother has stayed with him because she believes she has nowhere to go, because she believes she's wronged him by giving birth to me. Or wronged him by not being able to have more children. Or wronged him in some way. He's used his control over her to manipulate her into believing that. Trying to control people is the problem, not the solution."

"You think I was trying to control you when I told you to stand up to her? I wasn't."

"You were, though. You always want to fix everything. Because you do believe you can control things. This is why I never want to be in a relationship. I don't want to be controlled. I don't want to be with someone who uses my shame against me."

"Shame? How is there any shame in this for you?"

She laughed again and pressed a fist into her heart. "The shame, it's so deeply wedged inside me, it's part of me. There is no me without it. She's my mother, Vansh."

"I know. But you aren't her."

"Don't say that. Don't write her off. There's so much to her that you don't see. She just knows no other way to be. This is all she feels capable of and she's done the best she could with it."

He got up and sat down next to her. "Whatever else she did, there is one thing she's done that no one can fault her for. You." He tucked a lock of hair behind her ear. "I'm truly sorry for everything today. I'm going to be better. I swear."

The earnest regret flooding his heart seemed to finally reach her. Or maybe she was just too exhausted.

He wrapped an arm around her and she put her head on his shoulder.

"I've been honest with you, Vansh, you know that, right?" she said.

He didn't want to know what she meant by that, and he refused to acknowledge the hopelessness in her voice. In this moment she leaned into him with the kind of vulnerability he knew took all her courage, and he'd be damned if he wasn't there for her with his entire body and soul.

Chapter Twenty-Seven

*I*t was a full-time job not letting Vansh's indomitable hope seep into her. Fortunately, Hari was recovering well. He'd been diagnosed with panic disorder. He also had severe social anxiety and agoraphobia. But he had started therapy and was on medication and as much in love with Vansh as ever. Although Vansh insisted he was more in love with Naina.

The journey was for Hari to find his way to being in love with himself, as Sadiya had said with all her usual wisdom.

Naina searched Vansh's face across the coffee table as he worked with Hari on something. They were in Yash's apartment. Yash split most of his time between Sacramento and India's place, and his apartment sat mostly empty. Vansh had called him to ask if they could use it without giving it a single thought. The way the Rajes always did.

Yash had offered it up as an interim solution without asking a single question. They'd been using it as their makeshift office since they'd moved Hari there from the hospital two weeks ago.

After they'd moved in, when Yash had called to check in on them, Naina had been by herself.

"Did you want me to call Mehta?" he'd asked on the video call, studying her with gray eyes that were completely different from his brother's but had the same kindness and focus in them.

"No," she'd said. "Vansh and I got it."

A spark of surprise had brightened his eyes. "Ah," he'd said. She was used to these *ah*s now. "You're involved in Vansh's job-training app, then?"

"It's our app," she'd said without much thought.

"And Nepal?"

"Vansh takes care of the operations. Permissions, relationships. I focus on programs. Same as the app."

"Shit!" said the governor of California. "We've been best friends our whole life and this is the most you've ever said to me about your work."

"That's not true." Was it?

He gave her one of his *You dare to disagree with me?* looks.

"You never asked."

That made him give a surprised laugh. "We were such idiots."

"Idiots?" she said, unable to wrap her head around this new chatty Yash. Could people really change so much?

"You never allowed me any power over you and I never allowed you any over me. That's what we thought we needed to survive, to get what we wanted. We were idiots, Nai." He ran a quick hand through his hair. "Or maybe we were just waiting for the right people."

Wait, what was he insinuating here? "I'm really happy for you, Yash, you know that, right? But I am not you."

Another *ah* followed.

She wasn't interested. Enough with the *ah*s.

"I've got to go. Meeting."

He'd given another patronizing smile. "Of course. But may I say just one last thing?"

"I wish you wouldn't."

"All men are not your father, Nai."

With that unsolicited wisdom, he'd finally let her go.

She was still grateful for the use of his home.

Even though Hari was doing much better, he wouldn't stop agonizing over what had happened, no matter how many times Vansh apologized and told him it hadn't been his fault.

Hari was squeezed into the corner of Yash's gray leather couch. Naina and Hari exchanged a glance and Hari giggled. Naina made a Herculean effort not to.

"What?" Vansh asked, knowing full well what they were smiling about.

"It's violet," Naina said.

"With pink flowers," Hari said.

"Embroidered flowers," Naina said.

Every time Naina saw Vansh in one of these shirts, she could barely suppress the urge to climb him like a tree. Not that the urge hadn't been her constant companion for months now.

"They're lotuses. I happen to like lotuses," he said, running a hand down his shirt without a whit of self-consciousness.

"You really don't have to do this," Naina said.

He pointed a finger at her face. "Keep looking at me like that and I'll do it a million times over. I'll let Chandni Auntie paint roses on my cheeks if she wants."

Vansh had waited two days, as Naina had suggested, after that disastrous run-in with their mothers, and then he'd gone over and apologized to Naina's mother. When she had curtly accepted his apology, fed him some paneer kababs, and tried to send him on his way, he'd complimented her clothes and told her how much he'd always liked the things she wore.

What had followed was her giving him a detailed history of her lifelong love affair with clothes. She'd always been obsessed with fashion shows. For years she'd taken the over-the-top designs of big designers and tweaked them to make them wearable, made her own designs from them, and sent drawings to her cousin in India, who then had them made and sent them back.

A large part of Naina's childhood had been spent playing mannequin for Mummy's creations. What Naina hadn't known was that her mother's real love was fabrics. Appliqué, zardozi, and embroidery. Which shouldn't have been a surprise because Mummy's own clothes were always embellished with some sort of thread work. Naina had just never imagined that Mummy had done that herself.

As soon as she'd told Vansh about her passion, he'd asked her if the kurti she was wearing—with birds embroidered on the sleeves—was her work.

When he'd recounted his meeting with her mother to Naina, he'd sounded awed. "I've really never seen anything like it," he'd said. Which did not help with Naina's condition of wanting to climb him like a tree. Not even a little bit.

Mummy had given him an hour-long tour of all her designs, the ones in her closet and the ones on her iPad. Something she'd never shared with anyone, not even Naina. Probably because no one, not even Naina, had ever asked her about it.

Then Mummy had pulled out her stash of brightly embroidered shirts that she'd been working on and asked him if he would model them for her. When he'd said yes, that had led to her gifting them to him. Which he now wore because she had taken to calling him about their "modeling partnership" and seeing him in them made her face light up.

Whether she was punishing him or this was forgiveness, Naina didn't know, because her mother wasn't really talking to her. She was pretending that the disaster in the hospital had never happened.

Naina had expected no different. Embarrassment had been an integral part of Naina's life. This feeling of being naked in public, she should have been used to it by now. But she still felt scraped raw by the incident. She couldn't believe she'd let Vansh see her like that, the pathetic girl with a mother whose arm was in a sling.

But she'd had to tell him only once. Once. About why Mummy behaved the way she did. And he'd understood.

Maybe Naina was wrong that his wanting to fix things was about control. Maybe it was that he was able to empathize in this way, with connection rather than sympathy. Maybe that was what made him such a magnet for the Haris, and Nainas, and even Chandnis of this world. For the many friends he had across the globe.

She tried not to think about how she couldn't even hold on to the few connections she did have. She hadn't spoken to Yash, really spoken to him, in years. And Mina Auntie's reaction had crushed something inside her. Mina Auntie without her warmth tilted something about the world off its axis.

Vansh hadn't told Naina the part about modeling her mother's shirts. Naina had overheard Sid Dashwood and Vansh talking. Sid had been so amused by the story—and Vansh's new wardrobe—that he had offered to take pictures of Vansh in the shirts. Naturally, she'd been wrong about Sid too. The photographer had obviously also fallen prey to Vansh's charms. She'd admitted to Vansh that she'd been wrong and that Sid had not, in fact, had ulterior motives in making friends with him.

"I think you've atoned enough, Vansh. You can stop wearing the shirts now," Naina said, such warmth burning in her heart that she pressed a hand into it.

The way he looked at her told her that his wearing the shirts definitely had nothing to do with atonement and everything to do with her.

"Are you telling me to take my shirt off, Ms. Kohli?" Vansh said. "I think that's somewhat inappropriate in a work setting."

Hari giggled.

This seemed to ease some of the guilt obviously deeply lodged inside Vansh about what he'd put Hari through, and the two high-fived.

"The workday is almost done," Naina said, and Vansh whooped and Hari blushed.

Makayla was in Nepal and Sadiya had left for the day. Mariel was the only one who was a direct Omnivore employee, and she was the only one still going into Mehta's office.

With an email, drafted by his team of obscenely paid lawyers, Jiggy had put a hold on all future funding for the Nepal project. That meant their effort to fast-track the construction of the clinics had been fortuitous. It meant work didn't have to stop, for now. But you couldn't have clinics if you couldn't fund setting them up.

Jiggy had also claimed intellectual property rights to the app, since it had been created under the umbrella of Omnivore. Sadiya had already responded with suits.

"Alas, I'm pretty sure your friend Jiggy will appreciate you leaving your shirt on. We don't need to give him more reasons to be jealous and bitter," Naina said.

They had a call with Jiggy in ten minutes. Naina was not looking forward to whatever games he had left to play.

She didn't want to rely on Omnivore's funding to complete the project anymore. Vansh had agreed. They'd been trying to come up with an alternative.

"You're right," Vansh said. "Let's focus on enjoying the Jiggster's bitterness when we throw his strings-riddled money back in his face."

Naina sat up. "Vansh?" She slid a glance from him to Hari, who smiled and then gave a long yawn and stood.

"I wanted to be here when you told her about our fundraising plan, but these medicines knock me out." He also didn't want to be in the same room where he could hear Jiggy's voice. And the fact that he recognized what he could handle and verbalized it made Naina fill with pride.

"Way to keep a secret, Hari!" Vansh said. "It was supposed to be a surprise."

"Oops," Hari said, but he was smiling.

"That's fine. I think she's going to be excited enough that it will last until tomorrow. You can enjoy it then."

Tonight, it seemed, he wanted to enjoy whatever this surprise was alone. His eyes warmed as soon as Hari left the room, and her heart sent the most intense spark of electricity through her body.

"I love when you talk about me like I'm not here," she said.

Vansh pressed a kiss to her lips. "You're always there, Knight-lina. Always."

Before she could pull away because those words turned the buzzing in her body heavy and cold with fear, he pointed to the couch. "You might want to sit down for this." He sank into the couch in front of the laptop and pulled her into his lap.

She came willingly and dropped a kiss on his cheek. "You're cute when you're excited about work."

"Cute? That almost makes me not want to tell you."

"I mean cute in a wildly manly way. Tell me."

"Fine. Remember how you said that the way to help Hari is to ask him what he wants? What he likes to do? And remember how Shobi Kaki told us we needed to find a way to fund projects publicly and not through corporate philanthropic organizations? Well, I asked Hari, and he said the happiest he'd ever been was when he was working for Yash and digging into data to iden-tify people on social media who might have an interest in Yash's policies." Vansh opened their social media ad reach page, and his body vibrated with excitement under her.

"Hari's been coming up with an algorithm to target people

who might want to fund our project in Nepal. It's been three days and you're not going to believe the numbers we're at."

Naina's mouth fell open. Vansh navigated to their fundraising page and her shoulders started to shake. "Vansh . . ." How had he even done this? "I can't believe you did this."

"Well, Hari did this."

She turned in his arms and squeezed him in a hug, and he squeezed her back so tight it was a wonder she could still breathe.

"I don't know what to say," she said finally, feeling his heart pounding to match hers.

"You could tell me I'm the most brilliant man you've ever met and you can't live without me."

She laughed. Fingers threaded through his hair, she pulled away, something fierce burning inside. "Listening to me *has* turned you into the most brilliant man."

He waited. It had not escaped him that she hadn't touched the other half of what he'd said.

"Seriously, though, Vansh, this is truly brilliant. I can't believe we didn't think of this before! Have you told Shobi Auntie yet? She's going to be so excited. Do Sadiya and Makayla know?"

Turned out, they'd all been planning the surprise. So she could finally tell Jiggy to go to hell as ceremoniously as she'd been dreaming of.

And she did.

"You know you can't do this without me," Jiggy said on the phone, after.

"We'll figure it out. We rich kids do take our need to run around and save the world seriously."

There were monstrous amounts of paperwork to be done to transfer everything to their own foundation. Jiggy threatened to make things as difficult for them legally as he could. But Naina offered him the option of backing away without negative publicity. With so much of Big Tech on board with the app, attacking them legally on that front would be unimaginably stupid on Jiggy's part.

"Jiggyshasha is truly fucked," Vansh said when they hung up.

"You're a force of nature," she said. He was. And he'd get better and better. Because he would never stop trying. Already at twenty-six he was way ahead of where she'd been. The urge to be there for it was unbearable. But she knew it changed nothing for her.

"*We* are a force of nature," he said, and kissed her long and hard. Exactly the way she needed to be kissed in this moment. She had this moment. They had this moment.

"We are," she said. "But I'm not sleeping with you in your brother's home."

He jumped off the couch. "Then we'd better hurry and get to your place."

She followed him without a thought. All she could do was be honest with herself about what was possible. *And I've been honest with him.*

But the voice inside her that told her the crash was coming kept getting louder.

Chapter Twenty-Eight

Vansh couldn't tell if Naina had become progressively more withdrawn since that disastrous day in the boardroom or if his own need for her had become harder to control.

What was wrong with him? She was inside him, inside his head, his heart, all the time. All the damn time.

Don't think about the arrangement.

Don't think about what will happen when the arrangement ends.

A year? Tops?

What the hell had he been thinking?

At least she wasn't withdrawn with him when they made love. He'd never thought of sex as making love, but nothing else fit. It was the kind of intimacy Vansh had never experienced. It threw him wide open, made him more himself than he'd ever been. She made him exactly who he wanted to be, in bed and out of it.

How was he ever going to live without it?

When he touched her, when he was inside her, there was no distance between them. No part of her held apart. They were one. Body and soul.

He wanted that all the time. All the damn time.

And the work! The work they were doing was magic. All his life Vansh had done only what made him feel alive. But he'd needed it to be seen, to be on his family's radar. He'd gathered their approval like a child with a giant empty pillowcase on Halloween. Knowing only too well that they'd throw approval into his bag irrespective of what he did to earn it. Their approval had been their support and guilt. It hadn't been approval at all.

I'm proud of you too.

At least HRH had done him the favor of making his approval unattainable.

How can one of my children be stupid?

Well, Dad, stupid people didn't find a way to fund solutions to problems others only complained about.

He'd never been this connected to anything he'd worked on, and his family didn't even know about it. He didn't need their approval. He loved this work with all his heart.

This week, they'd moved Hari into his own place. He had a new passport and green card. He was planning a visit home next month to see his parents. The app was a success and they were able to pay him enough that he'd soon be able to buy his own place, or do whatever he wished.

"In that book of yours, *Emma*, what happens to her?" he asked Naina as she looked over some paperwork they were about to submit to Naman's office. They were in Yash's apartment, a.k.a. their temporary office, working long after everyone else had left.

She raised a brow at him, all the accusations she'd thrown at him—not entirely inaccurately—flashing guiltily in her eyes.

"The one who tries to be a matchmaker so she can feel good about herself and fill her boredom?"

She smiled, but there was an apology in her eyes. A *hot* apology. "She learns that having more privilege than other people doesn't mean you know what's best for them. She learns to admit her mistakes and listen to others, and it teaches her to listen to her own feelings too."

He laughed. "And she finds the love of her life and they live happily ever after."

He'd been joking, but her face said that was exactly what happened.

"You're kidding me," he said. "And this is a book you liked?" Which, come to think of it, gave him great hope. "You're a romantic, Naina Kohli," he said, and got all up in her face.

"You wish," she said, but she did kiss every last bit of breath out of him.

Before he could push the conversation any further, the doorbell rang.

"Were you expecting someone?" she asked, lips swollen, and he shook his head.

They had this paperwork to finish and then he was supposed to meet his sisters for dinner. But that wasn't for another hour.

The sound of a key starting to turn in the front door reached them, and they jumped off the couch as one. Vansh ran to the door just as it flew open. Three of his sisters stared at him.

What was going on?

"Oh. Hi, Naina," Nisha said as they came inside and saw Naina standing there, looking suddenly pristinely put together, fully in control of herself. Nothing like she'd looked a minute ago.

"Hi!" she said, and gathered the papers strewn around the coffee table into a neat pile.

Ashna and Trisha hugged her.

"What are you doing here?" Vansh asked, not bothering to hide his impatience.

All four women bristled at his rudeness.

"Since we're supposed to go to dinner in the city, we thought we'd surprise you and stop by early for a drink." Ashna held up a bottle of wine.

"Oh." Nisha slapped her forehead. "I forgot my cell phone in the car. I'll run out and get it while Ashna opens the wine. Vansh, want to join me?"

Not even a little bit, he wanted to say. But he'd had enough of Nisha and it was time for them to have this conversation.

He followed her down to the lobby. "What is wrong with you, Nisha? You know perfectly well your phone is in that big-ass handbag hanging on your shoulder."

"What is wrong with me? What is wrong with you, Vansh? You never talked to me like this before."

"I always talk to you like this." But she was right, he'd always pacified everyone around him. Stayed upbeat and kept the focus off himself, or at least off things that mattered. The way Naina had tiptoed around their mothers made a slow accusatory spin in his head. "I'm your brother. I shouldn't have everything I say weighed on some scale of preconceived judgments that you've suddenly decided to bring to all our conversations."

"Not all of them."

"Great. So this is about Naina. You're admitting to judging her unnecessarily."

"No! I'm admitting to judging her very necessarily. You've been spending every minute with her. It's weird."

Were his sisters always like this with Naina? He remembered their always being fond and respectful of her.

"I thought you loved Naina. You've been friends all your life."

"First, we did love her, then she lied to us. Second, she was only ever really friends with Yash. It makes sense now why she kept her distance from the rest of us. And third, she tied our brother up in an arrangement that almost caused him to lose his mind, not to mention the election."

"You want to think about what you're saying? It's the most preposterous thing I've ever heard. Yash also did all of that and you aren't treating him like he's a contagious leper. Nice going, Nisha!"

"Oh my God." She made a very Nisha face. One that said she had her big-sister-knows-best blinders on.

"I don't want to hear the rest of that thought." Pointing a finger at her face, he headed back to the stairs.

"You cannot possibly be serious." Of course she followed him.

He didn't turn around. "Not having this conversation with you. Whatever this conversation even is. Whatever you're thinking. Stop. And stop being rude to Naina."

"She dated Yash for ten years!"

He turned around. Nisha looked as determined as a tornado ready to lift up a house in Kansas and toss it across a rainbow. If she went anywhere near Naina with that unleashed determination, she would devastate Naina and any chance he might have of convincing her that they might have something. That realization was enough to calm him the fuck down.

The shrug he gave his sister was bored, almost lazy. "Really? How did I miss that? Does anyone else know?"

"Stop being a brat."

"Stop being a bully."

"Caring about my little brother does not count as being a bully."

"Your brother is not little anymore, if you haven't noticed. I have no earthly idea what you're insinuating. Naina is someone I've known—we've known—our entire damned lives. She's family. She's always been there for us. She's the only one who helped me when I was struggling with school and you all ignored it."

Nisha looked horrified.

"I understand why you did it. I'm not blaming you for it. She sat by Yash's bed the entire time he was recovering from the accident. You might have dropped her like a hot brick because you blame her for something our brother is just as guilty of. I, however, happen to believe that she and Yash were both being idiots and never meant to harm anyone. She's also a colleague. One who shares my love for the work we do."

"And there's nothing more."

"What the hell, Nisha! When did you turn into such a nosy auntie? There's this new thing going around: men and women working together, being friends. It's also, you know, the twenty-first fucking century!"

She narrowed her eyes. "Oh, so you're just colleagues. Friends."

He narrowed his eyes back at her but didn't dignify that with an answer and started walking again.

"Well, good, then you can act like that when we're at dinner."

"What does that mean?"

She shrugged.

"Actually, I don't want to know. You're acting like someone I don't know at all." He ran up the stairs and she followed him back into Yash's apartment, where Naina was studiedly chugging red wine to avoid the silence in the room.

Trisha and Ashna were doing the same. All his life he'd been proud of how empathetic and unjudgmental his family was. Even Ma and HRH, for all their Bollywood-star-meets-royal-prince vibe, worked hard to be open-minded and fair. They'd never had patience for bigoted or patriarchal behavior, HRH's attitude toward his youngest son's shortcomings notwithstanding.

Trisha might have been socially inept when it came to warmth, but she loved her patients and she would die for her family. Ashna might have been too shy with her feelings sometimes, but she would take the shirt off her back for anyone in need. They would both, along with Nisha, have bitten off the head of anyone who was being unfair to a woman because of her gender.

Why the hell were they doing this to Naina?

He went straight to her. "You all right?"

She gave him the subtlest warning glance, then looked away as though he were a bug she'd accidentally stepped on, inconsequential. "Why would I not be all right? I mean, I was until you asked me that. Is there something stuck in my teeth?"

Okay, fine, he deserved that. He wasn't supposed to behave like her boyfriend around people, especially their families. That was their deal. He got that, but he was her friend too. He could damn well behave like a friend around anyone he damn well pleased.

She downed the rest of her glass, and idiot that he was, it made him think about their first time, and that made him think about how much he loved when they were both a little buzzed when they were together. That in turn made him want her so damn badly he didn't know what to do with it.

"So I'll take my leave then. It was lovely to see you all." She threw a quick and very civil nod at his sisters.

Each of them returned it with varying degrees of awkwardness.

Vansh laughed, but it didn't do a thing to relieve the tension in the room or the pressure filling him up to exploding. What was happening to him? One minute he was turned on as hell, the next moment he wanted to shake his sisters. "I'm sure it was lovely to see them."

His sisters, all three of them, turned to him like lionesses. He could swear they bared their teeth at him. Naina just ignored the lot of them and picked up her bag.

"We need to finish going over those papers. We also need to look at the new numbers. Stay and we can finish up."

"Excuse me?" Nisha said, raising both hands as though she had no idea what to do with him. "We have a dinner reservation."

"I'll take a rain check. Naina and I have to send some paperwork out tonight and send some numbers to Shobi Kaki by tomorrow. She's helping with how to process overseas donations. We have to take care of this right now."

"No we don't. You go to dinner. I can look at it myself when I get home."

"No! I want to help."

The already palpable awkwardness turned intense. "Fine. We can do it tomorrow." Plastering the sweetest smile across her face, Naina started to leave.

The panic that grabbed him made no sense.

She was angry. Worse than that, she was hurt. He could see the hurt tearing at her under her skin and he was not leaving her when she was feeling like this.

"I want to do it now."

Color rose up her neck. Her gaze slid to his sisters and back to him. He could see her struggling to stay calm. With every bit of telepathy that connected them, she was trying to tell him to back off. To contol this thing raging inside him that he couldn't seem to stop.

"Why doesn't Naina join us?" Ashna said, finally feeling the need to speak up and invite her. Something they should have done when they had first brought up dinner.

"That's a great idea," Trisha said, determinedly not looking at Nisha. "Maybe you can both review this thing in the car and then we'll eat and you don't have to miss dinner." That was Trisha for you, filled with logical solutions. A little late, but thank you for trying, Trisha.

"What's the big deal about this dinner?" he said, moving so he was blocking Naina's way because she was all set to leave anyway. "We can do it another day."

"We haven't seen you in weeks, Vansh. You'll take off as soon as this project is over." Ashna threw a quick glance at Naina. "And we miss you."

Dear Lord. "I'm not going anywhere for a while. Let's just do this another time."

Naina's hand tightened on the strap of her handbag, but the rest of her appeared as calm as ever. Why was it bothering him so much, the way she was able to hide everything? "Vansh, you made a commitment to your sisters. Go. It's not a big deal."

Like hell it wasn't. "Why can't you come with us?"

Because I wasn't fucking invited. Their telepathy was working just fine, thank you very much. "Because this is your time with your sisters."

I don't want you to leave. "Actually that's not true. Aren't we meeting up with Neel and his cousin?"

Nisha's face transformed into an expression Vansh could not recognize, but murderousness was at least one part of it. Finally, she turned to Naina, sweet smile doing nothing to conceal the scream she had to be holding inside. "Naina, seriously, you should come. Sorry we didn't say anything before, but we assumed you had plans. Join us, please."

Now Naina threw him a look with a healthy tinge of her own murderousness. "I can't. I'm—"

"You can help Vansh check Neel's cousin out. We've been trying to set them up for years. She's a human rights lawyer. She just got back from working on a Habitat for Humanity project in Haiti."

All those years Vansh had spent missing his siblings, and it had come to this?

Naina's smile went wide and blank. "A human rights lawyer? A charitable mission in Haiti? She sounds totally his type."

He returned her smile. "So you'll come then?" Because that was the only thing that mattered. Being with her.

"Well, someone's got to help you check her out."

Nisha, Ashna, and Trisha picked up their jackets, their heads turning between Naina and Vansh as though they were at a tennis match.

Vansh retrieved Naina's jacket from the closet and held it up for her. Anger sparkled in her eyes as she tried to take the jacket, as though letting him help her with it was too intimate. It was, and he needed it. He needed to not tiptoe anymore. He wanted them to see her. He wanted more.

She shoved her arms into the jacket he was holding with far too much force.

"Who better than you to help me check a woman out?" he said behind her ear, everything he was feeling in his whisper.

She was far too adept at holding herself so no one saw the things she was feeling, but his body soaked up the shiver that ran down hers, every last tremor of it.

"I can't think of one single person," she whispered as they followed his sisters out to the car.

Despite himself, Vansh couldn't stop his hand from running down her back, from her long neck down her spine to the beautiful curve of her hip. They couldn't see him do it and the urge to touch her was too intense.

The fact that her legs faltered at his touch made everything okay, but just for a moment. Then she moved away from him, shoving herself into the third row of Nisha's van, right in the middle seat, leaving no space for him.

Don't even think about it. She glared at him when he tried to get in the back next to her.

"There's only five of us, Vansh, did you miscalculate? You don't have to crowd into the back row," Trisha said.

Vansh and Trisha both hated third rows. They made them carsick. Trisha had called shotgun.

Ashna threw Vansh a worried look, but it was so kind that he sat down next to her and felt Naina's body relax in the back row from the fact that he hadn't squeezed in next to her.

He threw a look over his shoulder. *Really?*

The fact that she didn't want him near her hit him hard. He knew why she didn't want his body touching hers with his family here. He knew how their bodies reacted to each other. He knew. Even so, the fear that rolled through him at the thought of not being wanted by her shook him.

"I thought we were picking up Neel and the human rights lawyer," he said.

"Bipasha," Nisha said as they slid into traffic. "Neel and she are meeting us there."

"Bipasha. That's a lovely name," Naina said, buckling herself in, attempting to insert a smile into her voice.

The Banana Tree was Vansh's favorite Malaysian place. It had the best roti parathas in the Bay. Sam, the owner, who was Nisha's friend, greeted them at the door and led them to a private booth in the very back. Naina threw another warning glare at Vansh, but it was more wary than anything else. This charade Nisha had trapped them in was exhausting.

It was obvious that Naina didn't want him sitting next to her, which made other things obvious too. How hard it was to keep their hands off each other. Even without realizing it, she kept angling her body close to him even as she tried to hold herself away. The sense that he was in over his head had taken root inside him weeks ago, and it had been growing and growing. Now it pushed all the way out and took over completely.

In the end, the exhaustion in Naina's eyes got to him and he backed off. He stood there letting everyone move and settle around the table. Neel was already seated next to his cousin, and between all the introductions and hugs, Vansh found himself seated between Ashna and the cousin. What the hell was her name again?

"Oh," Ashna said. "Didn't the two of you need to look at something in the car?" She got up and changed places with Naina, and now Vansh found himself between the cousin and Naina.

"That wasn't necessary," Naina said. "We can really look at it tomorrow." But the fact that he hadn't forced his way next to her made her soften.

For the next half hour, Naina and Vansh filled everyone in on the project as they ordered and poured enough wine into their systems that Naina relaxed.

Not touching you when you're this close is killing me. Maybe he shouldn't have texted her, but he did. "Sorry, our lawyer just sent the agenda for a meeting," he said as he looked down at his phone.

"Did she? Excuse me," Naina said politely, picking up her phone, and swallowed as she read his text. *Good, because if we survive this I'm going to kill you anyway,* she texted back, but her leg moved and touched his.

He smiled. *Do I get a last wish?*

You only ever want one thing.

Damn straight.

She was trying hard not to smile, but she didn't respond.

Ever thought what it would be like to come at a table filled with people?

He felt the heat on her face with his entire body. As though she were pressed against his bare skin.

Her eyes swept the table. Everyone was engaged in conversation. They were hotly debating what Yash should accomplish in his first year.

Her fingers touched her phone. They were shaking. Her cheeks were glowing like they did when he strummed her to full awareness, when she was close to release.

What? he typed. *Say it.*

I hadn't thought about it until now. She closed her eyes and swallowed as she hit send.

And? His fingers clutched his phone as he waited.

Show me. She swallowed reading her own words.

Vansh took a sip of his wine and his hand fell to his lap. Someone declared that Yash didn't have a choice but to address the fires first.

Naina set both elbows on the table and rested her chin on her hands.

They were close enough to the tabletop that it covered them completely. His thigh pressed into hers. His hand found the hem of her skirt and played with it. Thank God for flirty skirts.

"Everything all right with Jiggy?" Neel asked.

The cousin giggled. "That's a hilarious name."

A smile spread across Naina's face. "It is hilarious, isn't it? Vansh finds it hysterical."

"I do. I find it hard to control myself." His hand found its way under her skirt. "I can't stop convulsing . . . with laughter when I say it." The defined muscles of her leg shivered beneath her velvet skin. Her hand trembled on her wine, and she clutched the stem and took a slow, elegant gulp.

Her body was already ready, held rock steady to hide what was coming. His fingers trailed up her thigh, where taut muscle turned soft and hot, and found the silk of her underwear. With one pinkie he traced the edges that skimmed her skin. She had the most gorgeous underwear of any human on earth.

What color is it? he wanted to ask her.

She tapped her glass. "Red."

Before anyone could ask what she was talking about, she took another sip. "This red is really good."

"It is. It's one of Nisha's favorite cabs—what is that vinery we were at last year?" Thank the good judge for always knowing what to do with a conversation.

"Peju?" Nisha answered.

"Yes, I think that's it. Did the waiter take the bottle away?"

"He's getting us another. Is it a little dry though?"

"Not in the least bit dry," Vansh said, taking a sip with his left hand.

"I agree," Ashna said. "I thought it was a little on the sweet side."

"Definitely sweet." His fingers twirled the silk until it roped and pressed it into her folds.

Naina's lips quivered over the glass. Her clit quivered under his thumb. God, she was so wet, and swollen, and ready.

The waiter returned with a new bottle and everyone's attention turned to him. Well, not everyone's.

This waiter was a talker, and Vansh's family loved few things more than they loved talking about wine. Next to him Naina stiffened, then convulsed. Her fingers tightened on the glass, the muscle in her jaw worked, her thighs pressed together, but other than that not a hint that she was coming hard against his hand escaped her.

"God, Naina," he whispered close to her ear as his fingers soaked up the pulses that beat through her clit and thrummed through his blood.

The waiter poured her a glass, and she took a long sip on a gasp that sounded to Vansh's ears like his name screamed in the night.

"It's that good?" Trisha asked, taking a sip too and looking confused.

"Naina loves her cabs," Vansh said, pulling his hand away from her even as aftershocks shivered through her body.

He ran his fingers over his lips. He could have been just another man contemplating life and his friend's wine preferences. In reality he was a man savoring the taste of the most intoxicating woman he'd ever come across in his life. A man who'd just realized that he couldn't let her go. Not ever.

Chapter Twenty-Nine

Naina's legs still felt shaky in her heeled boots as she let herself into the restaurant's minuscule bathroom. Had she really just done what she'd done, with Vansh's family right there? Her inner muscles contracted just thinking about it.

What was happening to her?

Everything inside her felt different. It had been coming on for a while, this feeling of fullness, as though something had snuck inside her and infected her. The thick armor she'd worked hard to wrap around herself kept slipping off, but she felt too tired to pull it back on. Too greedy for the breeze that kissed her skin when it was exposed.

Most of dinner had gone by without her registering a single thing but Vansh next to her. Not all the wine in the world could compare with the intoxicating feeling of him.

Then his parents had arrived after dinner and joined them for coffee and dessert. How the hell were there families like this in the world? The kind that liked to be with one another? That ate and drank together and actually found enjoyment in it?

The rage inside Naina roiled to life, mingled with every bad memory from her childhood. How much more work did she have to do to get over this shit?

Well, getting involved with someone like Vansh was hardly the way to distance herself from the ugliness of her own family. It was akin to scratching at a scab. Satisfying in that moment, but it gouged out wounds in the long run. She scrubbed at the red wine stain on her white sweater with a wet washcloth. It faded but didn't disappear.

At least it had given her an excuse to get away from the familial banter that made her feel like she was choking. Not to mention the suspicious glances from Vansh's sisters and mother. His sisters' disdain Naina could bear, but to have Mina Auntie look at her like that, like she was a stain spreading on the pristine fabric of their family, it made Naina want to throw up.

Desperate for some fresh air, she pushed her way out of the restroom and then out the back exit. The unseasonably warm air hit her face and she filled her lungs.

Just as her insides were settling, the door opened behind her. Naturally his rich scent flooded through her before she heard his footsteps approaching. How had she ever thought he smelled like anyone else?

"There's the person I've been looking for." How was his voice so beautiful? So soothing that she felt the knots inside her start to ease?

"I've been with you the entire night, Vansh." She didn't turn around.

His arms wrapped around her waist, those ridged forearms pressing into the delicate knit of her sweater and making her breasts pucker like hungry babies. He pressed his face into her neck and she felt light-headed, as though the full moon above them were casting a spell that lifted them off the ground.

"But then you left. And all I can feel when you leave is this need." His lips kissed her skin, the gentle swell of his arousal pressed against her back. "This need that won't go away."

She should pull away, but the way he touched her was addictive, hit upon hit of a drug she couldn't get enough of. Her body was seized with a mix of complete and utter comfort in itself and overwhelming wildness.

"Someone will see, Vansh. Your entire family is here."

"Maybe it's okay if they see. Maybe I don't care what my family thinks." The way he held her was too possessive. Like wanting her was something he no longer cared to hide. Something he *couldn't* hide.

Her heart started to slam in her chest, the panicked dance that had taken to breaking out inside her unexpectedly throughout the day.

His body always picked up the nuances of her thoughts from her body, and he was about to pull away, or press closer. She'd never know which, because Nisha's gasp cut through the night and Naina sprang away from him.

Mina Auntie followed. Great. Just great.

Nisha had both hands pressed to her face as though she'd walked in on a stabbing. For once Naina was in agreement with her. Naina felt slashed open. How had she allowed this to happen? Why had she tangled herself up in an arrangement that was doomed from the beginning? Again.

"Vansh, beta, what is going on?" Mina Auntie asked, her eyes fixed on Naina even as she addressed her son.

"Vansh was just checking on me. Checking to see if I got the stain off. It's just that red wine is so stubborn, I can't believe how clumsy I was. But you wear white and this has to happen, right? I mean, why do we even wear—"

"What do you think is going on, Ma?" Vansh cut her off.

"Nothing is going on." Naina threw him a warning, but he looked so hurt by his mother's tone, so determined to fix this, it was like she wasn't even there. Like she didn't exist in the face of what he wanted. What he'd promised her he'd never want. Even though she'd made it clear it was not what she wanted.

"That's not what it looked like when I got here," Nisha said as though speaking to someone who might be taking advantage of her adolescent daughter.

"Nisha." Vansh threw his sister the kind of look she'd never seen him give anyone in his family. Outright anger. "Stay out of this. This is none of your business."

"What is *this* exactly?" Mina Auntie said, voice soft but determined to get answers.

"As I said before, it's nothing," Naina said. "There is not a single thing here you have to worry about, Mina Auntie. I was just leaving." She tried to skirt past Vansh but couldn't because he had her trapped between his family and the brick wall.

As if that wasn't enough, he took her hand. "This is not nothing and you know it."

She yanked her hand away from his. How dare he put her in a spot like this. How dare he manipulate her this way.

She'd known this would happen. She'd known.

What an idiot she was.

She pushed him out of her way and ran around the building.

He followed. Of course he did. "Naina!"

"No, Vansh. You don't get to decide what is or isn't nothing for me. I decide that for myself. Thanks for doing exactly what I knew you'd do. And thanks for doing it in front of an audience." Eyes distraught, he tried to reach for her again, but she held out her hand. "Not now, Vansh, please. I'm walking home. Alone. I need space. Please."

How dare he look wounded?

Mina Auntie came around the building, Nisha close behind her.

"Go inside, Nisha, Ma. Please." Vansh angled his body to block Naina from them.

Nisha was at least as stubborn as Vansh. "That poor girl Bipasha—whom you haven't said one word to all night—was invited here to meet you. The least you can do is say bye to her and let her know you're not interested."

"I never asked you to invite her," Vansh snapped. "And I never told her I was interested."

Naina couldn't stand this. *How did I let this happen?* The thought kept screaming inside her head. She started walking away.

He fell in step next to her and she stopped again. One part of her wanted to punch Nisha in the face. One part was grateful that Nisha was keeping her grounded in reality.

Sex is sex. We keep it separate from the rest of it.

How easily he had said those words. Had he ever intended to keep them? How had that been just a few months ago? It felt like years. It felt like her whole life.

Suddenly, Naina's body was encased in ice. All she wanted was for this to be over. "Nisha's right, Vansh. Go talk to the lawyer. She's right for you." Her heart should have crumbled. Maybe it did, but she could feel nothing. She was going to have to see him with someone else someday, and better to start building that muscle now.

"I was just touching you under a table. Do you think I give a damn for anyone else right now?"

Naina looked over her shoulder to see if Nisha and Mina Auntie had followed. They had, but they were far enough away that they hadn't heard Vansh.

She went back to them. "Mina Auntie, I'm so sorry. I really didn't mean to cause a scene."

Mina Auntie's eyes slid to Vansh and her face froze. They were in front of the restaurant now and people were entering and leaving. "Get yourselves together. This isn't the place for this conversation." With nothing more than that, she went back into the restaurant.

With an accusatory look at Naina, Nisha followed her mother.

"I'm sorry," Vansh said. "I shouldn't have said that in front of them."

"Do not follow me," Naina said, hoping her voice was firm, even though everything inside her wobbled. Then, just to make sure he understood, she added, "Do not come over later. I'm exhausted. Please."

We made a deal. You made a promise, she almost added, but that was not a bag she was ready to turn over and empty out just yet. Not here.

He took a step back. "Right. And you don't have the capacity to deal with me right now." Again, he had the gall to look wounded.

"I don't. And you promised to listen to me."

Anger flashed under the hurt in his eyes. She couldn't tell whom the anger was directed at. But she didn't care.

Turning around, she walked away, leaving him to his family and the human rights lawyer.

Anger was a good thing. Maybe anger would open his eyes.

The ten-block walk home was exactly what Naina needed. The breeze wafting up from the bay ruffled her skirt and she patted it down, feeling where Vansh's hands had trailed up her skin. It was a miracle he hadn't followed her, but she'd take the small victory.

When she passed Yash's condo, their makeshift office, her heart cramped so hard that pain radiated down her limbs. Had it really been only months since Yash's victory party on the Raje estate? How had Naina thought she'd ever be done with the Rajes? One was never done with the Rajes.

The disappointment in Mina Auntie's eyes was going to haunt her forever. If she'd been cold before, today she'd been downright livid.

As Naina approached her building, her eyes fell on a portly man leaning on the wall next to her door. A portly man in an expensive coat who made every bad feeling inside Naina expand and slither around even as it made the icy numbness return.

If she'd thought her evening had gone badly until now, this was about to make everything that had happened feel like a picnic.

What had she ever done to deserve this? Was it too late to pretend to not have seen him?

"Knightlina," he said, and a horrible shiver ran down Naina's spine.

"Please don't call me that."

"It is your name. It is who you are. Just because you changed it on a piece of paper doesn't make you someone else."

Was it even possible to feel this much hatred for a person who'd had a hand in your creation? Maybe *hatred* wasn't quite accurate. She felt entirely disconnected from him. Like they lived on two different planets and some grotesque time-space glitch had made it possible for them to be talking.

She stood there with her hand on the door, wishing she could go inside and have it slam in his face. But Mummy still lived with him. Mummy, who'd finally forgiven her and been excited when Naina talked to her this morning. She'd talked about maybe turning her hobby into something else. She'd sounded happy. And she still lived with him.

"I always knew you would bring shame on the family," he said in that ugly voice he never raised but that still somehow always made Naina feel like she was being screamed at.

Naina answered the way she always answered him, with silence.

"This is a little bit too vulgar even for you, don't you think?" he said, pushing.

Letting the door go, Naina turned to him. "I thought the only way I could erase the shame I brought on the family was by finding a man."

The laugh he gave was precise and cruel, Dr. Kohli in a nutshell. "You didn't find a man. You found a child."

Naina refused to wrap her arms around herself. She refused to let him see what his words did.

"The only thing women like you want is someone to control."

"No, that's what men like you want. All I want is a relationship that is not about control."

He spat out another one of those laughs, lighter on the precision this time and heavier on the cruelty. "Doesn't the fact that you can only have that with a man who is twelve years younger than you tell you something?"

Naina's arms went around her.

"Doesn't it tell you that you're fighting nature? All the things you want, how you want to live. It's against nature, against God, against our culture, against any civilized culture. Even though people like you keep trying to bastardize it under the guise of progress." His voice was filled with righteous indignation. The voice of a man who knew everything.

She looked him square in the eye. "Is it not against nature to hate your own child?"

He stepped back, surprised that she'd dared to contradict him. "What reason have you ever given me to love you? I always knew your mother had lost control of you. But this? You've seen the boy in diapers, Knightlina! Who doesn't think that's disgusting?"

The ugly coldness that had been the most pervasive memory of her childhood wrapped back around Naina. The armor she'd let slip crawled back into place, pressing tight against her skin.

"Well, you wasted your time coming out here, because you have it wrong. There is nothing between Vansh and me that anyone needs to worry about. We're colleagues. You're going to have to go back to being disappointed in me simply because I'm a girl and because you can't control me."

When she turned away from him, the rage was back inside her full force, an inferno. The sniveling sadness inside her was gone. The vulnerability she'd stupidly succumbed to, letting herself feel things she had no business feeling. All of it was burnt to ashes and scattered into the wind. The last thing that caught her eye was the satisfied sneer that distorted his face.

SOMETIMES ALL NAINA wanted was to be like the women in romantic comedies. She wanted to cry into her wine. She wanted to eat ice cream straight out of a tub in her pajamas while friends told her it was going to be okay. Instead she felt parched, desert sand where her feelings needed to be. Arid heat where her tears should have been.

She showered and changed into sleeping shorts and an oversized T-shirt, one that Vansh had worn. She hadn't washed it because it smelled of him. Once she'd put it on, she realized how bad of an idea that was and tried to pull it off, but that only made her smell it more, so she let it be. Just for a few moments longer, just until she scrubbed the stain off her sweater.

She'd been scrubbing and scrubbing at the stain when she heard her front door open. Only one person had her code.

"Naina?" Her name in his voice, as if it were color and his voice a paintbrush.

The advantage of having an apartment that was all of four hundred square feet was that she heard the front door close behind him. "Is it okay if I come in?"

Her lights were on, the water was on, so pretending to be asleep was out of the question.

"You promised you wouldn't come over."

"I didn't actually." He was standing in the doorway of her bathroom, wide shoulders filling it up, disregarding her wishes. Their eyes met in the mirror before her. His gaze took her in and softened. "I'm sorry."

Her hands sped up on the sweater, rubbing at the stubborn stain. The fabric tore between her fingers. "Shit." She loved that sweater and now it was ruined. She tossed it in the trash, fingers raw from scrubbing.

I told you not to come over but you didn't listen. The words danced on her tongue. The sense that he was too far away when he was just feet from her danced inside her.

"What are you sorry for exactly? The pissing contest?"

He blinked. She should have been used to the forest of lashes by now. But, no.

"Excuse me?" He had a way of speaking while barely moving his lips when he was hurting.

"Was this evening not a pissing contest?" She turned and leaned back into the vanity. It was the size of a pasta dish. They'd still had sex against it. Of course they had. They'd done it in every corner of her home.

Which meant she was going to have to move. The idea made her weary, but it was just another inevitability. Not putting her life back to rights was no longer an option.

"A pissing contest with whom exactly?" he asked.

"I don't know, Vansh, with yourself? With your siblings?"

"I am not in any sort of contest with Yash over you."

"Oh my God, that's not what I meant at all. But now that you've said it, are you?"

"Naina, sweetheart. Yash is never in my thoughts when I think about you. Tell me you know that."

She knew that. It didn't change anything. "What I know is that dinner today was you staking your claim, hard."

The honey brown of his eyes warmed, and she knew he was about to say something lascivious. He took a step closer. "If you didn't like it, we don't ever have to do that again. We don't ever have to do anything you don't like."

"You know I liked it. I like everything you do. That's the problem."

"How is that a problem? That's the point. The fact that we're magic together. The fact that we can't get enough of each other."

"Vansh! That's not how we were supposed to do this. You were upset with me because I didn't want your family to know. You practically told them."

"I'll take it back. This won't happen again." He looked scared and it ratcheted up the fear in her own heart.

She couldn't let that happen. She couldn't let fear become the center of her life again. "We were never supposed to have this conversation. You promised that we wouldn't have to."

"I'm sorry. I shouldn't have embarrassed you like that. Not in a public place."

"Vansh. Don't make this ugly. You know that's not what I'm talking about. You did not embarrass me. Not when . . ."

He tucked a lock of hair behind her ear, his touch sending a zing through her body as it always did. "When I made you come."

"Yes."

"Why don't you ever say it?"

His thumb on the shell of her ear, that was it, that was their only point of contact, and yet her entire body felt alive, fevered with hunger.

"Say what?"

"That I make you come like no one ever has. That your body is obsessed with mine. That you ache with the memories of the things I make you feel. That you wake up in the middle of the night touching yourself from how I make you feel."

"Is that what I am to you? Bragging rights? Look how obsessed I've made her. I've possessed her body and soul. I'm inside her all the time. That's what this is to you." She pushed away from him and went into the bedroom.

He followed. "No. That's all you want this to be to me, but it's not." He took a step closer to her, eyes filled with need. "Have

I? Have I possessed you body and soul? Am I inside you all the time?"

Without answering, she left her bedroom. That was not a room she could do this in, and she had to do this.

Vansh was light. She couldn't let him in a little bit. She couldn't contain him in a corner of her life. He'd get everywhere. He'd take over everything.

"No, you're not. Because if I let you in, you'll become all of me. There will be no more me left."

His eyes filled with understanding. He saw things no one had ever seen inside her. Things no one had ever cared to see. Things she'd sworn never to let anyone see.

He picked up her hand, warming her from head to toe, warming the coldest parts of her. Her dark, unreachable soul, her always-hungry-for-him body, all of it a molten mess from one touch. His gaze kissed their joined hands. He saw every bit of his power over her. Felt it. Power he'd gained sneakily with lies. She tugged at her hand, but she couldn't put enough force into it to pull away when he pressed it into his chest.

How she loved touching his chest. The warm, thick press of it against her palm. The comfort her entire being drew from it even when she tried not to. The sense of belonging that rested in the solid, beautiful planes.

"You feel that? It only beats like that when you're around." Her hand picked up the hypnotic rhythm beating against warm, hard muscle. "It's always beating. I'm always me. But when you're around it beats differently. Everything feels different. I'm me in a different way. But it's more me, not less. You make me myself in a way I want to be."

Snatching her hand out of his, she put distance between them. "Don't say that. You only want to be with me because I'm not interested in a relationship. Because you can't have me."

The way he looked at her said he heard something beyond her

words. He wasn't listening to her. "I want to be with you because you're what I've been searching for my whole life."

"You've known me your whole life, Vansh."

"No. You've been in my life, but I didn't know you. You were hiding behind my brother. I've been waiting for someone who makes me feel this way, the way I feel around you. I always knew I would know when I met that person, and I do know."

"So I make you feel good. That's all I am, just another thing in your life that feeds your need to feel good. All the time."

His Adam's apple bobbed in the strong, almost poetically beautiful column of his throat.

She'd taken a hard swing at him, she knew. The thing he hated more than anything was her writing him off like this. Pain brightened his eyes, but there wasn't a whit of anger in them.

"Naina." He tried to get closer, tried to hold her, but she couldn't let him. "It's too late to push me away. You're afraid of me taking over your life? What about the fact that you've already taken over mine? And yes, it does feel good. Better than anything has ever felt." He leaned into her again, like a magnet, their axes perfectly positioned for the force of attraction to be at its maximum.

The back of his hand stroked the skin of her jaw, suddenly the most erogenous part of her body. "Nothing feels as good as you. Nothing."

She removed his hand. He wasn't listening to her. "I can't be your instant gratification, your fix of the moment."

This time the pain that slashed through his eyes almost cut her off at the knees. He traced the space between them, the air saturated with yearning. "You know it's more than that. No matter how much you hate that it is. It is."

She stepped back from that declaration, from all the declarations he'd promised he wouldn't make but was making, because he didn't care what she wanted. It didn't matter in the face of his own wants.

His face twisted with new understanding. "If it were nothing, then would it hurt like this?"

"You promised this would not turn into more," she said. "You promised you would not ask for more. You broke your promise and now you want me to take the blame for the fact that you're hurting."

"I'm not the only one who turned it into more. You broke your promise to yourself." His kind, generous eyes softened again. "I'm not the only one hurting, Naina." He tried to touch her cheek again.

She shook her head. "Don't." Letting him touch her again was out of the question. She couldn't let him tear her open any more than he had. Already sewing herself back up was going to kill her. She felt like someone had put her arm in a sling, broken her.

Pain went through her arm, and she squeezed it. As a young girl, pain in her arm had woken her up at night. It had taken too much work to stop this, to stop hurting all the time.

His arm was suspended between them, reaching for her but not touching her when she didn't want it. But how long before that stopped? He'd already disregarded her wishes. He was here when she'd told him not to come. He only ever did what he wanted.

"I'm not asking for anything you don't want to give," he said, voice soft and precise. How long before it turned cruel? "But you're angry with me for making you want to give more. I don't know how to help you with that."

There it was. "I don't need your help. I can take care of myself. I don't need you to tell me what I'm feeling or how I should feel. I know what I want." And it wasn't a man who thought she needed his help to exist. "I know it's hard for you to comprehend things, but it's not that hard to understand."

His head snapped back as though she'd slapped him. For the first time he looked at her as though he had no idea who she was.

"Wow." He swallowed. "Thanks for that. But despite what anyone believes about how my brain works, I do figure things out every once in a while."

She took a few steps back, all the way back. Across the room. She'd hurt him. She knew that. She'd tried to warn him that she would, but he hadn't listened. "Then why can't you figure out that I want you to leave? I . . ." She had to say it. "I don't want this anymore. I'm done."

No matter how he looked right now, he'd be okay. He was good at being okay. His ease scared her. His ability to seek and claim happiness scared her. The fact that he thought he could seek happiness with her was absurd.

At least he'd figured out the kind of hurt she could cause. "Go." It was better than his figuring out how much he mattered. Because that was when he'd figure out how to use it, how to hurt her back. She'd rather be the one doing the hurting. Yes, that's exactly who she was. Her father was right, she was the one who had to do the controlling.

His jaw was tight with pain. "Fine. If that's what you believe will keep you safe. It's just as well. I thought I could be what you wanted, but I can't."

"And what is that?"

"An inflatable doll you can fuck and then let the air out of. So you can roll it up and shove it in that closet where you shove everything you don't want anyone to see." He walked to the door.

Then he turned to her again, his beautiful face so filled with disappointment it was like having her arm twisted until it broke.

"Isn't it ironic that you accused me of not being able to stick with things? Of using projects to feel good about myself? Turns out it was never about sticking with things, it was about letting things matter. Have you ever considered why you need to solve the problems of every woman in the world? Have you ever considered what *you* use your project for?"

"Why did you have to ruin it?" she whispered, trying to brace herself against the wave of pain that flowed from him.

His eyes were wet, those unreal eyelashes spiking and clumping with the tears he didn't struggle to hide. Unlike her. Her eyelids burned, but no tears would come.

"Now that I *have* ruined it, I'm going to ruin it some more. Because you were right, I need to learn to commit all the way when I take something on."

Don't. Please.

He ignored the plea she couldn't speak. "You pulled Yash into a fake engagement and kept your feelings in a bubble. That's the relationship you wanted. Clean and dry. I know that's what you wanted with me too. But for some reason you let your feelings out of the bubble with me. You felt things. I felt things, more things than I've ever felt for anyone. You were happy. And it was magnificent, wasn't it? But there's no place to hide from the fear."

"Don't you see? Happiness is a lie."

"Don't you see? Happiness is the only truth there is." He wiped his sleeve across his eyes, new resolve darkening them. "Well, there is one more truth."

"Vansh, don't, please."

He leaned back into the door, gaze locked into hers. "This is not how I wanted to tell you, but it is the truth, and I don't want to never get to say it. I love you, Naina. I love everything about you. The way your eyes glow when you're happy, your body and how it makes mine feel when I touch you. The way you stand up for me and for yourself and for everyone in the world. The way you see me. The way you open up and let me see you. I love how brave you are, how afraid you are. I love how your brain unravels the world without excuses. I love . . ." His voice cracked, but he kept going. ". . . love you. I love myself more when I'm with you. I know it's a burden you didn't ask for, a burden you don't want, a burden I promised to protect you from, but as much as I want to be with you, I can't lie about why anymore." He sucked in his lips and took a deep breath. "I love you."

Then he waited.

Eyes on her, seeking a response.

What did he want from her?

She was wrapped in a column of ice. Frozen in a way that no one could melt. Love was just something she didn't know how to feel. He knew that.

He knew it.

Silence stretched between them.

Endless.

Unforgiving.

Final.

Without another word, he nodded, his shoulders curving downward, hollowing him out. Then he left.

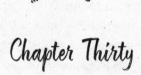

Chapter Thirty

*V*ansh stared at his laptop screen, where he was one click away from purchasing his ticket to Guatemala. His friend Amaan had been running a camp for American teenagers to work with the local villages to lay electrical lines for light bulbs. Physical labor outside the bubble of privilege that looked good on college apps. Amaan needed help with herding the kids. It was just the kind of thing that had always called to Vansh.

Young, unjaded people looking to find themselves. Small actions with tangible results. A bulb turned on, the egg of an endangered bird hatched, a building painted, a baby animal fed, a plastic bag pulled out of the ocean. Not big solutions but something he believed rippled across the universe and did something. Or undid something. How simple it had seemed.

SFO–GUA. The words flashed on the screen.

The most important thing he sought in a project had always been that it was far away from the place where he was nothing more than the youngest Raje.

Some might say the most insignificant Raje.

The child his father was proud of *too.*

Vansh had always prided himself on not caring. On not feeling insignificant or disappointing.

I've still been running away all my life.

All his life he'd been plagued by the sense that he had no purpose here. For the past months, he hadn't felt that once. He closed out of the website without purchasing the ticket. He couldn't leave their work unfinished. They were in the process of starting their own foundation. He'd messed up, but he'd find a way to make the foundation work.

Everything inside him told him to pick up the phone. Text her. Call her. Show up at her door.

The part that wouldn't stop haunting him was how much pain she'd been in when she threw him out. How afraid she was of losing control of her life. If he pushed her into a relationship, he'd just be doing what she was afraid of. She had to want this.

She didn't.

She'd called him stupid. Not in so many words, but she'd used something he struggled with to push him away.

For the hundredth time since he'd seen her two days ago, he dictated a text and erased it. Since he was staring into his phone, he couldn't ignore the text popping up from his mother. He hadn't been answering his family's calls. He'd told them he was too busy working on something important.

It wasn't a lie. He'd been taking care of both projects while hiding out in Yash's apartment. Naina hadn't shown up at work. He knew she wouldn't abandon work for too long. And losing himself in the endless tasks was the only thing that kept the pain of her absence from taking over.

The thought of going to the Anchorage and facing his family made him so angry he didn't know what to do with it.

Then the word *EMERGENCY* in his mother's text made him tap the family group chat open.

Drop what you're doing and come home. It's Esha. She's disappeared.

WHEN VANSH'S CAB pulled up under the porte cochere of the Anchorage, the driveway was clogged with cars. He ran into the house and found the family upstairs in the sitting room of Esha and Aji's suite.

Aji was red eyed and Ma was sobbing into a tissue. Ma never cried.

"Where's Esha? What happened?" Vansh's heart was thudding so hard he could barely breathe.

"She's . . . she's gone," Ma sobbed.

Only Ma, Aji, and Nisha were there, with Ram sleeping in his cradle. Where was everyone else?

"Gone?" Vansh ran into Esha's room. Her bright white bed was unmade, with pillows strewn all around.

"She's not in her room. We've looked all over the house. The rest of the family is combing the estate but we can't find her. It's been four hours. The longest she ever walks is two hours," Nisha said, face leached of color. "Aji went into her room to check on her while she was resting after her walk and found pillows arranged under her sheets."

"Pillows?" Did that mean Esha had run away? Why?

"She's been acting so different these past few months," Aji said. "Then her post-walk naps kept getting longer and longer. Now she's gone."

Vansh sat down next to his grandmother and put his arm around her. It was true Esha had been acting differently, but Vansh couldn't imagine her leaving them without a word.

And there were no signs of forced entry.

"Has anyone been through the security cameras?" Vansh asked.

"Yes, there's no sign of her. The only person who was here on the estate today was Sid Dashwood," Nisha said. "Yash and India tried to reach him to see if he'd seen anything, but he's not answering his phone."

"Yeah, Sid's not great at keeping his phone on. He was probably here to get some shots of birds." But discomfort prickled inside Vansh. "Let me try him."

He called Sid. Sid didn't answer but he texted immediately. *Esha is with me. We're back. Just hold down the fort for another few minutes.*

"Shit."

"What?" Nisha, Ma, and Aji said in one voice.

"I don't even know where to start. But she's fine. She's home."

Before they could respond to that, Esha emerged up the stairs and ran to Aji. "You're crying? Aji! I'm fine. I'm sorry. Don't cry."

Aji grabbed Esha and her sobs intensified. "Where were you? I almost died of worry." She kissed Esha all over her face.

Then Ma and Nisha were hugging Esha, stroking her arms, relief replacing the terror on their faces, even as tears streamed from their eyes.

"She's here," Ma said into her phone.

Esha wiped their grandmother's cheeks. "I'll tell you. I'll tell you everything. Stop crying first. Please." She turned around and looked at Sid Dashwood, who was standing by the stairs.

"Sid?" Vansh said. "Did you find Esha? Where was she?"

"Sid found me passed out on my walk. He was here to photograph birds."

Sid looked like he'd seen a ghost, not like someone who had just proved himself a hero.

Ma went to him and pulled him into the sitting room. Aji stood and grabbed his face and dropped a kiss on his forehead. "Thank you. Beta, I don't know how to thank you."

The look Sid threw at Esha was too complicated to be the look of a rescuer. The half-warning-half-pleading look she threw him in return was anything but the look of the rescued. What was going on?

The more they gushed at Sid, the more uncomfortable he looked. Before Vansh could figure out what was going on, HRH ran up the stairs.

"Sid found her," Ma said.

HRH, who was not given to hugging, held Esha so tight it was a wonder she didn't pass out again. Then he pumped Sid's arm. "I don't know how to thank you. You have no idea what you've done for us."

With another of those loaded looks at Esha, Sid pulled his arm away. "Actually, sir, I . . . we . . . Esha, please, I can't. I'm sorry."

The room's collective attention turned to Esha, who was shaking her head at him in the most un-Esha way. In fact, everything about her was most un-Esha-like.

There's something else Sid wants out of this. Naina's voice came back to Vansh like a sledghammer.

"Fine." Esha went to Sid and took his hand. A collective gasp rang through the room. She pressed herself into him and he wrapped an arm around her, setting off another gasp. "I didn't pass out while walking. I—we—Sid and I got stuck in traffic."

Everyone started talking at once. Esha stood tall and strong in the face of the barrage of questions. Something Vansh had never before seen.

She held up a hand and their voices died down. "Sid's been coming to see me for the past few months."

"Coming to see you?" Ma asked. "How's that possible?"

The relief on the family's faces was fast turning into outrage.

More speaking eye contact passed between Esha and Sid, and something inside Vansh twisted hard. Naina would've gotten such a kick out of this family drama scene. She'd have stood here looking amused-yet-envious. All her hyphenated feelings.

Vansh cleared his throat. "Sid was at the Anchorage a lot to see me. We were working together. He must have met Esha then," he said, and Esha smiled at him gratefully and he realized that Esha, of all people, might have tricked him.

"Excuse me?" Ma said, then turned to Sid. "Vansh invited you into our home and you thought it was okay to put Esha in danger?"

"Ma, please," Vansh said.

"He didn't know he was putting me in danger," Esha said.

"Esha, beta! How can you say that? How could you be so irresponsible?" HRH this time.

Then Ma turned to Vansh. "You brought him into our home and let him see Esha? What is wrong with you these days? Do you not care about your family at all anymore?"

The rest of the family chose that exact moment to make an entry. Trisha, Ashna, and various significant others crowded into the room.

"I'm fine," Esha said after she'd hugged everyone in turn. She seemed utterly comfortable with all that physical contact. "Sid and I went out and the traffic was terrible."

"What?" . . . "Where did you go?" . . . "Did you say traffic? Did you leave the grounds?" . . . "Did you say Sid?" . . . "How long has this been going on?" . . . "Did you tell him about your condition?" Another barrage of questions ricocheted like bullets around the room.

"Stop it!" Esha raised her voice. Esha, who used to crumple to the floor when anyone raised their voice.

The responding silence was deafening.

Vansh was the first to speak, because he was sick of this. "Has no one noticed that Esha is fine? She's standing there yelling at us. Esha . . . *yelling*! She just told us she's been sneaking out of the house." He laughed. "I mean, from where I'm standing we should be thanking Sid instead of biting his head off when Esha is obviously more *fine* than she's ever been!"

Esha grinned at him. "I'm fine. I really am. We just walked the Golden Gate Bridge. It's . . . it's so beautiful."

Vansh had to smile at that. Slowly the rest of them let tentative smiles spread across their faces. The fact that Esha had lived here for thirty years and never left the Anchorage blew Vansh's mind when he thought about it.

"I don't understand what is happening," their grandmother said, and Esha went to her and sat down next to her.

"I don't know what's happened either, but Sid showed up and everything changed. I . . . I feel . . . I feel . . ."

"Normal," Sid said, and everyone's glares returned to him.

Vansh went to him and squeezed his shoulder, because he wasn't about to be part of this, family or not.

"Vansh didn't know," Sid said, eyes on Esha. "I climbed up to her balcony before I ever even met Vansh."

"On the third floor?" Vansh whistled. "Wow. When?"

"Vansh!" Nisha said. "Stop acting like this isn't a preposterous violation. Esha, how could you lie to us?"

"I'm sorry," Esha said. "Honestly, I was so confused, am so confused by it, that I didn't know what or how to tell any of you."

"So the visions are gone?" Naturally Trisha was the one who asked the question that seemed to be on everyone's mind.

"Yes. It was slow at first. Just him. I could touch him, be near him, and nothing. Then the rest of you, everyone, it all just faded into whispers and was gone."

She came to Vansh and touched him. Put a hand on his chest. "Nothing," she said. "You're all on your own now."

"That's amazing," Vansh said. Seeing Esha like this, unafraid of the change in herself after a lifetime of being bound by it, shook something free inside him.

"But still, you lied to us," Ma said, and thew a wary glance at Sid. "Maybe you should leave and let us discuss this as a family."

"Of course she had to lie to us," Vansh said. "Look at how you treat someone you think threatens one of us."

"This is not about you, Vansh," Nisha snapped, and the rest of them turned to him.

"Oh, I know. This is about Esha, I get that. But Esha is fine. What's preposterous is the way you're all treating Sid."

"Vansh is right. Stop it. It's not Sid's fault. In fact, if not for Sid, I'd still be . . . God, you guys have no idea what it was like. There's so much I'd never have known." Esha laughed and looked at Sid with heat in her eyes, unconcerned with the judgment in the room.

"Esha obviously wants Sid here. It should be her choice," Vansh said. "Why do you think you get to decide who any one of us should be with?"

"Seriously?" Nisha said. "You're going to make this about your entirely inappropriate relationship with your girlfriend?"

"Nothing about what I have with Naina is inappropriate."

Ma made a pained sound.

"What is he talking about? Did he say Naina?" Aji said. "Yash's Naina?" Trisha and Ashna, who were sitting next to her, put their arms around her.

"Vansh? Beta?" HRH said, his voice uncharacteristically equanimous. "Your mother told me you and Naina have been spending a lot of time together. Do you think that's wise?" He sounded so calm that it was like being in a backward world with his parents swapping their usual roles.

"No. There is nothing wise about how I feel about Naina, Dad." He met his father's eyes. "I'm in love with her. Quite out of my mind in love with her, actually." And damn if his chest didn't hurt like someone had roundhouse-kicked the wind out of him.

His father blinked. Ma and Nisha looked horrified. If they clutched their figurative pearls any harder, they'd crush them.

"Naina? Yash's Naina?" Aji repeated, hand pressed to her mouth.

"Oh, Vansh!" Esha said, and wrapped her arms around him.

Sid looked completely out of place but also relieved at this fortuitous change in focus. "It was . . . um . . . really nice meeting all of you, but, I think this might be a good time to leave your family to this."

"Good idea." Esha went to him and dropped a kiss on his lips.

"We're not done with you," HRH said.

"Shree Kaka, I don't think you're ever going to be done with him," Esha said.

HRH rubbed his forehead. Esha was without a doubt his favorite, and seeing her this confident, this strong, was probably what he'd dreamed of since he'd scattered his brother's ashes thirty years ago.

"But," Esha said, "I think our Vansh problem needs to be dealt with first."

"Come in through the front door tomorrow," Aji said.

"God, please," Sid said, "I'd like that very much. Thank you." And with nothing more, he was gone with admirable speed.

Trisha and Ashna needed to get back to work too.

"You should be with whoever you want to be with," Trisha said, throwing a pointed look at Nisha.

"Will you apologize to Naina for us?" Ashna said, dropping a kiss on Vansh's cheek.

Then the two of them left with their partners and Neel.

"What is wrong with everyone?" Ma said, pinching her temples. "I can't believe Naina would do this. She promised there was nothing between you two."

"We didn't plan this, Ma. You know Naina, she doesn't even want a relationship. It just happened." Except it had also just unhappened.

"She is twelve years older than you!" Nisha said. "She's seen you as a baby."

"Really, Nisha? Neel had seen you as a baby too. You were in love with him in elementary school. Will you stop being a hypocrite for one moment?"

"Nisha is not older than Neel, and it's certainly not twelve years!" Ma said.

"This breaks you, Ma? This is the rock your feminist beliefs shatter on—that she's older than I am?"

Ma looked like he'd slapped her. "That's not true. It's not just that. It's Naina!"

"I know. Naina, whom you've always loved. And she loves you. Maybe even more than she loves me." A sad little laugh escaped him. "And it might be too late for this conversation."

Ma looked tortured. He knew she loved Naina. "She was in love with Yash. How can that not affect you brothers? It will tear my children apart."

"Mina," HRH said, but he was watching Vansh, studying him for something.

Vansh braced himself for disappointment.

"You know as well as anyone Yash and Naina weren't in love," his father said, something in his voice that Vansh couldn't wrap his head around. "At least hear our son out."

Vansh waited, not processing what he'd just heard.

"What do you mean it might be too late, son?"

Vansh blinked. "I messed up. I promised not to fall in love with her and then did. And she did too." Vansh knew exactly how arrogant he was. He also knew his faith in the fact that Naina loved him had nothing to do with arrogance. "She loves me enough that she won't go anywhere near me as long as there's any chance it will distance me from you, from all of you. That, along with the number Dr. Kohli has done on her, and . . ." He dropped into the couch. "She threw me out."

HRH came to him then and patted him on the back. That look in his eyes intensified, but Vansh didn't have the strength to label it as what it looked like: support.

Vansh had always befuddled his father. Disappointed him. It was something Vansh had always believed he could do nothing about, other than avoid it.

"And you're just going to give up?" HRH said, in his HRH voice.

"Shree! What is wrong with you?"

HRH sat down next to his wife and placed a hand on her back. "You're the one who's always telling me we have to listen to our children, Minu. He's found the one."

"But he's my baby, Shree."

"No, he's not. He's a grown man." His father slid Vansh a glance, an eye-to-eye look he didn't remember ever getting from his father. Or maybe he had and he just hadn't been able to see it. A lump started to form in Vansh's throat. "This reminds me of something," his father said.

Ma shrugged his hand off her back and turned angry eyes on him. "What? What does it remind you of?"

HRH looked at his own mother and took a breath. "Of another mother who thought her little boy was too precious for a girl who was the best thing that ever happened to him."

The lump in Vansh's throat grew hard to swallow around.

"It's not the same thing," Ma said.

"How is it not the same thing?" Aji spoke for the first time. "If my memory serves, it's exactly the same thing."

"She's the same person you were more than happy to have our other son be with," HRH said.

"She's twelve years older than him," Ma said again, but her voice wobbled. "God, I sound like a terrible person. Why is this so hard for me?"

"Because you've always been afraid of your children being hurt, but Vansh most of all." HRH looked at Vansh again in a way that Vansh didn't remember ever seeing. Possibly because Vansh had long stopped searching for things in his father's eyes.

"Because there were things you couldn't fix for him." He reached out and took Vansh's hand. "You know, there are very few things I regret in my life, but how I reacted to"—he cleared his throat—"his learning disability is something I regret every single day, and I'm grateful every day for how you schooled me. Because I was wrong. Vansh is the one who turned out to need the least care."

He wiped his eyes and fixed Vansh with the fiercest of looks. "Vansh turned out to be the most whole of our babies. All he's done is make the world a better place. The thing we hoped our children would do. We've known Naina her whole life. We thought she was such a great fit for Yash because of how driven she was, how focused on good outside of herself. We thought that was a lot like Yash, but, don't you see, Vansh is the one like her. They're united by passion and nature. There's something that's the same about them."

Vansh had teared up, but Nisha was the one sobbing the hardest. She pressed her hand into her face. "I've been such a bitch."

"You totally have," Vansh said, all the pain of the past three days gathering and sharpening inside him, but he rubbed her back. "I'm so glad you're all rethinking your stance on this, but I'm not sure if it's going to matter."

"Shit," Nisha said, her horror intensifying. "That's why you're looking like this." She waved a hand around his face.

"I don't know what you're talking about."

"You have stubble, Vansh," Esha said, as though making one of her clairvoyant declarations. "You do know how seriously you take grooming is a bit abnormal, right?"

Nisha smiled through her tears. "Also, I think that's a normal-sized T-shirt you're wearing."

"Also, your hair isn't defying gravity and the laws of physics," Aji said.

"So how are we going to get her back?" Ma asked, and HRH did the tiniest eye roll at Vansh that said, *See?*

He smiled at his father. *They're all nuts. How do we live with them?*

HRH smiled back, relief darkening his eyes. "Unfortunately, I have to get to surgery," he said. "But I want to talk to Naina. May I call her?"

"Let me talk to Vansh first," Ma said.

"Fine. I'll let your mother help you. I think she knows exactly how to handle this." He threw Ma a glance that summed up all the understanding in their marriage. "But make sure you do what it takes to win her back." With that HRH dropped a kiss on Vansh's head; squeezed Aji and Esha in a hug; gave his wife a full, on-the-mouth kiss that made them all groan; and then left.

Aji and Esha went into their rooms to rest. It had been a long day. Nisha left to go back to work. They all offered to call Naina and apologize, but Vansh told them they were jumping the gun.

Finally, he followed his mother to the kitchen.

"You said she doesn't want a relationship. Do you have any idea why?" Ma asked.

"Isn't it obvious?" Vansh said.

For a while Ma was silent, then she looked at Vansh, an odd flatness in her eyes. "You know, I knew she and Yash didn't have feelings for each other. That should have bothered me more, but I thought I saw something familiar in her. The way she was around Yash reminded me of when I first met Shree. Did you know I felt nothing for him?"

Vansh took his mother's hand. He had some idea about his mother's turbulent relationship with her own father, who'd forced her into being a child actor and then a Bollywood star. Vansh had picked up pieces from conversations, but this was the first time Ma was talking to him about it.

"It wasn't just Shree. I just felt nothing in general. It was the only way for me to survive my childhood. I was completely dissociated from my feelings. That's what the therapists called it later. It was good to find a word for it. I don't think Shree felt much more than sympathy for me either when we first met. He says it was love, but it was really his hero complex. He wanted to save me because what had happened to me was wrong and he felt violated by my violation. But then he did fall in love with me.

"I didn't feel anything in return for a long time. I had to feel things for me first. I had to fall in love with me first. Being the smart man he is, Shree realized that. For the first years of our marriage he gave me as much space as I needed to find things about myself I liked. My singing voice. My need to run. My love for decorating our home.

"He let me love those things without fear, and somewhere along the way I started to notice little things about him. How he never used force to get what he wanted. How he analyzed problems. How he never stayed quiet if he saw an injustice. How big his dreams were. How much he loved his family. How he thought about Esha constantly. How much wonder he had about her.

"The main thing was learning to see him as him, not as every other man I'd met. Not as my father. That was the first step, maybe the last one. Maybe that was the whole journey. Seeing him for him helped me separate how people had seen me from who I really was. And find the me who deserved happiness. Was capable of it.

"I know Naina is much stronger than I was then. I know she loves her work. She values herself. There's still a part of her that has to separate you from her father. I've seen how she looks at you. I recognized that and it scared me. But your father is right, that's because you've always taken care of yourself and that's made me feel somewhat helpless.

"Give her time. She knows who you are. It's her own experiences as a child that she has to reconcile for herself. You can't bamboozle your way through that."

Vansh had pushed Naina in front of his family without caring what she wanted. He'd forced his feelings down her throat when she'd been perfectly honest with him about hers. "I did bamboozle a little. But I didn't mean to."

"You know what the sweetest thing about you was when you were little? How easily you admitted you were wrong. It used to break my heart, because you wanted to take the blame for everything, things that were your fault and things that were not. You're always good at taking responsibility and setting things right, even when you bamboozle. I know she's going to see that."

He jumped off the bar stool and hugged his mother. "Thanks, Ma. I hope she does, but I think there's a little more bamboozling I might need to do first."

Chapter Thirty-One

*I*n her whole life no human being had said the words *I love you* to Naina. Not one single person. Vansh couldn't do this to her. The words had fallen on her like rocks in a landslide, dismembered her, and she didn't know how the parts that had flown from her would ever come back together. She'd been wrapped in her sheets rolled up into a burrito on her bed. For three days. Her eyes hurt from crying, her head throbbed.

You can't just say those words to me, she kept saying to him, but he wasn't there to hear them.

All her life she'd been terrified of this happening. Of a man doing this to her someday. Destroying her with a flick of his hand. She had expected to be more prepared.

Her bladder hurt too. She was having a hard time getting out of bed, even to make it to the bathroom. She had to get out of her apartment. For good. It was a mausoleum to her and Vansh. Like the damned Taj Mahal.

Someone had given her mother a miniature replica of the Taj Mahal once. Dr. Kohli had thrown it away, declaring it "too tacky." Naina had pulled it out of the trash and put it in her nightstand drawer. She wondered if it was still there. She'd completely forgotten about it.

Finally, unable to be pathetic enough to pee herself, she made her way to the bathroom. Crying on the pot was possibly even more pathetic than not making it there. She couldn't stop.

The knock on her bathroom door nearly killed her with fright.

"Vansh?" she said without thinking about it. He was the only one with her apartment code.

"Naina, beta?"

No! Please. She couldn't face her mother right now. Why was she here?

"I need a minute," Naina said, and splashed her face in an attempt to not look like she'd been sobbing for three days. It was a losing battle, so she gave up and went back to her bed and dropped into it, Mummy close on her heels.

"You smell bad." It was the first thing her mother said. She, on the other hand, smelled like roses and fresh paneer. Like Mummy.

"How did you get in here?"

"Your code."

She should never have given Vansh her code. Then again, the list of things she should not have done with Vansh was endless and a waste of time to recount in this moment.

Plucking a tissue from her nightstand, she honked into it before the snot leaked from her.

Why was he doing this to her? What had she ever done to deserve this?

Why had he sent Mummy?

Because he knew that anyone else seeing her like this would destroy her. He knew exactly what kind of mess she was right now.

The nerve.

"What do you want, Mummy?"

"The neighbors smell you and call cops. Then cops call Mummy. Like from-school calls for safety."

Naina poked her nose close to her shoulder and smelled herself. "It's not that bad." It was terrible. "My school never called you." Not once.

Her mother placed a hand on Naina's head. "You always very good girl." She was right. Naina hadn't done a single thing to add to her mother's troubles. Not once. "Even when you too young, you took care of Mummy. Thank you."

The tears got worse and the rage in her chest swelled so fast she gasped for breath. Once she'd left home, she'd abandoned her mother completely. Left her to fend for herself. Made choices that were the opposite of taking care of her.

Naina fell back on her bed, unable to stay upright anymore.

With a pat to Naina's knee, Mummy got up and went to her closet. The first thing her eyes caught were the cushion covers she had pulled from Naina's couch, and she froze. Then she shut the door and went into the bathroom and opened and closed some cabinets, then walked out to the corridor and started opening and shutting doors there.

She'd never been in Naina's apartment for more than a few moments. She'd never visited her in college or in any of her homes around the world. Ever. No one ever had.

Yash and she had been best friends since they were in diapers and he'd never been in a single home she'd lived in as an adult either.

"Did you know that Yash never visited any of my homes as an adult?" She hadn't meant to say it, but the words slipped out. "Ten years we were supposed to be together and no one ever asked me if he'd ever been to my home."

Mummy poked her head back into her room, a towel clutched in her hand. "Did you say something?"

Naina shook her head. Vansh had been here every night. He'd wrapped her ankle in ice when she twisted it. He'd pressed a heating pad to her back when her period gave her killer cramps.

He'd held her all night when she got angry and sad for no apparent reason. He'd fed her. He'd let her help him and correct him and scold him and call him names, and he'd listened. He'd fucked her in every room in the house and made her laugh and laugh as she shuddered and came. Again and again and again.

He thought she wanted to fuck him like he was an inflatable doll.

She wanted to fuck him. Period. At least one more time in her life so she would know to memorize everything and save it up.

As if she hadn't already done that.

"Can you continue mutterings in shower?" Her mother smiled a most un-Mummy-like smile, shoved the towel at Naina, pushed her into the bathroom, then shut the door behind her.

When had she come in here and started the shower? The entire tiny space was saturated with steam.

I've always thought washing someone's hair was the most erotic thing, Vansh had whispered behind her as he'd massaged her scalp, legs twisted around her as she sat in front of him in the tiny tub. *I've never washed anyone's hair, Knightlina.*

Don't call me that, she mouthed into the steam, no sound coming from her lips. The feel of his legs, those muscled calves under wet dark hair, the thick strong thighs. The way his muscles jumped beneath his skin when she touched him.

Every bit of him rubbed against her. No one wrapped her up the way he did, his body a down coat, ermine and cashmere squeezing out the cold in a blizzard. No one touched her as gently.

His fingers were worship, his lips a chant whispered into her soul.

"Vansh," she said out loud. Then, startled by the sound of her own voice, she looked around, but she was under the shower, the scalding water burning her skin. She was alone.

The taste of his name filled her mouth. It sank into her lungs. She wanted so badly to say it again, to taste him again, that she gave in to another wave of tears. How could everything inside her feel so parched, so sandy dry, when she was standing in a downpour?

Moving out of habit, she soaped herself, trying to wash it off, whatever this was that clung to her, on the inside, on the outside.

Mummy had left clothes on the vanity. Had time slipped? Was she ten again? Would she go out and find an arm in a sling? Would her eyes search for bruises in hidden places?

On legs that felt far too shaky, and feeling entirely too light-headed to not face-plant, Naina made it out of the bathroom and into her bedroom, where the memory of his cologne permanently lingered. Or was that her own skin? Had her own smell become indelibly mingled with his? How had she ever thought the brothers smelled the same? That Vansh was anything like anyone else?

She'd never felt this hunger for another human being, for the presence that grazed her senses and loosed the knots inside her.

When she went out into the living room, a bowl of rajma and rice was sitting on her breakfast bar, with a dollop of thick cream on top. Her favorite childhood comfort food, the opposite of diet kababs in her mother's book.

She started laughing. And couldn't stop.

Her mother said nothing, but her face said, *Oh, Naina. My poor, poor Naina,* as she pushed Naina onto a stool.

Naina's stomach growled. Hunger and a gag reflex working as one. Her mother put a spoon in Naina's hand and she started eating even as tears flowed from her eyes.

Every bit of dignity she'd possesed was gone. Just all of it gone. She was in the back of the Rajes' car as J-Auntie drove in silence. When she got home, she was going to find her mother gone. Her worst nightmare.

"Every man is not your father, Naina," her mother said. Simply. Sincerely. As though it wasn't thirty years too late for this conversation.

The spicy, buttery kidney beans mushed on Naina's tongue and mixed with long-grain rice, and she couldn't find her voice around it. So she ate. Until she felt just a little bit stronger. When her bowl was empty, she reached for the basket of naan and started shoving the puffy flatbread into her mouth one perfectly charred mouthful after another.

Rage swelled and ebbed inside her. Her stomach churned a little, that particular sensation from when you ate too fast and after too long.

"I know every man is not Dr. Kohli." She wiped her mouth on the brown napkins emblazoned with the yellow In-N-Out logo from her last meal here with Vansh. The paper and smell of restaurant napkins made the queasiness worse. "I just don't know how to separate the ones who are from those who aren't."

If Naina had thrown the rajma and rice in her face, her mother would have looked less devastated. Instead of outrage, or fluttering, or tears, she nodded. An acknowledgment. "You do. You do know how to make separate. I was one who didn't know."

The thick knot of thorns scraping the inside of Naina's throat became impossible to swallow around. She had to open her mouth to suck in a breath.

Her mother ran a hand over Naina's head, stroking her hair away from her face. A few months back, the touch would have made Naina uncomfortable. Drawing solace from it would have terrified her. Now she soaked it up.

How many ways had Vansh ruined her? She missed his touchy-feely-ness. By now he would have touched her in ten places. An elbow bumped into her arm, a finger trailed down her neck, a forehead pressed into her shoulder. The million ways he had of comforting her. Of telling her things about herself with his body.

"Why would you say all this to me now? Why are you even here? Why did you stay with him for so many years?" The question slipped out and she almost apologized, but her mother put a hand on her arm.

"That stupid question and I did not raise stupid girl." Her voice was too gentle for words that forceful.

"Oh, you raised a very stupid girl. If I wasn't stupid, I'd know how to navigate this. You. Him. I'd know what to do with all this." She circled her head with her hand, indicating the familiar buzz and crash of emotions that stormed inside her, that didn't sort or straighten out no matter how hard she tried. "Me."

"Of all women I know in world, only one know exactly what to do with herself, exactly how she wants, is you, beta."

"Why would you say that to me? Why would you lie to me?"

"Why you think everything I say is lie?" She patted her bun, then patted her heart. Reassurance, comfort she had to give herself. Because no one else had ever given it to her. The fluttering that had always annoyed Naina.

When Naina was a little girl, she had found it charming, the way she had found everything about her mother charming and comforting. Her mannerisms made her Mummy, and as long as she was around, Naina felt like she was seen, watched over.

"Actually I know why you think like that way."

Up until the Basketball Incident, they had been a team. Then Naina had given up. They both had. Her father had finally broken them both, in one fell swoop.

"Mothers tell to their children all time that they stay because for them. I thought that's why I stay. That's lie. Truth is, I should not have stay. So much I make you put through. So much it take from you. But no more. I cannot let him take away something that make you happy again."

This was about Vansh? "What happened to 'I don't like all such things'? What happened to 'Win Yash back'? What changed?"

Her mother went to the couch and sat down. The gray cushion

covers were gone. In their place were her bright Kathmandu covers. Mirrors catching the sunshine like happiness. She patted the
seat next to her and Naina went to her. Picking up a cushion, she
squeezed it into her chest.

Mummy's smile was all the things Naina had missed. "I didn't
expect from my marriage much. I just never did. Maybe that's
why Dr. Kohli became like that way. Because whatever he was,
I was okay with. Not like Mina and my other friends, who made
stand up and fight their husband."

She wiped Naina's tears. "I think I will be like this way: good
wife, and someday he will see. Only one thing there was that
I did expected. One thing I believed someday I get. A simple
'sorry.' At least once. Do you know not anyone has ever apologize to me in life? Never. Only you. All the time. When nothing
your fault. No one who ever make real mistake ever apologize to
me. When I was girl, my brother drive motorcycle over my toe. It
was accident but he never say sorry. My toe break, but he only tell
people how brave I was because I not cry. I think he feel sorry.
But he never say."

Her eyes were luminous with something now. "Do you know
who only person who ever really apologize to me?"

Naina's heart squeezed so hard, she didn't think she could
bear it.

"Your Vansh. He don't just apologize, he mean. Did you know
he make campaign for me?" She fanned herself. "A little too much
handsome he is, no? But most important, very brave. Not afraid
to admit wrong. Not afraid of be wrong. Not anything even little
like your father."

Vansh is not anything at all like anyone else in the world.

Mummy swirled a bejeweled finger in Naina's face, a perfect
circle that said QED, quod erat demonstrandum. "That. What
you just thinking about him. That truth. That how you feel about
him. Come on, beta, you are so brave girl. Same-to-same like

him. Not like Mummy. You're always fighting fighting fighting. Don't give up now when person for fight is yourself."

Naina found herself laughing through her tears. Vansh had put on some lotus-embroidered shirts and her mother was suddenly this new person? Seriously, that's all it had taken?

"I don't think I'm meant for this, Mummy . . . for domesticity. Women have worked too hard to have it be a choice."

"Yes. That's why when they get to make choice, when it not force on them, that beautiful thing."

What was beautiful was Vansh, and it wasn't just his perfect face and his flawless body. It was something deep inside him. Something that was a miracle given how everything on the outside would have been enough for any other person, but inside him was this drive to love.

Naina had always seen it as a drive to be loved. But he was loved. He just never took it without returning it a thousandfold. To everyone, not just those who coddled him. Mummy had not coddled him. He'd won her love.

He's too good for me. Too unsullied. Too bright.

Getting off the couch, Naina started pacing, glad to have the use of her limbs again even though they still felt like they were dragging behind her, her whole self made of balls and chains. The food was settling in her stomach. The metallic nauseated feeling kept rising and falling.

"You know what a mess I made with Yash. Because all this . . . what if it's just not for me?"

"I wish you never lie for so much long, but not all things between you and Yash lie. You best friend for full life. That is not lie. I was there. And that is not because you useful to him and him to you. That because you funniest, smartest, strongest person. You stand with him, always. Support, always."

Her eyes dimmed with guilt and she stroked Naina's arm again. "And you do that when Yash life is fill with all gifts you want and not have. Not once you hold grudge on him or on any Rajes or on any our other friends. You make others laugh even when you hurting. You force Yash to push ahead even when no one support you."

"Yash supported me too," Naina said. "So it wasn't exactly selfless." She dropped back on the couch, drained of every bit of energy.

"See, you care about what selfless and what not. All life, you pushing boulder no one care that sit in all women path. Don't write off to yourself. Don't make up value of yourself by one cruel man just because Mummy don't know how to deal him."

Cruel. All these years it had taken her, but she'd said the one word that said it all. *I hate him,* Naina wanted to say. *I hate him from the bottom of my soul.* Yet, she wished so badly that he'd been someone she could love.

Her mother pulled her head into her lap and she went willingly. Her Mummy smell, her Mummy warmth, all the things she hadn't experienced since . . . since that broken arm. How much she'd missed it. She'd thought her mother had lost her ability to love her daughter, but no, she'd only lost her ability to show it. Or Naina had lost her ability to see it.

Had one apology, one act of kindness from Vansh, really changed her mother so much?

"You not the same Naina who lie about Yash. Don't you see, beta, you change. I never seen you like this way."

She'd let him make her come in a restaurant. With his family sitting right there.

"You keep saying you not capable of love. But look at you. I think it little late. Already falling in love is done."

A laugh escaped Naina. Mummy was right. She'd changed, and when she didn't let the fear overwhelm her she liked who she was with him. Loved it, actually.

"But he's spoiled and indulged, and so smug it can be the most annoying thing."

"That describe pretty much all Rajes, no?" Mummy said, a happy gleam brightening her eyes.

"True."

But Vansh was also different from the rest of them in that he had no shell. He left himself wide open. What he knew to do was give everything. Unlike them, unlike *her*, he was not terrified of what it might cost him.

Suddenly she sat up.

How had it taken her so long to realize this? The fact that he'd sent Mummy here meant that he wasn't far behind. A smile spread across her face. Minutes ago she had felt like she'd never smile again.

"He asked you to come here."

"I never see any man look so much worried. So much miserable not look good on face like that."

He'd wanted to make sure Naina was okay. *I'm obsessed with your pleasure.* He was. But it wasn't just her physical pleasure. It was her happiness. God, what was she going to do with him?

Her mother wiped her cheeks, and she wiped her mother's. They were comforting each other like normal mothers and daughters.

"I think no other man do for you. Men like that Yash okay for women like that India. She with all yoga, he with all politics, all separate-separate. You need someone . . ." She wrapped her hands together, fingers firmly intertwined. "Someone who with you all time doing 'Naina, Naina'!"

Naina was laughing in earnest now.

"Is he downstairs?"

Her mother stood and took Naina's hand and pulled her off the couch. "How I will know?" she lied. "But he certainly come over when I'm leave and then you cannot be look like this way, all swollen face and in man boxer short. You should wear ghagra from dandiya party. You look best of all time in it. And his face become all . . ." She made the funniest smitten face. "*Dead.*"

"I'm not wearing a ghagra choli, Mummy."

"It be very romantic reconciliation, no?"

Naina blushed. Knowing Vansh, it was certainly going to be that. Maybe she should put on the ghagra just to make him laugh, but it was probably not smart to encourage her mother in this.

"I'll wear it another time."

Her mother studied her. "At least take hairs out of ponytail."

"Go, Mummy, he's been waiting for over an hour. Why didn't you tell me?" At least she knew him well enough to know that he wasn't too miserable, because if he'd brought Mummy here, that meant he'd already jumped the gun on believing he'd get Naina back.

Her mother went to the door. "At least put lipstick."

"Go!" She pushed her mother out the door.

And there he was, standing there, leaning against the wall next to the elevator. A sight that made her feel like she was taking a full breath after days.

"I'll wait if you want to go put on some lipstick," he said, his stunningly perfect grin nudging at his lips. It was his hope-filled eyes, however, that hooked her heart. They were exhausted, and he had stubble.

Mummy was laughing when the elevator door closed.

Grabbing his arm, Naina pulled him into the apartment.

He wrapped his arms around her, holding her close. "Naina." He said her name. That was it.

Everything inside Naina that had been floating in pieces fell back in place.

"I'm sorry," he said without pulling away, his scent, his heat, all of it sucking the pain she'd been carrying from her limbs. "I'm so sorry. I only thought about what I wanted. I'm sorry I pushed you. I don't want anything more than what we already have. I don't need you to love me back."

She pulled away and looked up at him. "You already know I love you back. Stop manipulating me." Then she kissed him, because she couldn't wait for them to get the semantics right.

Kissing him was exactly what she needed to do, because it made nothing else matter except what came after the kissing, which made her matter in ways she wanted, and needed. It made everything all right. All of it, because it was him.

"You smell beautiful," he said as they lay on her yellow couch wrapped up in each other, colorful cushions strewn on the floor around them.

She laughed. "Smart move sending Mummy over first to clean me up." Then she stroked his smiling lips, his dimpled cheeks, his heartbreaking but super-hot stubble. "I'm sorry I hurt you. There is no one on earth who understands me the way you do. No one who understands the world the way you do. I need that, your insight, your light. *You.* You were right. I was scared by how much I needed you and I didn't know how to handle that."

"You weren't wrong about everything. Not only was Jiggy interested in me for my last name, but Sid did befriend me because he wanted something too. You're never going to believe what was going on. He became friends with me because of Esha, can you believe that? It wasn't just my charm after all." He laughed a self-deprecating laugh.

"No! How is that even possible?" she said. Then more seriously, "No, Vansh. Jiggy is Jiggy, but Sid, Hari, you made it easy for them, you made them feel seen, let them in. The way you do for everyone, because people who are terrified of other people find it easy to trust you. Ask me how I know." She dropped a kiss on his lips. "I said horrible things to you. I'm sorry. I was trying to push you away and I'm so happy I failed." She waited. "Please tell me I failed."

For the hundredth time since she'd met him, she realized that having someone smile when they kissed you was the best sensation in the world. "Are you saying you want me to be more than an inflatable doll?"

She pressed into him. "I mean there are parts of you that are alarmingly easy to inflate."

His entire body shook with laughter.

"But yes, I want more. I want everything."

"I'm not sure. I think the matter needs further investigation."

"Investigation?" She blinked innocently. "Whatever do you mean?"

His hands were already working on an answer and her giggle got lost in a moan. "Can I have the rest of my life to answer that question?"

"God, yes," she said, and the game was on.

Epilogue

Sagar Mahal, the Sripore palace that had been the Raje ancestral home for centuries, was one of those places that time never seemed to touch. Not that Esha remembered much about it from her childhood. When Sid and she had moved to the Sagar Mahal a year ago, everything had felt shockingly new and yet as familiar as breathing. Since then, Esha had let new memories—her own memories—fill in the spaces left by a lifetime of other people's thoughts and feelings. It felt good to have her own. And she'd found the perfect thing to do with them: write stories.

Thus far only Sid had read her stories. He'd already jumped ahead to her publishing them and then planned out all the book signings she'd do around the world. It was nice to see him excited about the future. Everyone deserved to have that.

Sid had started a bird sanctuary on the palace grounds, working to replant a hundred acres of land with vegetation that provided safe haven to native birds. So, he was also excited about the present. Which might be the only thing better than being excited about the future.

"The red is absolutely gorgeous on you," Naina said, pinning the heavy pallu of the bridal sari that kept slipping off Esha's shoulder back in place.

Yes, Esha had chosen to get married in her aie's wedding sari. Every time she thought about it, tears threatened to ruin her makeup, and her sisters and sisters-in-law scolded her. So she was trying not to cry. She often joked that she'd liked it better when they had treated her like she was fragile. But having her family fight with her was the best thing ever.

"Should we all just take this makeup off and have a good cry?" Trisha asked, because she'd been sniffling so much that the false eyelashes on one of her eyes was hanging loose. "I hate that DJ has turned me into a watering can."

"Is that your way of telling us you're pregnant?" Ashna asked.

"God no!" Trisha said. "It just means that the man cries every time he feels something. And I think I've caught his feelings, which are contagious, by the way. Unlike being pregnant, fortunately. No offense."

"None taken," Ashna said. She was adorable with her baby bump in her sari. "You might be right, because Rico's kinda weepy too these days. Especially if you say the word 'twins' around him. I do it sometimes just to see him cry, because it's adorable."

They were all wearing saris from their grandmother's trousseau. Brocaded silks in a rainbow of colors. Nine yards instead of the modern six.

Naina's was a bright yellow, the sari Aji, and also Mina Kaki, had gotten married in. Mina Kaki had gifted it to her for Esha's wedding. It was another thing they couldn't talk about unless they wanted Naina to start sobbing too.

Nisha repositioned Trisha's eyelash and glued it down again. Then she went to Naina. "Why is your sari all askew?" she asked, squatting down in front of Naina and straightening out the pleats. "This is a mess. Oh my gosh, Naina! Is that why you were late?"

"I don't know what you're talking about," Naina said, but her face went flaming red. Naina had disappeared for a good half hour when she'd gone to "check up on the guys." "All I'll say is that Neel's not the only gavel in town, Nisha."

They all burst into laughter and Nisha smacked her with all the fondness of a lifelong friend.

Trisha laughed so hard that her eyelash popped off again. She pulled it off, then pulled the other one off too.

Then Nisha made quick work of re-draping Naina's sari. Nisha was the only one who'd bothered to watch YouTube videos on the ancient style of draping nine-yard saris, to make sure the professionals they'd hired to dress them knew what they were doing.

"Thank you," Naina said as the yards of silk and gold went back in place.

"Of course," Nisha said, tucking a loose lock of hair behind Naina's ear. "Good as new."

"Do you think the guys are ready?" Esha asked.

"Let me check," India said, hopping on top of the high windowsill, which was the only way to get a view of the garden where the wedding altar had been constructed. "Looks like they're all down there." She hopped off the sill with absurd ease, given that she was wearing a nine-yard sari. "They look like a rainbow."

Vansh had worked with Naina's mother to have the most ornate sherwanis made to match their significant others' saris. Chandni Auntie had come through spectacularly. And not one of the men had complained.

She'd moved out of her husband's house and into Naina's old apartment after Vansh and Naina had moved to Nepal for a few years. Although they traveled to San Francisco all the time to oversee the redeployment project that was being handled by their team there. They spent a lot of time here in Sripore as well working on Shobi Kaki's foundation.

The clock tower gonged and the door flew open.

"It's time!" Vansh said, his bright yellow sherwani making him look like an adorable banana.

One look at them all and he fell to his knees, dramatic as ever. "Have a care, ladies," he said, pressing a hand to his chest. "You can't go out there looking like this. Hearts will fail."

Naina shook her head, but her shoulders were shaking with laughter. She helped him up and kissed him full on the lips, to many hoots.

"Hey! It's my wedding," Esha said. "Let's focus."

"So it is." Vansh gave Esha a hug and dropped a kiss on her cheek. "By the way, have you considered that this wedding wouldn't be taking place if not for my matchmaking skills?"

"Of course it wouldn't, Baby Prince," Naina said, and they all laughed. "Ready, Esha?"

Esha nodded. She had never been readier.

Acknowledgments

Finishing *The Emma Project* feels like coming to the end of a vacation I had dreamed of my entire life, one that turned out to be exactly as much fun as I'd expected it to be. Nonetheless, leaving it behind is hard. Saying goodbye to the Rajes is hard, but also wonderful because they're out in the world now and always there for me to revisit. First and foremost, thank you to each and every one of you who accompanied me on this journey. I hope you had fun.

I would be lying if I said this book was hard to write, but I'd also be lying if I said that I could have written it without the support and encouragement of my Deadline Sisterhood. Jamie Beck, Priscilla Oliveras, Virginia Kantra, Barbara O'Neal, Liz Talley, Sally Kipatrick, Tracy Brogan, and Falguni Kothari, I have no idea how I survived this writing gig before I met you, but I'm deeply grateful that I get to do it with you in my corner now. Thanks also to Melonie Johnson, CJ Warrant, Clara Kensie, Robin Skylar, and Heather Lowry for helping me brainstorm this story from nothing more than the seed of an idea. And for bringing snacks and wine. And to Kristan Higgins, Christina Lauren, Nalini Singh, and Susan Elizabeth Phillips for your grace and generosity, always.

So much of my love for the Rajes comes from my California family. Thank you for the stories and for your passion for your home, Kalpana Thatte, Deep Sathe, Nishaad Navkal, and Emily Redington Modak. And for the insightful beta reads. Thanks also to my brilliant niece Devieka for her courage, candor, and insight into navigating dyslexia. I hope I honored your trust.

My thanks also to my publishing team: my editor, Tessa Woodward, for loving the Rajes and for always knowing exactly how to direct my messy drafts into stories I'm proud of; my agent, Alexandra Machinist, for her precious support; the entire marketing and publicity team at HarperCollins, especially Anwesha Basu and Danielle Finnegan; and the lovely and tireless Kristin Dwyer for finding the spots of sunshine for my books. And to every librarian, blogger, and bookseller who has shared my work, you are the columns, the spine; without you my dream would never stand, and I thank you with my whole heart.

Last but not least, to the best family in the world, Mamma, Papa, Manoj, Mihir, and Annika. None of this would mean anything without your pride, patience, and support. Thank you!

About the author

2 Meet Sonali Dev

About the book

4 Reading Group Guide

7 Behind the Book

Insights,
Interviews
& More . . .

Meet Sonali Dev

USA Today bestselling author SONALI DEV writes Bollywood-style love stories that explore issues faced by women around the world. Her novels have been named Best Books of the Year by *Library Journal*, NPR, the *Washington Post*, and *Kirkus Reviews*. She has won the American Library Association's award for best romance, the RT Reviewer Choice Award for best contemporary romance, and multiple RT Seals of Excellence. She is a RITA finalist and has been listed for the Dublin Literary Award. *Shelf Awareness* calls her "Not only one of the best but one of the bravest romance novelists working today."

She lives in Chicagoland with her husband, two visiting adult children, and the world's most perfect dog. ❧

Reading Group Guide

1. Vansh and Naina have what might be considered an untraditional relationship. Why do you think something like that works so well for them? What in their personalities and histories makes them perfect for each other?

2. In the previous book in this series, Naina was set up as an antagonist figure. Most of the Raje family still sees her in that light. How come Vansh doesn't?

3. Vansh's family, while sometimes annoying, is still very important to him. How does his reliance on his family both help and hinder in his quest for independence, respect, and love?

4. Naina and her mother have a very strained relationship. But they also show a great deal of love toward each other. How does each one express her love? What do you imagine their relationship could look like going forward?

5. Do you think it was fair of Naina to call Vansh's idea an Emma Project? Did your answer change at all over the course of the book?

6. What did you think about Esha and Sid's budding relationship? How did the more magical elements fit in with the rest of the story?

7. The themes of running away and separation from family run through this novel. Both Vansh and Naina have spent most of their adulthoods living away from their families. What does this homecoming mean for them? What does running away (for the first time) mean to Esha? What about Hari?

8. Vansh's preoccupation with his looks could be seen as pure egotism. But is there more to it? What do you think lies beneath that?

9. While Naina and Vansh's relationship in this book is loosely inspired by Jane Austen's *Emma*, it also is wholly its own. What do you think Ms. Austen would have ▶

thought of Naina and Vansh and the rest of the Raje family?

10. How do you feel about this story as the culmination of the series? What do you imagine comes next for the Rajes? ❧

Behind the Book

It is a truth universally acknowledged that a writer who starts a series must also end it someday. I always dreaded the day I knew was coming, and saying goodbye to the Rajes is still incredibly hard. It feels like the end of a grand love affair, and I'm struggling to let go. I wrote down the ideas for these books more than eight years ago. I had taken my children to their math tutoring class, and while I sat in the waiting room, I wrote down the premises and themes for the four novels. Pencil to paper, scratching away furiously. Four pages, one for each story. Seeds that would grow into the Raje family and the stories that have filled me up for the past decade. Add to that the fact that, for decades prior, I had been thinking about how to pay homage to Jane Austen and to bring under one story universe the novels that influenced me so significantly.

How do you let that go?

When I first read Austen in middle school, I often dreamed of those stories as my own. Me, with Lizzie Bennet's fearlessly opinionated spirit. Me, with Anne Elliot's undying love. Me, with Elinor Dashwood's strength to always do the right thing. Me, with Emma Woodhouse's popularity, confidence, ▶

and need to set everyone else's life to rights. All of it in my world with my parents and friends, in my city, and with my challenges. The very beginning of learning to tell stories comes from internalizing the storytelling of others. I didn't know it, but my dreams were cultural translations. They were retellings, although that word was not yet in my vocabulary. As I got older, I found these women inside myself, aspired to them, accepted them as part of me. As I wrote more and studied my craft, I also started to realize that the true genius of Jane Austen lay in how clearly she saw her world, how she never hid from the absurdity of it, and how she pushed at its rules without ever breaking them outright. She was a master class in subversion.

Even though the specifics of our worlds and what was ridiculous about them was different, the heart of that absurdity was still the same. So much so that it defied the fact that two hundred years had passed. Maybe that's why they call it the human condition. And maybe that's why all these years later, authors like me still feel the need to take those stories apart and find something inside them that speaks to us so very resolutely.

Marrying off daughters is not quite the do-or-die situation it used to be when *Pride and Prejudice* was written. But social class still causes us to meet each other from behind the curtain of our prejudices. Titles and their trappings are no longer the obvious dividing lines they were in *Persuasion*. But being persuaded into giving up on dreams because those around us deem them beneath us is still part of the journey for anyone who steps out of the bubbles they were born into. Breaking an engagement no longer costs us our self-respect and social standing. But getting stuck in situations where we're held ransom by the ambitions of those around us—and gathering the courage to identify and chase the parts that are ours to want—that's just as true today as it was in the time of *Sense and Sensibility*. These were the pieces that spoke to me, the paths that the Rajes organically called me to walk.

From the very beginning, Vansh was the essence of Emma. With all her gifts and privileges, but also the blind spots that come with those gifts. To me, *Emma* was always the story of a woman who had it all and assumed that it made her well equipped to solve the problems of those who had less than her. It is the story of growing into your own empathy. Matchmaking may not be quite the popular pastime it was when Emma strolled the halls of Hartfield with nothing but time on her hands, but the charity of the privileged to solve the problems of the not-so-privileged ▶

Behind the Book *(continued)*

and all the power play attached to that is more relevant today than it has probably ever been.

As I struggled to let go of this world and these characters that I've spent so much time with, a wise writer friend suggested I honor the gifts writing these books gave me.

The greatest gift, of course, was these characters. They let me take the questions Austen's novels threw at me and undertake the journeys to finding the answers. They made those struggles their own. With each of these stories, I had the burning need to say something, to walk in shoes different from mine. Each of these stories started out a tangled mess with no clear path to where it would all go. Jane's themes, my themes, my characters, her characters. But there was a beauty and an organic ease to how it all came together in the end. That magic moment when it became wholly my story, when it became its own story— that is something I will cherish forever.

I studied architecture in college, and one of my design professors loved to say that there are no original designs, no original ideas. The most worthwhile designs come from when you start at the point of genius where the masters left off and you build completely honest solutions from there. The art is in knowing how not to be beholden to the masters but to acknowledge their work as a springboard and to become faithful only to what you're trying to build, what you need to build.

That is the other gift. I wanted to say things about the world we live in. I got to say those things. Jane held my hand and then she let it go. That's what I honor: her holding my hand, and my learning to let it go. Much the same way her characters held my hand and taught me how to be me. My reward is the fact that I will always have these books, these characters to return to, a vision brought to completion. And the satisfaction that they are exactly what I set out to build, what I needed to build. ◠